Praise for *How Not to Fall in Love, Actually*

'A phenomenal cast of characters and some real laugh
out loud moments. Brilliant!'
Heidi Swain

'This superb debut is romcom at its very best.
I haven't fallen so in love with a bunch of
characters in a long while. Loved it'
Sun

'*How Not to Fall in Love, Actually* is a hilarious,
frank look at a modern girl's dilemma as she tries to
find harmony in life – laugh-out-loud comedy!'
My Weekly

'A charming, feel-good gem of a
debut novel that's guaranteed to leave you smiling . . .
An honest narrative and a fresh voice to tell it . . .
a great way to spend a lazy afternoon'
CultureFly

'More bubbly than a big glass of champers and just as fun.
How Not to Fall in Love, Actually is bright, breezy, and the
perfect way to beat back the winter blues'
Georgia Clark

'Full of heart and unique characters . . . It's original,
fresh and a little bit crazy, everything I love in a book'
Alba in Bookland, five stars

'This book had me laughing out loud so much. Pretty much all the way through in fact. Catherine has such a gift for humour. This is the type of romantic comedy I wish I had the talent to write'
Novel Kicks

With witty dialogues and a captivating plot, I read this refreshing and entertaining novel in two days laughing from the first to the last page'
Chicklit Club

'This book was really funny, it had emotion and a great story, but the humour really stood out. Definitely one to pick up when you need a good old rom-com'
Rachale's Reads

'Debut novelist Catherine Bennetto has written exactly my kind of romantic comedy: funny, engaging, clever, emotional, quirky, and truly uplifting'
NZ Book Lovers

'Can I give this book seven stars please?'
Goodreads Reviewer, Sozie

'It's a perfect rom-com and a highly enjoyable read. I think I have found a new author to love'
Goodreads Reviewer, Vicki

'Brilliantly written with the right balance of comedy that doesn't take away from the real narrative'
Goodreads Reviewer, Felicity

'This could be the next Richard Curtis movie. Read it! You will not regret it'
Goodreads Reviewer, Melodiacat

catherine bennetto

MAKE OR BREAK

**SIMON &
SCHUSTER**

London · New York · Sydney · Toronto · New Delhi

A CBS COMPANY

First published in Great Britain by Simon & Schuster UK Ltd, 2018
A CBS COMPANY

1 3 5 7 9 10 8 6 4 2

Simon & Schuster UK Ltd
1st Floor
222 Gray's Inn Road
London WC1X 8HB

Simon & Schuster Australia, Sydney
Simon & Schuster India, New Delhi

www.simonandschuster.co.uk
www.simonandschuster.com.au
www.simonandschuster.co.in

A CIP catalogue record for this book
is available from the British Library

Paperback ISBN: 978-1-4711-6576-4
eBook ISBN: 978-1-4711-6578-8
eAudio ISBN: 978-1-4711-7333-2

This book is a work of fiction. Names, characters, places and
incidents are either a product of the author's imagination or are
used fictitiously. Any resemblance to actual people living or
dead, events or locales is entirely coincidental.

Typeset in Bembo by M Rules
Printed and bound by CPI Group (UK) Ltd, Croydon, CR0 4YY

For Mama
(She will be SO mad if I don't put her
actual name, so to keep Mama happy:
For Tricia Helen Brown)

CHAPTER ONE

'Harry Styles.'

'That's not shameful!'

'I'm eighteen years older than him. Yes, it is.' Lana, my boss, looked at her Rolex; a fortieth birthday present from some boy-band member with a cougar fetish, and snapped her laptop shut. 'Right, enough "Shameful Shag" talk. Go home.'

'What?' I frowned and checked my phone. 'But it's only three thirty?'

Admittedly we'd done nothing since lunchtime except compare our updated 'Shameful Shag Wish List', stuff invites into envelopes for my parents' joint seventieth birthday/anniversary party and do a few moves on Lana's Pilates ball (January was a particularly slow month in the world of music video production) but still, 3.30 p.m. was two hours before my official finish time.

'Why don't I start on the rider for the *Feet of the People* shoot?' I said, flicking open my ever-present, neatly utilised Moleskin notebook. 'They're all vegan apparently and their manager requested there to be no meat on the premises. Also, weirdly, one of them won't sit on a used toilet seat, so we need to fit a new one in his dressing room and plastic-wrap it so he—'

'God, they sound awful,' Lana said, shuffling papers. 'And not even original – the plastic-wrapped new toilet seat is Mariah's thing. Anyway,' she waved her short-nailed, mani-cured hand. 'That's ages away. It's a horrible, rainy Friday. Go and get started on your weekend.'

'But—'

'In a few weeks it's going to be crazy.' Lana indicated towards the whiteboard calendar that covered an entire wall of her office where two months of music video production schedules were recorded in various colour-coded pens. Nothing but a handful of meetings and Elsie's twenty-sixth birthday – she was the other PA I shared the open-plan office with – were written in for the next two weeks. After that, each square representing a day was crammed with prep, shoot and edit days; voice recordings, CGI meetings and viewings. It did indeed look 'crazy'. 'We've got those vegan/toilet people,' Lana continued. 'I've pitched for Pink's new collab, and I'm still waiting to hear about Little Mix. We should take time off now while we can.'

I looked away from the whiteboard and stood at the end of Lana's desk, unsure.

'Go!' she said with a shooing motion. 'I'm five minutes

behind you.' She made a show of pretending to file documents I knew were just scribbled wish lists of embarrassing celebrity shags.

Half an hour later I stepped out of Balham station into weather so depressing it could make a Disney princess turn to drink. My phone beeped with a text from Lana.

I did actually shag him ;)

I laughed, happy that I genuinely liked my boss, then zipped up my parka and appreciated the lack of Friday evening commuters on the dreary mid-January walk to my sister's flat.

'Oh hey,' Annabelle said, as I let myself in her front door, not mentioning (or realising) that I was two hours earlier than usual. She continued searching through a Marvel Avengers school bag. 'We've got broccoli cheesecake stand-offs, Mum's repacking her packing and the cat is in the laundry, vomiting.'

'Poor kitty. Did he eat the broccoli cheesecake?' I shut the door with a smirk.

'Aunty Jess!' Seven-year-old Hunter appeared in the hall with a foam baseball bat tucked into his trousers, a fist full of kitchen utensils and a Thor helmet resting at a jaunty angle on his dark brown bird's nest. He pushed past his mum and launched at me for a hug.

'Hunter, why don't you try your broccoli cake?' Annabelle

said, emerging from the school bag with three unmatched socks and a lunchbox spilling crumbs.

Hunter made a face.

'I'm with him,' I said, setting my wriggly nephew on the ground and peeling off my coat and scarf. 'It should be illegal to say those two words together. It sullies the word "cake".'

'Broccoli is very high in—'

'Grossness.' I winked at Hunter.

'Fibre,' Annabelle countered, tightening her unintentionally model-ish bun and picking a path through some Lego. 'Mum thinks Katie is constipated because her midday "evacuation" had the wrong consistency.'

Annabelle and I rolled our eyes and sniggered as we arrived in the kitchen.

'Hi, Mum,' I said.

'Oh hello, Plum,' Mum said using the nickname I'd had since I was two. Apparently my tantrums were so vigorous (passionate) I'd turn a deep, fruity purple. She looked up from her open suitcase that sat on one end of the kitchen table; food, spilt water and Moana cutlery littered the other end. 'Shouldn't you still be at work?' she said, glancing at Annabelle's retro kitchen clock.

I took the baseball bat which was being wielded hazardously and put it on top of the fridge with the rest of the confiscated toys that had been repurposed as weapons.

'Lana let me leave early. There isn't much to do at this time of year,' I said, while coaxing Hunter into his chair. 'And, to make the day even better, Pete called and said he had to stay late at work because of some emergency, but he's coming here because apparently he has a surprise for me!'

'What kind of surprise?' Mum said.

Annabelle frowned. Despite the fact I was at her place every evening and most weekends to help with the kids, Pete, my boyfriend of six years, hardly ever came over. I shrugged and bent to pick up Katie, my three-year-old niece, who was on the floor playing with a rainbow-coloured xylophone. I signed and said, 'I love you' to her and she gripped my neck in an intense hug.

'And what kind of emergency would mean a PE teaching assistant has to stay at work late on a Friday?' Annabelle leant against the kitchen counter with a glass of something green and probably disgustingly healthy – but with her customary dash of something 'beneficial' (cannabis).

'I dunno.' I headed to the fridge, Katie kissing my cheek with three-year-old fervour. 'Maybe the soccer balls deflated.'

The three of us giggled. Pete took his job as a PE teacher's assistant at an International Baccalaureate school near Virginia Water *very* seriously. He was in a team of nine and was the most junior, but he may as well have been the private coach to David Beckham's kids. Having said that, the clientele at the private school weren't far off Beckham status. Pete had to wear a uniform and they had strict rules on facial hair, ironing and deodorant usage (must be used, must *work*, must not be Lynx-level fragranced), and I got in a lot of trouble if I bought the kind that resulted in white powdery pits.

5

I pulled a half-bottle of rosé from the fridge; Annabelle, being a semi-reformed substance indulger (cannabis oil is homeopathic apparently), didn't drink but always kept a bottle handy for Mum and me.

'Now, I'm leaving you with my iPad,' Mum handed Annabelle an orange-coloured hand-sewn pouch, 'and my phone. I'm not even allowed to take them in the car. Fancy that!' She handed over another pouch in recycled curtain fabric. 'If it rings, you answer and take a message.'

Annabelle nodded and sipped her drink.

'I have a mouthful, you have a mouthful,' I whispered in Hunter's ear, and pointed to his broccoli cheesecake.

Hunter nodded and we each cut off a piece of cheesecake. While Mum explained to Annabelle the intricacies of how she'd like her phone answered, Hunter and I silently mouthed, 'One, two, three' then shoved the squares of broccoli cake in our mouths.

'It tastes like toes,' Hunter said through his greenish-grey mouthful.

He held his nose to swallow and I pretended to vomit making him and Katie giggle.

'Here's a notepad for the messages,' Mum continued. 'And I got a nice pen.' She produced a fat plastic pen covered in koalas wearing Raybans then looked back into her suitcase and muttered to herself in German.

She'd been dipping in and out of it more and more lately. She usually only did it when stressed but recently Annabelle and I had noticed a definite change in her. She'd been acting weird. Well, weird*er.* We thought it was her impending seventieth birthday. Or the fact that Dad, also approaching seventy, wasn't showing any signs of slowing down. He'd flown past the usual retirement age with barely a glance out of his business class window. Which, seeing as he brokered the sale of islands to the rich and secretive, meant he was still spending weeks and weeks abroad. Or perhaps general senility was settling in. Whatever it was, it had her mumbling in her native tongue, weeping at adverts for insurance packages, mistaking a stranger's folded fur coat for a lap dog and asking to pat it, and booking herself on a ten-day silent retreat.

'They don't allow reading, Mum,' I said, scanning the contents of her suitcase and pulling out three self-help books and a herbal remedy magazine. 'Remember?'

'Or writing.' Annabelle plucked Mum's paisley notebook with its multi-coloured sticky tabs poking out at all angles from among the clothing.

'It is strict, isn't it? What will I do with all my thoughts . . .?'

'Ignore them,' I said.

'Observe them,' said Annabelle.

'You will feed my scoby, wont you?' Mum glanced towards the jar of glutinous bacteria she'd brought round that was sitting on the bench looking like something Jabba the Hutt might excrete after a particularly big night out.

Annabelle nodded. I gagged.

'And you'll listen to Eileen?' she continued while watching me extract various other tomes on herbal living from every pocket of her suitcase. 'I told Patrick I didn't want her

7

replacing me. She'll lose me my listeners! Doesn't know her walnuts from her worts, that woman. *And* I've seen her eat a Pot Noodle.' Mum looked at me, expecting allied horror. I gave her panto-style shock.

Mum had had a daily show on the local independent radio station giving 'Natural advice for the home and health' for twenty-five years. Patrick was her long-suffering producer. Mum had always been interested in alternative health, but Annabelle's unruly behaviour and my ADHD had propelled her firmly into a natural, preservative-free world. Yes, I'm mildly ADHD. Mum had treated my 'excitable nature', as she'd called it, with diet. I was gluten, grain, sugar and dairy free way before all the blogging beauties started doing it. And it worked. Although growing up it meant no kids liked to come and play at our house. The cupboards were full of raw nuts, almond flour cookie falsehoods and bowls of low FODMAP fruit.

The doorbell rang, and Hunter was off his chair and hurtling down the hall in seconds.

'That will be my driver.' Mum tossed the last few items in the top of her suitcase. 'Now, you'll remember Katie's tonic? I've put it in the door of the fridge. And I made more of Hunter's special muffins. Oh, and Katie needs—'

'Mum, she knows how to look after her own children,' I said, steering my mother away from her suitcase by her tiny shoulders.

'I do.' Annabelle nodded.

'And anyway, I'll be here.' I dropped the suitcase lid down and zipped it up.

'You'll come every day?' Mum fretted.

'I'll be fine,' Annabelle said.

'Yes. Every day. Like usual.'

'She needs help.'

'I don't,' Annabelle said.

'She's got her hands full, being—'

'On her own. Yes, I know, Mum.'

'But it's "no contact". I didn't really think about it till now. No contact for ten days. That's an awful lot of time to be out of touch. Perhaps I shouldn't go . . .?'

Annabelle's eyes widened over her smoothie.

I hoisted Mum's suitcase off the table, ushered her down the hall, thrusting her coat at her on the way, and bundled her out of the front door towards the waiting minivan. 'If there's an emergency they do let us contact you, you know. You're not in solitary confinement. Just a lentils-for-breakfast-lunch-and-dinner silent retreat. You'll come back calm and content, with terrible gas, and everything will be fine.'

'But you're an awful cook,' Mum said, watching me hand her suitcase over to the driver. 'You'll give them all E. coli.'

'I know how to order a takeaway,' I said.

Mum pursed her lips and began listing the perils of fast food while Annabelle stood in the doorway watching with relaxed amusement.

'Just go and have a good time with all your thoughts,' I said, guiding her into the van among the words 'sodium' and 'trans fats' and 'unethical mutton'. 'You'll come back transcended, or tranquil, or whatever they tell you you'll come back like.'

'Transformed,' she said through the open door, her eyes narrowing behind her large-framed glasses.

'Yes, transformed you shall be. You'll be a parrot of peace, or a sea-turtle of serenity, or a—'

'Goodbye, Jess,' Mum said in a clipped manner.

She slid the van door shut.

'Bye, Mum,' I said through the open window. 'I'll still love you if you come back a rat of restfulness.'

'*Halt den mund,*' Mum said with a scowl.

'Grandma, that's rude!' said Hunter, who was very good at German.

'Yes, it is,' said I, who was not but had a feeling my mother had just told me to shut my sausage-roll hole. 'Shame on you.'

Mum shook her head and closed the window on me and the drizzly evening. But I suspected mainly on me.

Annabelle waved from the front door. 'Have fun!'

Hunter waved a broken rake he'd somehow found and which I immediately seized before he started fencing with it. 'Bye, Grandma!' he hollered.

The driver reversed onto the darkened street and Hunter, Annabelle and I headed inside to the warmth of the kitchen. Moments later we heard the front door open and Mum appeared in the doorway.

'I just realised, without my phone I have no map.'

Despite the fact that the driver had sat nav and had been

there many times before, we recognised Mum's need for a modicum of control and spent another five minutes printing out directions to the Buddhist retreat in Devon 'just in case anything happens'. We said more goodbyes, coaxed her back to the van and then flopped at the kitchen table. The front door opened again and Mum stepped into the kitchen, wringing her bony hands.

'I forgot my phone,' she said.

Annabelle and I gave her a look. It took a few moments.

'Oh yes,' she said, worrying the tiger's eye pendant dangling over the top of her taupe turtleneck. 'Quite right. That's the whole point. Yes.'

It was the first time she was going to be apart from the kids since Katie was born. The anticipation of separation was clearly taking its toll on my grey-haired, herbal little mother who'd been Katie's secondary carer for three and a half years. She gave a plaintive look at the two children, Hunter submerging a Lego batman in his broccoli cake and Katie signing 'love you, Grandma'; got a bit teary, kissed Katie nineteen times, muttered something in German that possibly translated to 'I am dance scarf' but I couldn't be sure, as I hadn't kept up with my Deutsch lessons; said, 'OK, well, I'd best be off,' muttered to herself and left. Again. How she was going to keep her German trap shut for ten days I would never know.

'Is Mum worse?' I asked half an hour later, while standing in the doorway of the bathroom watching Annabelle bath Katie.

Hunter, my charge, could be heard singing a 21 Pilots song, far too old for his seven years, in the shower down the hall.

'She's losing the plot.'

'She never really had a firm grasp of it in the first place.'

'True.' Annabelle poured water over Katie's head, washing out the suds. 'You know she started crying on her show the other day when a caller asked about Bolognese stains?'

'Do you think she has a brain tumour?' I said, catching Hunter in a towel as he ran past naked.

'No.' Annabelle rolled her eyes and hoisted Katie out of the bath. 'Why does it always have to be so dramatic with you?'

'Brain tumours happen every day,' I said, indignant.

Annabelle sighed. 'I think it's Dad's work.'

'Mmmm,' I said, not really sure we'd pinned down the reason Mum was being so erratic.

Dad's career meant that he had always been relatively absent. Why would she suddenly be worrying about that now? Don't get me wrong, Dad was a fabulous father; doting, indulgent, firm, kind, playful and patient, and we all adored him, but most of my childhood memories contained just three of us: Mum, Annabelle and me. I would never tell him that, though, as his heart would be broken.

When we were young, and he was away, we didn't get to speak with him all that often. Time differences were awkward and not kid-bedtime or kid-manic-morning-routine-friendly. But when he was back it felt like we had his exclusive focus. We were never hustled to bed so that our parents could have 'adult time', nor did we have our child-ish questions limited to 'just one more'. As little kids he'd indulge us with game after game of Snap or Uno, or watch our endless tumbles on the trampoline, never averting his attention so that we'd have to say '*Dad! Dad! DAD! WATCH ME!*' As tweens and teens he'd listen patiently to our peer skirmishes and teacher grievances, spoiling us with his time and advice. Then, when a contract came in, he was off again and Annabelle, Mum and I would tumble along as usual; happy as a trio but looking forward to being four again. He'd once told me that he left a piece of his heart behind every time he had to go away. He was trying to comfort a tearful little girl, but in my child's mind I was terrified that each time he left his heart would get smaller and smaller until one day it would be gone altogether. Then he'd fall down dead, a cold, grey cavity where his heart used to be. Perhaps I did lean a tad towards the theatrical . . .

'Did I tell you I managed to book that Van Morrison cover band Dad wanted?' I said, releasing a dry, squirming Hunter who ran to his bedroom at normal Hunter speed: recently ejected cannonball. 'Lana knew someone who knew someone.'

'Great,' Annabelle said. She carried Katie out of the bath-room towards the living room while I hung up towels and bath mats and facecloths behind her. 'What am I in charge of again?'

'Ummm,' I hesitated. What *had* I let her do . . .? 'I think you're doing the . . . uh . . .'

Annabelle eyeballed me.

'You're doing the . . .'

In six weeks, eight days apart from each other, Mum and Dad would turn seventy. Which was also coinciding with their thirty-fifth non-wedding anniversary (as 1970s hippies they'd seen marriage as a joint governmental sentence of getting into debt, then trying to get out of it by retirement, so had shunned the official piece of paper and had a 'commitment picnic' in a field by the river Avon). Annabelle and I were putting on a big surprise party that both of them knew about. There was no way we could ever organise a surprise party with Dad's career being what it was. If a moneyed somebody wanted to buy an island, they wanted to buy it PRONTO. And Dad and his business partners dropped their newspapers, or their lattes, or their wives, or whatever they were holding and jumped on the nearest plane. I was saved from telling Annabelle I'd allowed her to be in charge of precisely nothing by the doorbell ding-donging through the house.

'That'll be Pete!' I said, skipping down the hall.

I flung open the door and there was my lovely boyfriend: neat brown hair, strong shoulders, medium height, more than medium-ly hung and, oddly, not in his work uniform but in a nice pair of jeans and his goose-feather parka.

'Hey babe,' I gave him a kiss, then registered my pink tartan suitcase and his big black backpack leaning against the doorframe out of the rain. 'What's with the luggage?'

Pete smiled and held up a printout. It took me a moment to read the particulars.

'*Cape Town?*' I squealed in a voice not unlike one of Alvin and the Chipmunks. Then I saw the date. 'TODAY?!'

'Actually, now,' Pete said, his handsome, clean-shaven face looking pleased with himself. 'As in *right* now.'

CHAPTER TWO

'We've got rubbish seats,' Pete said, examining the boarding passes with a defeated air as we joined the back of the long, long queue to board. 'Right at the back by the toilets.'

'Well, you should've checked in online.' I searched my handbag for my phone while also doing a check for liquids over 100ml.

'Hold this?' I said, holding out my handbag while turning my attention to my hastily packed carry-on tote.

When the handbag was not taken from me I looked up to see Pete's pained expression.

'Take it.' I jiggled it at his chest.

Pete looked around at the surrounding cluster of disinterested, impatient-to-board travellers. 'No.'

Admittedly the handbag was quite stand-outy. It was wicker and in the shape of a sitting camel with a decorative harness complete with tiny bells and multi-coloured tassels. I called it Alice.

'Women come with boobs, a vagina and a handbag,' I said. 'You wanna play with these,' I circled my hand over my lady areas, 'then you have to hold this.' I thrust him the bag.

Pete did want to play with those, so he begrudgingly took the handbag strap and held it by his fingertips, making himself look even more conspicuous than if he'd just held it like a normal person. I gave him an affectionate 'you're such a loser' headshake and went back to searching for my phone.

The rush to the airport meant I hadn't been able to text Dave, our flatmate, to tell him we'd be away for the next two weeks, allowing him to have his zombie-obsessed mates over to eat pizza and shun all things outdoor for the chance to stay on the sofa ripping apart the storylines of movies they'd seen three hundred times before. Pete abhorred zombie fests. And pizza fests. *And* Dave's mates. So Dave, my friend from film school who was currently working as a night shift dis-patcher for 999 until he became a director of 'epic zombie movies', kindly kept his 'fests' to a minimum. I'd also been unable to alert anyone to the exciting news that I was off on a last-minute trip to Cape Town to be bridesmaid for my best friend Priya's last-minute wedding. Or to thank Priya.

The week before, after I'd said we couldn't afford a trip to Cape Town at such short notice, Priya had called Pete. Apparently she'd offered to pay for the flights and put us up in her apartment if he could get us both some time off work. Priya was an actress on a Netflix show and had been in Cape Town six months a year for the past three years, so paying for two people's flights was an achievable and amazing reality.

But even if it wasn't, that was just how Priya was; she was generous even when we were poor film school students living in a basement flat that had mould, mice and a view out of the living room window of the ankles of people running for Cricklewood station. If Priya could afford only one beer she ordered it with two glasses.

During the tube ride to Heathrow, Pete had said that getting two weeks off work had been surprisingly drama-free. Lana had been only too happy for me to take my nearly expired leave, and the head teacher of Pete's school had a son who, in his final year at teacher's college, was gagging for the chance to cover someone's lessons. As he told me about the crafty co-ordinating Priya and he had been doing for the past three days I felt a rush of affection for them both. But only one of them was going to get lucky because of it. (I just want to be clear, that someone was Pete.) Images of us getting engaged (again, I'm talking about Pete here) had been filling my head on the journey to the airport. Surely the wedding and proximity to diamond mines would motivate *that* question being asked. We were at the end of our twenties and, unlike Annabelle with her two illegitimate children, or my commitment-picnicking parents, I wanted to do the marriage-before-kids traditional thing. Call me boring, but life was complex enough these days with software updates (seriously, must there be an update *every* time I turn on my computer?), austerity (something I was still intending to look up the definition of), and the fickle social challenge of trying to be the right kind of feminist, so why not keep the other stuff simple.

'If we'd come straight from Annabelle's, *like I'd planned*,' Pete stressed. 'We'd have better seats. I bet our chairs don't even recline all the way back.'

'Well, I'm sorry, but we had to go home,' I said, still digging around in my carry-on. 'I couldn't spend two weeks in Cape Town with yoga leggings, three gym T-shirts, my gym shoes, a nightie, nineteen pairs of underpants – did you think I was going to have an accident, by the way? – and the bra I wear when I'm hung-over.'

Pete looked upset I'd questioned his clothing choices.

'We made it, didn't we?' I leant towards him, abandoning the phone search and lowering my voice. 'And I got to pack the naughty knickers you like.'

'I guess that's something,' he said, thawing. 'So, you're really OK leaving Annabelle?'

Despite the fact that Pete thought Annabelle and the kids had outgrown the need for Mum and my daily assistance, I could tell his enquiry was genuine. Back at the house, when Pete had shown me the printed tickets to Cape Town my initial thoughts were sun, wine, Pete in board shorts tanning his sculpted torso, beach, sex, cocktails, sand, safaris, Pete's tanned calf muscles in safari shorts, and yet I'd hugged him and said, 'I can't go.'

'Wh … what?' Pete had stammered, looking mystified.

'I can't go,' I'd said, folding the printout in half and handing it back to my baffled boyfriend. 'Annabelle needs—'

'You to take millions of photos of elephants,' Annabelle had said, handing me my coat.

'But—'

'And giraffes.'

'But—'

She'd held me by the shoulders and said in a steady voice, 'Jess, get on that plane with your boyfriend and go watch your friend get married.'

'But the kids?' I'd said, looking at Hunter, who was helping Katie button up her pink pyjama top. His patience with his Down's Syndrome sister could burst your heart. It was the only time he ceased operating at Spinal Tap's level eleven. A knot of emotion caught in my throat as he slowly did the last button up then signed 'You did it!' to his sister, who grinned back at him.

'We'll be fine,' Annabelle had said with a look of firm determination. 'Go. I insist.'

Pete and Annabelle, admittedly not huge fans of each other, had exchanged appreciative acknowledgements. I'd chewed my lip. Could I leave her? She hadn't been without Mum or my help since falling pregnant with Hunter when she was a 24-year-old Art History student. Why did Mum have to be on her silent lentil retreat at the exact time I'd be in Cape Town? Dad was apparently somewhere in Scotland showing some blustery isles to a Russian, and who knows how long he'd be away this time. Not that Dad had ever been very effective in dealing with his wayward eldest. He was far too much of a softie towards Annabelle; the lovable black sheep of the family who did no right but could do no wrong.

As a child she threw temper tantrums; as an early teen she

got pierced; as a late teen she took drugs and ended up in rehab then got out of there and ended up at Anorexic Camp (it was called something else 'official' but Annabelle and I only ever referred to it as that). Those days were tense and because Dad was often away, and Mum was trying to contain the catastrophe that was Annabelle, I'd become an independent child. I'd ordered my own organic almond-meal birthday cake from the bakery when I was eight because Annabelle had been suspended for turning up to our private school with pink hair and Mum was trying to take the neon edge out of the hot pink with henna. She ended up turning it Fraggle orange and Annabelle had pre-teen-raged the house down.

When university entrance time came around she surprised everyone by nailing her A-levels and, after a gap year in Costa Rica where she came home with a back tattoo and a worryingly extensive understanding of cannabis oil, gained entry to an Art History degree. Then fucked that up by having an anonymous one-night stand, which only I knew to be a twelve-week stand, with her very 'nonymous' (what *is* the opposite of that word?) married professor. It resulted in a darling nephew for me but also meant Annabelle had to drop out of uni to care for him. The professor moved to Arizona with his family and sent Hunter cards and money and was ungenerous with both. When Hunter was four Annabelle went back to studying accountancy part time but then Daniel the superyacht skipper happened. He came, he impregnated (came again) then buggered off leaving Annabelle with a broken heart and a two-week-old daughter with Down's Syndrome.

Daniel adored Katie, though, and, having bought Annabelle a teeny-tiny flat in Balham just around the corner from his place, visited as often as his sailing schedule would allow. Which usually was only once or twice a year. But he didn't know how to be a father, much less to a child who needed as much careful attention as Katie. Her speech is delayed because of low muscle tone, which makes articulation difficult, hence the baby signing. So she has a speech therapist and regular physio. She has vision difficulties so wears adorable little elasticised pink bendy glasses and has regular trips to the ophthalmologist. Winter can be a tough time because weak lungs mean pneumonia is a concern. Her paediatrician is seen so regularly that she's almost family. It's a busy schedule of appointments, tests and therapies. Not to mention the unscheduled trips to the casualty department; which is why Mum and I have always been on hand to help. We all have up-to-date first aid training and have taken baby signing classes. Except Pete, so we make jokes at his expense that he attempts to be good-natured about. After Daniel broke up with Annabelle she swore off men and the family cocooned around her, breathing a sigh of relief. She's now thirty-three and totally on the straight and narrow. If by straight you mean 'cannabis oil in your smoothie', and your definition of narrow is 'Mum is her supplier'.

In the last year Annabelle had started making noises about not needing so much help, but it had become a routine nobody was ready to break. Mum would finish her radio show around 11.30-ish and head over to Annabelle's to help get Katie through to nap time while Annabelle did accounts at the kitchen table for her small handful of clients. I'd pop over most days after work and help get the kids through the evening routine before heading home to Pete, who'd invariably made a well-balanced meal and had started eating it by himself in front of the sports channel.

The queue to board shuffled forward a few steps and I considered laissez-faire Annabelle, hyper Hunter and love bug Katie being on their own until Mum got home in ten days' time.

'She'll be fine,' I said, more to comfort myself. 'She'll be fine.'

'She will.' Pete smiled, looking relieved. 'Like Annabelle said, the kids are older now and the alone time will be good for them.'

I stretched onto tippy toes and gave Pete a kiss, not worrying about the rub of red I left on his cheek. 'You're amazing. I love you very much and you are going to get *very* lucky later – Dad . . .?'

'No . . .' Pete mused. 'No, that's an inappropriate pet name. I'm going to have to put my foot down on that one.'

I smacked him playfully on the arm. 'Look.' I pointed ahead at the segregated business class politely drifting through the final passport check while our logjam of riff-raff battered each other with scruffy baggage and swelled towards the passport check waiting to be loaded into the back.

'Oh yeah,' Pete said, craning around the shuffling mass. 'I thought he was in Scotland?'

'Me too.' I dug around in my handbag again.

'Why don't you just yell out?' Pete said as I finally located my phone.

'Because,' I dialled Dad's number, 'he's miles away. And I might get arrested for causing a disturbance at an airport. They're very strict in these places now, you know. They might think I'm a terrorist.'

A Japanese woman to our side gave a condemnatory scowl.

'Keep your voice down,' Pete said. 'And why would a terrorist call out "Dad"?'

Her Japanese partner gave a condemnatory scowl.

'To distract everyone.' I craned my neck over the rabble and watched Dad register his phone ringing. He shifted his leather satchel and draped suit jacket from one arm to the other while patting trouser pockets, shirt pockets, carry-on luggage pockets, satchel pockets and suit jacket pockets, then eventually discovered it in the first explored pocket. 'You know, before letting off a bomb.'

We received matching condemnatory scowls as the couple moved away, and Pete coloured all the way down his neck.

'Hello, Plum.' Dad's smooth voice came down the line. 'How are you?'

'Great! How's Scotland?' I said with a smile.

I fully expected him to respond with, *'Actually, I'm off to Cape Town'*, for me to answer, *'Actually, so am I – turn around'*; for us to have a giggle, then try and wangle seats with him in business. But instead he said:

'Oh, fine. Lots of meetings, so not much time to get out

and about. Lovely views.' He said this as he looked out of the vast airport window.

My jaw dropped. He was lying. Barefaced, standing not fifteen yards from me looking at the Heathrow tarmac, lying. I turned to Pete but he was on his phone playing 'stick cricket' and therefore unable to register the dramatic event.

'Ah—' I managed.

Dad took a step towards the desk and handed his passport to the smiling business class steward. 'Plum, I'm sorry, I must go. I'm being called.'

'Uh . . .' I said, struck dumb by the development. 'But—'

'Bye, my love.'

'Yeah . . .' I croaked. 'Dad . . .?' But he had already hung up.

I watched him pocket his phone, smile to the young steward, take back his passport and disappear through the door beyond. Then re-emerge to collect his forgotten carry-on case.

CHAPTER THREE

'Why would he lie? Why would he lie?' I tightened my seat belt, but not so much that my stomach escaped over the top. 'Pete?'

'Yes?'

'Why would he lie?'

Pete shrugged and looked helpless. He'd been looking helpless ever since I'd hung up from Dad, grabbed the 'stick cricket' game out of his hands and had a mini existential crisis about my reality being ever so skew-whiffed.

'Why didn't you tell him you were standing behind him?' He moved his elbow away from a busy lady sorting her multitude of bags, magazines, iPads and Kindles into the cramped seating area.

Cabin crew were walking the aisles snapping shut the overhead lockers and making sure everyone had their seat belts fastened. I'd already tried to sidestep one of them and slip up the stairs to business when we'd boarded, but I'd been rumbled and was guided politely but firmly to my aisle seat. I searched through my carry-on bag looking for my elusive phone.

'Why didn't you call him straight back?'

'I don't know. He got off the phone pretty quickly. And I think I was too shocked. I don't think my Dad's lied to me *ever.*'

Pete looked sceptical. A female crewmember strode past us in thick-heeled pumps telling people to put their devices on flight mode and their bags on the floor under the seat in front of them.

'You know when you have that day where you find out your parents have lied about why Aunt Pip really went away for all that time; or told you your pimples weren't all that big and close together, therefore defining them as acne, but the doctor took one look and stuck you on medication at a strength that would mortify Armstrong; or that all the kids your age went to bed before *Will and Grace* and you found out it wasn't true? And you took your parents down from that massive pedestal and gave them a much shorter one that was easy to move them on and off of as you adjusted your view of them?'

Pete frowned.

'Handbag under the seat now please, ma'am,' another passing cabin crew said, giving me a smile that didn't reach her eyes.

I nodded and continued talking to Pete.

'Well, I never had that with Dad. If I asked him a question,

I knew, *knew*, he was telling the truth. He would look me in the eye and say "*yes darling, one of your ears is a bit lower than the other but you're still growing, and it'll probably even itself out eventually. But I love you even more with the wonky ears.*" And I believed him. And you know what? They did even out.' I lifted my hair and showed off my evenly allocated ear locations.

'Maybe it's a huge international deal with some- one famous?' Pete said, shifting away from his busy lady-neighbour who was getting liberal with a facial spray. 'And it needs to be a secret?'

'Hmmm ...'

Dad's job did involve a lot of high-profile clients and last-minute trips. Often he couldn't tell us who the client was, or any details about the acquisition, but I'd always believed we knew where he was. The plane gave a mini lurch and began reversing away from the terminal as another crewmember bore down on us.

Pete looked flustered. 'Put your bag under the seat,' he hissed.

'I just want to try and call Dad quickly,' I said, digging elbow-deep in my cavernous tote and finally coming out with my phone. 'He might still have his phone on.'

I had only managed to do the thumbprint thing when the cabin lady arrived at my side and said in a tight voice that I was to put my phone on flight mode and my bag under the seat in front of me *immediately*. A few people in the sur- rounding seats swivelled to gawp at the disobedient passenger and Pete got busy behind a magazine. Once we were well and truly airborne a bell sounded. The cabin crew clicked themselves out of their seats and began bustling around the service areas, walking up and down the aisle, putting their formal jackets in miniature wardrobes and doing other important things.

I unclicked my seat belt.

'What are you doing?' Pete said in a panicked voice, looking up and down the plane.

'I'm going to try and get up there.' I pulled myself to standing by the headrest of the seat in front then said sorry when I got a disgruntled scowl from the lady in the seat whose hair I'd accidentally pulled.

'You can't!' Pete said, flustered. 'The seat belt light is still on.'

'They're all walking around,' I pointed to the cabin crew. 'It's fine.'

Pete ducked in his chair, his cheeks flushed. The plane was still climbing, so the walk to the business class stairs was uphill. As I passed one of those kitchen / service areas a crewmember stepped into my path and her face registered polite outrage.

'Ma'am, the seat belt light is still on. You have to return to your seat,' she said through meticulously painted red lips. Her make-up was so thick that if she went in the sun it would harden and dry like a terracotta tile.

'I just want to pop up and see my dad,' I said, trying to sound rational and reasonable. 'He doesn't know I'm on this flight and—'

'Ma'am, it's aircraft security. You can't be out of your seat.'

Another crewmember stepped out from the service area, his face young yet severe. Some of the surrounding passengers stopped what they were doing to watch us.

'That's hardly fair,' I said, trying to smile my way through what was rapidly becoming an embarrassing situation. 'You're up and walking around. How come you're allowed and we aren't?'

'We're crew and we don't need a reason,' the lady said with an air of dislike.

'We're trained in the safety aspects of this aircraft and are required to be up to perform our related duties,' the young, severe man added. 'It's for your own safety.'

'What about your safety?'

'I'm taking you back to your seat, ma'am,' the severe man raised his voice slightly. 'It is the aircraft security code and you must comply.'

'Fine,' I said. 'But I think the aircraft law needs some revisions.'

'OK,' the man said, but the undertone was 'fuck you'.

A little while later the seat belt signs were turned off but a drinks trolley blocked my exit.

'Anything to drink, ma'am?' said an entirely new female crewmember with a genuine smile.

The face-spraying lady next to Pete took off her earphones, asked for wine and set about rearranging her magazines and notebooks and iPads and pens. Pete flipped down his tray table and requested water and when my turn came I ingratiatingly asked for a gin and tonic. I thought I'd explain to this nice-faced air hostess my need to get up to business, but before I could open my mouth, Face Spray Lady had bumped Pete's elbow who spilt his water over my tray table making me jerk my tonic can to the left just as I was opening it, and the nice-faced air hostess got drenched and became death-faced air hostess.

'Oh, I'm so sorry!' I said, looking at her sodden skirt.

'Sure you are,' she spat while dabbing pointlessly at her skirt with a miniature napkin.

I shot Pete a 'whoops' grimace. He gave my arm a brief squeeze of commiseration then fiddled with the entertainment remote. The face-spray lady sipped her wine, read her magazine and tapped at her iPad oblivious to the mess she'd gotten me into.

'I won't try going up there until the lights are off,' I confessed to Pete a little while later, as the smell of airline food wafted down the aisle. 'I think I'm on their radar as a nuisance.'

Pete looked up and caught wet skirt lady giving me a sideways glance of extreme distaste. 'You think?' he said with a cynical smile.

The food trolley parked next to us and Face Spray Lady made a fuss about chicken or beef as she wanted the sides that came with the beef but not the beef, Pete ordered the chicken and received it with a striking smile, twinkling eyes and a dash of flirting, and when I too requested the chicken I was icily told they'd run out and was thrust the sweaty beef casserole. Dinner service got cleared, another drinks trolley stopped by (I said no to a beverage hoping that by declining magnanimously I could get the crew back on side), and finally the lights were dimmed. I checked in with Pete, who wished me an unenthusiastic 'good luck' and donned his earphones, then unclicked my seat belt for my skulk up to business under the cover of darkness. Like a ninja. One with big boobs and no weaponry, lethality or co-ordination. I made it halfway up the aisle undetected and was approaching the galley, where the curtain had been pulled across to shield the snoozing passengers from the bright lights. I was close enough to hear the sound of cabin crew gossip when a woman one seat ahead got up, opened the curtain and asked for water, throwing a shaft of incriminating light on my passing form. The gathered cabin crew's megawatt smiles dropped and I was greeted with narrowed eyes.

'What happened?' Pete said as I slid into my seat, a sour-faced escort loitering a few steps behind, making sure I stayed put.

'I'm being victimised,' I said. 'Wet skirt lady has turned them all against me. Apparently I'm a "safety concern" and I'm to stay in my seat.'

Pete tried to suppress a smile as he laid a blanket over me.

'I think my basic human rights are being violated in some way,' I continued, allowing Pete to recline my seat. 'I'm going to look it up when I get off this plane.'

'But you're not going to try going up there again, are you?' Pete said, looking worried.

I thought about that for a minute. I tightened my seat belt further and flicked the inflight magazine with force. 'No. No, I want to sit here and think.'

'OK,' Pete said with relief, his fingers hovering over the entertainment remote. 'Do you ... want me to think with you?'

'Maybe he thought you said "How *was* Scotland" not "How *is* Scotland",' Pete said twenty minutes later in response to my 'Maybe he's buying a retirement apartment for him and Mum?' His earphones were hanging round his neck and the opening credits for a documentary about a footballer were on pause on his entertainment screen.

'Mmm ... maybe ...' I said, running that possibility through my shit detectors. It was plausible. Dad was a vague-ish sort of man so maybe he hadn't really listened to me properly. Maybe I didn't realise how vague, and he really had thought he was in Scotland? No, he'd definitely lied. Nobody could confuse Heathrow Tarmac with Scottish Highland. Not even my father, who once confused my sister's face cream with white sauce and ate it with his vegetables. 'I'm sure you're right,' I said, looking into his brown, concerned (or were they annoyed ...?) eyes. 'I'm just panicking.'

'You are.'

'Sorry for being a psycho.'

'I'm used to it,' he said with a grin.

I leant across and gave him a kiss. 'You can watch your documentary now,' I said, and Pete instantly did just that.

Within half an hour Pete was in a deep sleep. He was perpetually exhausted these days; the arduous trip from Streatham to Virginia Water was taking its toll. We'd had many discussions about moving closer to work, but I just didn't think Annabelle was ready to be on her own and I loved Pete for being so understanding about it. Although recently his 'understanding' had been wavering. His boss had given him more responsibility; he had to be at school early three mornings a week to take the senior boarders on a six-mile run before breakfast, and Pete had been suffering with the additional hours. Lana had wanted to train me up to be a producer, which would have meant more money, and more money meant Pete and I might be able to afford to buy our own flat. Or at the very least, not have Dave the Body Confetti (dandruff) flatmate. But I had turned her down. The producer role came with more money but it also came with more hours. Hours I was not yet prepared to spend away from Annabelle and the kids. I liked knowing that twenty-five minutes after I clocked off at 5.30 p.m., I would be walking through Annabelle's front door. Lana was supportive and had said the job was there when Annabelle and I were ready. Pete was less so. I rested my hand on Pete's and even in his conked-out state his thumb gripped my pinky. I decided that if Annabelle coped on her own this trip, we could start to look at flats on the other side of London. And maybe I would talk to Lana about the producer role.

Unable to sleep, I flicked through Pete's highlighted *Lonely Planet* and printed pages from TripAdvisor while coming up with all sorts of probabilities as to why Dad would have lied. The obvious ones, of course: affairs; drug deals; Dad had the sudden urge to tan; but none really fitted his MO. I kept coming back to how unlikely any of them were and that Pete must be right. Dad had thought I'd asked how *was* Scotland, he was talking in the past tense when he'd said 'Lovely views' and the only reason he was on his way to Cape Town was because the Russian had decided he didn't want a cold Scottish isle as a gift for his five-year-old, he wanted a warm African one with nesting turtles and endangered lizards for little Saskia to collect and put in her giant terrarium.

At 11.03 a.m. we touched down and before the pilot had even uttered the whole spiel about welcoming us 'to this land of sun and braais', and the lie that is 'we've loved having you on this flight and can't wait to see you again', I was out of my seat.

'Come on,' I urged Pete through the throng of bleary-eyed bodies un-creaking their limbs in the aisle and getting items out of overhead luggage.

'OK.' He yawned and allowed me to drag him forward by the sleeve.

Despite the lady next to him constantly fussing with face mists, flight socks, rehydration salts and various reading materials, Pete had managed to get about four hours' kip. I hadn't. Not a wink. I can function on little sleep during the week but will often crash at the weekends. Pete says the inability to stop myself falling into a coma-like slumber at 2 p.m. every Saturday is not 'functioning', but I know no other way. My family are nappers. We like to snooze. We must have been Mediterranean at one point in our ancestry, but no one's bothered to find out. Probably too busy napping. We were at the very back of the plane so it took us an inordinate amount of time to disembark. Once off the aircraft we trudged along the terminal corridors following signs for Passport Control. I scanned the crowds looking for Dad while dialling his number. And then my phone died.

'Can I have your phone?' I held out my hand while keeping up the brisk pace.

'What for?' Pete said, pulling it from his jeans pocket.

'I need to call Dad.' I rolled my eyes like, *hello*, what alternative universe have you been visiting?

'I don't have his number.' Pete rubbed at his eyes with a fist like a tired toddler. It made my heart melt.

'You don't?'

'Why would I?' he said, breaking into another yawn. 'I never call him and if I did he'd most likely have lost his phone again. Or forgotten how to use it.'

That was fair. Dad often forgot how to use a mobile phone between calls. The only number I knew by heart was Annabelle's. I dialled it.

'Hello?' she said.

'Dad was on our plane!'

'Cool,' Annabelle said in her usual nothing-phases-me manner. 'You guys going to hang out?'

'What? No!' I said. 'Dad was supposed to be in Scotland. Don't you think it's odd he's suddenly getting on a plane to Cape Town?'

'Did you speak to him?'

'No. The Air Hostess Gestapo wouldn't let me up in business.'

'I'd love to fly business,' Annabelle said dreamily. 'Just once. I wouldn't even care where I was going. I just—'

'Focus, Annabelle!'

'On what?' she said, amusement at the edge of her voice. 'The fact that Dad, who works overseas, was spotted getting on a plane? Shall I alert MI5?'

'Can you just call him?' I huffed. 'My phone died and Pete doesn't have his number.'

'No, you call him. I'll send Dad's number to Pete, OK? I'm taking the kids to the pools.'

'By yourself?' Mum usually helped Annabelle on Saturday mornings. She would stay with Hunter while he did his lesson and Annabelle would take Katie for a paddle in the toddler pool.

'Yes. By myself.' Annabelle said, and she'd gone from amused to annoyed.

Pete tapped my shoulder and pointed to his sports watch. According to Pete and Priya's secretly organised schedule I was due at Priya's bridesmaid brunch and we needed to get through Customs.

'OK, I have to go. Don't forget to send Pete Dad's number.'

'Doing it as soon as I hang up.'

We said our goodbyes as Pete and I arrived in the cavernous Passport Control. It was remarkably busy and Dad was nowhere to be seen. Pete's phone pinged with the text from Annabelle.

'Maybe Mum isn't actually on a silent lentil retreat?' I said as I dialled Dad's number. 'Maybe she and Dad have booked a dirty trip away and decided to keep it a secret?'

Pete wrinkled his nose.

'Nah, you're right.' I shook my head. 'It's not very them.'

'And too gross.'

'*Way* too gross.'

Dad's voicemail came on. I didn't leave a message, knowing full well that Dad never checked them. We skirted around people looking up at signs or conferring in foreign tongues about how to complete the Customs arrival forms and joined the back of another long queue. I kept looking for Dad, even though I knew business class would've been first off the plane and would have sailed through Customs already. At Baggage Reclaim I did the same, even though his frequent-flyer priority baggage status meant he was one of the first to receive his luggage, and was often already exiting the airport while economy clientele were still hobbling to the carousel trying to reinstate normal blood flow to their kinked extremities. We stepped out into the arrival hall and, while doing a cursory scan for Dad, saw a man holding a tatty piece of cardboard with 'JESS ROBERTS-SCHIELE' written in almost-run-out black Sharpie.

I pointed to his sign. 'Hi. That's me.'

'Hello, Jess!' The man grinned and held out a hand for me to shake. 'I'm Trust. Welcome to Cape Town!'

'Trust?' Pete said, shaking his hand also. 'As in *trust you*"?'

'Just like that,' the grinning man said and he seemed very satisfied with our comprehension. 'You Miss Priya's friends? Come for the wedding? You staying at her apartment?'

I don't know why he was asking, as he clearly knew everything but we said yes, yes and yes anyway.

'Give to me,' Trust said, taking my case and hoisting Pete's backpack over his shoulder, despite Pete's alpha male protestations. 'Come,' he said and made an authoritative track through the crowds.

The automatic doors to outside opened and we were hit by face-in-the-toaster-level heat. Not sticky and humid like I'd experienced in Majorca one summer but hot, dry and everywhere; back of the neck, behind the ears, behind the knees, nostrils. Everywhere. Africa was one big wood-fired pizza oven. We reached a parking ticket machine and as Trust fed in some ratty-looking notes he noticed me fanning myself with my open passport.

'This hot for you?' he asked with a smile.

I nodded. Trust, in jeans, closed shoes and a collared polo shirt in a fabric I deemed far too thick for this level of sun power, looked surprised.

'You wait,' he said and grinned. 'It's early now. Much hotter later.'

I decided I'd be wearing cheesecloth and netting for the duration.

'Come,' Trust said again, heading towards a covered car park.

We trotted behind him, weaving around people and trollies and luggage and vehicles and arrived at a white Transit van.

'No, no,' Trust said as Pete tried to help him with the bags. Everything he did was with a huge white grin. 'You get in.'

I was about to climb in, hoping the van had arctic-like air conditioning, when I spotted Dad wheeling his suitcase at the far end of the car park. I knew my father's unhurried gait anywhere.

'There he is!' I said, gripping Pete's arm. 'DAD!' I yelled, but it got lost among the concrete pillars and the reunited people chattering on their way to their cars.

'Where?' Pete's head swivelled left and right.

I gasped. 'He's with a woman!' A slim lady with a flank of shiny caramel-blonde hair walked alongside Dad in a cream and gold jumpsuit, which sounds a little Mariah Carey but looked very Condé Nast – Italian Coast feature. 'DAD!' I yelled again, watching him place his suitcase into the boot of a gleaming white Range Rover Discovery.

They were too far for me to run over. By the time I got even halfway they'd be driving out of the car park. I grabbed Pete's phone again and dialled Dad's number. It went straight to his answer service again.

'She's probably a client,' Pete said, finally spotting the pair, but as Dad's arm moved to the small of the lady's back his face creased with concern.

'We have to follow him.' I threw Alice (the camel bag) in the van's middle row of seats, jumped in after her and looked back at Pete expectantly.

CHAPTER FOUR

'Well, do *your* clients put their hands on the small of *your* back?' I asked Annabelle as I moved Pete's phone from one ear to the other so I could steady myself against the inside of the van door.

I'd called her as soon as Trust had crossed the car park and bumped over some barricades to catch up with the white Discovery, but an official-ish looking guy had leapt out of nowhere shouting in another language, shaking his radio and pointing to the squat concrete barricades with irate astonishment. Eventually, with a dismissive wave of his arm, Trust swung out of the car park leaving the man looking official-ish yet ineffectual, but the Discovery was long gone.

'One guy put his hand on my tit,' Annabelle replied down the phone. 'But he's no longer my client.'

'Is he now the father of your next illegitimate child?'

'Oh, ha ha. I'd be insulted if I could be arsed,' Annabelle said. 'But I can't.' She paused to tell Hunter to stop throwing his swimming goggles around then came back on the line. 'She's most likely a client. Dad's old-school, he probably guides all female clients by the small of the back. It's hardly going to be anything sinister. It's *Dad*, for god's sake. He wouldn't be able to navigate the logistics of an affair, if that's what you're thinking.'

It was what I was thinking. But I didn't say as much. She was right. Dad was ill-equipped to manage an affair. He was charmingly forgetful, endearingly vague and so calm that he could, and would, fall asleep anywhere. He'd once gone to see an airport chapel (him being curious as he'd never even known they were there), sat down in a pew in the darkened chamber and promptly fallen asleep for five hours. He ended up missing his flight home and his own birthday BBQ went on without him.

'Goats!' Pete pointed at a herd of untethered goats eating dusty grass a few feet from the edge of the craziest motorway I'd ever been on. And that included the A303 on the way to Glastonbury.

Vehicles that would've looked at home in a scrapyard wove left and right or sped up and slowed down, as unpredictable as bees on lavender. People cut in front of us or swerved towards us, but none of it seemed to faze Trust, who zipped in and out and from lane to lane like he was trying to replicate Julie Andrews' dance routine on the top of that *Sound of Music* alp.

'Are those houses?' Pete stared out of the window at thousands of structures that appeared to be nothing more than rusty bits of corrugated iron leant up against each other in the shape of a shed. 'Do people live in those?'

'It was different from client-touching,' I replied to Annabelle, while Trust said that yes, many, many people did indeed live in the tin shacks. 'I can't explain. They seemed more intimate.' I turned to Pete, who was gaping out of the window. 'Didn't they? Pete?'

'What's that?' he said, unable to tear his eyes away from a group of children playing football at the side of the eight-lane motorway. Rubbish lay in huge piles beyond them. 'That kid's in nappies!'

I looked out of Pete's side of the van at a group of children chasing after a raggedy ball. No adult was present and no barrier was there to stop the children, including toddlers, running in front of a precariously loaded bus traversing the two lanes beside us. Or the speeding car that looked like it had been on its last wheels in 1982. A pick-up truck passed us with scruffily clad African men crouched together in the open-backed trailer; their threadbare clothing flapped violently and their eyes were tiny slits against the wind and dust. A thickset white man sat in the spacious cab, his windows up and his air con mostly likely on.

'And wouldn't he have told us if he was flying somewhere else?' I continued.

'He doesn't always tell us, Jess. His clients change their minds all the time, you know that.'

'It still feels like something weird is going on.'

Annabelle made a dismissive noise at the back of her

throat. 'Don't be ridiculous. You're just prone to amateur dramatics.'

I sniffed my offence. There was nothing amateur about them.

Annabelle asked Hunter to help Katie with her water wings then came back on the line. 'Remember *Les Mis*?' she said, her voice muffled like she was trying to hold the phone between her chin and her shoulder. 'And the time with the beetroot and red velvet cake? Or those times you thought all of us were dead from thrombosis?'

I scoffed, annoyed that my past unfounded worries were being brought in to dilute the current concern. *Les Mis* was a legitimate panic. Mum and Dad had gone to the theatre with the neighbours and left Annabelle and me at home alone without a babysitter for the first time. They said they'd be back at 11-ish and at 11.17 p.m. I'd commenced phoning the hospitals and every friend in their phone book, convinced they'd been in a car accident. It turned out they were next door having several nightcaps and could see me through the windows on the phone in my nightie and just thought I'd snuck out of bed to ring the Santa hotline again. Beetroot juice and red velvet cake was a combination that had me booking in for an unnecessary (and extremely uncomfortable) colonoscopy, and thrombosis is a very real concern.

'He'll call back,' Annabelle continued, 'you'll go to the wedding, get a tan, visit some giraffes, and if Pete manages to locate his balls he might ask you to marry him, just like you've always wanted.'

Annabelle's entire side of the conversation had been audible to both Pete and Trust, and at that last remark I got a chuckle from Trust and an eye-roll from Pete.

'What?' I mouthed, raising my eyebrows, playing the innocent. Pete shook his head and turned towards the window. 'Can you just send Dad a text asking him to call you back? Pete's phone only has eight per cent battery left.'

Annabelle tut-tutted but agreed and we hung up just as the motorway narrowed into a boulevard lined with palm trees. Table Mountain, enormous and block-like, loomed to our left and the ocean, shimmering like it'd been sprinkled with crushed diamonds, came into view on our right.

'You see the zebra?' Trust said, pointing over his shoulder to the left, making the van drift into the other lane. A BMW glided away from us and various other cars sped up or swerved to accommodate the manoeuvre.

Pete leant across me and peered out of the window as I scrolled through his contacts and found Dave's number. We were approaching the city centre, yet there on a golden, grassy hill beside an urban metropolis, stood two zebra chewing the dry grass like a couple of eccentrically painted horses.

Dave answered in a sleepy voice. 'Sup?'

'Hi. Are you at work? I'm in Cape Town and I was wondering if you can look up a car number plate for me. Have you got a pen?' I said.

'You're in Cape Town?'

'Yes. Do you have a pen?'

'Where's Pete?'

'In Cape Town too.'

'Whoa, awesome.' He coughed a raspy smoker's morning kind of cough. 'How long you there for?'

'Two weeks. And yes, you can have your zombie marathon. You can have two full weeks of zombie marathons, now can you look up a number plate?'

Dave coughed again. 'Like I've said many times before, Jess, it's not CTU here. We don't have access to the government, I can't look up current hospital admissions and we certainly don't have access to the South African version of the DMV.'

'What about tracking a phone?'

'Nope.'

'Can you break into an email? Can you see where a passport is on some international database or something?'

'Nope and nope.'

'What *do* you have access to?'

'I can listen in on 999 calls,' he said in a weary voice. 'But only ones I've dispatched from my server.'

'That's it?'

'That's it.'

'How boring.'

'Tell me about it. So, what's going on, Jess?' he said in a patient yet knowing voice.

I filled him in on the Dad situation and Dave gently reminded me that I had the tendency to be a smidge psychotically, pathologically paranoid and got all, '*Remember the time you started worrying about sink holes?*' and '*I told you I couldn't smell*

47

any toxic gas but who ended up paying a huge fine for calling out the National Grid emergency services for what ended up being an overripe banana?' and I sighed and had to admit that perhaps the sleep deprivation and the sudden ripping away from Annabelle and the kids might have something to do with my heightened catastrophe radar. I hung up, handed the phone back to Pete and leant my weary head against his shoulder.

'Have I got time to go back to the apartment?' I said, checking my underarms. 'I smell.'

Pete put his arm around me and kissed the top of my head. Trust grinned in the rear-view mirror.

'You do smell,' Pete said with a smile. 'But no. The brunch started an hour ago and Priya said to take you straight there so you can do dress fittings and corsage ... painting ... or whatever.'

'But what about Dad?'

'You just have to charge your phone and wait for him to call back.'

'But what if—'

'Do you know what your mother would say right now?'

I eyed Pete suspiciously. Very rarely would he align himself with Mum's mode of thinking. He was a black and white, go-to-the-GP-if-you're-sick, watch-a-funny-movie-if-you're-sad kind of person. Mum's unconventional recommendations would fall on his selectively deaf ears.

'What would she say?'

'She'd say, "*You shouldn't worry about something you can't control*".'

My shoulders relaxed. 'She would.'

Pete continued with a rather cynical air about him. 'Then she'd tell you that worrying causes ulcerated colons, and that gluten glugs the mind and makes you negative and *"those electrolytes don't work, you know, Pete, you need to try my hydrogen water. Dehydration can contribute to erectile dysfunction"* and *"Pete, you do eat an awful lot of bagels, how's your mental health?"* and—'

'I get it,' I said, pulling him back from the brink of my mother-induced madness. 'I'll stop worrying,' I said, intending to do no such thing.

'Good. Because Priya's paid for these flights and she deserves to have an amazing wedding with her best friend beside her, bottling up all her feelings.' Pete gave a playful smile, knowing that my family, under Mum's self-help-book, organic-pillow-slips and om-your-pain-away leadership, don't do 'bottling up our feelings'.

We rounded a bend and the docks came into sight. A few miles off the shore lay a flat, white island, like a pancake floating on the top of the ocean. Traffic began to slow as we curved around high-rises pinging sunlight in our eyes and the city opened up in front of us. It didn't seem very big. More like a large, sunny town.

'How many people live in Cape Town?' Pete asked.

Outside his window children in tattered clothing and bare feet moved through the traffic, begging.

'Depends on how you count,' Trust replied.

'Riiight,' Pete said, giving me an amused look. 'How do *you* count?'

Trust chuckled. 'Fairly,' he said, making a quick lane change.

We left the boulevard and moved into a more urban area. People milled about on the sunny pavements. Priya had said Cape Town was a bubble in comparison to the rest of South Africa. Sure, crime was still there but for the most part everyone went about their daily lives the way we do in England. Just with more sun and cheaper plastic surgery. You still had to be careful, but perhaps no more than you did in certain parts of Hackney after dusk. We turned onto a road that followed the coastline while Trust chatted about how nice Priya was and how she never vomited in his van after a night out like the other actress. The sea was to our right, vast and shimmery. People bobbed about in kayaks not too far from the shore. Were they not aware South African waters were like an all-you-can-eat buffet for great whites? There was no way I was going to put even a toe in that water. It'd be like offering up a canapé. I'd be sticking to the nice chlorinated swimming pools thank you very much. I turned to look out of the other window at the lively pavement. Most people seemed to be in some kind of exercise attire. Packs of male cyclists in their weird cycle shoes and unforgiving lycra sat at outdoor café tables, their bikes in glinting metal stacks beside them.

Trust turned in his seat and grinned at our gawping faces. 'England like this?'

I laughed while watching a group of women in sherbet shades of tight activewear cross the road holding yoga mats and green juices, their arms bare and toned, their ponytails swinging down their backs. 'Not at all.'

I'd never seen so many slim, tanned women with perky boobs. I tracked Pete's gaze but it was focused on a park with an outdoor gym where muscled men were doing one-arm chin-ups and hanging ab crunches. One guy was doing handstand press-ups on top of the monkey bars.

'Every day these men are doing this,' Trust said, gesturing towards the beefy gymnasts. 'Very strong.'

'*Very*,' I said in an overly appreciative voice.

Pete gave me an under-appreciative look. We rounded a corner and a crescent-shaped white sand beach came into view. The sea, turquoise at the shoreline, deepened to a sapphire blue further out.

'Wow,' Pete breathed.

'This Camps Bay,' Trust said.

Boulders at either end of the beach were vast and smooth like the ones in pictures of the Seychelles. Some were the size of cars, others the size of studio flats. Busy cafés with outdoor tables lined one side of the street and the sea stretched out for miles and miles on the other. Breaking waves frothed themselves onto the shore, palm trees did their palm tree thing (which is instantly to make people feel good) and behind it all the craggy cliffs of some mountain range I'd have to look up the name of loomed dramatically. We inched along the beachfront watching men take surfboards off their roof racks, their wetsuits undone to their waists, showing off muscled, tanned torsos. Well I was, anyway. Pete's head was whipping around taking in all the people in their various states of 'sport'. They crossed the road in tiny, tiny outfits; they walked along the footpath in tiny, tiny outfits, or played with dogs in tiny, tiny outfits (the people, not the dogs). The sandy shore was swarming with couples playing beach tennis, groups playing volleyball and boys in their twenties throwing rugby balls or Frisbees, or hacky sacks. Pete observed the activity like a restrained puppy. I had the sudden realisation that Cape Town was going to be like a theme park for him. I wanted to sort out the Dad matter and then let my sports-mad boyfriend loose on the African outdoors. As Trust swung a left and drove up a steep winding road, Pete's phone beeped with a text from Annabelle.

Call me.

CHAPTER FIVE

'Did he call you back?' I said as soon as Annabelle answered.

'No, he texted.'

'And?'

'He said: "*It's lovely. Hope it's going OK with Mum away. Give the pumpkins a kiss from Grandpop. With clients now so turning phone off. Love Dad.*"'

My stomach sank. He was lying. 'So you asked him how Scotland was and he replied "*It's lovely.*"?'

'Yes,' Annabelle said, as Pete laid a sympathetic hand on my knee. 'Oh. No, wait . . .'

I waited.

'I asked him how the *trip* was.'

'Annabelle!'

Pete rolled his eyes and removed his sympathetic hand.

'Sorry,' she said, not sounding sorry at all.

I shook my head. 'Did you text him back?'

'Yes.'

I waited. It was like getting blood out of a banana. 'And what did you say?'

'Oh,' Annabelle said, and I could hear the dull click–click of her tapping at her phone. 'I said, "*OK. Have fun.*"'

'That's it?'

Annabelle could sense my disappointment. You'd have to be blind, deaf, dumb and dead not to.

'Yeah ...' she said. 'Maybe I should have asked him something else.'

'Yes, you should have. Ring him back.' I said, as Trust pulled up outside ornate metal gates in a long high wall.

'He said he was turning his phone off, remember?'

'God dammit, Annabelle!'

'Oh calm down,' she said. 'You've got yourself in a flap. He's with a client, Jess. A *client*. You've misread the whole thing and are just working yourself up. Did you pack the medicine I gave you?'

'No, Annabelle, your medicine is weed and weed is illegal.' Annabelle said her CBD oil was 100 per cent pharmaceutical and contained no mood-altering THC, but I wasn't so sure. 'I have to go now. I'm at the bridesmaid brunch. If you hear from Dad, call me, OK?'

'Sure,' Annabelle said with the slow assurance of someone appeasing a paranoid elderly woman at a retirement home. One who thinks her appliances are filming her in the tub.

I kissed Pete goodbye, hopped out of the van and, after speaking through an intercom, stepped through the automatically opening gates. A path wound through immaculate gardens towards an enormous white house. It looked like two huge glass and concrete shoeboxes on top of each other at opposite angles. I got to the end of the path and a man in a white suit directed me around the side of the house to the pool and gardens. Priya had hired the house for her family for the wedding weekend, which is why Pete and I were able to stay in her apartment. Her fiancée, Laurel, and her family had a house in another part of town. They'd meet the next day at the service and a day later head off on their honeymoon for two weeks. They may have been a British Indian lesbian and a white American lesbian getting married in South Africa, but they wanted to do at least *that* part traditionally. Pete had been very good at filling me in on all the proceedings during the plane trip. Interspersed with fielding my theories about Dad, of course.

'Jess!' Priya shot across the lawn. 'Oh my god!' She threw her arms around my neck. She was so tall my nose hit her collarbone. 'Thank you for coming! Thank you, thank you, thank you!'

'Thank *you* for the flights!' I said, gripping my best friend's thin frame in a tight embrace.

She waved away the acknowledgement and looked at me with familiar evaluation. Priya had always been able to tell when someone needed to 'talk it out'.

'You look a bit shit.' She slung an arm over my shoulder; I put mine around her waist (her height meant my arm had to angle upwards) and as we walked towards the other girls gathered under white brollies by the pool, I filled her in on the Dad situation.

I explained about the inappropriate touching, and gave Annabelle's theory countered with mine – he was having an affair with a woman named Maxima with caramel highlights and great sandals and they were going to start an eco-resort in Malawi. (My hypothesis had gotten more elaborate the longer I went without sleep.)

'God Jess, it's Teddy Roberts! He's *so* not having an affair!' Priya clutched her thin waist and laughed. She had a loud, honking laugh, which infected everyone around her. 'It's like that time you watched that old Ricki Lake episode and started worrying that Pete was your cousin and made him take that online DNA test!' She honked louder and pulled me into a tight hug.

In the face of her scepticism my anxiety waned. The champagne cocktail shoved in my hand before my bag was even off my shoulder also helped. Priya introduced me to two actresses from her show (I wondered which one was the vomiter who'd upset congenial Trust), and then I greeted her parents, cousins, sister and primary-school friend whom I already knew. We ate brunch, drank Pimm's and champagne cocktails for an hour then Priya took me inside to try on dresses. She wasn't having bridesmaids in the traditional sense; it was more in name than job requirement. Myself, her sister, her friend from primary school and two of the four cousins were being dressed in the same hue – blush – but in every other sense we were just one of the guests.

'Everything is super-casual.' Priya chatted animatedly as we padded across the marble floor to the master suite. 'We threw it all together in a couple of weeks. When we found out we had a hiatus in filming we just decided to go for it! I mean, who wouldn't want to get married in a place like this?' She was fizzing with excitement. 'Plus Cape Town is so gay-friendly, it just seemed right, you know, babe?'

I did and gave her a hug. I tried on the dresses; we talked hair, make-up, holidays and sex for a while then went back outside, lay on pool loungers and consumed Pimm's like it was water and we were desert wanderers. As it neared nap time I began to fade.

'Babe, go home,' Priya said when a snort-like snore woke me up and had the rest of the party giggling. 'I need you in top party form tomorrow, OK?'

She walked me to the gate where Trust was snoozing in the van. 'Wear whichever one you like,' she said as she handed over the dresses in a zip-up dry-cleaner's bag.

I nodded and climbed in the back of the van, my eyelids desperate to crash down and stay there.

'See you tomorrow when I'm a MRS!' Priya shrieked, then dissolved into her honking laugh.

Back at the apartment, which Trust helped me locate via security gates, access cards and keys, I found a note from Pete saying he was at the rooftop pool. I said goodbye to Trust, who Priya had told me was to be our personal driver for the next two weeks, had a quick cold shower to wake me up, changed into my bikini, balked at the sight of my body that had been under multiple layers since September and followed the apartment complex map to the pool. I found Pete on a lounger, his muscled chest glistening with sweat, a *Lonely Planet* at his side, talking enthusiastically with the pool attendant about paddleboarding at a local beach. Paddleboarding?! Was that not just a large floating platter upon which you stood, snack-like, above peckish sharks?

I hung out at the pool for a while, but between Pete and the pool attendant's conversation about leaping off mountains with a backpack that may or may not open out into a non-ripped, non-tangled, easily steerable parachute, or the best places to abseil (*duh* ... the answer is nowhere), I couldn't get a word in. I went back to the apartment, lay on the bed in my bikini and fell immediately asleep.

I woke an hour later with a taste in my mouth like I'd been sucking on one of Pete's gym socks. Pete lay asleep, shirtless, on top of the covers next to me. He looked so sexy but I decided against pouncing amorously on him, what with my breath akin to a sewer rat's undercarriage, and instead got up and pulled out my laptop. I'd been plagued by hallucinogenic anxiety dreams where Dad, in a tropical beach shirt, was with Mistress Maxima on her yacht in Jamaica flipping Malibu bottles behind his back to the sound of the song 'Kokomo'. Somehow my Dad had morphed into Tom Cruise in *Cocktail* and I needed to find out what was going on before I went 100 per cent crazy. I was going to email Dad and just ask him outright where he was. My logical self said I was wrong and everybody else was right but I had an illogical self who was currently front and centre and needed sedating. I opened my emails and saw one from Lana.

> Hi Jess, by now you will have arrived and hopefully have a cocktail in hand. I'm so glad you've finally taken a holiday. I've booked a night for you and Pete at a game lodge. You work hard and you know that I know you are more than just 'my PA' so please enjoy it. Unfortunately at such short notice they only had one date and one room available so I hope it fits in with your plans. All the details are in the attached confirmation form.
>
> BTW – in case you think I'm secretly super-rich and can afford to book nights at luxury lodges whenever I feel like it and you'd rather I just up your salary, calm down. I'm not rich. It's a comp deal from when we were out there for a shoot a couple of years back. I haven't found the time to use it so it's all yours. ☺
>
> Love Lana

I opened the confirmation form. Lana had booked one night in a luxury hut, all food and drinks included for the Monday before Pete and I flew back. We would have a private sunrise safari where we would get to see the Big Five and then meet rescue cheetahs at the game reserve's rehabilitation centre. I squealed and jumped up and down. I was going to touch all the wildlife and cuddle them and get all up in their faces! I tapped out a reply telling Lana I loved her more than Netflix and Zach Braff and the chocolate shelves at Wholefoods, then pressed send and tapped out one to Dad.

> Hi Dad, just wondering where you are at the moment. Miss you loads. Love Jess.
> P.S. I'm in Cape Town for Priya's wedding! Can you believe it?

I clicked send, then opened his company's website. In the Africa region, Barney and Irving Private Island Brokerage had three islands for sale in the Seychelles, one on Lake Kariba in Zambia, one in Mauritius and two in Madagascar. Satisfied that there was a legitimate reason for Dad to be in Cape Town, I closed down the webpage. But then the persistent niggly feeling reared again and I opened Google and typed 'Teddy Roberts, private island sale South Africa'. Nothing came up, so I tried a variety of 'Teddy Roberts, South Africa/ Edward Roberts, South Africa' options. Nothing obvious came up except an E. Roberts was having an exhibition at a gallery in Cape Town. I clicked on the link and it took me to a webpage for a restaurant/gallery called The Baroness, which I recognised from one of Pete's TripAdvisor printouts (it had been highlighted in pink which meant he'd thought I'd like it) and, according to Google Maps, was only ten minutes away.

I knew it was a huge leap (OK, a giant one that only a partially mad person might make) to think it might be Dad, especially considering the website had said the exhibiting pieces were 'various mixed-media erotica' and Dad only ever painted very average landscapes, but we needed to eat, so why not combine a little irrational investigation with a drink and a meal?

CHAPTER SIX

'It won't be him.' Pete fastened his seat belt, his eyes still crinkly from his nap. He wore a nicely pressed polo shirt, new chinos and his 'going out' trainers.

'I'm eighty-six per cent sure it's not going to be him either, but I need to find out what's going on and his phone is still off so what else can I do?'

'Oh, I don't know ...' Pete made a show of pretending to consider grand ideas as Trust steered the van out of our security gates, fist-bumping a guard through his open window. 'Maybe you could go to your best friend's wedding, climb Table Mountain, go to the beach and ... oh, that's right; understand that your Dad is just doing his job?'

I checked my hair in a pocket mirror. Underneath the heavy side fringe my hairdresser convinced me was going to nail 'sexy detective on American TV network', the heat was doing sweaty things to my forehead.

'What harm does it do? We'll look at the art, ask the

gallery owner about the E. Roberts exhibition, eat, drink then go home … and I'll do that thing you like,' I said with a saucy wink. 'Besides, I'm not sure I can climb Table Mountain.'

This was more of a concern to Pete than my father's potential lie/affair/illegal diamond trading/illegal arms trading/ illegal animal trading (yes, my anxieties had increased and yes, it sounded paranoid but we are who we are and I am the Princess of Darkness).

'Why not? It's the most recommended highlight!' Pete said, brandishing his ever-present *Lonely Planet* and his stapled printouts from TripAdvisor. Why could he not make bookmarks on his iPad like a normal Gen Y-er? Or, more importantly, why could he not use the iPad without a deep furrow in his otherwise smooth forehead and a torrent of annoyed huffs and puffs?

'Because of the snakes,' I said. A tremor of revulsion worked its way down my spine.

'Evil snakes!' Trust shuddered. 'Very many snakes.'

I gave Pete a pointed look. I definitely considered myself an animal lover when it came to every other creature on this planet. I didn't set mousetraps, I encouraged spiders to go outside (via the plughole) and I abhorred all things 'animal tested', but if I had the funds … oh, if I had the funds! You can forget Brexit; I'd have Snexit. Snakes exit planet earth. Preferably in a big robot-driven spaceship that would explode in space, obliterating those limbless swathes of evil. But other than that, all creatures were created equal, blah blah blah.

'They run away when they hear people,' Pete said.

'They run, do they?' I mocked. 'With their little feet?'

Trust chuckled.

'You know what I mean. I asked the guy at the pool. He climbs it every weekend and he's never, not *once*, seen a snake.'

'There are spiders too,' I said. 'Big ones.'

'Yes, Sisi.' Trust nodded gravely.

Pete gave me a look.

'And rabid monkeys and marauders and plague-ridden rats,' I added and then frowned because I seemed to be getting a walk up Table Mountain confused with the plot of an *Indiana Jones* movie.

Pete rolled his eyes. 'No there *aren't.*'

'And there's the mountain.'

'What about it?'

'It's very big.'

'That's the whole point!'

It's not as though I was averse to exercise. I loved exercising. I did a spin class and yoga and Pilates and yoga-lates. I didn't partake in anything running-related any more; these boobs were made for walking (as the song doesn't go). But I was truly, claw-your-own-skin-off, run-away-in-your-skeleton-screaming-like-a-hurricane terrified of snakes. And, according to Pete's *Lonely Planet*, which I'd read on the plane while he kipped, Table Mountain was crawling with them.

'Well, what about the environment then?' I protested. 'Won't the foot traffic be causing erosion which could lead to the entire tectonic plate shifting?'

Pete scoffed.

'You have heard of the butterfly effect, haven't you? A pretty little monarch flaps its wings in Kent and moments later a chunk of Australia breaks off. We end up with a whole new country and all the maps in the world need to be changed. Not to mention the koala families that were in side-by-side trees one moment and the next butterfly-flapping minute their trees are on different islands, separated by shark-infested ocean.'

Pete's discussion-wearied gaze weighed heavily on me.

'We clomp up there,' I waved in the direction of the monolith that was visible from every part of the city, 'changing the shape of that mountain with every step and who knows what could happen?! I'm only thinking of the koalas.'

Pete blinked. 'You'll love it.' He turned and looked out of the window. 'You just need to put yourself out of your comfort zone.'

I decided against replying. I was out of my comfort zone right now. Annabelle was at home without Mum or me to help and Hunter had probably googled how to make a bomb using window cleaner, a microwave and melted Lego pieces and the CIA would have tracked his internet search and would be bursting into the house right now; they'd find Annabelle's 'medicine' stash and the kids would end up in care and Katie would be signing for juice and her foster carer wouldn't know that Katie calls almond milk 'juice' (because she'd seen Mum squeezing the nut-milk bag, therefore thinks of it as being 'juiced') and they'd give her orange juice not knowing she'd end up with severe hives and respiratory difficulty. My stomach cramped. I dialled Annabelle.

'Hey,' she answered.

'Everything OK?'

'Yep.'

'What's Hunter doing?'

'He's . . .' Her voice sounded like she was craning her neck. '. . . eating an avocado with Marcus.'

'Who's Marcus?' I said, thinking CIA agent.

'My client. Remember? The guy with the sister. Mad Mandy?' Annabelle stopped. 'Oh god, he just heard me say that. He's got quite big ears.'

I rolled my eyes.

'Oh god, he just heard me say *that*,' she continued, still not clicking that lowering her voice might be an advisable option. 'He's—'

'OK, OK!' I said, stopping her from insulting Big-eared Marcus any further. 'I just wanted to check Hunter hadn't been googling anything incriminating.' Pete gave me a very strange yet not unfamiliar look. 'But if it's all OK I'll let you go. Heard from Dad?'

'No. You?'

'No, I'm following a lead right now though.'

'Following a lead?' Annabelle ridiculed. 'That fringe didn't make you Kate Beckett, you know.'

'I'm going. Goodbye,' I said, hanging up and adjusting my fringe. It SO did make me Kate Beckett.

*

Trust turned down a side street and pulled up in a 'no parking' bay outside a dove-grey building with purple window frames. The purple doorway was framed with blue Perspex glitter hearts the size of saucers. A strip of green AstroTurf lay across the footpath from the doorway to the road like a red carpet and electric-orange velvet barriers attached to brass poles flanked either side.

'Many famous people come here,' Trust said.

I leapt out of the van into the heat of the afternoon. While I waited for Pete to put his *Lonely Planet* in his ever-present backpack and climb out after me, I considered the building. There was no signage, just the glitter hearts, the AstroTurf and an outdoor ashtray on a stainless steel pole. According to some of my googling, James Franco was seen here downing shots and dancing on tables with model-esque locals a few months previously. Trust told us to text him when we wanted to leave and drove off looking for somewhere to park and wait (snooze).

'Right,' I said to Pete. 'Let's get this over with.'

'After you, Miss Marple.'

'Detective Beckett,' I said, flicking my hair and following the AstroTurf carpet to the entrance.

The door opened into an intimate space by South African standards but perhaps what an English home would consider a large reception room. Tables of all shapes and sizes were painted glossy white and surrounded by differently styled chairs, also white and shiny. The wallpaper was an opulent patterned burgundy and ornate gold picture frames displayed tongue-in-cheek paintings of renaissance-style characters holding loaves of bread suggestively. A small raised stage took up the back wall and housed a polished black piano. Along the left-hand side of the room ran a flamboyant gold rococo bar, behind which stood a sandy-haired guy speaking baby language to a bichon frise. The bichon frise lay on a tasselled velvet pillow on top of the bar, luxuriating in the praise.

'Oh hi,' the bar guy said, looking up from his *amour* and noticing us standing in the doorway. He was English, which surprised me. 'Can I help you?'

'We're looking for the gallery?' I said, walking closer.

A brown shaggy dog trotted by me and I stooped to give him a scratch behind his hairy ears before he continued towards a door behind the bar, probably the kitchen considering the clanging sounds emanating from there. Pete followed me and narrowly missed treading on another dog lying partially under a table.

'It's through there,' the guy indicated to a closed door opposite the piano, his grey eyes flicking between Pete and me. 'But it's not open. Where're you guys from?'

'London,' I said. 'I'm Jess and this is Pete.'

'Jimmy,' the guy said, offering his hand over the bar. He wore a white T-shirt, kind of grubby, and his forearms were tanned and muscled. 'I'm from Richmond. Are you here on holiday?'

'We're here for a wedding,' Pete said, a bit more blokey than usual. 'Thought we'd tag on a bit of holiday.'

An ugly chihuahua/pug-type dog wheezed and waddled past and I picked it up. 'Aww, how cute is he?!' I said, hugging it and holding the dog's face up to Pete. It immediately sneezed and covered Pete's polo shirt in viscous snot.

'Jess!' Pete screeched.

'Ooops!'

Pete gave me a death stare and I hid my sniggers behind the wheezy, snotty dog.

'Here,' Jimmy said, passing over a filthy-looking dishcloth, trying to supress a laugh. 'And he's a she. Lucy.'

Pete looked at the filthy dishcloth and Lucy's snot and appeared to be wondering which was the lesser of the two evils.

'We were wondering about an artist you're exhibiting?' I said, putting Lucy back on the floor before she gave Pete another coating.

'*You* were wondering,' Pete said, dabbing at his shirt with a corner of the cloth.

'I don't know much about the exhibitions,' Jimmy said, glancing at Pete, then checking the levels of a liquor bottle. 'I'm just the barman. You'll have to wait until we're open. How long are you here for?'

'Two weeks,' Pete said. 'Wedding is tomorrow, then we're seeing what Cape Town has to offer.' He handed Jimmy back the filthy rag.

'You guys are going to love it!' Jimmy said, cracking into a wide grin. 'There's so much to do!'

'I've been reading about it.' Pete fished his *Lonely Planet* out of his rucksack, eyes a-sparkle. 'I want to go shark cage diving, and there's a triathlon next week, and we want to climb Table Mountain.'

I snorted. '*You* want to.'

Pete rolled his eyes. I rolled my eyes right back. The barman seemed to find us amusing.

'They have the best nightlife here,' Jimmy said. 'And markets and beaches and festivals. Oh man, the festivals! There's this one where the bands are on the banks of a river and everyone floats on the water in rubber rings, drinking beer! You'll want to come back, two weeks isn't enough to fit it all in.'

Pete looked pained at the thought of 'not fitting it all in'.

'Can we just see the gallery?' I asked, trying to get the conversation back on track despite the fact that a very clear picture had filled my head of Pete floating past me on a rubber ring, his abs tensed pleasingly and his straight-toothed grin shining in my direction.

'We're not open yet,' Jimmy replied.

'But surely the gallery is?'

Jimmy shook his head.

'But it's daytime?'

'I don't make the rules. I make margaritas!' Jimmy held up a bottle of tequila, the worm banging against the side. 'And if you come back when we're open I can make you one on the house.'

'Sounds great!' Pete said.

'I don't want a margarita, thanks,' I said. 'I want to speak to someone about an exhibition. Is there anyone here I can speak to?'

'The gallery isn't open. The bar isn't open. The restaurant isn't open. *We're* not open,' Jimmy said, but not unkindly. He flashed a wide grin to Pete. 'Persistent, isn't she?'

'You have no idea,' Pete smiled back.

I shot him a look that said *you're supposed to be on my side, punk, and if you want any future blowjobs you'd best keep that in mind.* Pete gave me a repentant smile because he did want future blowjobs.

'What kind of gallery isn't open during the day?' I asked.

'This kind.' Jimmy emptied one bottle into another. 'T.I.A.'

'Huh?' I was starting to lose my 'Kate Beckett' coolness.

'T.I.A. This Is Africa. It means . . . things don't make sense. That's the only thing that makes sense.'

'That things don't make sense?'

'You got it!'

'So, the gallery isn't open until night time?'

'Nope.'

'Because it's part of the bar/restaurant/dog hotel you've got going on here?'

'Exactly.'

'So, if I want to see if it's my father's work in that exhibition . . .?'

'Who's your father?' he said, looking interested.

'Teddy Roberts?'

'Never heard of him.'

'How about Edward Roberts? Or E. Roberts?'

Jimmy shook his head.

'You've got an exhibition for an E. Roberts starting in just under two weeks and you've never heard that name?' I said, sceptical.

'I told you, I'm just the barman.'

'Then why did you ask who my father was?'

'Seemed polite at the time.'

'That was thirty seconds ago,' I growled.

Jimmy seemed unperturbed. 'If you come back tonight Frankie will be here and will be able to answer any gallery-related questions.'

'Can't you just take me in there?' I didn't know what I thought I'd find. An incriminating self-portrait of my father perhaps? But the website had said E. Roberts was exhibiting a collection of erotic nudes, so I put that mental picture in the mental shredder. Twice.

'I'm not allowed in there any more,' Jimmy said.

Pete and I frowned.

Jimmy glanced towards the kitchen then leant on the bar. 'My brother shows in there sometimes, and once,' he paused. 'Twice.' He paused again. 'OK, every time . . . I've sneaked in before opening and put some real piece of shit up on the wall with his name under it.'

I giggled and, encouraged, Jimmy continued with a twinkle in his grey eyes.

'You know that drawing of the dog that has a story that helps you draw it . . .? About a guy in a cave with bees and a bear or something?'

'Yes,' I said, captivated.

'No,' Pete said, confused.

'Well, I did one of those on the back of a menu then taped it to the wall and called it *Dog's Dinner*.'

I sniggered.

'Another time I dropped tomato juice on a napkin and pinned it to the wall with a green drawing pin. They loved that one.' Jimmy grinned. 'My brother didn't. His art is quite serious.'

'What kind of art does he do?'

'Takes photos of bridges.'

'Brilliant,' I said, with growing admiration for stubbly chin, scruffy shirt, practical joker Jimmy.

'Anyway . . .' He picked up another half-filled bottle and wiped it with a cloth. 'Like I said, I can't help you but you can come back later tonight and talk to Frankie if you like.'

'Will do,' Pete said, taking my hand in his and giving it a gentle tug towards the exit. 'See ya, mate,' he said to Jimmy, who raised his arm in return. 'We'll come back for that margarita.'

I followed Pete outside, who'd begun flicking through his *Lonely Planet*, but then remembered a photo I had in my phone and rushed back to the bar.

'Have you seen this man in here before?' I said, holding the screen towards Jimmy, watching for his reaction.

For a tiny instant I thought I spotted recognition behind his eyes, then he frowned and shook his head.

'It's a pretty terrible photo,' he said, getting back to his bottle-cleaning.

This was true. It was out of focus, shadowy and Dad was dressed as Santa, his elasticised beard pulled down under his chin and his hat on wonky. But Jimmy had recognised him. I was certain of it.

'Are you sure? *Really* sure?' I pressed.

'Two fucking portions of salmon starter?!' A woman's gravelly voice with a strong Afrikaans accent travelled out of the kitchen, then a diminutive lady with a messy grey chignon, wearing a blue and white striped catering apron over her chef's shirt marched into the restaurant, cursing and pulling a packet of fags from her apron pocket as she went. 'What do I pay you for? You're fucking useless! Saturday night and only two salmon starters? Two?! Two fucking portions isn't going to feed anybody!'

The lady barrelled past me without acknowledgement but as she reached the front door she said, 'Jimmy, what have I told you about having your lady friends visit?' then tugged open the door and stalked through, lighting her cigarette.

'I'm going to kill her dead this time,' said a young Hispanic guy as he emerged from the door behind the bar, his catering apron barely covering his wide chest and his face like thunder. 'I'll put arsenic in her cigarettes, I'll feed rat poison to her dogs, I'll put acid on her eye mask. I will kill her, Jimmy.' He pronounced the 'J' more like a 'Y'.

'I'd better go,' Jimmy said with an apologetic shrug. He turned, slung an arm over the Hispanic guy's meaty shoulders and sweet-talked him back to the kitchen.

CHAPTER SEVEN

'So are they going to say *"the bride may kiss the bride"* or something?' Pete said as we jumped in the back of Trust's van the next day.

'No, they'll say *"you may now kiss"*.'

Trust eyed us from the rear-view mirror. Priya and Laurel were going to have some kind of equality-type ceremony that involved vows of mutual respect, lots of flowers (Priya was obsessed with colour, yellow being her favourite), a traditional Hindu walk around the fire pit and lots and lots of laughter. Pete nodded and processed the information. He loved Priya. Absolutely loved her. But he'd never been 100 per cent comfortable with her being a lesbian.

'I just worry I'll say the wrong thing,' he'd stressed to me once when he was drunk in a taxi on the way home from one of Priya and Laurel's infamous (and boozy) pot luck dinners.

'What, like, *"This is a lovely salad; are those pine nuts YOU BIG CARPET MUNCHER?"*' I'd replied, and Pete had dissolved into embarrassed drunken giggles. And hadn't been able to eat pine nuts with a straight face ever since.

I'd told Priya about it the next day. She'd thought it was hilarious and now every meal we had at her flat contained pine nuts. And that was why, sitting in Pete's lap, was his wedding gift; a little jar of pine nuts tied up with a yellow ribbon.

The wedding was at a winery forty-five minutes out of Cape Town. We travelled through dry, open landscapes with jagged mountain ranges showing grey-blue in the distance. Heat pounded through the windows despite the van's air-conditioning blowing a noisy gale. I smiled at Pete, the memory of the night before playing in my head. After we left the RSPCA/gallery/bar/restaurant, Pete had asked Trust to swing by a place he'd read about. It was a big restaurant on the edge of the water where tables, sofas and bar leaners sat on sand. Yachts moored close by, their occupants lounging on deck listening to music coming from the outdoor speakers. Pete had gotten me tipsy on an amazing South African red (not sure of variety, definitely don't care) and then we'd gone home, shagged and Pete had fallen dead asleep. I'd gotten up to check my emails but there was nothing from Dad; it wasn't unusual, he often took a few days to reply. So I'd started a Google search for things to do in Cape Town. Pete liked his *Lonely Planet* and TripAdvisor recommendations but I preferred to scour Instagram and do intensive Google searches. By the time I crawled in beside Pete, I had more places I couldn't wait to visit than we had time to see. I'd snuggled next to him and felt a heat in the pit of my stomach when, in his sleep, his hand stroked my thigh. I would think about climbing Table Mountain. I really would. Pete wanted to climb it and I wanted to *want* to.

Trust swung the van off the main road and drove down a tree-lined drive towards a white building with round gables which, according to the *Lonely Planet* Pete was reading aloud from, was typical of Cape Dutch architecture and was about three hundred years old. Trust dropped us by a little chalk-board sign that directed guests to the picnic area and drove off to snooze in the van under the trees.

We followed a winding path through gorgeous gardens and when we reached the picnic grounds, stopped in our tracks. The vast lawn was emerald green, dense and short-clipped in a standard similar to a luxury golf course. Hammocks hung between grand old trees with drooping branches which gave dappled shade to the white and grey beanbags dotted about the lawn. Tables with linen tablecloths had been placed in various areas, each with jars of rustic bouquets of herbs and wildflowers. Yellow bunting hung between trees, marking out the wedding party area, and the expansive lawns stretched out towards the mountain ranges in the distance. The sky was blue, the air was warm and the only sounds were laughing, chatting and the tinkling of wine bottles on glasses. My favourite kinds of sounds.

'Wow,' I said, taking hold of Pete's hand. I couldn't believe I was actually there. About to watch my best friend get married in the most beautiful setting I'd ever seen. It was so romantic and joyful. 'Let's get some wine!' I said, keen to get in the thick of the merriment.

With a rosé for me and a local craft beer for Pete, we walked over to a group of people who looked like they might be the most fun. Pete has the tendency to be shy whereas my philosophy is everybody is a potential new friend. Just walk up and find out if you like each other. And anyone who thinks I'm weird for introducing myself is not my kind of person anyway, so no loss.

'Do you think most of the people here are gay?' Pete whispered as we neared my chosen group of new best friends forever.

'I don't know. Why? Will you talk differently to them?' I affected a serious expression. 'Will you put on a lesbian accent?'

Pete, trying to look irritated, chuckled. 'You are *so* annoying.'

I was delighted to find that South Africans are super-friendly. The wedding wasn't big, maybe about fifty people; only a handful of Priya and Laurel's friends and family could make it out at such short notice, and the rest were people they'd met while working on the show. The local guests were a good-looking bunch; hot guys with man buns, beardy chins, blocky sunglasses, big smiles and big personalities. The girls were beautiful, friendly and funny with smooth skin and long manes of blonde or caramel hair. Everyone looked like they had just been on holiday: tanned, thin and happy. In London people only looked like that for the week following a Spanish mini break where they'd starved themselves beforehand then worked intensively on cultivating an 'I've-been-on-holiday' tan.

Within an hour I'd met nearly all the people I didn't already know, and the chime of a bell told us the ceremony was about to begin. We sat on linen-covered hay bales in the shade, watching as Priya and Laurel danced down the aisle to the sound of Stevie Wonder. They stopped under a pagoda heavily adorned with flowers of every colour imaginable. Priya beamed in her floaty yellow dress, her make-up natural and her hair like liquid chocolate flowing over her shoulders; Laurel, with her blonde angular bob and her pixie nose, wore an ivory playsuit with lace panels, which had a sort of cape that flowed from her capped sleeves. It was awesome. And sort of Bowie-as-a-hot-female-spaceship-captain, which isn't a recognised clothing style but SO should be. If anyone could pull it off it was tall, slender, grinning, 'fuck it let's do it' Laurel. She worked in the writer's room on Priya's show and they'd been inseparable since the day they met three years previously.

'They look so happy,' Pete whispered, as the celebrant said something that made Laurel and Priya turn to each other and grin.

I grabbed his hand, intertwining my fingers with his. 'Don't they?' I dabbed under my eyes with a scented tissue that a cute flower girl had handed out earlier. All I could ever ask for the people I loved was for them to feel joy. And my best friend was quivering with it. I couldn't have been happier if I'd been given a basket of puppies and a bikini line that never needed waxing.

Priya and Laurel's vows incited hilarity and emotion, and after a hysterical walk around the fire pit, where traditionally the groom leads the bride but with two brides and not enough planning meant Priya and Laurel had attempted the circuit side by sid, resulting in Laurel on the inside going half-pace and Priya on the outside skipping double time and tripping on her hem, Priya's honking laugh signalled it was time to party.

'Where've you been?' Pete asked as I arrived next to him at the bar a few hours later, hot and a bit sweaty from all the dancing with all the friendly people.

I stretched onto my tippy toes and kissed his cheek. 'Dancing.'

'Well, do you want to know where I've been?'

'Where?' I said, slipping my phone out of my bag and checking for emails and texts from Dad. Nothing.

'Talking to an American actor from Priya's show about himself.' He took an icy-cold beer from a lady behind the bar with a twinkly 'thank you' and turned back to me. 'For *an hour.*'

I slid my phone back in my bag and gave Pete a sympathetic look while asking the bar-lady for a rosé with extra ice cubes.

'I pretty much know his jock strap size, the glucose levels of his last blood test and the thread count of the sheets at his mother's house, and I one hundred per cent guarantee he won't even remember my name.'

'Aw, poor baby,' I said, curling an arm round his waist and giving him a squeeze. 'How do you always manage to find the one twat at an event that is almost ninety-nine per cent twat-free?'

'It's a gift,' Pete said, mock grimly.

I laughed then stopped as 'You're the One That I Want' from the *Grease* soundtrack came on. 'Oooh, let's go dance!'

Pete's eyes widened in horror. He used to be way more fun, but as he's gotten older he's become more serious. Like now that he is thirty it isn't cool to replicate Sandy and Danny's synchronised 1970s strutting. Which was exactly what Priya and Laurel were doing, and I wanted in!

'Right,' I said as I took my giant glass of rosé from the lovely wine-supplying lady with a big thank you. 'You're coming with me and we will find you a non-twat to talk to, OK?'

With our drinks condensating (it's a new word) I led Pete into the crowd of non-dancers, got him talking to some friendly folk then kissed his cheek and raced back to the dance floor to join the John Travolta pelvic pumping that had now morphed into everyone dancing like backpack kid.

As the sun dipped, I left the dance floor (a grassy patch marked out with pink and silver bunting) to call the RSPCA bar and ask to speak to Frankie. I was having so much fun with Priya and Laurel and all their friends, but the nag of my father's whereabouts and why-abouts was at the back of my mind, pulling me back from complete abandon.

'The Baroness, Jimmy speaking.'

'Oh hi,' I said. 'You again.'

'I'm sorry?'

'It's me. The girl from last night.'

Uncomfortable stammers came down the phone line.

'Not that kind of girl!' I laughed. 'It's Jess. I came in with my boyfriend and was asking about an exhibition?'

Jimmy laughed. 'Oh yeah! So what's up?'

'I was wondering if I could speak to that guy Frankie you were talking about.'

'Well firstly, Frankie is a girl. And secondly, we're not open yet so she's not here.'

I looked at the time on my phone. It was only 5.23 p.m. but felt much later. I guess that's what afternoon drinking did to your perception of time.

'Are you ever open?'

'Yes. At eight p.m.'

'That's late for a restaurant.'

'We're more of a nightclub-type restaurant.'

'Right.'

'Why don't you pop by later and you can talk to Frankie and I'll make you guys that margarita?'

'I can't, I'm at a wedding.'

'Then why are you calling here?! Go back and have more

free champagne and dance to the Bruno Mars medley that's bound to come on at some point.'

After I'd worked up a South African sweat leaping about to said Bruno Mars medley, Pete called me over, his cheeks flushed with alcohol and excitement.

'Jess! Come meet Goat!'

I wobbled towards a man who had the physical stature of a London bus on its end. He was literally rectangle-shaped and, from the looks of his strained dress shirt, all muscle. His meaty hand made the beer bottle he was holding seem like a prop for a Ken doll.

'Hi, I'm Jess.'

'Goat,' he said, shaking my extended hand. 'How're you liking South Africa so far?'

'It's hot,' I said, and although it wasn't funny Goat laughed, loud and chesty.

'Goat says he can take us up Table Mountain tomorrow,' Pete said, a hopeful look on his face.

Goat had a proud one. I'd realised that mentioning Table Mountain to a Capetonian made them flush with pride. It was like you'd paid a compliment to their favourite child.

'Is Goat your real name?' I asked, avoiding any climbing commitment just yet. I was planning on having a hangover tomorrow. And wanted to eat that hangover away at a steampunk café I'd seen on Instagram.

'No, it's Adrian.' Goat adjusted his considerable weight from one wide spread foot to the other. 'But only my mum calls me that. I've been Goat since I started climbing as a boy.'

Another tanned man in a button-down peach shirt and giant aviators arrived beside Goat. 'Goat is called Goat because he can climb anything,' the new man said.

'Then wouldn't you be better being called Monkey?' I giggled. 'Aren't they better climbers?'

'Goats climb mountains,' Pete said, worried I was going to embarrass him in front of these ever so manly men. He lowered his voice. '*Mountain* Goat?'

'I reckon a monkey could climb a mountain better that a goat, they're more limber.' I mimed a monkey mountain-climbing, stumbled, then under Pete's alarmed gaze, stopped and took a swig of my warm wine.

'He's a beast! ' the new man said. 'He looks as unlikely as a goat does at being able to climb mountains. But despite their "un-limberness",' the new man winked at me, 'goats are very good climbers. Like my bru here.' He clapped a hand on Goat's meaty shoulder.

'All right,' Goat blushed under his surfer's/climber's/general-outdoorsy tan.

The two mates began talking about a seven-day hike they had coming up. They were sleeping under the stars and aiming to get to an especially high, especially danger-ous peak and it was evidently 'brutal'. Pete's excitement ignited at the words 'high', 'dangerous' and 'brutal'. Mine powered down. I made polite excuses and wandered off to cuddle Priya and request the 'Mahna-Mahna' song from *The Muppets* that Priya, Laurel and I had a whole routine to.

*

'Goat is picking us up at five a.m.,' Pete said, as we climbed into the back of Trust's van at the end of an extremely fun, love-filled wedding.

I wondered when Trust ever had time off. He seemed to be in the van day and night, at our beck and call and it was not something I was a) used to or b) comfortable with.

I checked the time on my phone. 11.29 p.m. 'Babe, I'd rather climb it when I've had a proper sleep. And haven't been drinking. And when I've done some kind of training. I can barely walk up the apartment steps!'

'But Goat only has tomorrow morning free.'

'Why do we have to go with Goat?'

'He knows the way.'

'So do I,' I said, trying to defeat a hiccup. 'Up.' I pealed into giggles, which made Trust chuckle twelve octaves lower. 'And we have the post-wedding BBQ at Priya's.'

I opened Alice and began to eat some liberated wedding food.

Pete frowned. 'There's plenty of time.'

'I was talking to a girl at the wedding who said her parents had this snake called a Cape Cobra in their garden,' I said, my mouth full of grapes. 'And then another girl said one came into their kitchen. And another said they see them all the time on their lawn.'

Pete gave a weary shake of his head.

'It's true! They all have snake stories! And do you know where all these people live?'

Pete shrugged.

'Around Table Mountain. And do you know what they call that snake?'

Pete, again, shook his head.

'The two-step snake. As in, it bites you and two steps later you die. And I bet it's a lot more than two steps from the middle of that mountain to a syringe full of anti-venom.'

'You're probably right,' Pete said with a small smile.

'And this other girl's dog, a Cape Cobra bit it and it died. Immediately. And it was a Rottweiler. One of those big ones that look like Mike Tyson in a flea collar.'

'They disappear when they hear humans,' Pete said, and admirably he was maintaining his patience. 'Just stamp as you walk.'

'So not only do you want me to climb that massive mountain, but you'd like me to do it stamping like a North Korean soldier?'

'It takes Goat and his mates fifty minutes to climb. So we'll probably do it in an hour and a quarter.'

'You want me to stamp upwards for an hour and a quarter?' I hiccuped and dropped grapes all over the floor of the van.

Pete looked at the state of me. 'Maybe an hour and a half.'

As I bent to pick up the grapes I was suddenly struck by a brilliant idea. 'I've been suddenly struck by a brilliant idea,' I said, righting myself. 'Why don't you go without me?'

Pete opened his mouth to protest and I held up a palm, perhaps a little too close to his nose but my depth of field was shaky.

'Just listen. You go without me *this time*, and for the rest of the holiday I'll practise stamping up the apartment steps and just before we leave we can climb it together.'

Pete could see the merit of my proposal. Especially since it had been delivered interspersed with hiccups. Trust dropped us off and we security-swiped ourselves into the foyer at the bottom of our apartment block. Pete pressed the lift button.

'Uh-ah,' I said, shaking my index finger. 'Up.' I pointed at the stairs. 'Training starts now.'

Pete laughed. 'Really? Now?'

'Come on.' I stamped my first step. 'All hail Kim Jong Ju-Ju!' I said, doing an attempt at a North Korean salute, which looked more like the beginning to Madonna's 'Vogue' dance. 'What *is* his name anyway . . .?'

It took us at least twenty-five minutes to drunkenly climb all six flights of stairs. During which I sang the bits I knew to Yazz's 'The Only Way is *Up*', Wham's 'Wake Me *Up* Before You Go-Go' (and had a brief moment of sadness about George), 'Moving on *Up*' by M People, 'Get *Up*, Stand *Up*' by Bob Marley, 'Start Me *Up*' by the Stones, 'Straight *Up*' by Paula Abdul, '*Up*town Girl' by Billy Joel and '*Up* Where We Belong' by some old people. By the time we got inside we were breathless with giggles and stamping and had upset two sets of neighbours. We fell into bed, shagged once and fell asleep.

CHAPTER EIGHT

I was partially aware of Pete leaving at 5 a.m. but didn't wake properly until the much more respectable holiday time of 10 a.m. I padded across the cream tiled floor to the living room to check my phone. I had a couple of emails from Mum and Dad's friends RSVPing to the party, one from the caterers asking to quadruple-check the food list (it contained three distinctly different, uncomplementary menus: Mum's grain/sugar/dairy and fun-free items that the rest of us had mostly given up eating, Dad's traditional 'meat 'n' veg' fare and Hunter and Katie's kid-friendly treats) and no emails from Dad. I had a text from Pete saying instead of the fifty-minute walk they were going to do a three-hour one, leaving the fifty-minute one (that I was intending to do in a leisurely two hours in a snake-proof, air-conditioned suit the internet was yet to provide me with) as a new experience for both of us. He said he'd meet me at Priya and Laurel's BBQ. I smiled and flicked on the kettle.

With a hot coffee in a patterned mug, I slid open the doors to the balcony and got comfy on a lounger in the morning sun. I dialled Annabelle while soaking in the sights and sounds of the busy harbour. Annabelle answered and we exchanged updates on the party. We locked down the menu, agreeing to disagree that Brussels sprouts were a good choice (old people farting en masse? I wouldn't be staying long) and then I asked if she'd heard from Dad. She hadn't.

'If you're so worried about it why don't you call his office?' Annabelle said.

'Nah.'

It was a pointless exercise I'd tried many times before. The secretaries at Dad's London office had to remain discreet about their high-profile clients, so only ever took a message and said they'd have him call us.

'Who's that man I can hear?' I said, not wanting to get off the phone just yet. I was feeling a bit homesick for my usual routine of being there over the weekend, having Katie cuddles and cleaning whatever Hunter had got stuck to the walls/floor/ceiling/cat.

'Marcus.'

'What's he doing there again?' I said, checking the time in England. It would be 9.30 a.m. Annabelle usually only did her accounting work in the afternoons or evenings when Mum or I were around to help with Katie. Although with us both away perhaps her schedule was totally different.

'I'm helping him with his new business.'

I began to worry. What if Marcus's new business took all

of Annabelle's attention and Katie started having breathing problems and nobody noticed because they were nose-deep in Marcus's books and had found his 100-flavour popcorn café was spending too much on organic vanilla dust? I forced myself to exhale. That would never happen. Annabelle was a sharp-eyed mama bear and nothing would ever, *ever* make her compromise her precious children. But oh my gosh! What if he intended to be the next to nail and bail? To fornicate and evacuate? To bump hips and jump ship? To hit it and quit it?

'What are Marcus's intentions?' I said stiffly.

'Oh, well, he thinks he should be renovating one of his sites but with the current business loan rates so low and his equity levels, I'm suggesting he diversify—'

'No,' I said, thinking Annabelle sounded extremely money-knowledgeable, and also, renovating? What happened to the popcorn café? 'His intentions with *you*?'

'What are you talking about?'

'Does he have romantic intentions? Or sexy-time ones?'

'You're on speakerphone.'

I cringed. Then coughed my dignity back in check. 'Hello Marcus,' I said formally.

'Hi,' a soft Welsh voice replied.

'How . . . how are you?' I attempted. 'Business going . . . is it going? Annabelle, can you take me off speakerphone please?'

'Oh sure,' she said, then came back on the line a bit louder than before. 'There you go.'

'You should tell people when they're on speakerphone so they don't make an arse of themselves. Do you know this Marcus very well? He might be a psycho or a pervert or a money launderer or—'

'I can still hear her,' Marcus said in his soft voice.

'He can still hear you,' Annabelle repeated matter-of-factly. 'I think I've got the volume quite loud.'

'Annabelle!'

'Marcus is a property developer. He buys big old houses and renovates them to become private childcare centres. He's not a psycho, or a pervert, or a money launderer. From what I can see from his books so far, anyway,' she chuckled and I heard Marcus laugh softly in the background.

The thing about Annabelle, which is something she doesn't seem to be aware of, is that she is beautiful. With her olive skin (something we both got from Dad), cupid's bow lips, rich chestnut hair and huge brown eyes ringed in lashes so thick and long I used to call her Camelbelle, she looks elegant and vulnerable. Like a French Bambi. With wrist tattoos and a small scar from a septic home eyebrow piercing. And despite her chaotic youth, she moved about her adult life with a measured peace. She doesn't expend any unnecessary energy. Perhaps she'd used it all up sneaking out of her teen bedroom, lugging backpacks full of Carling across south London and scaling nightclub walls. And, most worryingly, Annabelle is not wary of men. She's wary of who *she becomes* around men, and even though there is no scientific evidence, she still harbours a fear that her wayward years have karmatically caused Katie's Down's Syndrome and Hunter's 'hyperactivity' (the family ADHD). She is pragmatic and says there is no point blaming men as a whole, which is refreshing and enlightened and all that, but it means she doesn't have her shit detectors on. I felt she needed reminding of the dangers of the unknown (penis).

'Advancing males need to be heavily vetted, not heavily petted.' I repeated the helpful motto I'd come up with after Daniel had poked and revoked.

'Marcus is not an advancing male. He's a client,' Annabelle said airily.

'AS LONG AS HE KNOWS THAT,' I said so Marcus could hear.

There were some muffled noises like Annabelle was covering the mouthpiece and making unknown gestures.

'I do,' was Marcus's distant, somewhat uncomfortable, reply.

An hour later I threw my beach bag in the back seat and clambered next to Trust in the front of his van.

'This OK?' I said at his shocked look.

'Yes, Sisi!' He broke into a brilliant white grin and drove towards the security gates.

'When do you get a day off?' I asked, competing with Trust's music.

'Oh,' he shifted in his seat and turned the radio down. 'Maybe one day if you don't need me I get a day off. But Miss Priya, she says to look after you, so that's what I do.'

'Do you like your job?'

'Yes. Very much. I like to drive.' He shot me a sideways amused look.

'Are you married?'

'No,' he said and his voice was warm and chocolatey. 'Not married yet.'

'Oh,' I replied. 'Girlfriend then?'

Trust gave a slow chuckle. 'You ask many questions.'

'Yeah, I know. I can't help myself.' I said. 'So ... *do* you have a girlfriend?'

'Yes.' He smiled. 'She's pregnant. And I have a daughter. Two years old.'

Trust and I chatted all the way to Priya's and I was stunned to find out he lived in a small township. Like the ones Pete and I had seen sprawled out on either side of the motorway. I was embarrassed to find myself inspecting his clothing. His striped polo shirt was box fresh and I wondered how they did their laundry in those tin houses. Trust was surprised that Pete and I had been together so long and had no children. He was twenty-two but he didn't know how old his girlfriend was because she was an orphan. They guessed she was between twenty and twenty-five.

'So you not married yet?' Trust asked as we turned up the steep, winding road that would take us to Priya's white house in the hills.

'No, not yet,' I said, thinking fond thoughts about my mountain-scaling boyfriend with his mountain-scaling thighs straining against his mountain-scaling shorts. 'But we've talked about it. One day.'

Trust raised his eyebrows.

'Soon, hopefully.'

It was a little jarring to exit the van at Priya's giant, shiny holiday rental after hearing where Trust lived. With thoughts of the advantages of birthplace I followed the fastidiously tended garden path round the house to the pool area, and saw family and people I'd met at the wedding lounging in beanbags on the grass or sitting at outdoor tables under brollies. Laurel was in the pool riding a huge inflatable unicorn, singing along to an Imagine Dragons song while Priya sat on the edge with her feet in the water, laughing. The vibe was that of hung-over relaxation. Nothing like the fizzy anticipation of two days previously.

I scanned the garden with my new snake data. Flat lawn edged in manicured box hedging, various palms and lush trees behind that and behind *them* steep banks that eventually became the cliffs and rock faces of Table Mountain, home to lethal serpents. Snakes were everywhere in South Africa, yet people just lived their lives as though it wasn't a big deal. Like Australians. They still went camping and did other outdoor things, knowing that 73 per cent of their wildlife is deadly and mean-spirited. OK, that statistic is made up. But it seems plausible. The point was, I was in Cape Town on a magnificent lawn with luxury travelogue views but could be two steps away from death at all times! The only way to deal with the anxiety was to start drinking. Luckily it seemed to be everyone else's plan also, so within an hour we were cocktail-merry and sunbathing or swimming or eating and laughing by the pool. I sent Lana one of those annoying pictures of your bare knees with the pool and the blue sky in the background and she sent one back of a watery-looking coffee and her computer complete with boring spread sheet.

Laurel and Priya got everyone involved in a game of Marco Polo and I couldn't stop laughing at Laurel's clumsy attempts to move around the pool with her eyes shut. I climbed out of the water and collapsed on a lounger next to Priya, who was watching Laurel with adoration as she slipped under the surface mid-open-mouthed 'Marco Polo' call and emerged spitting out water.

'So, I'm an old married woman now,' she said, turning to me and sliding her purple D&G glasses on top of her head. 'When is it yours and Pete's turn?'

'Oh, I don't know,' I said, getting comfy on my stomach, a grin starting to form at the idea of it being my turn to trip and stumble round a fire pit. Or was that only for lesbians? Or Hindus? Or Hindu lesbians? 'We've talked about it but I think Pete is really distracted with work at the moment. And he's so tired from the commute. I don't think he has the brain space to be thinking about that right now. Maybe at the end of the holiday when he's relaxed we can talk about it again.'

Pete hadn't wanted to talk marriage until he had got a bit further in his career. But positions at his school were coveted and very rarely came up. Someone would have to leave for him to be promoted, and in the three years he'd been there no one had even contemplated moving on.

'Talk shmalk. How unromantic. You should do it, babe.

Just propose. Do it! Do it *tomorrow*,' she urged. 'There's no need to wait for the guy. You can totally propose. Tradition schmadition. I did it!'

'Yeah, but you're a girl marrying a girl. Tradition is right out of the wedding window.'

Priya snorted with laughter while looking at Laurel in the pool. 'So . . .? Are you going to do it?'

'I *could* ask him, I guess . . .' I said, running the idea through my cocktail-compromised brain. If Annabelle coped on her own while we were away and we started looking at moving across town then he might be more receptive to the idea. My skin tingled with delight. 'Maybe I could do it at the top of Table Mountain on our last day here?'

'Perfect!' Priya said. She flipped her glasses down over her eyes and lay back. Then she shot up again, raising her glasses. 'Did we just decide that you're going to propose to Pete? Here in Cape Town? In like, a week and a half?'

'I dunno . . . maybe . . .' I said, not feeling wholly in sync with my sensibilities.

'OMGEEEEEEE!' Priya pounced on my lounger. 'Let's get drunk!'

'I'm already drunk,' I giggled, trying to keep my bikini top on amid Priya's overzealous hugging.

'Then let's get drunker!'

CHAPTER NINE

Around 1 p.m. I realised Pete hadn't arrived so checked my phone and saw I had a missed call from him. I spread my towel on a lounger in the shade, lay down and dialled his number.

'Hey!' he answered. It sounded like he was in a car. 'Did you get my message?'

'No, I just phoned you back. How was the hike?'

'Oh my god, Jess,' he said. 'It was unbelievable! It's this track called Skeleton Gorge. It goes through a ravine and at the top there's a lake! Heaps of other people were walking it and they were cheering each other on and singing. And *everybody* seems to know Goat.'

'Sounds amazing! I can't wait to see the photos,' I said and felt a pinch of guilt I hadn't gone with him. 'So are you on your way here?'

'No, the hike is one-way so we're in a taxi back to the car at the other end. But Jess,' he lowered his voice like he didn't want his fellow passengers to hear him. 'Goat and his cousin are going snorkelling with seals and they've invited us along. We can swing by the BBQ and pick you up in half an hour?'

'Snorkelling with seals?' I laughed. 'In the ocean where sharks hang out? And isn't it totally freezing?'

Priya had said the ocean in Cape Town never gets above an icy fourteen degrees, which confirmed I was never going in there.

'You won't be freezing, you wear wetsuits.'

'A dark shiny wetsuit? Sort of like a dark shiny seal?'

'Jess—'

'You want to swim *with* seals, dressed *as* a seal? If a shark is heading out for lunch you'll be the slowest seal on the menu.'

'I really want to do this,' Pete said, a small plea in his voice. 'My god, this place is amazing! Please come?'

'I can't.'

'Come on, Jess, I thought this trip would be a great time for us to, you know, reconnect and stuff.'

'What?' My stomach dropped. 'You think we're disconnected?'

Pete sighed. 'Look, I'm just saying that this time here is a great opportunity for us to spend some proper time together. Between my job and Annabelle we hardly spend any time together. It's important.'

'Oh, right. I agree. Totally. It's just, the thing is, I'm a bit tipsy.'

'You'll be fine.'

'Probably more like a lot tipsy. If they did a breath test,

hey … do you think they do breath tests for snorkelling? They should. You could totally drown if you were so drunk you used your snorkel as a straw – I mean, it looks like one big straw and for a drunk person—'

'Jess?'

'Yes?'

'Are you coming or not?'

'I'm not,' I said. 'You go though, OK?'

'Are you sure?'

I looked across the garden. Priya was gathering players for a game of pool volleyball, Laurel's head was thrown back in laughter at something somebody had said and the elder family members were gathered around a table under a white brolly, getting along famously.

'Yeah, I'm happy here by the pool,' I said, raising my hand to be included in the volleyball game.

'You're two steps away from death at all times, remember?' Pete joked.

'Ha! Then I'll have to stay in the pool, won't I? Snakes can't swim, right?'

'Yeah, they can.'

'God! It's not safe anywhere! Online flights to South Africa should come with a warning. Like a pop-up box that says, "*Are you sure you want these flights? Please check the left box if you are OK with imminent death at all times. Enjoy your flight.*"'

'You're a weirdo,' Pete said with warmth in his voice.

'Pete?' I said, getting serious.

'Yeah?'

'I love you and I don't want you to be eaten.'

'I won't be. Have you seen the size of Goat? They'll definitely go for him before me.'

I heard Goat make laughing protests in the background. We arranged to meet back at the apartment and I hung up feeling like Pete and I had two very different holidays in mind. I shook my head. I would go home, buff my starting-to-tan skin, put on something short and flirty and take Pete to one of the restaurants Priya had recommended.

Trust dropped me back at the apartment at 5 p.m. I looked at the lift, inviting and quick, especially with an afternoon of cocktails in my system, but instead turned, and with my sandals dangling from my hand, began a barefoot, stamping ascent to our sixth-floor apartment. Priya and Laurel were leaving for their 'tech free' honeymoon at an eco-resort at 3 a.m. the next day. They'd return the day after Pete and I left, and Priya had given me strict instructions to enjoy the apartment, hit all the places she'd listed, trust in Trust and have a 'fucking good holiday, babe, you deserve it'. An hour later Pete came home fizzing with exhilaration.

'Hey!' he said, dropping his gear bag and launching himself onto the bed where I was looking at my inbox void of emails from Dad admitting to having joined the South African diamond mafia. I got a waft of manly sweat and sea salt when he kissed me. 'Look at this!'

He pulled his phone out and, with eyes gleaming, showed me a picture of him on an inflatable boat with a gigantic outboard motor. The sun glinted off soft undulations on the ocean's surface and Pete sat on the boat's edge with a mask and snorkel pushed on top of his head. He looked ecstatically happy.

'Did you see seals?' I asked.

'Did we see *seals*?' Pete grinned.

He swiped through photo after photo of endlessly clear blue sky, sapphire ocean, hundreds of seals, the fins of a pod of dolphins, penguins, dramatic cliffs and colonies of seabirds. I felt truly jealous. I was disappointed in myself for being scared of sharks (and jellyfish and swordfish and undetonated 1940s underwater mines and spontaneous tidal rips). And a bit upset Pete had gone on the trip when he was supposed to be with me at the BBQ. If he'd waited until the next day I'd have gone too. Perhaps not in the actual water dressed as lunch, but at least on the boat trip. I decided to agree to whatever was Pete's next desired pursuit. As long as it didn't involve sharks or water or heights or caves or snakes or— STOP! I would do whatever he suggested.

'The Cederberg climb?' I said as we took delivery of our tapas-style dishes.

The Uber driver had dropped us off outside an old factory building (I'd told Trust to go home to his family) and we'd taken a glass exterior lift up to a seventh-floor exposed-brick-and-pipe/black floor-and-ceiling restaurant. The interior was dimly lit, so the 360 views of the harbour and city were the focus. It was intimate and lively at the same time and the two glasses of champagne, flippy summer skirt and Pete's interest in my low-cut top had made me feel sexy and excited about life. But then Pete had mentioned, in a leading and hopeful manner, that there were spaces on the seven-day trip, and my life-loving mood had taken a nosedive.

'Is that the one Goat was talking about at the wedding? The one that was brutal and dangerous and all that?'

'It's a measured risk,' Pete said in a measured tone.

'How *exactly* do they measure it?' I said, getting out my phone and googling The Cederbergs. A quick scroll told me what I needed to know. 'They have snakes and cliffs and scorpions and leopards. You don't want to go, do you?'

'Leopards are shy. You'd be very lucky to see one.' Pete popped a dumpling in his mouth, avoiding the question.

'Pete?' I said, putting my phone to the side and looking directly at him.

'I think it's an amazing opportunity.' He shrugged one shoulder.

'But it's for seven days,' I said, trying to reign in my mounting frustration. 'Today you said you thought we needed to reconnect? Going away without me is not "reconnecting". It's the total opposite.'

Pete sighed like he'd known what my reaction would be and had already been getting aggravated by it. 'I just feel so energised by this place. Like I'm in the right place for *me* for once!'

'For once? What does that mean?'

'I feel ...' He glanced at the people either side of us. '... stifled sometimes. Like I could be doing these amazing things but I can't because of my job and where we live and stuff.'

'Where we live? England, you mean? You want to move to South Africa – is that it?'

'No,' Pete sighed. He picked up another dumpling from one of the shared platters and plopped it on the mini plate in front of him. 'It's just that most of our life seems to be organised around Annabelle and Streatham and driving to my job and it's just so ... so *regulated*.' He looked up at me. 'Don't you ever feel like you've had a door open to you for the first time and you can suddenly see so clearly that you've been living a half-life?'

At Pete's mention of Annabelle I realised I hadn't called to see how Katie's therapy had gone. It was the first time Mum wasn't there to pick Hunter up from school. Had the lady from the nanny service known Hunter couldn't eat normal biscuits because he'd go supersonic and end up leaping from the tops of large furniture items like a demented flying squirrel? I clicked back into Pete's monologue about how the world is a vibrant, exciting place that must be climbed on and swum in and run along. Planet Earth was one big jungle gym and he wanted in on it.

'I mean,' he looked at me, 'are you happy just being a PA and going to work and yoga and Annabelle's, and for every week just to be the same?'

'I'm not just a PA, and you know it!'

I looked at him; dark rings under his eyes, pale English skin that had pinked under that day's sun and an expression of desperation. Or was it exasperation? We'd been on heaps of holidays together but never before had we seemed on such different wavelengths. Before Annabelle had Katie, Pete and I would hit all the major European cities. We loved walking, seeing the sights, climbing the ancient steps, eating all the food. We'd been happy with our regular mini breaks to Paris and Barcelona, and our once a year medium-sized breaks to Turkey or Greece. When Katie came along Annabelle needed help and we'd pretty much dropped our lives to be there for her. I knew we'd get back to how we'd been before. One day. It hadn't happened yet, though, and I didn't realise Pete was feeling so frustrated. I leant across the table and grabbed his hand. He was tired and just needed a few days to relax into holiday mode.

'Shall we skip dessert and just go home?' I asked, giving him a flirtatious look from under my lashes. 'I've got the best day planned for us tomorrow.'

Pete gripped my hand and nodded but he looked resigned. Our eyes met across the table full of picked-at food and tea lights, and I tried to push down my feelings of uneasiness.

CHAPTER TEN

The next day we got up early and ate breakfast at a steam-punk café. Huge vintage machinery with shiny copper piping and multiple levers and cogs took up the majority of the warehouse-like space. Waiters in waistcoats adorned with chains and leather straps, top hats and/or vintage aviation goggles on their heads and iPads in holsters took orders from lively locals with bundles of cheer and personality. The coffee menu had strange things like egg-white shots or orange juice infusions, and I ended up trying far too many and chittered incessantly like a coked-up Warner Brothers' chipmunk. I think I was also trying to compensate for Pete's slight downturn in temperament. It was something we were both trying to overlook but it was there, loud in its silence.

'What did you think of the egg-white coffee?' I said as we hopped into Trust's waiting van. 'It felt like I was drinking, sorry, but a coffee that someone had ejaculated in.'

Pete made a face. A justifiable face. And yet I carried on.

'Not that I've ever drunk a coffee that someone has ejaculated in.' I clicked in my seat belt. 'Well, not *knowingly*, anyway. I mean, I could have. But I'm sure I would have been able to tell. It's a very distinct consistency, isn't it?'

Pete glanced towards Trust then looked at me with his eyebrows raised so high they were almost in his hairline.

'Sorry,' I made an '*I'm-being-a-bit-gross-aren't-I*' face. 'I feel a bit wired. I think I've had too much coffee.' I shot Pete a sideways glance and lowered my voice. 'Too much cum coffee,' I muttered, and then giggled behind my fist.

We walked off the generous breakfast along a clifftop footpath, busy with Capetonians and their dogs. The sea pounded below us and I pointed out (after googling the correct collective noun) a murmuration of starlings twisting and folding in on itself, some risk-loving paddleboarders and a host of great whites that mostly (always) turned out to be rocks breaking through the rolling surface of the ocean. Pete walked beside me trying to muster enthusiasm but I could tell his heart was elsewhere. Surfing an avalanche or diving for toxic-shelled crabs, perhaps. We ran through our individual ideas for the rest of the trip.

'I think we should go shark cage diving. And ziplining. And I *really* want to try canyoning,' Pete said. His eyes had shone when he'd mentioned the Cederberg climb again.

'I'm pretty keen to visit some more wineries. And animal sanctuaries. And I'd *love* to go to a festival while we're here,' I said. *My* eyes had watered when he'd mentioned the Cederberg climb again. I was really trying to understand his new need for going to the top of things or under things or off the edge of things. He'd never been into this type of stuff before – just your regular 'go to the gym/lift some weights/Map-My-Run-and-share-it-on-Facebook' type stuff (I'd been very disappointed that he didn't take on my suggestion of running in the shape of a dick and balls like I'd seen on Bored Panda and sharing *that* map on Facebook). I wanted to share his enthusiasm but it felt forced, whereas his was real and desperate.

'Why do you keep checking your phone?' I asked a few hours later as we reclined on a blanket in the stippled shade of a giant tree.

The remains of a winery picnic lay between us and I was feeling warm and fuzzy due to the delicious and criminally cheap rosé. A shallow river bubbled past us and other pic-nickers paddled in it or sat on the banks drinking wine and chatting, their feet cooling in the clear, cool water.

Pete glanced at his phone again before putting it face down on the blanket. 'It's just Goat. He's posting pictures of his hike.'

I looked at the time. It was 3 o'clock. And a Tuesday. 'Doesn't Goat have a job?'

'It *is* his job. He's a social influencer, so makes money from posting. He's got airlines and travel companies and sports-wear companies sending him places. And he gets paid for it!'

I nodded. At work we had a pool of paid influencers we used when promoting a new music video. You generally had to be 'somebody', though, before you were paid to post.

'How'd he get to be that?' I said, popping the last circle of chorizo in my mouth.

Pete's face lit up as he spoke. It turned out Goat was something of a celebrity in South Africa. He'd been on *The Bachelor* and while he didn't find lasting love (apparently the girls had descended into out-and-out sluttery), he did emerge victorious; Goat's gentlemanly rebuttals had gained him a huge following. He was now a well-known semi-celebrity and didn't work in the conventional sense but instead got paid to play and post. Luxury tour companies, champagne-makers, cars, protein powders, hair gel, nightclubs, sports clothing, wine; basically everyone wanted a piece of Goat. So he climbed the mountains, leapt off the cliffs, wore the watch, drank the champagne, blended the paleo smoothie, did the hashtag and the money rolled in.

'I was thinking I could do something like that but for kids,' Pete said. 'Have an Instagram aimed at teens and pre-teens. Get kids interested in something else other than selfies and Snapchat. Make them excited to be young and healthy.'

'That's an amazing idea,' I said, feeling affectionate and proud. I moved some picnic debris out of the way and laid my head on Pete's lap. 'Is there anything like that at the moment?'

'I don't know.' He instinctively began twirling my hair around his fingers. 'But imagine being paid to go on all these adventures!'

'Goat gets paid because he's a personality. You'd have to do it for a while to build up a following before you'd make any money from it.'

'Hmmm,' Pete mused. 'If I went on the Cederberg climb it could be an excellent starting post.'

I sat up, instantly irritable. 'Can you stop talking about that climb? You can't come on holiday with me then fuck off for a week. What would I do in Cape Town by myself?'

'Sunbathe?' he said, knowing I found sunbathing tedious. 'Hang out with Priya?'

'Priya is on her honeymoon, *remember*?'

'I really want to do this,' Pete said, throwing a screwed-up paper napkin in the picnic basket.

'And I really don't want to have a holiday in South Africa by myself,' I said, glaring at him from behind my dark glasses. I couldn't believe he was saying this. I didn't want my boyfriend not to do all these things he clearly felt so instantly drawn to; it's just none of them involved me. And this was our first holiday together in ages! 'What about the game reserve Lana booked? We'd *never* be able to afford to do that. Do you know it has baby rescue cheetahs that we are allowed to *TOUCH?!*'

'You'd still enjoy it,' Pete said, looking mildly conflicted.

'By myself? Are you kidding me?!'

'You spend all your time with Annabelle and I never *ever* complain. Why can't I do this one thing?'

I stood and began packing up our picnic debris. Pete stood and did the same.

'Annabelle needs help,' I said, gathering all the empty boxes that had contained our food and tossing them in the picnic basket. 'She's a solo mum battling addiction demons every day.'

'Annabelle has two illegitimate children and puts drugs in her smoothies.'

'It's CBD oil and it's legal and medicinal!' I said. 'She takes it for her anxiety!'

'Annabelle is the least anxious person I have ever met.'

'Proof that weed works.'

'I thought you just said it was CBD oil,' Pete snapped.

I let out a frustrated groan. Pete glanced at the other picnickers but no one seemed to notice our heated exchange.

'You want to run off on a trip with people you barely know when there are diamonds in ethically run mines waiting to be put on the fingers of people who you've loved for six years!' I stopped tidying and looked at Pete. 'This is our first holiday together in three and a half *years* and you want to spend most of the time apart?!'

Pete threw a paper plate on top of the picnic basket and stormed off. The pathways from the picnic area to the car park meandered through painstakingly tended kitchen gardens, velvet-petalled roses and heavily laden fruit trees. Instead of the romantic stroll I'd been hoping to take, sipping on the last of our rosé and chatting about the rest of our holiday, our future, whatever, we marched through in uncomfortable silence until we reached Trust dozing in the van in the shade.

'I'm going on the trip,' Pete said fifteen minutes into our icily quiet car journey, his face dark and determined. 'I might not get another opportunity like this.'

'I can't believe you.' I shook my head.

'I have to do this. I *need* to do this,' Pete said, steely. 'I feel like I'm becoming who I'm supposed to be.'

'Oh *god*. You're climbing some rocks to "find yourself" now?'

'So what if I am? I'm not stopping you pursuing your dreams.'

'This has been a dream of yours for precisely two days!' I said, louder than I intended. 'A month ago you wanted to go back to teacher training and get your master's. Now you want to climb rocks and tweet about it?'

'Instagram.'

'Same shit.'

Trust sat in the front absorbing every bit of our conversation.

'I'm sick of being the sidekick in the Annabelle and Jess show.' He fixed me with an accusatory look. 'Aren't you sick of being there day in, day out, not living your own life?'

My eyes welled up. What was Pete saying? It felt like all of a sudden, since meeting Goat and his cliff-climbing cousin, he was disappointed in what we'd become. What *I'd* become.

'Don't you have dreams?' he continued. 'Wishes?'

I turned sharply away from him, fighting back the tears. My dreams? *My* wishes? I wished I could be one of those people who remember quotes from books and are able to quote them at the exact right moment instead of googling them later and going, '*oh that's what I should have said!*' I wished, catching a whiff of myself, that natural deodorant actually worked. And all I dreamed of was an ordinary life.

One where my family was happy and my niece didn't end up in hospital every time she got a cold. One where, when Annabelle was fine, Pete and I would go on camping holidays to Cornwall with a bunch of friends and a bunch of vodka. We'd have regular brunches with Priya and Laurel, and Sunday afternoons at the local pub where the landlady knew our names and drink orders and didn't mind our corgi puppy sitting at the table in his tartan sweater. I wanted to be in a relationship like my parents', where the only thing they fought about was how to fold a fitted sheet. And now I felt stupid for wanting all that. Pete had wanted to run the PE department at a fancy school and I'd just wanted a happy life, spending time with people I loved. And I thought that was a good 'want'.

'Am I supposed to want something grand?' I said, turning back to him. 'Something "worth fighting for"? Or striving for? Or making a vision board for?'

Pete gave me a look of contempt.

'All I've ever wanted is my family, friends and boyfriend around me. To have children one day, and get some pets. Ones that don't shed so Katie won't get respiratory problems when she comes over. To perhaps run my own little business like Annabelle has, against all odds, managed to do. And to take evening classes. Like pottery and lead lighting and nude drawing.' (I really just wanted to see up close what kind of person chooses to pose nude for strangers.) 'I want us to buy a place of our own just outside of London yet commutable enough to go in and visit friends or see *Matilda*.'

'How many times do you have to see that show?!'

'Some people have grand aspirations like social media dominance or getting their book published or owning a PR company that allows you to rub shoulders with the some-bodies of the current world. And some people just don't. And I'm OK not being grand.' I looked at Pete. 'I thought you knew that about me. I thought you *liked* that about me.'

Pete put a hand on my shoulder but I turned away from him and he let it fall. We drove the rest of the journey in silence, and when Trust pulled up outside our apart-ment building Pete thanked him then jumped out and headed inside.

'You can go home now,' I said to Trust as he helped me out of the van.

'But this evening?' he said, passing me my bag.

I shook my head. 'Maybe another night.' I'd booked us a game of cave mini golf, which was exactly as it sounds: mini golf played inside a cave, followed by dinner and a movie at an outdoor theatre. You watch the sun set over the city and then get given squidgy day beds and fluffy blankets and are served dinner while snuggled under the stars. I'd chosen tonight because they were showing the documentary on Lance Armstrong. Pete had wanted to see it for years but we'd always watched something else. I'd been really looking forward to it. And it was just the kind of thing Pete would have loved. Well, the old Pete would have loved it. This new adrenaline enthusiast probably only wanted to watch a movie if it was projected onto the side of K2 and viewed from a paraglider.

'Why don't you have the day off tomorrow?' I said as we walked to the apartment doors. Pete must have already gone up, as he wasn't in the foyer.

Trust looked concerned. 'You sure, Miss Jess?'

'Absolutely,' I said with a tired smile. I gave him a hug, which surprised him, then said goodbye and headed inside.

CHAPTER ELEVEN

Is there anything more lonely than lying next to someone you feel you're losing? Yes, of course there is. Get a grip. Being homeless, friendless, family-less, moneyless, foodless and moisturiser-less would be way worse. But none of that was happening to me, and it was pretty shit to try and sleep knowing the person next to you was wishing they were elsewhere, their back a wall of hostility.

Pete got up at 4.30 a.m. and the front door clicked behind him ten minutes later. I'd barely slept all night. I'd tried counting sheep but it wasn't a system that worked for me. My sheep always intended to jump over the fence the way they were supposed to but at some point they'd get bored and move into pirouetting and cartwheeling. Next thing I knew they'd be getting out Bluetooth speakers, turning up some ska music and would start parkour-ing over the fence, flipping mustangs or donning Evil Knievel helmets and shooting themselves out of cannons.

Around 6.30 a.m. I dragged open the bedroom curtains, climbed back under the covers and watched the sunrise from my bed. The horizon was the colour of an actual orange, then merged into buttercup yellow, banana yellow, lemon meringue pie yellow, before ending in the kind of pink and purple you see in the 'girls' aisle at a toy store.

I took a few photos on my phone but they did no justice to the intensity of the colours. It was like someone had rubbed wet crayons all over the sky. The need for coffee eventually dragged me from watching the harbour wake up. The coffee tin was empty so I threw on some clothes and plodded through the waking streets to a cool-looking café I'd spotted a few times from Trust's van.

A smattering of diehard coffee addicts sat at tables tapping at silver laptops, appraising their neighbours and looking intensely millennial. I ordered an almond milk cappuccino with an extra shot, then sat at an outdoor table and called Pete.

'Hi,' he answered, his voice subdued but with a hint of warmth. 'You're up early.'

'Couldn't sleep.' I picked at a groove in the table top. 'Babe, I don't want to fight.'

Pete sighed. 'Me neither. I'm really sorry I left without saying goodbye. I thought you were asleep.'

At home, even on the days when he'd left extra early for work, he always kissed my cheek and murmured a goodbye.

'I was faking.' I chewed my fingernail. 'I just ... I don't understand why you had to go on this trip. We're supposed to be on holiday together. I can't believe you just ... went.'

'I'm sorry, Jess,' Pete said. 'It's ... I think we've changed. What *I* want has changed.'

My heart felt like it had dropped to the pit of my stomach.

'Since when? Since meeting Goat three days ago? So now you're a completely different person?'

'No.' Pete cleared his throat and continued in a low voice. 'I've been feeling like this for a while.'

A while? Pete and I had been together for six years but were friends for many years before that. We had both been in the school running team and were just as fast as each other. I would beg my teachers to let me run in the boys' races and Pete and I would be neck and neck. Our parents became friends by the edge of the racetrack and still had dinner with each other every month or so. Pete and I remained friends through secondary school and university but then I hit twenty-three and my functional runner's breastlettes blossomed to the double Ds I dragged around with me now, and Pete began to look at me a little differently. As did Mum. 'Where did you get these?' she'd asked in a clipped tone that made her German accent more pronounced. 'Have you been in Harley Street, young lady?' Mum had compact, efficient German boobs; Annabelle had delicate Bambi boobs (was Bambi a boy ...?), and it wasn't until Dad produced an old photo of his aunt with big Cornish fishwife bazangas that Mum believed I hadn't come back from a season being a chalet girl in Chamonix having had a boob job. I'm not sure how I got on to the subject of my great aunt's boobies but the point was, Pete and I had been 'Pete and I' for a very,

very long time. We were happy. And now he was telling me he felt differently.

'If you've been feeling like this for a while, then why did you agree to this trip?' I said, still reeling.

'Because I couldn't turn down a free trip to South Africa,' he said. 'And Priya insisted.'

'Priya is going to rip your balls right off when she finds out that you've left me here.'

Pete let out a tight little sigh. 'And I knew if I could get you to leave Annabelle you'd have an amazing time. You never allow yourself to do what *you* want because you're always helping her.'

'What I *want* is to help Annabelle!'

'But what happens when she doesn't need your help? Then what do you want? *Then* who are you?'

There was a silence while I processed what Pete was saying.

'And I'm sorry,' he continued with a loaded sadness. 'But I don't think I can wait around to find out.'

I swallowed. 'Oh my god.'

'Jess,' Pete said in a consolatory tone. 'We hardly spend any time together. I thought this trip might help us reconnect but—'

'You keep using the word "reconnect" yet I'm here and you're not,' I spat. 'You want to know what *I* thought? I thought we'd be having an amazing holiday *together*. I thought we *might* go back to London engaged.'

'I know,' he said. 'But I think ... I think being here has

only highlighted our differences.' He sounded uncomfortable. He'd never been much of one to talk about emotions. 'I think we should—'

I heard a girl's voice in the background.

'Who was that?'

'Who was what?'

'That girl's voice. Who was it?'

'Oh.' Pete lowered his voice and it sounded like he was covering the mouthpiece. 'That's Goat's cousin.'

'Goat's cousin is a *girl*? You never said Goat's cousin was a girl!'

'I never said it was a guy.'

'I thought this was a boys' trip. You didn't even invite me!'

'You wouldn't have come,' he hissed. 'You don't even want to walk up Table Mountain!'

I wasn't usually a jealous person. In fact I'd go so far as to say I was never a jealous person. Growing up I'd had lots of male friends. Boys were fun. And during those hideous teenage years, when girls become irrational she-devils, I'd found myself gravitating more towards their keep-it-simple, wanna-share-a-pint nature. I never thought a boy couldn't have an innocent and platonic relationship with a girl and I was never jealous if Pete was friendly with other females. But this seemed different. It felt like he'd purposefully kept something from me. None of the photos from his hike or the seal trip had her in it. Only him, Goat, cliffs and the god damned, (admittedly breath-taking), wildlife.

'What the fuck, Pete?! You lied to me!'

119

'I did not,' he said, exasperated. He said something else but the phone cut out.

'What? I didn't hear you.'

He tried again but all I heard was 'oh oh eh oh-oh'. He sounded like he was doing the vocal on a New Kids on the Block chorus.

'What was that?'

'The reception's getting bad. I'd better go,' he said, the reception now crystal clear. 'But I think we need to talk when we get home—'

'Need to talk?' I said, suddenly angry. How dare he utter the dreaded 'we need to talk' words over the phone when he was about to fuck off out of mobile coverage for a week?! 'Are we breaking up?' I said, incredulous. This couldn't be happening. What about the ethical diamonds? What about my potential proposal at the top of Table Mountain, sweaty and breathless and hopefully free from snake damage?

'I don't know,' Pete said quietly.

'Jesus.' I whooshed out a mouthful of air and with it went my anger, replaced by sad reality. 'I can't believe this.'

'I should go.'

I didn't know what to say.

'Jess?'

'Yeah.'

'I'll call you when we're back in range, OK?'

I hung up, dropped the phone on the table and sat with my hands curled on my lap, then snatched up my phone again and began to search. Goat's real name was Adrian and he'd been on *The Bachelor*. It didn't take long to find his full name, Adrian Du Plessis, and to find his Instagram profile. I scrolled through his pictures – he really did post abundantly – until I found ones of the seal trip. I swore audibly, which made the man wearing loafers without socks at the table next to me purse his lips. Her name was Giselle. She was a tanned, smooth-skinned, honey-haired model with pillowy lips, lovely teeth and dental-advert-worthy pink gums. Her hair was swept off her heart-shaped face in two inside-out French braids, the tail ends falling over her toned shoulders. In one photo she sat on the edge of the boat, her arm slung over Pete's shoulder, their wetsuits peeled down to their waists and her red string bikini holding up tanned C-cups. Pete grinned beside her. I clicked on Giselle's Instagram handle '@adventuregirlSA' and scrolled till I found a picture of Pete. She'd clearly been enamoured with him because there were plenty. Pete and Giselle in wetsuits. Pete and Goat in wetsuits. Giselle and Pete in the water with seals. Goat and Pete changing out of their swimmers (Goat's bottom was visible and by the amount of likes, the internet definitely approved).

'Almond milk cappuccino,' a voice said, and my coffee was placed in front of me.

I murmured a thank you and looked from a photo of Goat, Pete and Giselle (#selfie #newfriends #hotenglishboy) to my coffee. The barista had made a perfect heart in the foam.

'Hey!' a vaguely familiar voice said. 'How's it going?'

I looked up and saw Jimmy from the dog hotel/bar/gallery/restaurant grinning down at me.

'Whoa.' His brow furrowed. 'Are you OK?'

Jimmy had a friend with him. They were both looking at me. I was looking at them. They had tight leggings on and I felt the need to make a joke about it. But I couldn't find the funny words. I couldn't find any words.

'It's Jess, isn't it?' Jimmy said. 'This is my brother-in-law, Diego.'

I looked at brother-in-law-Diego, not really seeing him. Pete was on a seven-day trip with a model who knew how to inside-out French braid and didn't save them merely for big nights out but casually wore them on snorkelling trips with my boyfriend. Diego and Jimmy looked at each other. Pete was sleeping under the stars with a model who liked to climb shit and get sweaty. I realised I hadn't said anything so tried to talk, but I hadn't decided what words I wanted to say so my mouth moved and I just sat there. Pete had been snorkelling with a model who had nice gums and the kind of armpits that looked like they'd never had a stubbly day in their life.

'You aren't OK,' Jimmy said, pulling out a chair opposite and sitting down. 'Is your boyfriend here? What's his name? Paul?'

I glanced at the heart in the coffee.

'Pete,' I said, looking back at the picture on my phone. 'He's gone ... up ... very high ... big rocks. Brutal rocks. With Giselle the French-braiding cousin.'

Jimmy turned to Diego. 'There's something wrong with her.'

'I can see that,' Diego said, glancing at his watch meaningfully.

'I can't just leave her.' Jimmy turned back to me. 'Can we take you back to your hotel? Where are you staying?'

I pointed across the road in the direction of the harbour. It looked like I was pointing to a juice bar. Jimmy and Diego looked at each other. Diego shrugged. I noticed how tremendously muscled and colourfully dressed he was, and then went back to looking at the foam heart, now sinking into the coffee.

'Is it near?' Jimmy said, tapping my inert arm. 'Did you walk here?'

I felt so, so tired. I shut my eyes for a moment. Perhaps I'd just have a snooze at the table.

Diego and Jimmy commenced an analysis of the situation. Diego thought I was one of Jimmy's 'floozies' and Jimmy let him know that the girls aren't his floozies. Most of them are his friends. But I was neither his floozie nor his friend; just a girl who'd been a little weird about the opening times of the restaurant. I'd seemed nice, if somewhat tenacious, and I'd had a boyfriend with me who was perhaps a tad uptight but probably a decent chap. As he wasn't here and I seemed pretty sad about something, he was potentially the cause and it was their duty to help. Diego did some sighing, said 'another girl with a broken wing' under his breath then mentioned he needed to get home and have breakfast before his next class.

'I like breakfast . . .' I said, opening my eyes. I hadn't eaten since lunch the day before and with the lack of sleep I'd begun to feel woozy.

Jimmy looked relieved I'd spoken a full coherent sentence. 'Do you want to have breakfast with us?'

I looked from Diego to Jimmy, contemplated saying no and going back to my empty, foodless apartment, realised I was at a café so could just eat here next to Mr-Pursey-Lips-No-Socks, looked back at smiling Jimmy and nodded.

'Great!' Jimmy stood.

I looked at his tight leggings. 'Will you be wearing those?'

Jimmy cracked into a delighted grin. 'Offensive, aren't they?'

CHAPTER TWELVE

Unusually for me I was pretty quiet during breakfast. But then I'd had no sleep, was potentially breaking up with the man I'd been planning on proposing to and was sipping coffee on the balcony of a stunning house with two virtual strangers in questionable leggings. Fortunately, Jimmy talked enough for the three of us.

I learnt that Jimmy wasn't good at keeping up with his laundry, hence him wearing Diego's multi-coloured leggings that displayed far more anatomical detail than is strictly acceptable at the breakfast table. I learnt that Diego was the partner of Ian, Jimmy's older brother. That Diego and Ian weren't officially married but had been together for years and owned pets and the lovely house I was currently sitting in, so may as well have been, which is why Jimmy introduced him as his brother-in-law. I learnt that Jimmy had come to South Africa to check out Ian's boyfriend, had gone travelling, spent all his money and now lived in

their basement and worked at the doggy daycare centre/
gallery/bar.

I learnt that Diego owned a gym down the road called
SWEAT 2000. And that Jimmy's older brother, Ian, was an
engineer so worked 'grown-up' hours and couldn't go to a
yoga class then sit on his balcony overlooking a white sandy
beach on a sunny Wednesday morning, having smoothie
bowls and paleo granola in leggings so bright and tight they
ought to be hanging in Katy Perry's dressing room.

And from Diego I learnt that Jimmy was single because he
was too fussy, that he needed to 'get his life sorted' and that
he sang 'How is Julia?' instead of 'Halleluiah' till he was eleven.
I also learnt that Jimmy adored his brother-in-law and, despite
his 'older-brother-ish' jibes, his brother-in-law adored him.

After breakfast Jimmy and I stayed on the balcony listening to the activity on the beach below us with a second
round of coffee.

'So how was the wedding?' Jimmy asked, tipping his head
back in the hot morning sun.

I frowned before remembering I'd called him to ask
about the exhibition. Which then reminded me I'd forgotten all about the little nest of meat-eating crickets that
was my father's potential affair with a South African wine
estate owner who had a side job raising funds for the critic-
ally endangered Pickergill's reed frog. I'd put a little more
thought into that when I was home. After a nap.

'It was beautiful,' I said, remembering how happy my best
friend had been that day. It felt like weeks ago.

'Got any pictures?'

I gave him a weird look.

'What?' he said with a shrug. 'I like weddings.'

I showed him a photo of Priya and me hugging in the late-afternoon sun, our cheeks flushed with wine and joy.

'You know Priya Jensen?' Jimmy sat up and took the phone. 'Man, she is so hot!'

'She is so lesbian.'

'Lesbian?' He handed back my phone then lay back and put his feet on the weathered antique coffee table. 'Her wife hot?'

'Yes, I suppose so.' I watched him wriggle into a comfortable position and close his eyes. 'If tall blondes with button noses are your thing.'

Jimmy opened his eyes and gave me a look that said *does a bear like non-GMO, free-range salmon?*

'Yeah, she's hot too,' I conceded.

'Two hot lesbians …' he said dreamily, shutting his eyes again.

'You know, lesbians don't generally like to have sex with men. That's the whole point of being a lesbian. They live a penis-less life and are quite happy about it.'

'Shh …' Jimmy said. 'You're ruining my fantasy.'

'I'm just saying, a newly married lesbian couple don't generally sit around thinking, "*Oh you know what will make tonight great, let's have sex with a cute guy.*" Do you sit around thinking about having a hot night with Ryan Gosling?'

Jimmy wrinkled his nose. 'No.' Then he opened his eyes

and grinned. 'Unless Eva joined us, then I'd do whatever with whoever.'

'I'm sure they'd be delighted to know.'

'I might tweet them,' he said, shutting his eyes again, the effect of another fantasy playing at the edge of his lips. 'And I just realised something.'

'What?'

'You called me cute.'

'Well, you are,' I said, not worried by what I'd said. I was merely stating an obvious fact. Jimmy, with his SA tan, surfer's arms, grey eyes, mischievous grin and unkempt blondish hair was undoubtedly good-looking. And by his easy confidence I was pretty sure he knew it. I looked over at him and he was grinning. 'Don't get a big head about it. You just got born pretty – it's no achievement on your part.'

Jimmy laughed. 'Cheers,' he said chinking his coffee mug against mine. 'You're a real charmer.'

A little later, after he'd quizzed me about Pete and I'd shut up like a clam near a shucking knife, Jimmy looked at his watch and said he had to be at a writing class, but he could drop me back at my apartment on the way. We walked through the house that Ian had designed himself, and which screamed casual beachside elegance. It clung to the side of a cliff and had many levels which all looked out through floor-to-ceiling glass at Clifton Beach, a white sand paradise with frothy surf and beautiful beachgoers. The kitchen was clearly the heart of Diego and Ian's life and housed a huge marble island surrounded by eight designer stools. An extra-long dining table in untreated wood sat below two giant antler chandeliers. Weathered leather chairs for eighteen surrounded the table and conjured up images of Vikings with tankards of mead. Two long white sofas, covered in plush cushions in all shades of vanilla, cream and white, and two armchairs surrounded a deep fireplace. Everything in South Africa was supersized. LA on steroids. They didn't just have mountains, they had behemoths with flat tops; they didn't just have flora and fauna, they had bushes with three-inch spikes (I'd nearly had an accidental nose piercing at the winery picnic with Pete the day before), elephants, rhinoceros and a two-step snake. They didn't have floor-to-ceiling windows, they had triple-height glass walls in houses overlooking oceans that weren't just blue but cerulean, with waves that didn't just crash on the beach but could boom over the sea wall and wash away a Fiat. I followed Jimmy past a large utility room where an African lady of about fifty stood sorting through washing.

'Morning, Pamela!' Jimmy said, bouncing into the laundry and giving her a hug from behind.

She tutted and batted him away with a smile. He introduced me and then we carried on walking along window-filled hallways and down wide-spaced stairs.

'If you have a housekeeper who does laundry why are you wearing those monstrosities?' I said, pointing at the leggings.

Jimmy laughed. 'I'm thirty-one years old. I don't want someone picking my dirty clothes off the floor. If I can't get them to the laundry room I deserve to suffer this humiliation.'

'That's very mature of you.'

'I'm training myself for full adulthood,' he said, then flung open some heavy double doors. 'This is my room.'

Light flooded a room the size of my flat three times over. One whole wall was glass with, yet again, another view of the ocean. A California King bed dressed with fluffy white linen (unmade) was to one side and to the other, surrounding a plush rug, sat a keyboard, drum set, two guitars, a bunch of sound equipment and a massive xylophone.

Jimmy pointed to a green shaggy fake fur sofa against an exposed brick wall. 'That's Oscar the Couch,' he said and cracked up.

The snowy-white bichon frise I'd seen at the bar stood up from a silk floor cushion and trotted over to Jimmy.

'And this is Flora,' Jimmy said, picking up the ball of fluff and talking in nonsensical lovey-dovey language.

My upper lip curled. 'Get a room.'

'This *is* our room,' Jimmy said, without removing his face from Flora's curly coat. 'Feel free to leave if you can't handle witnessing true love.'

I giggled and crossed the room.

'What's that all about?' I said, pointing to a calendar that was still on December, hanging on the wall above a messy desk. The calendar had a photo of Jimmy looking startled while coming out of the bathroom, a tiny towel evidently only just managing to cover his bits by the time the camera clicked.

'That,' Jimmy said, taking the calendar down and handing it to me, 'is a little Christmas tradition my brother and I have.'

I flicked through the pages. Each month showed a different photo of Jimmy in a state of surprise or annoyance. Or nakedness.

'Nice,' I said when I came to a picture of him, totally nude, sitting in a very dark room with his brow creased in annoyance and his mouth in the middle of saying '*FUUUUUCK*'. He had one hand trying to shield his manly area and the other outstretched as if to stay STOP.

'We sneak up on each other and take photos,' Jimmy said. 'The aim of the game is to catch each other in an unflattering state and at Christmas we give each other a calendar of all the pictures. The ultimate goal is to get a "poo shot".' Jimmy pointed to the toilet picture. 'Ian won last year with that one.'

'THAT'S YOU DOING A POO?!' I screeched, only then realising he was sitting on a toilet. 'Gross!' I shoved the calendar back at him.

Jimmy sniggered, flicked to the correct month and re-hung it. He stood back, appraising the January photo. He was in the shower and could only be seen from the waist up. His eyes were stretched wide and his mouth open in shock.

'That's when Ian flicked the shower to ice cold,' Jimmy said, tapping the picture and turning to me with a severe expression. 'Diego took the photo while Ian did the tap. It's against the rules to use an assistant so officially that one doesn't count.'

I laughed in the face of his seriousness.

Jimmy glanced at his watch. 'Shit! I gotta shower. Be five minutes.'

I flopped on Oscar the Couch and in exactly five minutes Jimmy emerged in a cloud of steam and began rummaging in a pile of clothes on the floor of his wardrobe, a towel wrapped round his waist.

'Can you play all these?' I indicated to the instruments, averting my eyes from his muscled torso.

'Yeah,' he said, his voice muffled by the mountain of clothing he was nose deep in. 'I'm classically trained on the piano but I get by on most instruments.'

'I used to be able to play the theme tune to *Magnum, P.I.* on the xylophone. My old music teacher had a thing for big tashes.' I stood and picked up the sticks. 'Can't remember what these are called though.'

'That's a marimba,' Jimmy said, pulling a T-shirt over his head then crossing the room and taking the hitty things from me. 'And these are mallets.'

He grabbed another two mallets and launched into a jovial little tune reminiscent of 1980s new wave music.

'Wow!' I said, impressed. 'What's that song?'

Jimmy shrugged but looked modestly delighted. 'Something I wrote.'

'Cool. If I could wake up one day and choose an instant talent it would be to read music and play any instrument.' I frowned. 'Or to make myself invisible. Or to never sweat. Or to be able to dance and not look like I'd been born with half my joints fused together and an itch I can't reach. Or to . . .'

Jimmy was looking at me with a strange expression.

I cleared my throat. 'That was amazing!'

He grinned, handed me the mallets, grabbed some shorts from the floor and ducked into the bathroom again.

Jimmy's car was a battered green Mitsubishi hatchback with a 1980s power ballad CD stuck in the player.

'So, do you know anyone in Cape Town?' Jimmy said as we drove along the winding coastal road listening to Whitesnake, the sun glinting off anything and everything, making the city shine like a disco ball.

'Just Priya and Laurel and they're on their honeymoon.'

'Priya and Laurel ...' Jimmy said, getting lesbian-dreamy again.

'Stop it,' I said. 'You're soiling their honeymoon with your hetero fantasy vibes.'

'Hetero fantasy vibes?'

'It's a thing.' I checked my phone. No text from Pete and no emails from Dad. 'My dad might still be here somewhere, I guess. I haven't heard from him yet.'

I'd told Jimmy about my concerns that Dad was here under dodgy circumstances, and he pointed out that there were a lot of mega-wealthy people in Cape Town and that half the clientele at the bar he worked at probably owned private islands. We pulled up at the security gates to the apartments and I directed Jimmy to the foot of our building.

'Thanks for breakfast,' I said, giving a small smile. 'It's kind of weird I came to your house and I don't even know you.' Now that I was back at the apartment complex without Pete, it made me realise I was alone for the next week.

'No problem.' He watched me for a moment. 'Why don't you come to the bar this afternoon?'

'What for?'

'If you come before five Sylvie won't be in yet and I can sneak you into the exhibition space.'

'Who's Sylvie?'

'The boss. That tiny smoking psycho you saw the other day.'

'Oh, right. She seems scary.'

'She is. Which is why I can't get caught. So, come at five – we'll go in, look around, then get out, OK?'

'Really?' I said, my spirits lifting.

He nodded. 'If the exhibition is in two weeks then the paintings are probably already in the storage area. I don't know what you think you'll find but if it will put your mind at ease . . .'

'It will, thank you!'

I slid out of the car, thanked him for breakfast again, got the lift to the sixth floor (Pete and his stair-stamping could get fucked), had a long shower then climbed into bed and had myself a four-hour, dreamless nap.

CHAPTER THIRTEEN

'They're quite . . .' Jimmy glanced at me. 'Vagina-ry.'

'Yeah . . .' I said, suddenly aware I was in a darkened storage room looking at erotic etchings, which my father may or may not have drawn, with a near stranger. I replaced the framed sketch I was examining on the floor against the wall. 'They're no Georgia O'Keeffe, though.'

'Who?' Jimmy asked, putting down the one he was scrutinising a little too closely.

'She painted extreme close-ups of flowers that were, supposedly, "representative of the female genitalia",' I said in my art history teacher's voice.

Jimmy locked the storage room door behind us with a reflective look on his face. We crossed the small exhibition space looking at the current artist's work – sepia photographs of decaying buildings.

'There's a South African artist, Reshma Chhiba, who made a walk-in vagina,' Jimmy said, shutting the gallery door behind us as we exited into the restaurant. 'It was set up in an old women's prison and it screamed and laughed at you as you walked through it.'

I screwed up my nose. 'I don't think I know you well enough to have a conversation that includes my dad and walk-in vaginas.'

'Who *do* you know well enough to have that conversation?'

'Good point.' I climbed up on a bar stool while Jimmy went behind the bar. 'Did you go and see the screaming vagina?'

'Noooo,' Jimmy shuddered. 'Too frightened.'

I laughed.

Jimmy opened a bar fridge and began checking the stock off a printed list. 'So, do you think those drawings are your dad's?'

'No,' I said, shuddering at the memory of one I'd seen titled 'Her' that was ultra-intimate and ultra-bulbous. 'He used to like to paint, just landscapes and sunsets and stuff. I can't really imagine him doing anything that . . . clitoral.'

Again Jimmy shuddered.

'But if he's here having an affair with a South African ex-model-now-arms-dealer then perhaps I don't know him as well as I thought I did.'

Jimmy raised his eyebrows. 'I didn't think it would be your dad. Frankie said the artist's a local.'

'It was a long shot.' I drew a figure eight on the bar top with my fingertip thinking about Dad somewhere in Africa (possibly pretending he was in Scotland), Pete on the top of some Cederberg rocks (pretending he wasn't a primary school PE junior teaching assistant from Streatham) and Priya: loved-up and on her honeymoon. I felt Jimmy watching me.

'You want a margarita?' he said.

'You aren't open yet.' I frowned. 'Won't you get in trouble?'

'It's OK if it's for medicinal purposes.' He produced a tequila bottle.

'And what ailment does tequila fix?'

'Irritable bowel.'

The next morning I came to much like Dracula but worse-looking. My tongue was so tacky I almost had to lever it off the roof of my mouth with a shoehorn. My eyelids were weighty and immovable, like the slammed-shut iron doors in the *Titanic*'s boiler room. I made viewing slits by pulling my eye sockets down with my fingertips. The resulting hazy sight had me clutching the covers to my, thankfully clothed, chest and shuffling to a semi-sitting position, my head pulsing and screaming like the shrill 'wee-ooo, wee-ooo wee-ooo' of a failing nuclear reactor.

'You took advantage!' I rasped through alcohol-ravaged vocal cords.

I was wearing a baggy T-shirt (not mine) and knickers (mercifully mine but unmercifully back to front). I'd clearly been sexually interactive.

Jimmy rolled onto his back, the covers falling across his bare chest. 'No.' He yawned and rubbed at his eyes with curled-up fists. 'No, I didn't "take" advantage. You were giving it away freely. Thrusting it, in fact. I had to fight you off.'

That didn't sound like me at all. 'Liar!' I said, thinking sinister thoughts. 'You probably got that waiter to put something in my drink!'

'You mean Toler?' Jimmy said, hoisting himself to the same semi-sitting/half-slumped position as me. 'Yeah, you thrust your advantage at him too. He was horrified. Thinks boobs are disgusting jiggly things.'

I returned his mirthful look with one of revulsion.

'I don't, though.' He grinned. 'I love 'em. But I didn't think it was appropriate to accept your admittedly kind of gross and sloppy advances, considering you have a boyfriend and all.'

Pete! I needed to check my phone.

'Can you face the other way please?' I said, scanning Jimmy's bedroom for my clothes and bag.

My back-to-front undies were uncomfortable in the extreme. Certain areas were being separated and flossed. Had I put them on that way? Had Jimmy re-dressed me after I'd shoved my advantage all over him? A cold wave of embarrassment shot down the back of my neck. This was so unlike me. I had a boyfriend! I had standards! I had a knicker situation that needed rectifying!

'Sure,' Jimmy said with an amused grin. He turned on his side and picked up his phone. 'But I saw everything last night.'

'I don't want to talk about it,' I said, my cheeks flaming. 'I have a boyfriend, you know.'

'Yes, I know,' Jimmy said, but his delivery was dubious. 'You told me all about it last night. You told everybody all about it last night.'

I ignored his ambiguous tone, checked he was facing in the other direction then quickly rearranged my knickers before sliding out from under the covers. My clothes were in a pile on the floor by Oscar the Couch. A memory flashed in my head of Jimmy at his keyboard singing REO Speedwagon's 'I'm Gonna Keep on Loving You' and me dancing around the room. Had I done a strip tease? Oh, please make me not have done a strip tease.

'You did a strip tease, you know,' Jimmy said.

'Shut up,' I grumbled.

I tore off the oversized T-shirt and quickly threw on the bra, sleeveless blouse and jeans I'd been wearing the night before. They smelt like alcohol and made me gag. I looked up as I pulled my hair into a ponytail and saw that Jimmy had a clear view of me dressing in the reflection of a full-length mirror. He grinned.

'I told you to look away!'

'Not true,' he shook his head. 'You told me to *face* the other way. This,' he waved at the wall with his perving mirror, '. . . is the other way.'

'Oh. My. God.' I said, snatching up my bag. I flopped on Oscar the Couch and scrolled through my phone while Jimmy tried to regale me with last night's activities.

'I shouldn't have let you have the shots,' he mused.

'No, you shouldn't have. I don't usually drink spirits. I get hyper if I drink a lot.'

I'd sent Pete nineteen messages and he hadn't replied to any of them. But he had said the Cederbergs were most likely out of range. I read through the messages with mounting dismay. They'd gotten increasingly indecipherable and desperate and culminated in one that called him a 'Goal wannabe' (I think I'd tried to type 'Goat') and Giselle a 'rock-cock-collector with dumb plaits'.

'Yes,' Jimmy said, his eyes smiling. 'Yes, you were definitely "hyper".'

I uttered a weak groan.

'I told you I was cutting you off,' Jimmy continued, while getting out of bed and rummaging through the pile of clothes at the bottom of his wardrobe. 'But you just went and downed drinks off other people's tables.'

'I don't want to talk about it,' I said, my dignity beginning to resemble a half-chewed prune.

Pete was going to get back into range and his phone would ping-ping-ping with garbled abuse. Giselle would sit next to him thinking, '*No wonder he left that psycho behind.*'

'You told Sylvie you wanted to be just like her when you grew up. Except not short and not a smoker. And not scary.' Jimmy pulled a pair of shorts over his boxers while I cringed. 'You told Toler you wanted to be like *him* when you grew up. Except not gay. You told Frankie you wanted to be like her when you grew up. Except not gay. Which, by the way, she isn't.' He ran his hands through his mussed-up hair. 'And you told *me* I needed to grow up.'

Frankie! I remembered meeting her and asking about the man who'd done the 'pussy pictures', as I'd taken to calling them last night. She'd said he was a friend of Sylvie's neighbour and was currently in Mozambique with his family. So that drew a line under that.

'And,' Jimmy was still talking. 'You dance like a honey badger.'

'How do they dance?' I said, looking up from my semi-abusive, fully desperate text messages with an air of hopelessness.

Jimmy did some kind of jolting jazz-hands movement, his hips shunting mechanically left and right and his gaze watching invisible fairies.

I narrowed my eyes. 'I think that looks very cool.'

Jimmy plopped next to me on the furry sofa. 'Do you remember anything about last night?'

I frowned. I remembered Jimmy making me margaritas before the restaurant opened. I remembered Sylvie arriving and having a husky-voiced rant at Jimmy about lady friends. I remembered Jimmy saying I wasn't his lady friend and that I was there for the job trial. And I remembered how he then got me folding napkins, setting tables, putting in fresh bin liners and doing all his boring jobs to 'throw Sylvie off the scent'. I remembered the restaurant eventually filling up and being captivated by the festive vibe of the place. Especially for a Wednesday night. The clientele (mostly over forty) were the somebodies or former somebodies of Cape Town. They sported even tans, thin limbs and plastic surgery gone those two procedures too far, where they all started looking like they were from a human subspecies. Homo-meltedo, perhaps. Everything about them was a tad off kilter, like looking at faces through a wet window. People were shown to their tables but as the evening progressed, the table became where you left your glittery clutch. Everybody was up visiting other people; chatting and air-kissing and calling each other 'my angel'. I'd decided it must have been a way to show off the full length of your gym-honed body. Why waste all those hours you spent working out sitting at a table only being viewed from the cinched waist up?

Sylvie would march diminutively through the throngs at various points in the evening, still in her generic catering apron, her grey hair in a casually flung-up banana clip, dramatically ripping up bills the waiters had delivered, ordering shots for the whole restaurant or screaming at Jimmy for playing a song she hated. The customers loved her and she clearly enjoyed being the (psychotic) centre of attention. I sat at the bar with Jimmy, who was evidently a favourite of the female and mostly gay male patrons. At one point in the evening, when I'd been making a zigzagged trip to the toilet through women so tall and thin they looked like they'd been digitally stretched, I passed a lady who I was sure said, '*The first time Arnold Schwarzenegger fucked me was a complete surprise.*' Upon my return to my favoured barstool Jimmy assured me I'd heard correctly and that the woman, Heather (who was forty-seven but with mountains of plastic surgery that made her look forty-six and vaguely aquatic) fucked all the visiting celebrities she could ensnare and gave everybody a 'blow-by-blow' account after.

By the time food service was over and the real partying had begun I was stag-do-in-Benidorm-level drunk. The restaurant became more of a bar/nightclub, the dogs left the humans to their debauchery and Jimmy stepped out from behind the bar and took up residence at the piano, rocking tunes from the late 1980s and early 1990s that had the clientele rubbing their thin forms against each other. Heather ended up on the table giving us all a view of her comprehensively waxed areas. From what I could remember Jimmy was a fantastic singer and, with his shirtsleeves rolled up, his top buttons undone and his cheeky grin frequently flashing my way, I'd found him incredibly attractive. Which might explain the late-night strip tease in front of the Sesame Street sofa. I looked over at him, my cheeks roasting under his amused and unwavering gaze.

'Nothing past when I fell off the stage while singing that Rodriguez song.' I dropped my aching head into my hands. 'I feel like a lobotomist has taken out my brain and given it to Michael Jordan who is bouncing it around a concrete basketball court in the Chicago prospects, and bits of gum and cigarette butts are lodging themselves in the grooves of my cortex.'

Jimmy looked at me, his eyebrows raised.

'My head hurts.'

There was a knock at the door.

'Come in!' Jimmy said, giving me a consolatory pat on the back.

Diego walked in sporting a lycra ensemble so bright it caused blinking and potential seizures, assessed the messy room – me in last night's clothing looking ashamed and ill, shirtless Jimmy looking calm and relaxed, and the empty beer bottles on the floor I'd only just noticed – and assumed a 'business as usual' expression.

'Breakfast?' he said, looking from Jimmy to me.

'If you could ask anybody anything and not worry about causing offence or getting in trouble, what would you ask?' Jimmy said, then spooned in a mouthful of Diego's exceptionally delicious cinnamon and apple millet porridge.

We were sitting on the balcony around the same glass-topped table as the previous morning, Jimmy chatting ceaselessly and aimlessly. The South African sun glinted off every shiny surface, the surf pounded the beach and with each mouthful of porridge my hangover was seeping away.

'I'd ask Kim Kardashian if it feels weird to sit on her arse,' I said, pouring more home-made lemon and ginger tea. Diego and Ian's lifestyle was a homage to the paleo way of living. Mother would definitely approve. Jimmy, it seemed, ate whatever came his way with no judgement. If somebody was offering, he was eating. 'Like, when she sits down does it feel like she's sitting on a mini inflated lilo, all wobbly and unstable, and when she wants to sleep on her back does she have to do it in the bridge position?'

Diego grinned.

'Excellent,' Jimmy said, nodding his affirmation. 'I'd ask a policeman how often a fart wafts out when someone they've pulled over winds down their window.'

'Gross,' I said.

'Everyone farts in the car.'

'And what about you?' I asked Diego once we'd deliberated over how often police fart-wafting might occur.

He pushed his empty porridge bowl to the side, picked up a small paring knife and began peeling a mango with practised dexterity. 'I'd ask what happened between you two last night.' He raised a thick yet well-managed eyebrow.

'Nothing,' I said firmly.

'She did a strip tease,' Jimmy said at the same time.

'Shut *up*!'

'And woke with her knickers back to front.'

'Jimmy!'

'And it was a G-string.'

I punched him on the shoulder.

'Nude-coloured,' Jimmy said, laughing while dodging my ineffectual punches. 'With a tiny bow at the front.'

'That certainly sounds like nothing happened,' Diego said, devouring the mango. He glanced at his chunky watch. 'Gotta go.' He shoved his chair back and collected his dishes. 'Can you take Flora and Lucy for a walk? I've got back-to-back classes today and Ian has gone to Pretoria for a conference.'

Jimmy nodded and turned to me. 'Got plans?'

CHAPTER FOURTEEN

'The exhibition isn't Dad's,' I said, plodding one foot in front of the other on the sand.

'Shocking,' Annabelle said down the phone. 'But I already know that because you called me last night.'

'I did?'

'Yes. You called at about two a.m. to tell me how some hot guy called Jimmy knew all the words to the Dennis Leary "Asshole" song.'

Jimmy, walking next to me and able to hear Annabelle's side of the conversation, cracked up.

'And that Pete was away with a goat and a gazelle and that you hate Goat, who evidently is a guy, and you hate Gazelle, who is a *girl*, and you hate deers ...'

I glanced at Jimmy, who seemed to be appreciating his eavesdropping session while Annabelle continued her recount of the call.

'... and I told you it was "deer" not "deers" and that I

thought a gazelle was actually an antelope and you tried to google the difference between deer and antelopes and you hung up on me.'

'Sorry,' I said in a small voice.

'Gazelle is a really weird name, though. Is everyone in South Africa named after animals?'

'That's not her name. It's Giselle.'

'Jesselle?'

'No, *Gis*-elle. Like male jizz and *Elle* magazine. *Gis*-elle.'

Jimmy sniggered.

'Right,' Annabelle said. 'So, it's a bit crap about Pete.'

'Yeah,' I said. 'I don't know where all this "must-climb-to-the-top-of-all-the-rocks" has come from. Why have humans become such creatures of extremes? "*Must go to London to walk where* millions *have before me*",' I said in a dramatic documentary-style voice. '"*Must go to the wilderness where* no man has ever gone before". Nobody wants to just go somewhere ordinary, where an average amount of people have been. Like Staines.'

Annabelle laughed. 'Hey, thanks for the dinners. You didn't need to do that, I know you don't have much spare cash.'

I shot an embarrassed glance to Jimmy, who smiled warmly back. I'd jumped online when Pete was packing in determined silence for the Cederbergs and ordered three each of Annabelle, Hunter and Katie's favourite dinners from a delivery service. Just so I could feel I was still helping out in some way.

'CAN YOU ASK FOR THE PEAS TO BE ON THE SIDE OF THE PIE NEXT TIME?!' Hunter's high-decibel boom came down the line. I heard some muffled instructions. 'THANK YOU, AUNTY JESS!'

'Why isn't he at school?' I said, looking at the time on my phone and noting it would be 11 a.m. on Thursday morning in England.

'He's got a little cough.'

'A cough?' I did some panicking. What if Katie caught it?

'He's fine,' Annabelle said and briskly changed the subject. 'So, I think Pete is just feeling frustrated. He'll come round. You've been promising to move for ages now. Maybe he's just sick of waiting.'

'Waiting for what?'

'To get your own flat on the other side of town like you promised you would.'

'But I can't leave you. What about Katie?'

'She is pretty adorable,' I could hear the smile in Annabelle's voice. 'But we're good. I'm coping fine without everyone – an Americano please?'

'Who are you talking to?'

'Marcus. We're at Wandsworth Common. He's showing me his new site.'

'How come you're seeing Marcus's new site?'

'He wants me to check out his renovation plans. Oh hey, Hunter wants to ask you something.'

The line went muffled for a moment and then Hunter was on the phone, his mouth too close to the speaker. 'Aunty Jess, is it night time where you are?'

'No, it's daytime. It's only two hours later than where you are in England.'

'But Mum said it's summer there?'

'Yes, it's a different season but I'm just below England so that makes it nearly the same time of day.'

'You're below us?' Hunter said, and I could tell he was moving his head around by the varying volume of his voice. 'I can't see you.'

'Can't you? Ask Mum which way south is.' I waited while he asked Annabelle and came back on the line. 'Are you facing south?'

'Yes,' Hunter said.

'I'm waving now. Can you see me? I'm the one in the white top,' I said, and waved towards where I thought north was. Jimmy stopped walking and looked up at the cliffs, seeing who I was waving to. 'Can you see me?'

'No!' His chesty breathing was loud in my ear.

'I'm still waving,' I said, waving harder.

'She's being silly,' Annabelle said, coming back on the phone. 'Oh god, he's running around looking for you.' She giggled. 'I'd better go, Marcus is running after him and Katie is running after *him*. Oh god, and now a dog is running after Katie. Do you think if I ran after the dog we'd look like we were doing some kind of interpretive theatre? Oh shit, gotta go, Hunter is bothering a lady in a white top who isn't you. She does sort of look like you though . . .'

'Oooh, can you get her number? I've always wanted a doppelgänger so I can play tricks on people.'

'Sure,' Annabelle said, laughing. 'Bye!'

I hung up giggling then looked at Jimmy. 'I'm the normal one.'

'If you say so.'

We walked a few paces watching surfers tackle the curling waves.

'So what are you going to do for the rest of your holiday, then?' Jimmy said, carrying Flora across the sand.

Flora got 'tired' and would frequently sit directly in Jimmy's path. Jimmy would carry on chatting, pick her up and continue walking, Flora tucked under his arm, taking in the superior view with an air of entitlement. When she wanted to get down she'd paw at his chest with a single snowy-white mitt. Jimmy, still talking, would place her on the ground and she'd trot ahead, her black nose held high, her self-possession higher. It was a relationship of silent understanding. I was not enamoured by Flora. She looked at me with haughty indifference and I was disappointed with myself for being rattled by a ball of arrogant fluff. I identified more with Lucy: the ugly, sweet-natured chihuahua-pug cross who'd sneezed on Pete. She'd labour behind us on the beach, never requiring a grander viewing platform, wheezing and dripping snot from her interbred mooshed-in nose, her buggy eyes watering and her tongue flopping out of the side of her mouth like a wet sock. She'd come when you called, sit whenever possible and flop on her back and open her legs with shameless appeal for belly rubs.

'I'm going to have such an amazing time that when Pete

gets back he'll wish he'd been here doing all the fun stuff with me instead of at the top of some dusty rocks with—'

'The sunrises there are out of this world—'

'With the snakes and the vicious wildlife—'

'My mate saw a leopard. Said it was the most amazing—'

'And the precarious cliffs and the—'

'The views are unbelievable—'

'Will you shut up!'

Jimmy looked startled for a moment then grinned.

'Anyway,' I said, shooting Jimmy a pretend glower. 'I'm going to do all the awesome Cape Town things I've wanted to do my whole life, since three days ago when I knew I was coming on this trip.'

'Cool!' Jimmy put Flora down for her next instalment of pretentious promenading. 'Who with?'

'Myself.'

'And what are you going to do?'

I named a bunch of things I'd read about with Jimmy screwing his nose up as my list went on.

'I can't allow any of that to happen,' he said with a firm sweep of his arm.

'OK,' I said with a curious grin. 'What do *you* think I should do?'

He stopped walking and faced the ocean, watching a couple of morning kayakers whoosh along the crest of the waves. Didn't anybody have a job in Cape Town? The beach seemed to be in a constant state of activity.

'OK,' he said, looking out to sea. He appeared to be

doing some thinking. 'I only work evenings and have most of my days free, so how about I show you the Cape Town locals love?'

I did some thinking of my own. What about Pete? What *about* him? I kept defaulting to what Pete would think but was starting to realise that he might not be up his mountain range worrying about what I thought. The fact that he'd been unhappy for a while was slowly sinking in and that I, in my 'Annabelle needs me' little world, had failed to notice. Him going on this trip was perhaps his way of letting me know he thought we were over. I grappled internally with this notion.

Pete doesn't care what you do. He's hanging out with little miss neat braids.

That's not very nice – she's probably quite lovely.

I don't care – who are you to tell me Giselle is lovely? Whose side are you on?

I'm on your side because I am you.

If talking to yourself is a sign of being crazy, what does it mean to be arguing silently between yourself and a meaner version of yourself, imagining what each one looks like and thinking your negative side dresses better and wondering if she got her pencil skirt at All Saints?

Jimmy was watching me. He seemed to sense my internal chatter. If only he knew it was a full-scale production with costume, make-up and a set design that needed looking into. Who chose the geese-in-a-field wallpaper?

'Why would you do that?' I asked, looking at Jimmy.

'Because I can't see you hanging out at the top of Table Mountain with a bunch of tourists in white sneakers and matching anoraks.'

I gave him a 'no, really' look.

'Because it's pretty shit of your boyfriend to just take off with a goat and a gazelle and leave you here on your own.'

I gave a rueful smile. It was pretty shit. I was trying to serve it up better – 'it would be good for us as a couple for him to "find himself"/we are individuals/nobody said couples have to do everything together etc., etc.' – but shit is shit, no matter the platter.

'I only have one rule,' Jimmy said, clicking his fingers for Lucy to come.

She'd given up on the whole walk thing a few paces back and was sitting on her arse drooling on her own feet.

'Oh yeah?'

'No more advantage-thrusting.' He grinned, then affected a dramatic confession, palm to his chest. 'It makes me feel really uncomfortable and I feel like you don't respect me—'

'You're such a loser,' I said, shaking my head and smiling.

I felt surprisingly content when Jimmy and I arrived back at the house and put down two bowls of (filtered) water for the dogs. Flora lapped it delicately while Lucy slumped her whole smashed-up face in and looked in danger of drowning. I watched Jimmy arrange her in a seated position. I was putting the next few days entirely in his hands and I was quite fine with it. He would work in the evenings, but I could use that time to skype Annabelle and catch up with the party-planning. While Jimmy made coffee, I sat at the island and chatted to Pamela as she rearranged the cushions on the already tidy sofa. When she left the room, laughing at Jimmy who'd asked her not to move the fake dog poo he'd put on Ian's side of the bed, I looked around at the light-filled space that seemed to be perpetually ready for a photo shoot and asked Jimmy why they needed a cleaner every single day when most people in England had one once a week, if at all.

'Everybody has housekeepers here,' he said with a shrug. 'It's normal. They're part of the family. She does the laundry, changes the sheets twice a week, irons, washes cushion covers and beats dust out of everything. And does the shopping.'

I gasped, making Jimmy nearly spill our coffee. 'Like groceries?'

'Yeah,' Jimmy said, bemused.

'Oh no. I couldn't have someone choosing my avocados. I'm an expert avocado chooser. What if they got one with a bruise?'

'Well, I guess the sky would fall down,' Jimmy said, getting back to pouring coffee.

'I *knew* it.' I said, and grinned at his expression. 'So, what am I in for in the next few days? Tell me your daily routine.'

Jimmy raised an eyebrow.

'I like to know what's happening,' I said with a shrug.

'Well,' Jimmy said, getting comfy on a stool next to me, 'usually, if I don't wake up next to a randy girl with her undies on inside out—'

'Back to front,' I corrected.

'I wouldn't be so quick to point that out.'

I narrowed my eyes. 'Continue.'

Jimmy laughed. 'As I was saying, after I wake up I like to get out and do something physical, a run, a walk, a climb or something. Sometimes Diego makes me go to a yoga class – remember the dodgy leggings?' he said, making an 'eek' kind of face.

I sniggered.

'Then I come home and sit out on the balcony eating breakfast and drinking coffee and watching the waves.'

'Sounds a bit ideal.'

'I work on my music, go to my writing class, meet up with mates. Normal stuff.' He grinned and grabbed an iPad that was sitting on the table top. 'I like to keep abreast of what's going on at home ...'

I looked over his shoulder at the screen. 'That's the *Daily Fail*.'

'Yes,' he said as he clicked on a picture of a reality TV star attending a movie premiere in Leicester Square with a stare so vacant, a dress so tiny and a split so high you could see that not only was she not wearing underwear, she was as hairless as polished steel. 'But I like looking at the pictures. It reminds me why I stay here.'

I read over his shoulder. The girl in the 'article' was defending her 'LOOK AT ME! ENVY ME! LUST AFTER ME!' outfit, saying it was 'empowering to wear what she wanted'.

'Why is it empowering to be that level of naked in public in the middle of January?' I said. 'Do you know what I'd do if I wanted to feel completely empowered as a woman attending a premiere in London in minus one degrees with all the photographers crouching down low to get a fanny shot?'

'Tell me, I'm fascinated,' Jimmy said, not fascinated.

'I'd wear a dress made out of a duvet. And it would have a hood made out of memory foam so that when you're in there watching yet another probably very average Johnny Depp film you can rest your head back and sleep instead of pretending you give a shit in a tissue dress and earrings so adorned they remind me of the cutlery drawer. How does she not stab herself when she turns her head?'

Jimmy shrugged, his eyes beginning to glaze over.

'I'm not going to walk around uncomfortable and naked and call it "empowerment". I'm going to be warm and cosy.' I lifted my coffee cup with an air of having said something profound.

'You done there, Germaine Greer?' Jimmy said, turning his attention to the iPad again.

I sipped my coffee. 'Yes.'

'Oooh look, somebody from some reality show stepped out in Chanel trackies and a Louis Vuitton cap,' Jimmy said drolly, while scrolling past some pictures of a woman walking along a street. 'Her glasses are Chloe and her tote is Marc Jacobs. Thank *god* I know.'

As Jimmy continued to flick through varying questionable online newspapers scanning 'articles' about which nobody was wearing what, eating where and dating whomever, I checked my phone. I was still holding on to the hope that Pete would call. Or text. Or send me a picture of the view saying, 'wish you were here'. But perhaps he didn't. The thought stung. Perhaps he really was 'becoming who he was meant to be' and I was not meant to be beside the new him.

I checked my emails. I had one from Dad!

> Hi Plum, Lovely to hear from you. Having a very busy time. Clients ended up wanting to view an island on a lake in Uganda. Then a couple by Madagascar. Been flying all over the place. How wonderful you are in Cape Town. That's lovely. I stopped by there on the way to Uganda. I hope you and Pete have a wonderful time. Give my love to Priya and her friend. Am tired and looking forward to coming home and also the 'secret' party! Do you and Annabelle need any help? How about money? Just ask Mum. Love Dad.

Overjoyed the whole Dad-having-affair-with-ex-Victoria's-Secret-model-who-now-opens-orphanages-in-her-native-South-Africa thing was unfounded and noting that, yet again, my overactive Princess of Doom imagination had run away with the muse of Shakespearian dramatics, I tapped out a reply. I said the wedding was amazing, Cape Town was stunning and that the party-planning was all going fine. I didn't mention that Pete was sleeping under the stars with snakes and leopards and goats and gazelles. I told him I was flying home Saturday week and that the party was running exactly to plan. Of *course* it was; I was in charge. I sent Annabelle a text telling her that I'd heard from Dad and all was well and got a sarcastic reply implying my lunacy levels needed checking. With my shoulders less burdened, I put my phone on the counter, picked up my coffee and tuned in to Jimmy saying that Taylor Swift had written another thinly veiled song about people who'd slighted her.

CHAPTER FIFTEEN

The next morning, I watched the sunrise from bed again then jumped in the shower and got an Uber to Jimmy's (I'd given Trust the next few days off), arriving just in time for a Diego protein pancake stack. Diego informed me, after gushing over the multi-coloured lilies I'd bought him ('my favourite, sweet girl! How did you know?!'), that 8 a.m. was not an hour Jimmy saw often, so I got comfy on a stool and gratefully accepted a coffee. I was pouring pure maple syrup over my pancakes and telling a fascinated Diego and a confounded Pamela how my mother, in the interests of digestive health analysis, liked to weigh herself before and after a poo, when a man who looked like an older, more respectable Jimmy arrived in the kitchen. He was wearing tailored trousers, a slick belt, a crisp white shirt and had freshly washed hair. He looked like he belonged on the cover of *GQ*, whereas Diego, in phone-box-red leggings and a tight turquoise tank, belonged in a Richard Simmons video.

'Hello,' he said with a twinkly smile. 'So you're the English girl who looks like Kate Beckett that Jimmy's been talking about.' He extended an oft-moisturised hand. 'I'm Ian, Jimmy's brother.'

He was very similar to Jimmy, just older and with less of an up-all-night-let's-see-where-the-day-takes-us air than his younger sibling. He had a calm, even face: earnest, but interestingly so. He looked like he should be reading the breakfast news and that his favourite parts were the stories about dogs who skateboarded or a man whose home-grown squash resembled something suggestive.

'How are you finding Cape Town?' he asked. It was everybody's favourite question. It was said with a look of eagerness, keen to see if you loved it as much as they did.

'I love it so far,' I said, and Ian nodded like I'd passed a test.

Diego poured coffee while Ian opened cupboards, checked his phone and filled Flora and Lucy's bowls, at the same time as making enquiries about my Cape Town plans and checking that Jimmy was treating me well. At the sound of her food being plopped into her designer bowl, Lucy fell sideways off the sofa and panted and snotted her way across the room. She made it to a foot before the bowl then sat down and wheezed, looking forlornly at the food that was so close yet so far.

'Where's Flora?' I asked, picking up Lucy and setting her down in front of her meal of chicken risotto.

'That dog!' Diego said, ladling fruit salad into a Tupperware container. 'She thinks she's Jimmy's girlfriend.

It's icky. She goes to work with him and guards him from all the girls he brings home.'

Ian gave Diego a sharp look from behind the refrigerator door. Pamela, tending to some bubbling vegetable stock, glanced in my direction.

'Not that he brings home that many,' Ian said, placing a container of quinoa next to the fruit salad box. He gave me a compassionate smile that creased the lines around his eyes attractively.

'Oh, we're not like that,' I said, waving my hand and sliding back onto my stool in front of the pancakes. 'He's just showing me around while my boyfriend is away.'

I thought I caught a look from Diego, but then he turned to put more healthy snacks in little Tupperware containers and add them to Ian's growing pile. I watched as Diego explained the health benefits of each and every box, then they checked their evening arrangements: somebody was coming over for dinner and was bringing their new partner, who was a pescatarian. They argued tenderly over who would pick up the fish, each trying to take ownership of the job so the other wouldn't be put out. They were incredibly sweet together.

'I'd love to stay and chat some more but I have a meeting,' Ian said, looking at his watch. 'Will you have dinner with us one evening?'

'I'd love to,' I said.

'Oh, and can you find out what book he's reading?' Ian said, watching Diego put the Tupperware containers in an insulated bag. 'Not the decoy, I found that already.'

'Decoy?'

Diego rolled his eyes while filling Ian's thermos with coffee.

'About two years ago, I spent the whole weekend on the sofa reading a book I just *had* to get to the end of. *The Girl on the Train*. You know it?'

I nodded. Who didn't.

'Well, Jimmy had ants in his scruffy pants that day.' Ian rolled his eyes. 'I don't know why; he was new here and didn't know anyone, I guess. He was frustrated I wouldn't go surfing with him, or drink coffee with him or play Trivial Pursuit with him—'

'A big baby, that boy,' Diego said in a matronly yet fond manner.

'He stomped downstairs and didn't come back for a few hours. Then just as I was probably a quarter from finishing he pranced into the room and blurted out the ending.'

'Agh! I thought they were going to kill each other!' Diego said, throwing his meaty arms to the heavens, making Pamela chuckle. 'Then Ian did it to him, and Jimmy back again and now they have hidden books and decoy books and write the endings on bathroom mirrors! I don't know what to do with the pair of them!'

Ian laid a placating hand on Diego's arm, took the offered bag of snacks and smiled in my direction. 'The decoy book is an Ian Rankin, so if you can find out what the real one is I'll be forever indebted.' He squeezed my shoulder, made me promise to find a night to have dinner with them then turned to Diego, checked he really was happy to collect the kingklip fillets, discussed what sauce would best complement them, and then they walked to the front door deliberating over playlists.

An hour later I was sitting at the kitchen island sipping a second coffee and sharing my gossip from the music industry with Diego (he was desperate to know which famous singer requested a young man dressed as a lifeguard in his green room) when Jimmy's voice preceded his arrival in the room.

'I just did a fart in the shower and the heat cooked it nearly solid. I had to punch my way out. Man, it was gross,' he said, then blinked as he entered the kitchen and saw Diego and me smirking and Pamela giving him a look of disgust.

For the first time since meeting him he looked mildly embarrassed.

'Charming,' I said, with a look of repulsion.

Diego chuckled.

Jimmy tightened the white towel around his waist and recovered his general composure. 'Why are you here so early?'

'The day is a-wasting, Jimmy boy,' I said, sliding off the stool and guiding him away from the fridge by his bare shoulders. 'Let's get on with it!'

Jimmy threw a 'what's happening' look at Diego, who raised his bulletproof coffee (black coffee with – ew, gross – butter and coconut oil in it) and said, 'The lady wants to see Cape Town.'

*

'So where are we going?' I said ten minutes later as I followed Jimmy to the car.

'An SA adventure,' Jimmy opened his rear passenger door with an unhealthy-sounding screech of rust and age. He threw a mess of towels, swimmers, drink bottles, hats, sunscreen and bags onto the back seat and jumped in the front, slamming the car door with a metallic thud.

'Will it make the journey?' I said, trying to replace the cover to the speaker which fell to the floor when I shut my door. 'I don't want to have to push this heap around Africa.'

Jimmy leant across and felt my bicep. 'You seem strong enough,' he said and turned the key.

The car coughed and shuddered itself alive.

'You touched my boob,' I said, over a Foreigner song.

Jimmy grinned like a boy who'd put a whoopee cushion under Grandma's dining chair. 'I know!'

The sun beat down on us as we backed out of the driveway; the smell of salt air, hot grass and a spluttering exhaust pipe filled my nostrils. We drove down the steep hills from Ian and Diego's place towards the sea and followed the road through ever-busy Camps Bay beach, then wound our way along the coast. Jimmy pointed out seals, colonies of gulls, diving groups and shark flags.

'What in the name of Jesus and all his minions are shark flags?' I said, craning to see the green flag flapping high on the cliff above us. It had an outline of a great white on it.

'It's a warning system,' Jimmy said casually. 'A white flag

means a shark has been spotted, a red flag means high shark alert, black is bad spotting conditions—'

'Spotting conditions?'

'Yeah. They have people out looking for sharks.'

'What an awful job!' I shuddered. 'So, what does a green flag mean? No sharks – you're good to go in the water?'

'No, it means the spotting conditions are good.'

'That's it?' I balked. 'Just good *visibility*? Good conditions for you to spot the shark and hopefully die of fright before the shark has a chance to crush and shred your entire body with its nineteen rows of serrated teeth and its 1.8 tons of bite force?'

Jimmy glanced away from the road to give me a strange look. 'So, no surf lessons for you then?'

'Not even a molecule of a toenail in that water.'

We didn't talk as Jimmy navigated a precariously winding road. Crumbly steep cliffs went up on one side, with nets strung over the road to catch falling boulders, and a precipitous drop to the rocks and frothy surf below us on the other. The ocean went on and on, the sun beating down on it and turning the water various shades of sapphire and turquoise depending on how deep it was. I felt like I was on the edge of Africa, which, according to my little Google Map search, I kind of was. I pointed it out to Jimmy.

'Yep,' he said. 'If you leapt off the cliff and swam straight out you'd hit Uruguay.'

I peered at the horizon. 'Another time maybe.'

Once we were off the edge of Africa and traversing a

mountainous range covered in low, brushy bushes, Jimmy turned up the volume and sang along, loud and proud, to his jammed 1980s CD. He knew every 'oooh', 'aaahh' and 'hey baby'.

After a few songs he turned to me. 'You're mouthing all the words,' he said. 'Just sing it.'

'Nooooo,' I shook my head. 'I can't sing. *At all*. None of my family can. We're tuneless, cloth-eared, musically impoverished beings.'

'So?' Jimmy laughed. 'Nobody should feel too self-conscious to sing Def Leppard in the car. It's one of life's simple and free pleasures. Do it!' He winked then sang, throwing in an effortless harmony, a look of unassuming happiness across his face as he hit the steering wheel in time to the drumbeat.

I watched him as the chorus approached. With Jimmy's nod of reassurance and the salty wind whipping my hair around, I joined in, spectacularly out of tune but, as instructed, nice and loud and definitely carefree.

I screeched the chorus in fluctuating tones of off-key, sounding like an opiate-abusing dolphin recovering from a stroke. Jimmy stopped singing and watched me, his mouth half open. I immediately ceased my carefree vocals.

'Hey!' I glowered at him with embarrassed irritation. 'You said . . .!'

His features quivered, trying to contain his escaping laughter. 'No, keep going. You're doing great,' he said, attempting a look of encouragement, his eyes watering.

Tentatively I started again with Jimmy looking side-ways at me.

'I might just turn it up a bit though ...' he said with false casualness. He swivelled the volume knob to max, then grinned.

We drove through places with names I couldn't pro-nounce: Noordhoek, Kommetjie and Fish Hoek, and some I could: Cape Point, Simons Town and Kalk Bay, all the while listening to a backing track of Poison, Bon Jovi and Joan Jett. We saw ostriches and zebra and big scary birds. At one point we had to slow down to allow a troop (another collective noun google) of baboons to cross the road. Some mothers carried babies on their backs that were so cute I wound down my window to see if any of them wanted to hold my hand, or give me a cuddle, or come and live with me and eat cut-up banana from a bowl at the kitchen table and be my best friend forever, and was swiftly told to wind it back up because baboons know humans have food and aren't afraid to get vicious to get some.

'Respect,' I said solemnly, making Jimmy laugh.

At a place called Boulders Beach Jimmy pulled into a car park and said we needed to stretch our legs.

'No, you can't touch or cuddle or take any of them home,' Jimmy said as we arrived on the white sand beach and I gasped in delight.

Huge smooth boulders sheltered the tiny beach, making the aqua water millpond still, and in among the families playing on the icing-sugar sand were penguins. Hundreds and hundreds of little black and white penguins, no taller than my knee.

'Oh my god!' I squealed, as a couple of them waddled past me, entered the water and paddled around some kids wearing water wings.

Everywhere I looked humans and penguins were enjoying the beach together. Humans picnicked, and next to them penguins sat; humans swam, and next to them penguins floated; humans stood at the edge of the water watching their children, and penguins stood at the edge of the water watching whatever they were watching. It was the strangest sight I'd ever seen. We stayed for about an hour observing the penguins waddle along the beach, paddle in the shallows and bask on the rocks with zero fear of humans. Sadly there were rangers stopping me touching, cuddling and smuggling a couple home.

Once back in the car we followed yet another coastal road beside the wild ocean and got out at a loud and busy white sand surf beach. I bought us a couple of ice creams from a man hefting a cool box from one collection of sunbathers to the next, and we sat on the sand and watched surfers catch wave after terrifying wave.

'So how long have you and your boyfriend been together?' Jimmy asked once he'd given his sticky fingers a thorough licking.

'Six years,' I said.

'That's quite a long time.'

'We took a three-month break at one point to "see how

it felt",' I said. 'It was Pete's idea. He thought we were too young to be together for such a long time or something.'

'But you got back together, obviously.'

'Yep. Pete thought I'd freak out about being apart but I ended up having a thing with a guy from work.' I grinned. 'And another couple of guys.'

'Reprehensible!' Jimmy said, affecting disgust.

'Pete did too but he doesn't know I know,' I said. 'When we got back together we promised not to tell each other about anyone else we'd dated but Pete's friend had been telling me everything the whole time. He'd slept with a girl from his gym, went on a few dates with a girl who turned out to be completely psycho and got an unsolicited blowjob from his friend's slaggy cousin from Manchester. When he woke up the next morning he found out he hadn't been the only guy in the flat who'd had a surprise horny visitor that night.' I giggled. 'I think he was horrified. We got back together a week later.'

Jimmy laughed.

'What about you?' I said.

'Girlfriends?'

'Yeah.'

'A few,' he said. 'None for a while. Maybe I should look up that girl from Manchester . . .' He grinned and watched a surfer who'd caught a particularly huge wave and was riding it all the way in to the beach.

'That's my mate,' Jimmy said, standing up and waving.

After a few minutes four good-looking guys, all tanned

and salty and dripping, ran out of the surf, their boards under their arms, and joined us. There were a lot of boisterous '*hey, my bru*'s, then Jimmy introduced me.

'Jess, this is Sam, Gus, André and Bryn,' Jimmy said, and I immediately forgot who was who. 'Guys, this is Jess.'

I got a host of damp, strong handshakes and I ignored the knowing looks they threw Jimmy's way.

'What are you doing here, mate?' one of the guys asked Jimmy as we walked across the sand to the car park.

'Thought I'd pick up lunch and show Jess the studio,' Jimmy said, stopping at his car while the guys walked on, carrying their boards, their suits stripped down to their waists, showing off firm chests. 'The usual?'

The guys gave thumbs up and disappeared.

'Doesn't anybody have a job in Cape Town?' I asked Jimmy as we pulled out of the car park.

'Those guys are artists. Creators, really. They own a studio together and take time off when they want to surf and see their kids and stuff. It's a pretty sweet set-up.'

With a back seat full of fish and chips, we parked outside an old building painted mint green. After punching in a code on a pin pad Jimmy pushed open a barred security door and we climbed some concrete stairs and arrived in a place so weird and wonderful I loved it immediately. Music blared from speakers by a leather bar with a glass top that was a real fish tank. Perspex rococo-style mirrors hung on the walls with LED lights in their clear frames that changed from blue to yellow to pink to blue again. Skulls painted bronze, gold and neon yellow hung from the exposed beams on chains and held weeping lush plants. A ceiling light the size of a kids' paddling pool hung low in the centre of the room and seemed to be made of hundreds of realistic-looking crows in various states of flight.

'Hey!' I said pointing at a sofa just like Oscar the Couch but in shaggy pink fur.

'That's how I met these guys,' Jimmy said. 'Diego commissioned Oscar the Couch as a Christmas present for Ian. When I came with him to pick it up I had to break it to Diego that it wasn't exactly to Ian's white-and-cream-coloured tastes.'

'Aw, poor multi-coloured Diego,' I said, walking past a table that held candles shaped like human bones, kewpie dolls and full-sized, old-fashioned liquor bottles.

'Luckily I knew someone who would love it. Me!' he grinned. 'That was a great Christmas. I gave Diego a really cool pair of socks and a framed picture of me on the sofa.'

'Let me guess, you were naked?'

'Maybe,' he laughed and walked towards the bar area. 'Lunch!' he hollered, and set about spreading the fish and chips across the top of a table-tennis table.

Sam, Gus, André and Bryn appeared from various parts of the warehouse-like space. All dressed and clean-smelling, their wet hair pushed off their tanned, smiling faces. Just as we were about to eat, André's wife and baby turned up and they headed into a workroom with their food. Sam received a phone call and went and sat on a flocked black chair in the corner by the bar to chat and eat. The chair's legs were black casts of human legs and its arms actual arms, with hands balled into fists. It was the kind of thing that would make you scream if you saw it in a darkened room. Or a lit room. Actually I was suppressing a scream right now.

'So how do you guys know each other?' Bryn said from a stool at the bar. He was the tallest of them all, with a messy crop of blond hair, a broad chest and a host of wrinkles from a life spent on the waves.

'Jess turned up in my bed with her undies on back to front,' Jimmy said with a wicked grin.

'I did not!' I threw a chip at Jimmy.

'Lucky Jimmy,' said Gus, laughing from his chair, which was a huge cube of wood painted glossy red; his lunch sat on a metallic side table shaped like a Hawaiian hula girl holding out a drinks tray.

After eating and chatting the guys went back to work while Jimmy showed me around a handful of rooms that led off from the open space. In one, Bryn and Gus were working on life-sized arms of Darth Vadar and Luke that would eventually be mounted on the wall like giant arm-shaped sconces. The lightsabers they held really lit up.

'If you can think it we can make it,' Sam said with a grin when I asked how he came up with the idea. 'A guy in America ordered these for his kid's bedroom.'

He pointed to the bust of a bison made out of white resin hanging high on the wall. Its horns were lava lamps, glowing a multitude of colours. 'That's Jimmy's favourite,' he said.

'It is,' Jimmy said. 'If I could afford their stuff that'd be my first piece.'

My phone rang and when I saw it was Pete calling I left the workroom and sat on a stool at the bar.

'Hi,' I said down the phone line.

'Jess?' Pete said through the noise of wind and bad reception. 'Can you hear me?'

'Yes, are you all right?'

'I'm fine. I got your millions of abusive texts, though,' he said, sounding superior. 'And Giselle saw them, too.'

'What's she doing with your phone?'

'She was taking a photo when they all came through and I asked her to read them to me.'

'Texts between you and me are private!' I hissed down the phone, glancing at Jimmy, who smiled and waved at me from the workroom.

'She's actually really nice and what you said about her was really mean.'

'Well, I obviously didn't think she'd be reading my texts, did I?!'

'Look, I know I didn't leave in the ... circumstances but ... and you ...'

'What? You're breaking up.'

Crackles and wind came down the line.

'Pete?' I waited, but could only hear the wind, the crackle and snatches of Pete's voice reprimanding me through the bad reception. Then the line went dead.

I went back to the workroom, where music blared and the

guys worked and laughed and teased one another. They were like school friends doing woodwork class all day.

'You all right?' Jimmy said.

'Yeah,' I said, but it was obvious my mood had dipped after the phone call.

Jimmy watched me for a moment then grabbed my hand and dragged me across the warehouse. 'I challenge you to a game of beer table tennis.'

'What?'

He pulled two beer bottles from behind the bar, flicked off the lids by doing some kind of manoeuvre with the mouth of each bottle, thrust one in my hand, a paddle in the other and said, 'Drink with one hand, play with the other. Try to win.'

I grinned. 'You're on.'

After an hour I was laughing and puffing and giggling, and Jimmy looked at the time and said we needed to go. We said goodbye to everyone, and just as we were leaving Gus ran up and handed me the bottom half of a skull that was painted gold and made out of some kind of resin.

'To remember us by,' he said. 'It's a chip bowl.'

Pete would hate it. I, on the other hand, couldn't think of anything I loved more at that very instant. Except baby hedgehogs, because who doesn't love them? Psychopaths. That's who.

On the drive home I called Annabelle to tell her about the penguins and the baboons and the dead snake we saw on the road that Jimmy insisted on stopping next to so we could look at its guts and beer table tennis, and Annabelle made sat-isfying '*I'm-so-jealous/that's-gross/sounds-hilarious*' comments.

'Did I tell you Mum phoned yesterday?' she said.

'How? I thought they weren't allowed any contact.'

'They aren't. One of the other guests smuggled a phone in. She said she thought they were using food deprivation to play mind control games. And that she was getting a bit jumpy from all the gunshots.'

'What gunshots?!'

Jimmy gave me a worried glance.

'It turns out there's a rifle range next door to the retreat.'

'Well, that's great council planning.'

'Anyway, she was worried about that lady covering her radio show and wanted me to try and get the listener stats or something, then one of the guides found her and the phone got confiscated. I heard her call him a fascist before she got cut off.'

'We need to get her out of there! What if she's accidentally signed up to some cult and comes out thinking she's had alien intervention or agrees to a mass suicide pact thinking it's an environmental protest march?!'

'Oh, I don't think so . . .' Annabelle said vaguely.

'You don't sound worried. Why aren't you worried?'

'She'll be fine. She could do with some mind control. Be cool if she did make contact with aliens, though. Hey, I gotta go OK? Bye!'

'Aliens?' Jimmy said once I'd hung up and commenced chewing my fingernail.

'Bit extreme?'

Jimmy bulged his eyes to indicate the affirmative.

I laughed. 'I have a tendency to go straight to catastrophe mode.'

'I've noticed.'

'I can't help myself. I always think everyone is dead if they don't answer their phone. And most of the time, OK, all of the time, *so far*, people call back and say mundane, totally reasonable things like they were in the shower or in the queue at the supermarket, or in the toilet, or their phone was in their bag and they didn't hear it. But you know what? The one day I don't worry and think, '*Oh they must just be busy, happily busy and happily alive*' will be the day somebody is dead. And who'll be sorry then, huh?'

Jimmy's eyes flicked from the road to me.

'Well, a lot of people will be and it will be awful and very sad and life will never be the same again, but the point is, I worry to keep people alive! You're welcome.'

Jimmy laughed, turned up Whitesnake and we sped towards the apartment.

CHAPTER SIXTEEN

The next day was Saturday and, after a brief chat on the phone to Hunter about Marvel versus DC and why unicorns are perceived as nice when really, they are weaponised horses, I'd received a call from security saying Jimmy had arrived. I'd clattered down six flights of stairs in my flip-flops, jumped into his car and we'd screeched out of the complex because Jimmy was 'starving'.

'It's probably got a huge queue!' Jimmy said, his voice elevated above the noise of the bustling crowd. He pulled me forward by the wrist. 'Hurry up.'

Jimmy was keen for me to try a particular kind of sandwich and the stall was evidently at the very back of the covered, busy marketplace. I shuffled closer and followed his broad back through masses of young people in tiny shorts and trendy waistcoats. He'd taken me to a market popular with locals that was set in the grounds of an old biscuit mill. To get there we'd driven down dodgy streets lined with squat buildings that had bars across broken windows. Car guards, which were a thing I'd now gotten used to, jostled with each other to guide us towards parking spaces we could clearly see ourselves. Once parked, they'd ask for ten rand to 'keep the car safe'. We'd stepped out into insane heat despite the fact that it was only 10.30 a.m.

'We'll try some of those later, too,' Jimmy said, pointing to an experimental gin stand where jugs of gin containing a variety of botanicals sat on a cloth-covered trestle table, beads of condensation dripping down the glass.

As we hustled through the market I spun my head left and right, tying to take it all in: giant sizzling paella pans, a vegan stall selling exotic mushroom kebabs with a vast array of vibrant sauces, huge queues at coffee carts, supersized blooms I was sure Diego would love, gin stands, juice stands, craft beer stands, and the bustling, laughing, smiling crowd. Everybody was beautiful, and it was hard to tell if it was the strong Dutch ancestry or if plastic surgeons were seen the way someone in the UK sees the hairdresser.

'Nobody here has fringes,' I said loudly as I swiped my heavy fringe off my face and clipped it back while trying to keep my elbows out of the eyes of the people in the crowd. 'And the reason is twofold.'

A girl in a panama hat and pink plastic sunglasses walked between us with two plates of mountainous salad and I skipped to catch up with Jimmy, who was on a mission.

'One, it's bloody hot,' I said, sidestepping a guy who turned away from a stall with a mouth-watering paper plate

of hash browns, eggs, bacon, hollandaise and roasted tomatoes. 'And two, they're all Botoxed and wrinkle-less so the
forehead is a thing of pride.'

'What is the point of all your blather?' Jimmy said, glancing back at me.

'I'm growing out my fringe and getting Botox.' I spied
someone with a crepe the size of a large pizza, dripping in
lemon juice, loaded with berries and glistening with sparkly
sugar. 'Oooh, shall we get one of those?'

We passed food stalls with queues of hungry, chatty,
laughing people; pizza was passed to the hungry customer
on a square of cardboard; oysters in their shells sat beside a
plastic cup of prosecco on a rough wooden board. Everything
looked worthy of an Instagram snap. We finally reached
Jimmy's desired stall and joined the back of a big line of
customers.

'I'm so excited,' Jimmy said as we neared the front of the
queue. When he was next in line he became deathly silent,
focusing intently on a man with some tongs loading meat on
to the guy in front's bun.

With a huge roast lamb sandwich balanced on a flimsy
bamboo platter, we zigzagged back through the crowds and
found a spot we could both squeeze into at a long bench table.
People stood or sat in groups eating and drinking, chatting
and laughing. There was no pushing or shoving or looks
of gross impatience or irritation at the crowds or queues.
Everybody seemed happy and relaxed. And I could see why.
With the abundance of amazing food and drink on offer, and

the knowledge that outside the entrance to the market was yet another sunny Saturday with palm trees and white sandy beaches, why wouldn't you be? After devouring our food we went back to the gin stand and emerged into the sun with jars of sparkling elderflower and gin. Giant cubes of ice tinkled against the sides and big sticks of South African plants stuck out of the top.

'It's hard to drink the gin without being stabbed in the eye with the stick,' I said, raising my voice over a live band, in response to the look Jimmy was giving me as I tried to sip from my gin jar at a weird angle.

'When does a twig become a stick?' he said, pulling out the soggy sticks/twigs and appraising them like an *Antiques Roadshow* aficionado.

'Is that a trick question?'

'No. I just want to know if there is a size frame. Like when a house becomes a mansion. What's the deciding factor? Floor plan, size, amount of windows?'

'We can just google,' I said, getting out my phone.

Jimmy frowned.

'What?'

'The modern day access to everything has stopped all awesome conversations where you can debate over things for hours. Now we just google the answer and go, "*Oh, all right then. Grand. Want another drink?*"'

'You think a conversation about sticks was going to be awesome?' I raised my eyebrows. 'And yes, thanks.'

'"*Yes thanks*" what?'

'I'd like another drink,' I grinned. 'But one with no sticks this time.'

'Twigs,' Jimmy corrected.

We headed back into the market, taking more time to savour the atmosphere. It felt vastly different from the food markets in Europe with their breads and cheeses and olives, which were also there among the Afrikaans dishes, but mostly the food was fresh, innovative and, in my mind, all restaurant quality. It was a foodie heaven, and I was quickly realising that a Capetonian's attitude to life was one I greatly admired and aspired to. Food, friends, music, sun. Such simplicity. We spent another happy hour sipping cold craft beer then wandering through the market, buying things Diego might like, gifts for Annabelle and the kids and sampling as much as our bellies would allow.

'Now where?' I said, leaping back into Jimmy's hot car with a bag of gifts and snacks. I immediately wound down the windows. His must be the only car in South Africa without air con.

I looked at Jimmy, who hadn't answered but was regarding me with sincere satisfaction.

'What?'

'You're having fun, aren't you?' he said.

'I'm having an amazing time!' I said, beaming back at him. 'So, what's next?'

'A little drive,' Jimmy said, pulling out into the busy streets. 'You like mojitos?'

'Does Samuel L. Jackson have cheekbones to die for?'

*

'This playlist contains a lot of the same songs as the stuck CD,' I said after half an hour of driving.

Jimmy had brought a portable speaker and was playing songs from his phone because he thought I may have tired of listening to 'The Final Countdown' and 'Hit Me With Your Best Shot' sixteen times in one day.

'I know,' Jimmy said. 'I have a thing for the eighties.'

'I figured,' I said, turning up Prince. 'You know when I was little I thought this song said "When *Dougs* Cry"?'

Jimmy laughed. 'Why would Dougs cry?'

'I dunno ... maybe their wives left them.'

'Yeah, that happens to Dougs a lot, I hear.'

I sniggered.

Jimmy looked over at me. 'I thought the guy from Toto was singing 'I bless *Lorraine* down in Africa.'

'Why would he bless Lorraine?'

Jimmy shrugged. 'Maybe she did something nice? Like took them out to dinner when they arrived in Africa and didn't know anyone?'

'Wow. You should definitely write love songs.'

I got out my phone, linked it to the speaker and the rest of the journey we listened to show tunes while I marvelled at the scenery.

'Here we are,' Jimmy said, pulling up in front of a ramshackle place, its perimeter marked out by concrete Grecian-style pillars, wrought iron gothic-style rusted gates, French Caribbean shutters, their pink paint flaking off, and heavy Cuban doors, painted vibrant blue and lush palm trees.

'What is this place?' I said as we walked through the entrance to the courtyard. Random pieces of architecture from all kinds of eras had been used to make a mismatched, low-slung building open to the elements. We walked across the sandy courtyard busy with people in shorts and sunglasses drinking cocktails at brightly coloured tables.

'Just a bar,' Jimmy said, leading me inside. 'Mojito?'

'Yes please,' I said, looking around.

Beaded chandeliers of all colours hung from the ceiling and the floor was sand. Male bartenders sported Che Guevara berets and the females wore flower garlands in their hair and bright red lipstick. Hanging from the middle of the room was a swing, upon which a girl sat chatting to her friends who were sitting on old sofas around her. On every available surface was a faded religious effigy or dramatic candelabra dripping with years of undisturbed wax.

'My friends at the studio made those,' Jimmy said, pointing to some arms holding torches sticking out from the wall behind the bar.

We found a place outside at a brightly painted outdoor table under a bamboo pagoda that was adorned with multi-coloured beads, beer bottle tops and bunting. Jimmy kicked off his flip-flops and dug his feet in the warm sand.

'So, what kind of writing class are you doing?' I said, relaxing against the back of the wicker chair.

'Scriptwriting.'

'What kind of script?'

Jimmy gulped his non-alcoholic cocktail. 'It's an animated kids' musical about the animals on Wimbledon Common. I'm trying to get it finished to submit for an internship-type course at a production house in Soho.'

'In London?!' I said, and I seemed a lot more excited about it than someone who had known a guy for six days and who also had a boyfriend (who, admittedly, was being a bit arsehole-y) should have been. I looked at my drink. Perhaps it was time to ease off . . .

Jimmy smiled. He looked entirely too handsome in the sun with his tanned arms resting casually on the sunshine-yellow table. 'Yes, in London. If I get on the course there's potential for a job in the writer's room afterwards. But the submission date is just over a week away and I haven't finished it yet.'

I felt bad. He was spending all this time with me when he could have been writing. I told him as much.

'Nah,' he said, dismissing my concern with a squeeze on the shoulder that left my skin tingling. 'It'll be a long shot anyway – there's only three places. They'll take on people who've written something "*culturally relevant to the current climate*", or something "*supernatural with a dark twist and an unreliable narrator*". They probably won't even look twice at my little script with the talking badgers and the adders who sing Alice Cooper's "Poison".'

I laughed. 'I think it sounds wicked.'

I asked him why he'd stayed in Cape Town. Although with my feet in the sand, Cuban music wafting from outdoor speakers, the sun on my shoulders, the tang of sea spray in the air and the sounds of other happy drinkers, it was a no-brainer.

'I kind of ran out of money so I didn't really have an option. But then I made friends and Sylvie let me play at the bar and I've got my scriptwriting class, which I really love.' He shrugged. 'There's just so much to do here.'

'Have you been on a safari?'

Jimmy shook his head.

'You've been here three years and you haven't even been on a safari?' I said, shocked.

'When you live somewhere you never end up doing all the things the tourists do,' he said. 'Like in London, how many times have you been to a West End show?'

'I've seen *Matilda* six times.'

'Really?'

'*The Phantom of the Opera* four. *Wicked* twice, and I'm pretty sure the cast from *The Book of Mormon* are sick of me mouthing along to every word.'

Jimmy gave me a look.

'You like the eighties, I like show tunes,' I said. 'We're equally uncool.'

'Or equally cool.'

'Let's go with that.'

Jimmy looked at his watch. 'I gotta get back.'

In the kitchen we found Ian and Diego dressed all in white: jackets, shirts, trousers, shoes. Including white sunglasses for Ian and a white flat cap for Diego.

'You two off to your NSYNC appreciation night?' Jimmy said, walking past laughing.

Diego looked at Ian then glanced down at his outfit. 'What's in sync?'

'It's a boy band,' Ian said, adjusting his belt. 'Ignore him, you look great.'

With a menacing look from Diego, Jimmy hustled downstairs, leaving me in the kitchen watching Diego and Ian fuss with their all-white ensembles, which were a requirement for something called Dîner en Blanc; an elegant, outdoor picnic at a secret location with a secret celebrity host and a secret band. It sounded fabulous, and Diego and Ian promised to take me to the next one if I was ever back in Cape Town. When Jimmy ran back up he found us sitting on the sofa with flutes of champagne, nibbling on the titbits I'd bought at the market and in mid-discussion about his love life.

'He never has a girlfriend because he shuns all the decent ones that show interest in him,' Ian said.

'He's too fussy,' Diego said, like an old school matron.

'I am not *too* fussy,' Jimmy said, his car keys dangling from a finger. 'I'm the right amount of fussy.'

'You didn't keep seeing the yoga instructor because ...?' Diego said.

'She thought Brexit was a biscuit,' Jimmy replied.

'And what about the one who played the violin and was off to climb Mount Kilimanjaro?'

'Obsessed with trail mix.'

'The one last month who stayed for three days and didn't

pass the test?' Diego said, appraising Ian's outfit and brushing non-existent dust off his shoulder.

'She stayed for three days and didn't pass the test. Duh.'

'What test?' I said, thinking it was more than a little weird if future girlfriends had to sit an exam.

Jimmy turned to me. 'It's called the Tarantino Test. Does she understand *Pulp Fiction* on first watching? No? Then she's out. Yes? Then she's a potential keeper. Well, she's through the first round anyway.'

'Did you understand it first time?' Diego asked me.

'I don't understand it now, and I've watched it fourteen times and read the plot on Wikipedia.'

'Then you're out,' Jimmy said with a wry grin.

'Oh, I'm *so* upset,' I replied.

'And of course, there's the music,' Diego said. 'What are you into?'

'The last three songs I Shazamed were by ex-One Directioners.'

Jimmy's expression implied that I needed to reassess my life choices.

'And what happened to that girl with the big . . .?' Diego made hand gestures to imply substantial boobs, making Jimmy shake his head slowly. Diego turned to Ian. 'Maybe he's just frightened of commitment?'

'Maybe he's just too annoying,' Ian said with a grin.

'Maybe his obsession with another girl got in the way,' I said, nodding my head in the direction of Flora, who was perched on an armchair watching the gathering with snooty mild interest and looking like an exploded Tampax. (*Un*used. Don't be gross.) I swear her eyes narrowed when I spoke.

Jimmy appeared shocked at my disloyalty.

'You just need to put yourself out there more,' Diego said, taking a sip of his champagne.

'And try to be less irritating,' Ian added with a grin.

'Stop trying to "sort" me, Pet Shop Boys!' Jimmy stalked to the front door. 'Come on, Judas,' he said to me.

Diego and Ian fell apart laughing. I hugged them both goodbye, told them they looked fabulous and raced out after Jimmy.

'They seem to think you've had too many one-night stands and not enough "relationships",' I said in reply to Jimmy's query about what his two-faced brother and meddling brother-in-law had been saying about him.

'Those two are a couple of old prudes,' Jimmy said. 'And anyway, how many one-night stands are too many?'

'Can you count them on one hand?'

'Yes,' Jimmy said.

I gave him a dubious look.

'Well, one of mine. One of yours.' He pointed to a passing jogger. 'One of his, maybe.'

As Jimmy pulled into the apartment grounds he turned to me. 'So, you want to hang out tomorrow?'

'Are you kidding me? I'm having a fab time! That is, if it's OK with you? I mean, you don't have to. You might think I talk too much, or I'm not adventurous enough because I don't want to go in that pool of violence you people call the ocean and what about your script deadline? You should probably—'

Jimmy leant across me and opened the car door. 'I'll see you tomorrow then,' he grinned. 'Now get out, I'm late.'

I jumped out and waved until he was out of the security gates and no longer in sight.

CHAPTER SEVENTEEN

'Is there going to be a day when I wake up and you aren't here with your perky face?'

'Yes. In precisely six days. And you'll be very sad to see me go.'

Jimmy grinned and tried to pull the covers up but I pulled them back. A tussle ensued.

'Up you get,' I said, giving his bare shoulder a shove. I stood and flung my arms about. 'Places to go, people to meet, wine to drink and food to eat! Heeey, I'm a poet and I didn't know it.'

'You're tiring and need rewiring,' he said, circling his finger around his temple.

'*Very* good,' I said with admiration. 'You're implying insanity, but I care not. Hey!' I gasped. 'What happened to Flora?'

As Jimmy shot up and worriedly looked in the direction of Flora (who was absolutely fine) I yanked his covers off.

'Sneaky,' Jimmy said, yawning.

Flora sat delicately on her plush throne looking at me with an expression I interpreted as, '*Don't involve me in your petty games, silly girl.*' I shot back an expression that required no interpretation and said, '*You're so fluffy I don't know which end is arse and which end is face. And I can play any games I want to, you piece of dryer fluff. You don't get to me. Stop looking at me like that! Stop it! Stop it, you—*'

'You don't like my dog, do you?' Jimmy stood next to his bed in his boxers, a towel in one hand and his phone in the other, evidently taking a photo of me in a battle of wills with the canine version of Regina George from *Mean Girls*.

'So, what are the plans for today?' I asked, watching Jimmy rummage through his clothing pile.

'Well,' Jimmy said with another yawn, 'we are going to have a relaxed day. Because it's Sunday. A holy day. We shall drink wine because Jesus liked wine. And that is a religion I can get on board with.' He located some shorts and walked towards the bathroom. 'We shall do a little interacting with some wildlife,' he laughed as I clapped my joy. 'Then have lunch at a winery and, because it's Sunday, we can nap in the sun. Do you like to nap?'

'More than I like Jason Bateman,' I said.

Jimmy gave me a look.

'I like him a lot.'

I jumped in the front seat and saw a sheet of A4 taped to the dashboard in front of me.

SONGS FROM THE SHOWS ARE BANNED it said in red pen.

I turned to Jimmy, who was grinning. 'Fine!' I said, ripping it off and laughing.

To the soundtrack of *Rock of Ages*, which was both showtune-ish and 1980s, we embarked on another hot drive and arrived at another busy car park. I climbed out of the car and followed Jimmy towards a lake with swans floating beneath weeping willows. I saw a sign for wine-tasting and was just letting my homing device kick in and lead me there when Jimmy called me back.

'We're going here,' he said, and pointed to a sign that said '*Up close and personal encounters with eagles, hawks, falcons, porcupines, owls and SNAKES*'.

'Not happening,' I said, jabbing my finger at the word snakes, the cold sweat of terror already making its way down my spine.

'If you don't hold a snake I won't take you to the winery.'

'We're at a winery. Ha! I'll drink here.'

'This place is on the tour coach circuit and will be crawling with tourists in approximately ...' He looked at his watch. 'Thirty minutes. You have to book way in advance. But good luck!'

We paid the entrance fee in a little wooden shack then wandered into a grassy area surrounded by pens and open cages. The first thing I saw was a fluffy rabbit bounding freely across my path.

'Now *that* I will hold.'

'If you can catch him,' a voice said behind me. I turned

and saw a guy of about twenty-five in cargo shorts and an 'Eagle Encounter' T-shirt. 'You can start here if you like,' he said, leading us to a nearby smallish tree. 'If you can find a chameleon you can hold one.' He pointed out where the bird show was, where we could play 'chase' with the porcupine, then he went back and sat under a tin roof shelter where some other tourists were holding brown owls and bearded dragons.

Jimmy and I spent a happy half hour searching for chameleons, putting them on various parts of our clothing and watching them change colour, then moved on to other birds and lizards. We fed raw meat to eagles, got chased by a 'domesticated' porcupine, then approached the tin shelter near the entrance where the baby owls and lizards were. Jimmy walked up to a large tank.

'Jess,' he said. 'Come and see Charlie.'

The young guide, sitting on a wooden table, his sturdy boots on a chair, turned in his sitting position, a lizard on his forearm. 'You can't hold Charlie today. He ate recently and is still digesting.'

I walked up to the tank and saw a huge speckled brown and cream boa constrictor with a rugby-ball-shaped lump in the middle of his long body. He lay very still, just the tip of his tongue flicking REVOLTINGLY in and out. Immediately my body went into fight or flight mode. I chose flight and tried to back away and bumped into Jimmy's firm chest.

'What did he eat?' I asked, wondering if that bunny was still bounding around.

'A rat,' the guide said. 'We've got a freezer full of them.'

I shuddered with disgust.

'But you can hold Felix if you like?'

'Who's Felix?' I said, smiling and stepping towards a super-fluffy, super-cute baby owl perched on a branch next to the guide.

'Him,' the guide said, pointing to a super-fuzzy, super-disgusting tarantula in a tank next to Charlie.

'Nah, I'm good,' I said, stepping back and hitting up against Jimmy again, who laughed.

We hung out with the guide for a bit, as far from Charlie and Felix as possible, taking it in turns to pat the owls and lizards, then Jimmy looked at his watch.

'You hungry?'

'Do zebras have a black penis?'

Jimmy frowned. 'Do they?'

'They do,' the guide said.

Jimmy turned to me. 'You're gross.'

I grinned. 'Let's eat.'

We drove for a few minutes, then Jimmy pulled off the main road and we bumped down a hot and dusty dirt track, arriving at a leafy parking area next to a large manor house. A softly rolling lawn stretched out in front of the house, with a smattering of large trees providing much-needed shady spots. There didn't seem to be anybody around.

'This is a winery?' I said, looking out at the field devoid of any formal seating.

'Yep,' Jimmy said. 'Find a spot and I'll be back with our picnic.'

Jimmy came back from a building behind the manor house with a picnic basket, a chilled bottle of chardonnay and a tartan blanket. We lay on the ground in the shade of a huge tree. Only a handful of other picnickers were visible in other shady pockets so far away we couldn't even hear their conversations. No one came to top up our wine glasses or ask us if we'd like any more smoked fish pâté. If you wanted more wine, you went to the building behind the manor house and bought some. If you wanted the bathroom, it was inside the manor house, which was full of antiques and high-ceilinged rooms but empty of people. It was just the sun, the grass, the wine and us. It felt like we were lazing about in the grounds of our own private mansion. When we'd finished eating we lay back on the blanket, the half-bottle of chardonnay and warm sun making us relaxed and sleepy, and chatted comfortably, Jimmy telling me more about the musical he was writing and what it was like growing up in Richmond.

'When Ian and I were kids we used to bike all over Richmond Park and Wimbledon Common,' he said, his eyes closed and his head resting back on his arm. 'We spent nearly every weekend there kicking balls, climbing trees and looking for lizards or adders or moles. I used to give the animals personalities and make up stories about their homes. I guess the idea grew from there.' He opened his eyes. 'The badgers are going to be a Kiss tribute band.'

'Music is a big part of your life, huh?'

'Yeah. Sometimes to my detriment.'

'How?'

Jimmy moved to lying on his side, propping himself up on his elbow. 'I've only really had one serious girlfriend. Back in London. I had to break up with her though. I couldn't see it going anywhere, and I just didn't think it was fair to stay together when she was starting to look at bridal magazines and I was still reading *Time Out* and the travel section of the newspaper. I was a bit immature I guess, and didn't know how to let her know so I just became distant, hoping she'd break up with me.'

'How original.'

'She went mental when she realised I was using words from Elvis's song 'Always on My Mind' to break up with her.'

I frowned my non-comprehension.

He sang a few lines about not treating her as well as he should have in a gravelly voice that did goosebumpy things to the backs of my arms, and then grinned in a guilty-looking way.

I laughed. 'She had a right to go mental.'

Jimmy went and got another bottle of wine, only having half a glass of it himself so he could still drive, then told me about how his mother had died when he was two, so it had been just his dad, Ian and him growing up. Despite not having a mother his childhood had sounded fun, albeit quite boyish, with camping and fishing and tadpoles in their drink bottles and plastic wrap over the toilet seat.

He said his dad had never remarried and I got the impression that their relationship was now strained, but he didn't elaborate. There was a lull in the conversation while Jimmy and I both shut our eyes and appreciated the feeling of full bellies and the sunshine on our bare legs.

'You have Mondays and Tuesdays off, right?' I said after a short while in which we'd both dozed.

'Yeah,' he replied, with a curious tone.

'Do you want to come to a game reserve with me tomorrow?'

Jimmy opened his eyes and looked directly at me. I blushed under his inquisitive gaze.

'My boss booked it for Pete and me, but he's off ...'

'Being a jerk,' Jimmy said, his face unexpectedly and unusually hard. 'Sorry,' he said, looking embarrassed. 'I didn't mean it.'

'Yeah you did,' I said. 'It's OK. He is being a jerk. But I think I have to take some responsibility.'

I told Jimmy about Annabelle and how I'd sort of put a hold on my life, and by default on Pete's as well, to help her out and it seemed Pete may have decided I wasn't worth waiting for.

'Fool,' Jimmy said, emphatically.

'You think?' I said, unconvinced. 'It's hard to figure out who's in the wrong. He's waited around while I've spent all my time with Annabelle, so maybe I don't have a right to be upset about him doing his own thing now.' I shrugged. 'I don't know ... It's like my relationship has become one big grey area.'

Jimmy looked at me.

'So, what do you think?' I said, lifting my voice to raise

the mood. 'You want to come and bother some more wild-life with me?'

'Maybe . . .' He glanced at his watch. 'We'd better head off, I've got my class to get to,' he said, standing up and stretching, the muscles in his arms flexing.

Forty-five minutes of companionable banter later, we pulled up at the apartment.

'So, what do you think about the safari?' I said, gathering my things from the floor of the car. 'You want to come?'

Jimmy smiled. 'Yeah, why not.' He glanced at the clock on the dashboard. 'See you tomorrow then.'

I looked at him, eager for me to get out of the car so he could get to his scriptwriting class before his bartending shift.

'What?' he said with an inquisitive half-smile.

'I just always thought of musicians as . . .'

'Struggling? Tortured? In possession of great forearms from all the "rock"?' He said the last word with a single thrash at his air guitar.

'Losers.' I grinned. 'But you're really—'

'Hot? Sexy? Talented?'

'Motivated.' I patted his rock 'n' roll forearm then jumped out of the car.

Jimmy smirked and swung the car out through the security gates with a wave out of the window.

Once inside and showered I sat on the balcony with an ice-cold rosé and got comfy for a nice long chat with Annabelle. While the phone rang and rang I let out a long, easy sigh. Then got the excited fizzies because I realised I was content.

The phone kept ringing. Eventually I ended the call and fought back anxieties that Annabelle and Hunter and Katie were in some kind of boating strife. Mainly because a) they didn't own a boat, b) I was sure Annabelle would call me if she were drowning, and c) it was madness, and I had only very recently let out a long, easy sigh with excited fizzies and I wanted to get back into that blissful state.

My phone buzzed with a text.

> Cant anser fone. Having peepel for diner.
> Hands in minst. This is hunter.

Followed by at least thirty-five random emojis.

Hands in minst? Before I had a chance to reply another one came through.

> Mince.

And a further ten emojis all of the skull, fire and poo variety.

Having people over for dinner? Who was this Annabelle, who was coping and having coffees on the common with Marcus the property magnate and putting on dinner parties for friends I didn't know she had? I sent a text saying, 'Have a good time' then lay back on my lounger, drumming my fingertips on the edge of the wine glass, contemplating what to do with my evening. I could email Lana and see if there was any work I could catch up on? I could work on Mum and Dad's party? Who was I kidding, the party was 110 per cent organised months ago. What to do ...

'More lady friends?' shouted Sylvie, Jimmy's scary little boss, as she stalked past me in the open doorway, a lit cigarette in her hand.

Jimmy looked up from behind the bar. 'She's no lady,' he said with a grin.

I quickly skipped inside, away from Sylvie's scary, scowling form and grinned as I approached the bar. 'I don't know why I keep coming here.'

'I do!' Jimmy sauntered over to the piano and broke into the song from *Cheers* about everybody knowing your name and always being glad you came. 'Ricki, in with the harmonies!'

Ricki, polishing glasses, raised an unenthused eyebrow.

'Only you know my name. And you mostly call me "Oi".'

'Ricki knows your name, don't you Ricki?'

Ricki raised his unenthused eyebrow again.

Later, round about the time Heather liked to get on the table tops and give her anatomical demonstration, Jimmy, at the piano, launched into a gravel-voiced version of Tom Jones' 'Sex Bomb', but changed the words to Jess Bomb and sang the whole song with his sparkly eyes on me. I've always loved watching people do what they're good at. I find it intensely attractive. Michael J. Fox in all those *Back to the Futures* really gave it his all with his youthful cheekbones and the bounce in his tiny step; a scientist hovering intently over his petri dish; Jimmy at the piano, enjoying himself so effortlessly whether the audience was there or not. I wondered if I looked attractive hunched over the computer entering catering numbers, my brow creased and my tongue probably sticking out.

Just before 1 a.m. I got tired and called an Uber. I waved goodbye to Jimmy, who was still at the piano. He winked, mouthed 'see you tomorrow' then launched into a Billy Joel song that had Heather writhing around a man I recognised from the local news channel.

CHAPTER EIGHTEEN

The next morning I was up a little later with a small but non-hampering hangover. Coffee helped me achieve full cognitive aptitude and I was in the middle of packing for my night at the game reserve, the mid-morning sun streaming in through the open doors to the balcony, when I got a call from Annabelle.

'Hey!' I said, cheered by hearing from my sister. She needed me! And then I gave myself a minor congratulation for my first instinct not being panic that something had gone wrong.

'Hi, I just got a call from someone at Mum's retreat.'

My self-congratulation stopped short and images of Mum being accidentally shot by someone at the rifle range while trying to flee the lentil dictatorship flooded my previously peaceful mind.

'Oh no! What happened?'

'Nothing. Apparently, she's loving it and she's staying on to do a five-day guilt workshop.'

'Are you sure she isn't being forced?'

'No, she wants to stay.'

'That's what all captors say,' I said darkly. '"*They stayed of their own free will*"; "*they were permitted to leave at any time*"; "*the bars on the windows are for their own protection*", and "*they were kept in a cellar under the laundry because of the threat from acid rain*".'

'Pfft,' was Annabelle's only reply.

I had to agree with her argument.

'Anyway, what's Mum got to be guilty about? Forgetting her "Bag for Life" one time?'

Annabelle giggled. 'Maybe she neglected to let her "yellow mellow".'

'Accidentally not buying non-irradiated herbs?'

'Thinking the chicken in the KFC ad looked tasty?'

'Harbouring illicit thoughts about wanting to use normal shampoo full of chemicals and actual cleaning properties instead of baking soda and vinegar?'

'Ahh, Mum,' Annabelle said with a smile in her voice. 'I hope she's enjoying herself.'

'Yeah, me too.'

'Anyway, she's due back the same day as you.'

'Oh, I didn't think about that. Are you going to be OK?'

'We're doing great,' Annabelle said, and by the tone of her voice I knew we were not discussing it any further.

I changed the subject and continued packing one-handed. 'Do you think it's weird to go away with a guy I don't really know?'

'You seem to know him pretty well.'

'But he could be a secret psychopath.'

'Yes. He could be. They're very good at hiding it, I hear. He's probably been planning your death since the day he met you.'

'Great. Thanks.'

I spent most of the day by the pool and at 2 p.m. Trust and I pulled up outside Diego and Ian's to pick up Jimmy.

'Do you mind if I do a bit of work?' was the first thing he said as he came out to the van with his bag and a stapled script about an inch thick. 'My tutor gave me heaps of really great notes and I want to work on them while it's still fresh.'

'Of course,' I said with admiration.

So, for most of the two-and-a-half-hour trip, Jimmy worked on his script while Trust and I chatted and took turns playing each other songs we liked. Trust liked a lot of hip-hop and RnB. Trust did not like the soundtrack to *Annie*.

At 4.30 p.m. we drove down a dusty, potholed road and under a huge archway made out of intertwined branches. Trust parked up outside a collection of stubby-looking circular buildings with thatched, peaked roofs and hopped out to greet the waiting staff with wide smiles and fist bumps.

'A drink, ma'am?' a lady with a tray of drinks said.

Glasses of champagne, juice and water were on offer, all weeping with condensation.

'Thank you,' I said, taking a stem of champagne. I grinned at Jimmy, who did the same.

Trust and a porter took our bags away while another man smiled and said, 'Follow me'. He took us into a plush reception building, where we signed some 'arrival forms' (waivers in case we were eaten) and were offered cool facecloths and water bottles from a fridge behind the thatched reception desk. Once we were all signed in, the smiling man led us through a covered walkway with elaborate rock gardens on either side, densely planted with the kind of spiky, sturdy specimens that thrive in arid conditions. He showed us the dining area, a huge round room with curved glass windows from floor to ceiling on one side that showed a view of a giant turquoise pool, a field of short, pale and patchy grass and beyond that, drinking from a muddy-looking pond of water . . .

'ELEPHANTS!' I screeched, jabbing Jimmy on the arm and nearly spilling his drink. 'Do you see?! Do you see? Oh my god, there's a baby!'

'I see, I see,' said Jimmy, more amused by my reaction than the elephants themselves.

'Can we go down there? Can we touch them? Are they tame?'

The man with the wide smile laughed. 'No, we cannot touch them. They trust their rangers, but we just watch and enjoy. See their rangers?' the man said, pointing a few hundred yards from the elephants to a clutch of dry-looking trees.

'Yes,' I said, squinting. Two men stood underneath the tall trees in the patchy shade. I thought I could see rifles hanging casually over their shoulders. 'What do they do?'

'They follow the elephants. We must protect them.'

'From what?'

'Poachers,' the man said with a brief expression of severity. Then he brightened. 'Come, I show you your accommodations.'

We followed the man through the dining hall and into a sumptuous hunting-lodge-styled lounge. The head of a huge antelope-type thing, its horns twisted like a corkscrew, sat above the deep fireplace, its eyes black and glassy. With the intensity of the current heat I couldn't imagine the fire ever having to be utilised. A log-framed bar ran the entire length of the room and wicker fans spun lazily above us. A waistcoated bartender poured chilled beers into iced pint glasses for a handful of hot and sweaty guests. Again, one side of the room was all glass, showing a different view of the elephants. I couldn't take my eyes off them, drinking and swinging their trunks from left to right. It didn't feel like they were real.

Only ten days ago I was in Balham on my sister's doorstep, the drizzle soaking the cracked, filthy footpath behind Pete, looking at a printout that said I was going to Cape Town. And now, here I was, looking across African grasslands at elephants. Elephants, doing their elephant thing, in Africa, where elephants are from.

'I think elephants are my favourite animal,' I said.

'How old are you?' Jimmy handed his empty champagne glass to the bartender with a smile and a 'thanks, mate'.

'Twenty-nine.' I flicked my fringe. 'And a quarter.'

Jimmy laughed and we followed the man out of some

French doors to another covered walkway. He pointed to the pool and the pool bar (definitely getting a visit from me), showed us through the high-tech gym (*not* getting a visit from me), and then we walked out in the sunshine along an elevated broken shell path that circumnavigated the grassy field. The man ran through our itinerary as he walked ahead of us, frequently turning and grinning at our gaping, astounded expressions; drinks were available at any time in the lounge bar or at the pool bar or delivered to our room, all included in our stay. It was suggested we get an early night because we had to meet our personal safari guide at 5 a.m. out in the car park. We passed huts on stilts, each a few metres from the other, all facing the watering hole and the elephants, which I was still mesmerised by. We reached the end of the path and the man stopped at a short set of shallow steps and stretched out an arm, welcoming us to our hut. It was the last one and, where all the other huts had a veranda at the front facing the watering hole, ours also wrapped around the side, giving us an uninterrupted private view of the African plains as well. Jimmy and I climbed the stairs and walked along the veranda. Two chairs sat facing the private vista, a table between them with a champagne bottle waiting in a bucket of rapidly melting ice.

'Zebras!' I said, pointing out a herd of zebra in the distance, grazing on the side of a barren, dusty hill. 'Oh my GOD! They've got babies too!'

The man chuckled. 'Many babies.'

'I love their stripes!! I can't believe it! I think zebras are my favourite animal!'

Jimmy grinned and walked past me then stopped. 'Jess, look.'

Past the chairs, at the very end of the veranda, jutting out over a rock ledge, bubbled a huge spa. Two thick towels sat on a rock alongside it. Jimmy and I looked at each other, wide-eyed and stupidly, uncoolly overexcited.

'We hope you will enjoy your stay with us,' the man said, his satisfaction at seeing our excitement evident in his wide grin. He handed Jimmy a key and backed off the balcony and down our little steps. 'Please use the phone should you need anything. Welcome.' And with that he left us.

'Are you freaking kidding me?!' Jimmy said, standing next to the spa and looking out across the hot plains and the reddish mountains far in the distance. 'Is your boss super-rich?'

'Not at all!' I squeaked, fizzing with my good fortune. 'It was a comp deal that she didn't manage to get around to using. She's going to be gutted when I tell her what she gave up! Poor Lana.' I giggled and picked up the bottle of champagne. 'More bubbles?'

I poured us a glass each and we headed inside to check out the cottage.

'Oh,' I said, stopping at the foot of a big, rustic four-poster bed with luxurious white sheets and enough pillows to open my own branch of Peter Jones. 'I didn't actually think about the sleeping arrangements.'

Jimmy looked around the rest of the room and I followed. Two armchairs sat at the foot of the bed, their rustic frames made out of thick logs of wood, their cushions in a chic

African black and white pattern. There was a stone fireplace in the corner, an antique, leather-topped writer's desk with lush stationery, binoculars and a phone, a mini fridge with mini bottles of all sorts of drinks and some luxury chocolates, a walk-in wardrobe that led to a gold-tapped bathroom with double sinks and a rock-walled shower with two gold shower heads, and that was it. We arrived back at the bed.

'We could ask to change rooms?' Jimmy said, but he lacked conviction.

What sane person on a limited budget would walk away from a luxury cottage with a spa and private views of a game reserve?

'Lana said she booked the last room available but we could ask ...?' My heart wasn't in it either. I walked back outside and looked at the champagne bottle, the spa and the view, then looked back at Jimmy standing in the doorway with his glass of champagne, his aviator sunglasses reflecting the incredible view behind me. 'The bed is huge. We could just build a pillow wall down the middle?'

Jimmy smiled and chinked his glass against mine. 'Done.'

'Now this,' I said, floating on my back with my sunglasses on in the aqua infinity pool. 'Is my kind of South African swimming. Full of chemicals, cleaned daily, no chance of something toothy and violent getting intimate and with a swim-up bar.'

Jimmy, floating past me, his chest tanned and muscled, uh-huh-ed his agreement.

'Shall we swim up?'

Jimmy and I sat on the in-pool stools, drank cocktails and laughed with the bartenders. We stood in the water and leant against the edge of the pool, the early-evening sun warming our bare shoulders and watched wildebeest, which had joined the elephants at the watering hole. As the sun lowered we headed back to the cottage, got changed for dinner and spent fifteen minutes watching the impossibly large, flaming sun fall towards the dusky blue mountain ranges on the horizon. I observed the zebra through the binoculars and kept saying, 'I can't believe I'm actually here', until Jimmy pinched me and told me to believe it and shut up. We finished the champagne and watched the sky change colour and intensity with every passing second. Then, with a spray of perfume for me and a dab of cologne for Jimmy, we walked over to the dining hall, our skin still warm from our time in the sun.

Dinner was exquisite, and the staff seemed to thrive on the guests' collective excitement at what the next morning held. It was still hot outside when we left the dining room and walked the crunchy shell path to our cottage. We ambled slowly, looking up at the curve of stars above, and our arms brushed against each other. Jimmy's little finger almost hooked mine but he let it go and continued walking, looking upwards. We took turns in the bathroom then stood beside the bed, me in my leopard-print pyjama shorts and a vest and Jimmy in his boxers and a T-shirt.

'Do we really need a pillow wall?' Jimmy said. 'The bed is massive.'

'Probably not.'

Jimmy smiled and began taking the decorative pillows off the bed and tossing them onto the armchair. 'Anyway, you promised you'd do no more advantage-thrusting and I want to be able to believe you.'

'I'll do my best,' I said, laughing. I climbed onto the bed and slipped under the sheet.

Jimmy flicked off the light and jumped in on his side. We'd left the curtains open, as the man who'd shown us around had suggested, enabling us to lie in the moonlight and see the stars through the French doors.

'Thanks for inviting me here,' Jimmy said, lying on his side facing me.

'Thanks for showing me around Cape Town,' I said.

We looked at each other in the moonlight. Had I not had a boyfriend, I really couldn't see myself getting through the night without thrusting my advantage. But, even with my future with Pete uncertain, I did have a boyfriend. One who, up until this trip where he'd instantly morphed into an adrenaline junkie who found me boring, I thought I'd end up marrying.

Jimmy seemed to sense my thoughts. He smiled. 'Goodnight,' he said. In place of a kiss he patted me on the top of the head like you would a good dog, making me laugh.

'Goodnight,' I said, patting him on the head and turning over.

The sheets were the silkiest I'd ever lain on and felt unbelievable against my sun-kissed skin. I willed myself to go to sleep but after half an hour I was still wide awake, the past week with Jimmy running through my head, making me smile in the darkness. I could feel Jimmy's awake body next to me. His breath was measured and his movements precise. I swallowed then shuffled backwards across the expanse of cool silk sheet until my back hit his. There was a brief moment where his muscles tensed. Then his body relaxed against mine.

CHAPTER NINETEEN

'It's so early and yet you're smiling.' Jimmy yawned. He stood in the car park, shoulders hunched in protest, wearing the provided puffa jackets with the game reserve logo on the breast. 'Only psychopaths smile at this hour.'

'I'm so happy!' I squealed, jumping from foot to foot to keep warm but also because my body wanted to bounce and leap and skip. I was going to see all the animals!

Jimmy grinned and shook his head, his face half-disappearing into his hood as he did so. Other guests stood around the car park in various states of chilly wakefulness. There was the American guy I'd seen downing far too many beers at dinner and talking to his wife in an increasingly loud voice, only now he was sitting on a rock wall, eyes closed, resting his head on his resigned wife's shoulder. Then the mid-range-awake people, like Jimmy, who were amenable enough but cross them and you might just get a finger in the eye. And then me: Tigger on laughing gas. A handful of open-sided jeeps suddenly swung into the car park and guides in beige shirts, army green multi-pocketed trousers and sturdy black boots jumped out of each truck. They'd obviously been prepped as to who they'd be driving, and each guide walked over to a group of guests with confidence.

'Jess and Jimmy?' A tall guide with a kind face offered us his hand.

'Yes!' I said, still bouncing.

'I'm Ngoni,' he said in a deep, comforting voice. A voice I felt I could trust to keep me safe from a charging rhino. He indicated for us to follow him to his jeep. 'I'll be your guide today and you can ask me anything at any time.' He stopped at the jeep and opened the passenger door. 'Sit wherever you like.'

The jeep was open on all sides, including the back, and had a green canvas roof. Behind the driver were five tiered rows of bench seats. My excitement got away from me and I launched myself at Ngoni, flung my arms around him, pinning his arms to his side in a hug, then flew at the jeep and propelled myself over the benches in a bid to get to the very back because the seats were higher off the ground and therefore further from the snakes.

'She's not normal,' Jimmy said, getting into the jeep and clambering gracelessly over the seats. He made to climb over the last row and sit next to me but I slammed my hands down on the vinyl bench that was designed to fit about four people.

'This seat's taken.'

Jimmy looked around at the other guests all getting in their own jeeps. 'By who?'

'Me! I want to be able to move from side to side and see all the animals.' I smiled ingratiatingly and slid back and forth along the bench seat to demonstrate.

Jimmy, only just coping with the extreme early morning, a time when his body clock was telling him he would normally only have been home from working at the bar for two hours, narrowed his eyes and sat on the seat in front of me. 'This OK?' His tone was leaning towards intolerance.

'Actually, could you go forward one more?'

Jimmy looked at me, incredulous.

'Your big fat head might block my view of something.'

While Jimmy moved forward not one but two more rows, Ngoni and the other guides finished up whatever they were discussing in a huddled group in the middle of the collected jeeps and jumped in the front of their respective vehicles.

'It can get cold out there before the sun comes up, so you might want these,' Ngoni said, passing us some heavy woollen blankets from the front passenger seat.

Watching animals in the African plains from under a woolly blanket?! The day couldn't get any better. I gratefully took the blanket that Jimmy tossed over his shoulder, draped it over my legs, pulled it up to my waist, tucked each side in, then sat up, straight as an A-grade student, and waited.

Ngoni grinned from the front. 'You ready?'

'YES!!' I literally screamed.

Jimmy shook his head and smirked. Ngoni chuckled, started the engine and swung the jeep out of the car park. In a convoy of six open vehicles we bumped down a hard-packed mud road, following the line of an extremely high wire fence and stopped at a set of gates. The driver of the front jeep pressed some buttons on a keypad at the entrance and the gates slid open. Once through, the jeeps dispersed in different directions and within moments the others couldn't be seen or heard. A cool wind whipped up as we drove and I buried my chin in my jacket. The booking information Lana had sent along with her email had said to bring gloves, woolly hats and thermals, and when I read that information in the apartment in Cape Town, sitting in direct line of the air conditioning and still sweating along my top lip, I didn't think it possible to be freezing in Africa. But freezing it was and I pulled the blanket higher and tucked it tighter. We lurched down a rutted track. Bushes with thousands of inch-long spikes scratched at the canvas roof of the jeep. The sky was still dark but you could sense the burgeoning dawn in the sounds of birds and the silvery glow coming from behind the far-off mountains. Ngoni deftly navigated the terrain while imparting his knowledge of the plants, the plains, the weather, the bugs, the origin of the game reserve and the conservation and anti-poacher policies they adhered to. After about twenty minutes the sky had lightened to a white-ish blue. Low streaks of wispy cloud lay like grey chiffon scarves across the horizon. Ngoni pulled the jeep over beside a bristly bush and pointed across the expansive scrubland. In the distance, loping across the plains, its silhouette blue-grey against the whitening sky, was a solitary giraffe.

The bristly bush was partially obscuring my view, so I

clambered over the seats and sat in the one behind Jimmy. In unison we leant out of the side of the jeep. A breeze chilled the tip of my nose.

'Oh my god,' I breathed.

It was that single image that made me fully comprehend that I was in a very foreign country. Not the baboons, or the penguins, or the heat, or the beaches, or the weird accent I'd come to find melodic, or the other languages spoken in the streets that had clicks I found impossible to replicate, or the cheap yet delicious wine. A giraffe walking by itself, doing its own giraffe thing, on a vast scrubby African plain, was what made me realise where I was. And how lucky I was to be there. I breathed out the longest sigh of extreme content.

'This is pretty cool,' Jimmy said in a low voice, his eyes on the lolloping giraffe.

'Over here,' Ngoni said quietly, pointing in the opposite direction.

Jimmy and I spun in our seats.

The head of a giraffe appeared behind a huge bush, maybe only fifteen feet from us. Ngoni cut the engine, which gave me a brief internal panic. What if a rhino suddenly charged us and we wasted valuable seconds restarting the car? The giraffe moved slowly, elongating a huge blue-ish tongue and curling it around the spiky branches before swallowing down the leaves. Then next to him another head appeared. And then another. Ngoni spoke about the giraffe's digestive system, how and why it dined on the most unpalatable of plants, and imparted various other fascinating facts, all delivered in a low, respectful voice. Within a few minutes six giraffes were moving around the jeep, eating from the bushes and glancing our way indifferently. I'd seen pictures of giraffes, of course; I'd read alphabet books where G was for giraffe, I'd watched *Madagascar* with Hunter and Katie, and I'd been to the zoo and seen them standing as far from the public as possible, eating hay from the ground; but being so close, looking at their exotic markings, their weird longs legs and their freakish necks made them a completely different creature to me. They were graceful yet ungainly and seemed the most polite of animals. The herd moved around the jeep and I tracked them with my gaze till I was looking at them over Jimmy's shoulder. Inside I was a ragtag bag of confusing emotions. I was elated at being in Africa, so close to these incredible creatures; I was sad that Pete wasn't with me, but happy that Jimmy was; I missed Hunter and Katie, and felt guilty for not being with Annabelle, but I also had a new feeling. A dizzying freedom of doing exactly what I wanted in that exact moment. I felt like simultaneously whooping and weeping and clapping and crying.

I looked at the back of Jimmy's head. His hair curled at the nape of his tanned neck. If he lived back in London it probably would have been dark blond but here in Cape Town it had been bleached to a golden colour. I wondered how the trip would have differed had Pete stayed with me. I'd still have made him sit in front, not blocking my view, but would I have been so relaxed as I felt right then? Would he have been embarrassed by the horde of naive questions I threw at

Ngoni? Would he have wanted to look like he already knew all the answers?

I leant forward and whispered in Jimmy's ear. 'I think giraffes are my favourite animal.'

Jimmy chuckled then turned his head and kissed me on the cheek. Startled, I looked into his eyes, smiled then sat back in my seat and looked out of the side of the jeep. Jimmy continued to face the front but I could tell, by the movement of his muscles, that he was smiling.

'Ready to go?' Ngoni asked us after a long while where we just existed alongside the giraffes. 'You have enough pictures?'

I'd barely taken any, preferring to just watch the animals be themselves but quickly took out my phone and snapped a few more to send to Hunter, Katie and Lana when I got home.

'Ready,' I said.

I could have stayed there all day, close enough to hear the giraffes breathing rhythmically through their huge nostrils and crunching down on the barbed branches.

We drove on and stopped next at a wide-open flat area where a herd of zebra and a herd of buffalo were mingling at the edge of a murky stretch of water. From my seat I was straining to hear Ngoni, so I moved a row closer and sat next to Jimmy. Ngoni seemed to have an endless amount of knowledge. It didn't matter what questions we (I) fired at him, he answered them all with a pile of information that always incited more questions. On my behalf, anyway. Within the hour we'd stopped at various spots to view buffalo, rhino, hippo in a lake from afar (because they were the most dangerous animal of them all), kudu, gemsbok, eland and zebra so often they became common. I'd clambered closer row by row until I was in the front with Ngoni, engaging in ceaseless conversation while Jimmy sat in a middle row enjoying the scenery. Ngoni mentioned that the springbok is South Africa's principal member of the gazelles and I stiffened at the word that triggered images of French braids, pink gums and nice armpits. But as we turned a corner and a family of elephants came into view, flanked at a respectful distance by their rangers, I forgot all about Giselle and her plaits and watched the majestic, emotionally intelligent, community-minded animals protecting their young while pulling great branches from trees. They were huge. I loved them and wanted to jump out and hug them and take them home and feed them apple segments and have them sleep in my bedroom and cuddle me with their trunk. When we'd had our fill of elephants we drove with a bit more speed towards a set of gates. Beyond a fifty-foot-wide perimeter was another set of gates. It all looked very Guantánamo Bay.

'What's this?'

'The lions,' Ngoni said.

'But we've got no sides to the jeep!' I said, scanning the jeep for hiding places.

'You're safe with me,' Ngoni grinned his uber-white grin. 'No need to worry.'

I looked at his single rifle propped between the seats and tried not to imagine a blood-splattered, limbs-torn-from-torso-type situation where more than one lion attacked from more than one side of the jeep. But luckily no lions were visible as we drove though the dusty area. We made our way through another set of gates, parked next to an open-sided tower on stilts and were told to exit the jeep.

'Don't worry,' Ngoni said, noting my hands gripping the seat with white knuckles. 'This is an enclosure within the enclosure. Lions can't get in here.'

Ngoni led us out of the jeep and up some steep ladder-like steps. At the top we were greeted by a man and a woman, and asked if we'd like coffee or tea. A white cloth was spread over a large waist-high centre table and linen-lined baskets held fresh croissants, pastries and fruit. From the top of the tower we could see the sun, pale yellow, rising above the mountains, turning the sky peachy-pink.

'Listen,' Ngoni said, coming to stand next to Jimmy and me with a white teacup wafting hot steam into the cool air.

At first, I heard nothing but birds chittering and bugs making clicking noises, but then a single roar echoed across the scrubland. And then another and another.

'The lions are waking,' Ngoni said with a grin.

He left Jimmy and me to appreciate the moment alone. The breeze was still cool but the coffee warmed my hands. I looked at Jimmy leaning against a wooden post.

'This is probably one of the best days of my life,' I said, resting my elbows on the edge of the tower wall and sipping my coffee.

Jimmy mirrored my position and smiled. 'Me too.'

Shoulder to shoulder we gazed down from the tower and listened to the lions. We watched the sun change the colours of the sky and light up the plains, then ate fresh croissants and sipped coffee until Ngoni said it was time to go again. We drove out of the safety of the fenced-off tower and back through the lions' enclosure, this time driving right through the middle of the lions. It was the only time Ngoni did not stop the vehicle but instead made a steady track through them and I found myself letting out a tense breath when we reached the double gates and left them behind.

We watched animals for another hour or so, this time Jimmy and I sitting side by side, our thighs pressed up against each other, then, when the sun was high in the sky, Ngoni drove us back to the car park. As we exited the jeep I felt like I'd experienced something meaningful. I hugged Ngoni again and this time he hugged me back. An early lunch was ready for us, which we ate by the pool. We were so tired we barely spoke. After lunch we were taken to the cheetah rehabilitation area. I loved learning all about the animals and again asked far more questions than anybody else; after some time all the other guests remained quiet, certain that I would eventually ask the same question they had in mind. At 2 p.m. Trust arrived in the car park; he'd stayed in the drivers' accommodation somewhere on the grounds, and took the bags from our weary arms. Half an hour into our journey Jimmy and I were asleep against each other.

CHAPTER TWENTY

'Aw, man!' Jimmy's voice reverberated off the inside of the freezer where he was immersed almost to his armpits trying to locate some 'epic' frozen yoghurt.

He'd started talking about it as soon as we'd woken and by the time Trust dropped us off outside Ian and Diego's he was salivating like one of Pavlov's particularly hungry dogs. He'd bidden Trust a hasty but genuine thanks, burst through the front door, dumped his backpack on the floor and made a sweaty beeline past Diego and Pamela, prepping a meal at the kitchen island, to the freezer.

'That bastard!' Jimmy said, brandishing the open container in Diego's face.

Diego smirked. 'He was pissed about the grapes.'

'What's going on?' I said, handing Diego a box of fresh raspberries I'd bought from a man at the side of the road and walking around to look at the cause of Jimmy's distress.

In the bottom of the empty organic frozen Madagascan

vanilla yoghurt container was a crude drawing of a hand with an extended middle finger.

'Jimmy ate half of Ian's grapes and Ian was not happy,' Diego said to me, his hands in a glass bowl, massaging kale.

'He said to leave him half,' Jimmy said, looking anguished. He brandished the yogurt container at Pamela, who was chopping up mountains of basil, and she smiled and shook her head.

'You know what you did,' Diego said to Jimmy with a look of reprimand. He turned to me again. 'He ate half, all right. Of each grape.'

Jimmy dumped the frozen yoghurt container in the recycling bin while Diego, Pamela and I shared a covert chuckle.

'So, sweet girl, if I make you sangria will you stay and tell me all about your trip?'

I grinned.

'I'm going to unpack,' Jimmy said, defeated. He grabbed his backpack by the straps and scuffed his feet across the room, his bag banging against the backs of his tanned calves.

'I'd give your room a once-over,' Diego said to his receding back.

Jimmy turned in the doorway. 'Why?'

'After Ian found the grapes he spent quite a bit of time down there. He had glue, food colouring and glitter with him.'

Jimmy groaned and trundled, heavy-footed, out of the room.

*

Around 6 p.m., Ian came home and we all partook of Diego's chilled sangria while sitting in the early-evening sun on the balcony. Jimmy, who'd spent an hour scouring his room for booby traps and had ended up throwing out all of his bathroom products for fear of glue/food colouring contamination and raging upon discovering his drawers and the pockets of his hanging clothes filled with pink and orange glitter, sat beside me, the sinking sun making him squint attractively and turning his skin a deep golden colour. Although he was usually in possession of a graze of accidentally stylish stubble, it had grown thicker over the past two days on safari and as he rested back on the outdoor sofa, his arm stretched out across the backrest towards me, he looked roguish and striking.

'Oh, what a princess!' Diego said, looking at a photo of Katie dressed as Elsa on my phone. He showed it to Ian.

'Princess,' Ian confirmed with a smile.

Jimmy wriggled in his seat, his face showing discomfort.

'How are you going there, squirmy?' Ian said, a knowing glint in his eyes.

Jimmy, who'd showered and changed into fresh clothes, stood and shook his shorts, sending a flurry of orange glitter over the balcony floor.

'It's itchy,' he said, frustrated.

Ian looked extremely pleased with himself.

'*She's* beautiful,' Diego said, turning the phone to face me. 'Is that Annabelle?'

I nodded.

Jimmy sat back down next to me and rested his hand on

my knee. It was a familiar, intimate gesture that he wasn't even aware he was making. I liked the warm weight of it.

I watched Jimmy's smiling profile as he told Ian and Diego about the safari and how I'd wanted to take every animal (except the gazelles) home with me. Ian noticed Jimmy's hand and gave me a twinkly smile, making me blush.

Diego and Ian asked lots of questions about my family, my job, my childhood. I could tell they were being careful not to enquire about Pete, which was something I appreciated. As the two of them moved on to pictures of the safari, their heads touching as they scrolled through the phone, Jimmy turned to me.

'Do you want to come to a festival on Thursday?' he said, removing his hand from my knee to pull at his shorts, releasing more glitter. 'We've got a spare ticket because my mate dislocated his shoulder sandboarding.'

'Sandboarding?'

'Like snowboarding but on massive sand dunes.'

'Doesn't anyone just stay still in South Africa?'

'Not really,' Jimmy said, grinning, and then he told me about the festival and how it was in the countryside about three hours' drive away and was on, actually *on*, a river. 'So, you keen?'

'It sounds amazing but I can't,' I said. 'Pete's due back tomorrow.'

'Oh yeah,' Jimmy said. 'Forgot.'

Across the table Ian was watching our exchange. He smiled when he caught my eye.

'They had babies!' Diego said as he came across a photo of the elephants. He continued to scroll through, asking questions and showing the screen to Ian. When he came across a couple of the hut we'd stayed in he raised his eyebrows. 'Only one bed . . .?'

Jimmy grinned and shook his head.

Pamela and Diego served prawns and salad for dinner and we sat outside on the balcony exchanging stories. Through the calm contentedness I felt a sadness. With Pete coming back I realised it would mean not seeing much, if anything, of Diego, Ian and Jimmy.

After dinner had been cleared away and we'd had our aperitif we all started yawning. Diego stood and said he needed to get to bed as he had an early class.

'Will we see you again, sweet girl?' he said, his thick eyebrows sloping.

'I don't know . . .' I said, feeling sad. It seemed unlikely. 'Maybe not . . .'

'Well then, come here!' He held out his arms and told me to keep in touch, to be sure to update him with any more music industry gossip and to remember to email him the link for the podcasts of my mother's radio show. 'And we shall skype and text and you absolutely *must* come back!' He gave me one last extra-firm squeeze, then Ian took his place.

'I'm sure this won't be the last time we see you,' he said, glancing at his younger brother. 'Make sure you keep in contact.'

I nodded and hugged him while Jimmy looked on with a

strange smile. I had to hold back tears, which was weird and a bit unexpected after knowing people for only a week, but Jimmy, Ian and Diego had been so open and welcoming it seemed like I'd known them much longer.

Amid a flurry of blown kisses Diego and Ian left for bed. Jimmy and I sat side by side on the balcony sofa, finishing off the last of the sangria and watching the lights from the container ships move across the horizon. After half an hour Jimmy could barely contain his yawning. I gave Lucy an extra-big scratch on her tummy, gave Flora a curt nod, jumped in Jimmy's car and, fifteen minutes later, we drove through the security gates to the apartment. Jimmy pulled into a space and put on the handbrake instead of stopping at the doors, keeping the car in gear, like he usually did.

'I guess I won't see so much of you now that your boyfriend is getting back,' he said, looking across at me. It seemed significant that he hadn't used Pete's name.

'Guess not.' I looked at my hands.

'That's sad,' he said, and the simplicity of the statement nearly undid me.

We sat for a moment in the dark.

'I like you,' he said, looking across at me. 'A lot.'

I didn't say anything back. I couldn't. My feelings were all mixed up. Instead of telling him how I felt, that I liked him too, that I'd had the happiest week I'd ever had, that I'd been so relaxed in his company and had slotted in to Ian, Diego and Jimmy's life so effortlessly I felt like I'd known them for years, I took his hand.

'We can still keep in touch,' I said.

Jimmy gave me a look. We all know how that goes. If you haven't forged a strong enough friendship, people you meet on holiday just fall out of your lives.

'I'd better go,' I said.

Jimmy nodded.

'But I'll call. And text. And Facebook-message.' I said, forcing a smile.

Jimmy smiled back. Then lifted my hand to his lips and kissed it.

'Bye, Jess,' he said.

I leant across, kissed his cheek and jumped out of the car. I waved and watched his shitty Mitsubishi with one working tail light drive through the security gates and down the street.

CHAPTER TWENTY-ONE

The next morning, I sat in the middle of the bed under a starched white sheet watching the cerise and orange sunrise blister up behind the harbour. Once the sun was fully up and the Monet-esque sky had turned a pale blue, I made a coffee, opened the doors to the balcony, slid back under the sheets and watched gulls swooping down towards the docks while anticipating Pete's arrival home and wondering what feelings it would bring. He'd been away for a week in a country that had awakened something in him that neither he nor I knew had been there.

A little later I pottered around the tiny kitchen, lamenting my lack of putting anything in the fridge for breakfast. I missed my routine of getting up and heading to Jimmy's, hopefully arriving in time to eat paleo pancakes and share music industry gossip with Diego, while waiting for Jimmy to emerge bleary-eyed and bare-chested. I texted Jimmy, asking what Lucy was up to and just to say 'Hi', then went into the bathroom. Moments later my phone pinged. I skipped back to the bedroom in just a towel, harbouring a thrill in my chest that Jimmy had texted back so quickly. But it was from Pete.

> Hey, heading back now. Trip was amazing. Goat has to swing by a kitesurfing event in Langebaan this afternoon on the way home. He's sponsored by them so we have to go. Plus we get a free day on the boards! Will be back late. Think it's about 2 hours drive from Cape Town. Will call when reception is better. We keep going in and out of range. Hope this text gets to you. Pete.

I looked at it for a few moments and then felt an intense sting that not only was he not coming straight back, he hadn't even asked how I was. For all he knew I'd been alone for the past seven days, going to all the touristy places, unable to turn to someone and share the joy of the new experience. I threw the phone on the bed and jumped in the shower.

'And he didn't even *call* to ask if I was OK!' I paced the room in a bra and pants, my hair twisted up in a white fluffy towel and my phone to my ear. 'I could have been bitten by a snake and be lying on the apartment floor bleeding from my eyes (that's a boomslang, by the way; you don't die immediately but you bleed out from your eyes, nose and fingernails like a scene from *Kill Bill*), or have swelling limbs, bursting blood blisters and cardiac arrest (that's the puff adder, a fat, lazy snake that hangs out in people's gardens), or be lying in a pool of sweat and saliva, dead from asphyxiation caused by complete body paralysis (that's the black mamba, a vicious little bastard). And what about the safari?! I could have been rammed by a rhino; I could have been shot by a poacher who thought I was a rhino (although I didn't wear grey on purpose for that very reason); I could have fallen out of the jeep and landed on a rock in an unlikely yet lethal angle causing immediate death. I could have choked on biltong. It's so freaking chewy, I can't believe they eat that stuff! Have you ever tried it? Ew, gross. Seriously though, Annabelle, not only did he *not call*, he didn't even ask in his text how I was or if I'd been having a good time?!' I stopped in front of the bedroom mirror. 'On a side note, I'm really tanned.' I recommenced pacing. 'So, what should I do? Should I dump his ass? Should I be happy he's found things he loves doing – even if he's involved me in precisely none of them and has suddenly turned into this selfish asshole? I should break up with him, right? But we've been together for six years! *Six years!* How can he change so much in one week? What should I do? OK, so call me when you get this. Love you.'

When I hung up I had no anger left. How cathartic it was to be able to yell and rant uninterrupted to a non-judgemental answer machine! I dialled Jimmy.

'Hi,' he said, his voice croaky.

'Hey! Whatcha doin'?'

'Sleeping.'

I checked the time on my phone. It was 10.17 a.m. – a time Jimmy and I would usually be cruising along hot roads in his shitty Mitsubishi, taking turns to show how supremely cool we were in our music choices. 'Why so late? Big night?'

'This is the time I usually sleep in till,' he said through a yawn. 'I got up early when you were here because I didn't want you to be alone in one of the greatest places in the world.'

I fell for him a little bit just then. 'Oh.' I didn't know how to respond without sounding gushy so I barrelled on through the moment. 'Pete isn't coming home. He's going to Langebaan.' (I pronounced it 'lang-barn'.)

'Lunga barn.' Jimmy chuckled softly. He sounded like he was still lying down. 'You OK with that?'

'He's going so I have to be, I guess,' I said. 'What are you doing today?'

'Working on my script. Submission cut-off date is in four days and I'm quite behind.'

'Oh,' I said. 'So, you can't come out to play?'

Jimmy laughed. 'No, I can't come out to play.'

'Bummer,' I said.

'Why don't you come here?' Jimmy said. 'Diego should be home soon, so you can hang with him. And I can stop and have lunch with you?'

'I'd better not. I don't want to distract you.'

'While you are dazzling company, I'm pretty sure I'll be able to concentrate with you nearby,' he said. 'Come on, Diego would love to see you again.'

I thought about it for a moment.

'And so would I,' he added.

The big gates to Ian and Diego's buzzed open and as I walked up the path past the Buddha heads and the black sculptural ball that had water running over it and was supposed to be relaxing and meditative but just made me want to go to the toilet, I saw Jimmy standing at the open door in shorts and no T-shirt and I felt my face stretching into a wide grin.

'I'll have a coffee with you but then I'd better get back to work,' he said, shutting the front door behind me. 'That OK?'

'Of course!' I said. 'I can make the coffee, you keep working.'

I pottered around the kitchen getting out Jimmy's favourite mug: a white one with Queen lyrics around the side, and my favourite: a pale blue one with a happy cartoon cow on it. I'd never actually made anything in their kitchen but I'd watched Diego every morning so knew my way around by proxy.

Jimmy had set himself up at the kitchen island and it was littered with notes and script pages, pens and his laptop.

Over coffee Jimmy told me a bit more about the festival he was going to the next day. It sounded completely mad to watch a concert while floating on a river in the middle of nowhere. I really wanted to go but it had been sold out months previously, so, although Jimmy still had a spare ticket for me, we wouldn't be able to get Pete one.

'Do you ever wonder how many murderers we walk past

in a day?' I said as I reached the end of my coffee. 'I saw a man dragging two heavy plastic bags down the street and I thought – they could be filled with heads. *Mine* could have been one of those heads! Amazing when you really think about it. How close we come to death each day.'

Jimmy blinked. 'OK!' he said, straightening a pile of notes officiously. 'I'd better get to work. Do you need something to read? Here,' he said, sliding a pile of *Interiors* magazines towards me. He gave me a quick smile that said, 'you do that, and I'll do this' then hunched over his script.

I ignored the magazines, cupped my chin in my upturned hand, my elbow resting on a pile of notes, and watched Jimmy flick his attention from his laptop screen to his script pages to his notes and back again. When it became apparent my staring was bothering him (he told me to stop staring), I picked up my phone and scrolled through Facebook for a bit. All my friends in England were bemoaning the January weather and their self-imposed ban on drinking and socialising for the month. I couldn't relate, what with my winery-visiting and the ceaseless sunshine. They were in hibernation and I was feeling a sense of liberation. I wondered if those two words were opposites and liked how they rhymed, so got on Google and found that 'aestivation' was actually the opposite to hibernation. But as it meant 'the prolonged torpor or dormancy of an insect, fish or amphibian during a hot dry period', I thought it sounded *exactly* the same as hibernation – just in the summer instead of the winter – and decided to email the Oxford English Dictionary and suggest they look into the matter.

I put my phone on the counter, swivelled in my stool and looked out of the open glass doors to the beach below. Paddlers paddleboarded, surfers surfed and sunbathers stretched out their toned, tanned forms on brightly coloured towels. I swivelled in my seat again and turned my attention to a fruit bowl, picking up each piece of fruit and testing it for ripeness. That done, I scanned the room. Behind the fruit bowl on a carved wooden stand was a new recipe book. *Balance Bowl Recipes*, the title said in swirly red letters. And underneath, '*Nutritionally balanced meals in one bowl. Balanced, Beautiful, Beneficial*'.

'You know squirrels?' I said, frowning at the pages of the recipe book of one-bowl meals mathematically balanced by the correct quantities of magnesium and carbohydrate and whatever.

'Not personally but as a concept, yes,' Jimmy said with a grin. He continued to look at his laptop, his right hand subconsciously banging a pen on his script like a student in a boring science class.

'They eat nuts.'

Jimmy gave me a sideways glance.

'How come we're told to have a multi-coloured, five-a-day, varied complex carbohydrates, proteins and fats diet and a squirrel can just eat nuts and be perfectly healthy? Do squirrels get allergies? Do they get cancer or diabetes? Where do they get their vitamin C from?'

'Why don't you google it?'

'Good idea.'

The room fell silent save for the scratch of Jimmy's pen

on A4, the ever-present squawk of gulls and the pounding of surf coming through the wide-open doors to the balcony.

'Huh. I was wrong,' I said, reading from my phone. 'Squirrels eat dirt too. And bark. And some fruit and insects.'

I put my phone on the countertop and watched Jimmy strike out a couple of lines on his printed page and write down the side in barely legible markings.

'How do you get your ideas?'

'Dunno,' Jimmy said, his eyes scanning his stapled script pages. 'They just turn up, I guess.'

I picked up a piece of paper with a bunch of notes all over it. 'You know that saying "*Pluck it out of thin air*"?' I said.

Jimmy took back his page of notes and put them on the other side of his laptop, out of my reach. 'Yes.'

'Do you think that means Everest air? Because it's so thin up there? Like saying, "it's so difficult to get what you want you have to go to the top of Everest and pull it out of the sky up there"?'

Jimmy laughed then turned back to his laptop with a grin. 'You are so distracting.'

'Sorry!' I said, making an 'oops' face.

We grinned at each other.

'Wow, you've written so much,' I said, flicking the corner pages of his script like a pack of cards. 'What's the word count? Must be massive.'

'Around eighty thousand I think,' Jimmy said, sliding the script out of my reach and pushing an *Interiors* magazine into its place.

I picked up the magazine and began reading.

'Do you ever think there are too many words?' I said after reaching the end of a very wordy, highfalutin article that said nothing more than '*designer goods are best*'. 'I sometimes think there are too many. I mean, environmentally it'd be wise to lose some. If only for the environment. *Remonstrate.* No one needs that when 'protest' will do in much less time, effort and space.'

Jimmy sniggered and scribbled more notes. 'Shhhhhhh.'

Silently chastising myself for being unable to keep quiet, I went back to the magazine, but it was boring. I honestly didn't care if monochrome table settings were back or not. I looked at Jimmy, absorbed by his pages of notes. 'I should go home.' I slipped off the stool and reached for my bag on the floor. 'I'm distracting you.'

'No, you're not!' Jimmy placed his hand on my arm. 'Stay.'

I looked back at him, uncertain.

'Diego will be here soon.'

'Yeah, but—'

'And I like having you here.' He smiled and his earnest expression sent a bloom of warmth across my chest.

'Are you sure?' I said, looking pointedly at the huge pile of notes he had to get through.

'Definitely,' he said with a firm nod. 'Why don't you watch a movie?'

'But you won't be able to concentrate.'

Jimmy shook his head. 'I don't even hear it. It's like white noise.'

'If you're sure?'

'I am,' Jimmy said, taking my bag from me and putting it on the stool on the other side of him.

'All right.' I smiled.

I made my way towards an armchair that had an inviting shaft of sunlight but Flora, up until then curled in a tiny ball in the corner of the sofa, lifted her head, jumped down and scampered ahead of me. She leapt onto the armchair, turned around and sat, her front paws resting just off the edge of the chair, giving me a black-eyed little stare that said, '*My seat.*'

I narrowed my eyes and returned her look with one that said, '*You're a dog, you belong on the floor.*'

'*You're new. You sit on the floor.*' She glared back.

'*Dogs shit in public.*'

'*Humans have pap smears.*'

'*Dogs get thermometers up their arses.*'

'*You have to wax your vagina.*'

'*You have to* lick *yours!*'

'Stop fighting with my dog.'

I turned around and saw Jimmy looking highly amused by Flora's and my stare-off.

'She started it,' I said, searching for and eventually finding the TV remote sitting neatly in a mother-of-pearl tray alongside some glass bowls full of shells, a couple of expensive candles and a silver candle-snuffer. I looked over at Jimmy, who was still watching me. 'Back to work!' I said with a 'go, go' flap of my hand.

Jimmy laughed and turned towards his script pages. Ignoring Flora's sniff of triumph, I curled up on the sofa and tried to figure out the TV. After a few minutes of getting nothing but a black screen with 'HDMI 14' in a little box in the corner I flicked it off and picked up another magazine. It took an embarrassing amount of time before I realised it was in Afrikaans. And was for gay males.

'Learning anything?' Jimmy said.

I turned in my seat to see him grinning.

'I couldn't work the TV.'

Jimmy hopped off his stool and grabbed the remotes. 'What do you feel like?' he said, pushing a few buttons and getting an alphabet tile search page on the screen.

'Hmmm ...' I said, putting the magazine to the side. 'I think I feel like watching something where they wear capes.'

Jimmy frowned. 'Like *Superman* or *Batman*?' He began navigating the alphabet tiles with the remote, spelling out B-A-T.

'No, the old-fashioned swoopy ones. Like they wear in *Harry Potter*.'

'So, maybe something medieval-ish then? Like *Robin Hood Prince of Thieves*?'

I wrinkled my nose.

'How about *Lord of the Rings* or *Twilight*? Vampires wear capes, don't they?' He deleted B-A-T and put in a T-W.

'No, that sounds depressing. Something fun like *Harry Potter*. With the *magic* of *Harry Potter*.'

Jimmy stopped typing. 'So, you want something that has

capes like *Harry Potter*, is fun like *Harry Potter* and has magic like *Harry Potter*.'

I nodded.

'Do you just want to watch *Harry Potter*?' Jimmy said with a twitch of amusement on his lips.

I thought about it for a minute. 'Yes.'

Jimmy, eyes wide, turned towards the TV to begin typing in *Harry Potter* as the front door opened and Diego and Pamela walked in carrying groceries in cloth bags.

'Sweet girl! You're back!' Diego said, dropping the bags on the kitchen counter. I stood to meet his burly hug.

'For the love of Tom Petty, god bless his talented soul, can you please entertain this noisy girl,' Jimmy said.

'It would be my pleasure.' Diego wrapped an arm around me and guided me to the kitchen. 'I'm going to teach you my mother's, god bless *her* talented soul, recipe for salmon.'

Jimmy packed up his writing things and headed down-stairs while Diego flicked on an Afrikaans radio station and he and Pamela sang along to it while attempting to teach me how to cook. Ian came home for lunch at 1 p.m., Jimmy took a break and we all ate poached salmon on the balcony. Jimmy cackled in delight upon hearing that in the middle of a very serious meeting that morning Ian's phone had rung, and Ian had been very unimpressed that Jimmy had changed his ringtone to Right Said Fred's 'I'm too Sexy'.

Ian and Diego left at the same time, giving me another round of goodbyes and hugs and promises to keep in touch; then at 4 p.m. Jimmy bundled me in the car, his bartending clothes lying on the back seat, and drove me home before heading to work.

'So, I guess this is another goodbye?' he said, this time pulling up at the doors like usual.

'Yeah, maybe,' I said, not knowing if Pete would actually make it back from the kitesurfing event tonight. 'No. I dunno.'

'How about we just do, "see you later" then?' Jimmy said, smiling.

'OK,' I said, unwilling to get out of the car.

I sat there for a moment, looking at the interior of the car I'd spent so much time in. The sand on the floor, the various bottles of suntan lotion, the spare sunglasses with scratched lenses he kept in the cup holders. David Coverdale from Whitesnake coming through the speakers, calling himself a drifter.

'Jess?' Jimmy said.

'Yeah?'

'I gotta go to work.' He gave an apologetic shrug.

'Yep, sorry,' I said. I opened the car door with a sigh. 'OK, well, have fun at the festival tomorrow. I'll call you to say goodbye before we fly.'

Jimmy smiled and nodded.

In the apartment I changed into my bikini – I was now an even golden colour – and headed to the rooftop pool with a book that I didn't intend to read. Instead I lay on the lounger, the late sun low enough to beam straight into my eyeline and thought about Jimmy and Pete, my flat and my job, and if

Pete and I would try to sort things out. And if I even wanted to. Just as I was about to nod off my phone rang. It was Pete.

'Hi,' he said. I could hear the sound of pounding surf and wind. 'You OK?'

'Yep,' I said.

'OK, great,' he said. 'Look Jess, Goat is the guest of honour at this kitesurfing party tonight.'

'Oh yeah?'

'So, the van is staying here. But I could look at getting a taxi back ...'

'Right.'

'But it's like, in the middle of nowhere and ... I mean it would probably be really expensive, if I could get one, not that I'm sure I could, but if I did it's about two hours' drive so I reckon I wouldn't get in till really late ...'

'You want to stay away another night?'

'No,' Pete said quickly. 'Well, yeah. It makes more sense, don't you think?'

'I guess,' I said, my voice devoid of any emotion. I'd lost the inclination to give a shit.

'The thing is, there's another kitesurfing event all day tomorrow. So, if I stay tonight I may as well stay for the day tomorrow too. And I reckon they'll end up staying the next night as well because of how long the event goes on for, so ...'

'So, you're saying that if you stay tonight then you may as well stay two nights and you'll be back on Friday, the day before we fly out?'

'Well ... yeah ...' he said, managing to sound contrite.

'Fine. Whatever. See you when I see you.'

'Jess—'

I hung up.

Without saying it out loud, we were both aware that our relationship was pretty much over. Pete had left after four days of the trip and was coming back the day before we left. I looked up Giselle's Instagram page and scrolled through her pictures. She'd posted a lot of photos and a lot of them were of Pete. Nothing incriminating, but they clearly enjoyed each other's company and she certainly seemed smitten with him. Stupid girl with a stupid name that sounds like a species of antelope and is derived from the Germanic word for 'hostage'. Yes, I looked it up one night.

Back at the apartment I called Jimmy.

'That spare ticket still available?'

There was a beat where Jimmy was quiet, then he spoke with a smile in his voice. 'Yeah, yeah it is.'

CHAPTER TWENTY-TWO

'Good morning ma'am, is that Jess?'

'Yes,' I said down the apartment phone. I could hear laughter and cheers and the sound of a car radio in the background.

'This is security at the front gates. I have Jimmy here.'

I heard a cacophony of voices repeating, '*Hi Jess! Hi Jess! Hi Jess!*' I giggled, told the security guy to let them in, grabbed my daypack and skipped out of the door.

Jimmy and his friends only had a day pass to the festival so we were leaving early, and when I stepped out of the apartment building at 7 a.m. and crossed the paved drive to the waiting van the air was fresh on my bare shoulders. In the van were Gus and Bryn from the art studio, their girl-friends, the Hispanic kitchen hand from Sylvie's and another guy who was unbelievably good-looking whom I'd not met before. They were all jammed in with their tanned limbs, big smiles and their rough-and-ready stubble (not the girls).

Every other available space was filled with inflatable rubber rings, water bottles, boxes of beer, colourful towels, straw hats and spare pairs of board shorts. It was an explosion of summertime supplies. I sat next to Jimmy and was introduced to the people I didn't know.

'Can I borrow your phone?' Jimmy said.

I raised my eyebrows at the phone in his hand while trying to find enough space for my feet.

Jimmy rolled his eyes. 'Ian changed my phone to Greek and these bastards,' he shot his friends in the back a good-natured scowl, 'won't lend me theirs so I can figure out how to change it back.'

'We're Team Ian!' his friends hooted.

I giggled but handed over my phone. I was definitely Team Jimmy.

After we swung into a café and picked up iced coffees and fresh juices we were on the road amid in-jokes, singing, friendly ribbing and laughter. We made only one toilet/refreshment stop at a dusty roadside place that looked like it ought to have been on Route 66 in the 1980s. The heat as we clambered out of the van and tossed all the tumbling summer paraphernalia back in was intense even at 9.30 a.m.

An hour later we turned off the highway onto a dirt track and then drove through a grassy field to join a queue of cars, pick-ups and vans all looking like ours: dusty, full of tanned people and inflatable dinghies and emitting music and laughter. It took forty-five minutes in the slow-moving queue to reach the entrance of the festival. We handed our tickets to a girl dressed in a tie-dye vest, cut-off black denim shorts, cowboy boots, two flower leis, one pink, one yellow and a straw panama hat with another multi-coloured flower lei wound around the crown. She had gold temporary tattoos down her thin, tanned arms and greeted us all in Afrikaans first then English. Similarly dressed men and women directed us to park in a field on the edge of a high bank.

'Wow,' I said, once I'd extracted myself from the sweaty van and stood on the edge of the field.

The view down to the festival site was like nothing I'd ever seen. The river was wide and flowing gently, with one side bulged out to form a tranquil lagoon, perfect for accommodating floating concertgoers. It was a browny-golden colour, not murky like the Thames but clear, and festooned with hundreds and hundreds of inflatables in every size, shape and colour the Internet could provide. There were unicorns and pandas and killer whales, small orange dinghies and floating armchairs. Five girls in bikinis lay on their stomachs on top of a double blow-up mattress. There were traditional lilos in all sorts of neon hues and rubber rings in all dimensions from one-person size all the way up to a giant one that had ten people straddling its circumference. I even saw a blow-up paddling pool floating on the river with some guys who were rapidly sinking but seemingly not caring.

Along the grassy banks people had set up various brollies and sun shelters, and it was here that people kept their cool boxes full of alcohol and food. The stage was a wooden platform jutting out over the water with a huge canvas canopy. Music floated out over the valley and mingled with the whoops and cheers of hundreds of tanned and happy people all splashing and drinking and dancing. I trotted back to the van, loaded up with as much as I could carry then followed Jimmy and Bryn, who each carried a handle of the very heavy cool box down the dusty path towards the water. Within twenty minutes we'd found a spot next to another group of Jimmy's friends, set up our shade shelters, peeled off our clothes to reveal our swimmers underneath, reapplied suntan lotion and were mixing drinks and cracking open cans of beer. Jimmy introduced me to so many people I couldn't remember all their names, and within half an hour we were floating on the river, beers in hand, hats on heads, bumping into people we knew and people we didn't.

'I think we should raft ourselves together so you don't get lost,' Jimmy said, pulling me towards him. He'd brought two dinghies, one for him and one for me and we'd filled the bottom of each one with water to keep us cool.

'Good idea,' I said, gazing across the hundreds of people in inflatables laughing and drinking around me. 'Are there snakes here?' I said, noticing a group of people who were standing in the waist-deep brown water at an ingenious floating raft bar; a square sheet of wood had been attached to floating barrels and on top of this, plastic bottles of various spirits with proper shot measure dispensers had been gaffer-taped upside-down to the side of an upturned crate. On top of the crate in cartons of ice were the mixers. A collection of people stood in the water and leant against the floating platform with plastic cups of crudely mixed cocktails like they were standing at the bar of a pub.

'Yes, heaps of them,' Jimmy said, tying his dinghy to mine with a plastic flower garland he'd been given by a giant lilo of floating girls.

'Great,' I said, scanning the crowd of death-chancing revellers.

We floated in a large group, all taking turns to hop out and do a drinks run back to the cool boxes on the river's edge. I came back from my turn, my arms full, the beer cans freezing against my skin, to a large group of girls on floating whimsical creatures all giggling and laughing and giving Jimmy and his friends a lot of attention. I passed the drinks around just as the gaggle of beauties sailed off in their flotilla of long limbs, whitened smiles and laughter.

'They're all Jimmy's exes,' Gus said as he cracked his beer open with a satisfying hiss.

Gus's girlfriend slapped his arm. 'Don't listen to him,' she said to me, obviously mistaking our relationship for something it wasn't.

'He's talking shit,' Jimmy grinned and drenched his mate with a strong swoop of his arm.

'Mate, you've definitely slept with half of them,' Gus said and bobbed down in his giant floating rubber ducky to avoid another wave of water from Jimmy.

'Half?' I said, clambering back in my dinghy and looking

back at the girls. 'There's nine of them. Have you slept with 4.5 of them? Which one did you half-sleep with?'

Jimmy laughed and splashed me with a wave smaller than the one he'd shot at his friend.

'Did you only put half in?' I said, ducking from another splash.

After many hours of drinking, floating and talking I looked over at Jimmy, who was lying back in his dinghy appreciating a moment to himself. His resting face was one just on the verge of smiling; the kind of smile where you've just seen a good friend unexpectedly or you're waiting for the punch line of a joke. I looked in the minimally reflective bottom of my empty beer can and arranged my face into various resting positions.

'What are you doing?'

I turned to see Jimmy giving me a very strange look. 'I'm trying out a new resting face,' I said. 'I think my current one says *"you're an idiot"* and I'm trying to put a more positive vibe out there.'

Jimmy frowned then yanked my dinghy close to his. He jammed his head right next to mine so he could see himself in my beer can mirror. 'What's mine?'

'I eat crayons,' I said, and Jimmy tipped me out of my dinghy.

When the heat of the afternoon hit its peak, Jimmy and his friends started making moves to get out of their dinghies and rubber duckies and head to the mermaid pool.

'What mermaid pool?' I asked, making slow progress through the busy river, dragging my dinghy behind me.

'It's a pool at the bottom of a waterfall. It's really deep and cold, so perfect to cool off before we go to the main field.'

The main field was where the evening part of the festival would take place. Apparently, some semblance of health and safety kicks in at this point, where they've realised that inebriated people, darkness, rivers and loud music are not a good public welfare mix.

'Where is it?' I said, as we reached the water's edge.

'Up there,' Jimmy said, pointing to a steep rocky mountain upriver.

I looked up and worried about the size of this waterfall. 'Is there a way to freshen up without jumping off a waterfall?'

Jimmy grinned. 'Nope.'

'Do you ever think the crevasses look like giant rock vaginas?' I said, looking up at the juts and ravines of rugged rock in the looming mountains as we made our way up the mountainside.

'A rock vagina?' one of Jimmy's friends said. 'Ow.'

'Are there snakes up here?' I asked as we trudged upwards, collectively puffing.

There were seven of us in our group, but hordes of others had had the same idea and we trekked up over the dusty rocks in a convoy of people hoping to sober up a bit before starting to drink again.

'Yes,' Jimmy said from behind me. 'This is Africa. You

are just going to have to assume there are snakes every-where we go.'

My heart embarked on snake-induced palpitations. I tried to calm myself with the rational tête-à-tête I'd had with many a local: they are shy creatures and will keep away from humans (except the puff adder, who is so lazy it will just lie wherever the fuck it wants and attack you if you get too close); locals hardly ever see them (except for all the people who see them all the time in their fucking gardens); you'll hear it hissing as a warning and know to stop walking (unless you're walking in a convoy of loud drunk people all singing and laughing and telling jokes), and my favoured rationale . . .

'They have anti-venom, right?'

'Yeah,' Jimmy said. ''Course.'

'Except for the coral snake,' Jimmy's friend puffed. 'No anti-venom for that one.'

'No anti-venom?' I said, scrambling over a big rock to keep pace with the girl ahead of me. 'Why would they have a snake with no anti-venom?'

'They're very rare,' Jimmy said. 'Don't worry.'

'A guy saw one yesterday,' the guy with the comfort-ing snake information said. 'On the edge of the river near the stage.'

I turned to glare at Jimmy, who wrinkled his nose and shook his head.

After a hot twenty minutes, where the last ten were so steep you had to grip dry twisted branches and have help getting up and over crumbly jagged rocks, we reached the top covered in a fine ochre dust. A tiny breeze gave infinitesimal respite from the late-afternoon heat. We walked along the crest of the ledge until we reached an area where we had to go down a steep rock face. I could hear the rush of a waterfall as we helped each other down with fireman's grips and instructions on where to place your foot. Once we'd navigated the brittle rock face, we joined a group of others waiting their turn on the top of a smooth boulder that jutted out over the mermaid pool, its depth apparent by the dark blue of the water, which became almost black in the centre. A tumble of frothy water fell from a high ledge to the right of us, into the pool.

'... three, two, one!' a group of friends chanted and a guy in neon-green board shorts ran off the edge of the smooth boulder and into the abyss shouting something in Afrikaans on his way down that made everyone laugh.

As Jimmy and his friends moved into a sort of line, I inched past all the people towards the edge of the rock.

'Fuck!' I said and shuffled backwards.

'You OK?' Jimmy said, holding my elbow protectively.

'I'm not jumping off that!'

The boulder we were standing on was large and bulbous, not allowing you to see the part of the pool you'd land in. You had to leap out far enough so that you didn't land on the rock you'd just jumped off. It was like an ant trying to leap off a rotund apple. I could see the far edge of the pool, with its jagged rocks, and I could see the ripples of the people who'd just jumped. But the jumpers only became visible, swimming towards the left where the mermaid pool became shallow and people lolled about in the waist-deep water, five seconds after I'd heard their landing splash. I'd counted. I'd also counted how many seconds between leaping off the boulder and landing in the water. To obtain the length of the drop with the seconds between jumping and landing, I'd also need the jumper's body weight and a physics degree. I had neither, but by my calculations the estimated fall was TOO FUCKING FAR.

'WOOHOOO!' a girl hollered as her friends finished their countdown and she launched off the rock, her tanned quads flexing with the effort.

She disappeared and far too many seconds later I heard her touchdown splash. From my dizzying height it seemed the drop was at least nineteen stories high. Of a very high-ceilinged building. But I could have been paranoically wrong. It's been known to happen.

'What if I leap too far out and land on the rocks on the other side?' I said as we moved forward, my heart hammering.

Jimmy looked amused. 'You won't.'

'How do you know?' The jump was a leap of faith and I was feeling particularly faithless.

'Because you're not Wonder Woman,' he said. 'There is no way you'd be able to jump that far.'

'I used to be very good at long jump, I'll have you know,' I said. 'Before I grew these anchors,' I muttered under my breath while glancing down at my boobs.

One more person and it would be Jimmy's turn. And then mine.

'OK,' Jimmy said, as the girl in front was counted down. 'Just watch me and do the exact same thing.'

I nodded. The girl in front leapt. Moments later we heard her splash and then when she came into vision, swimming to the edge of the pool, Jimmy's friends began their rowdy countdown.

'Ten, nine.'

'You can do this,' Jimmy said in my ear, then he grinned and moved into position.

'Five, four, three, two,' they hollered.

Jimmy glanced back at me, gave me a wink then on 'one' took a three-step run and jumped. The last thing I saw was the muscles round his tanned shoulders rippling as he disappeared beyond the edge of the boulder. It seemed an age before I heard his splash and then he came into sight, his powerful arms pulling him through the indigo water. He reached the shallows and looked up with a grin.

'Go Jess!' he yelled. 'You can do it!'

I stood, frozen on the smooth boulder, inches from where it curved downwards towards the water. 'I can't! Oh my god, I can't do it!'

'Yes, you can!' he hollered.

People behind me started counting down from ten.

'Which part do I jump off?' I shouted back.

'Nine, eight!'

'Like which *exact* bit of rock? What if I jump too soon?'

'You won't! Just do it!' Jimmy's voice echoed off the sheer rock walls.

'Six, five!'

'What if I jump too late?'

'Four, three!'

'Somebody ought to make some kind of "jump here" marker!' I screamed. 'If I survive and I ever do this again I'm going to do some Pythagoras and get back up here and make a jump mark so no one ever jumps too late and skids down the rock face on their back!'

'Hurry up!' Jimmy said, through laughter.

'Two, one, GO!'

'Jump, Jess!' Jimmy called. 'Just jump!'

I felt immense pressure, my heart was going mental. I was sweaty and dusty and boiling and terrified. The crowd behind me started chanting.

'Jump Jess, jump! Jump Jess, jump!'

'There's a coral snake!' Jimmy's friend suddenly yelled.

'WHAT?!?' I ran at the edge of the rock, grabbed the seat of my bikini bottoms so as not get carved in two, and leapt. Time slowed, and I felt like I was falling and falling and falling and never going to reach the pool, when suddenly I plunged through the surface and sank into water so cold my breath got knocked out of me. Everything went dark. I plunged deeper and deeper.

'*Oh well, I did kind of like my life,*' I thought, as I sank lower and was enveloped by cool darkness. '*I never got to sleep with Bradley Cooper, but I did get to see* Matilda *six times and I really liked that day at school when I was nine and I wore that polka dot ruffle skirt and David Sanders told me I looked pretty. Now where's this light at the end of the tunnel everyone talks about? Actually, where's the tunnel? Death needs to come with a map. Oh, hang on; I'm going back up. Oh OK. No light this time. I still have a chance with Bradley!!'* And I broke through the surface and saw Jimmy's grinning face, his eyes sparkling with pride and his arm outstretched. I grabbed his hand and allowed him to pull me into the shallows, checking quickly that my bikini was still present and doing its job.

'I did it!' I was so overjoyed at having survived I leapt at him and threw my arms around his neck. 'Oh my god, I can't believe I did it! Did you see me?!' I looked in his face, and became aware that my breasts, with only a thin layer of wet lycra, were pressed up against his warm chest.

'Yes, I saw you,' he said, looking into my eyes.

CHAPTER TWENTY-THREE

Back at the river site people were deflating their whales and unicorns, folding towels and gathering empty beer cans and plastic cups. Some were moving in the direction of the tents and caravans, some were taking stuff back to their cars and some were heading to the main field where a band was already playing. The euphoria from the jump had me chatting ceaselessly on the walk back from the pool, which had been a nice, steady, manageable gradient as Jimmy and I had fallen back from his group of friends. Once we'd packed the van ready for a quick getaway at the end of the night, and changed into evening attire (Jimmy doing it amid a cascade of glitter and bad words about his brother), we walked over to the main area, where it was set up more like a traditional English festival in a field. The only difference was it was warm and dry, and you didn't have to wear wellingtons and a see-through rain poncho that you'd picked up at a pound store. And Alexa Chung wasn't going to walk past and make you feel unworthy, fashion-wise.

Caravans serving food and drinks dotted the perimeter of the field and once we had a couple of beers each, we found a spot towards the back of the field and faced the stage. I didn't know any of the bands but I enjoyed the music and loved being under the stars with a huge bunch of friendly, welcoming people. Jimmy's group swelled as the night grew. Everyone knew someone who knew someone, and people came and went throughout the night. A handful of beautiful girls flirted with Jimmy. He had all the time in the world for them. But it became apparent that he had more for me. He kept checking if I was all right, if I had a drink, if I could see the band, if I liked the music and making sure I wasn't getting tired. It was a heady feeling to have someone be so attentive.

Jimmy drank all night but he didn't get messy, just sparklier and, if possible, more smiley. He was one of those rare people who become chilled-out and happy with drinking rather than boisterous and obnoxious. It was the kind of drunk I aspired to be. Although I was pushing thirty, so maybe I should have been aiming for self-restraint rather than being a cheerful inebriate.

'I think I'd like to cultivate my personality without alcohol,' I said to Jimmy as we walked back from a caravan that served beer in bendy plastic cups. 'You know there are some people who are really cool and they don't drink? Like Michelle Obama. I bet she's cool without drinking. I think I'm only cool with liquor.' I hiccuped and spilt beer down my leg. 'I'll start tomorrow.'

'I think you're cool all the time,' Jimmy said as he threw an arm around my shoulder.

We walked back to where Jimmy's gang of friends had been but the crowds had moved, so we stood at the edge of the masses and listened to the music. I was enthralled by a band with a bouncing frontman playing from a guitar made of an old petrol can, and an African woman who sang like an angel and could high-kick her leg up to her forehead. They were obviously an SA favourite because the crowd went crazy. Halfway through the night I stopped drinking. The portable toilets were disgusting and I was frightened a snake might bite my vagina if I went in the bushes like everyone else. Around 11 p.m. a DJ took to the stage. Laser lights streaked out over the crowd and everyone was jumping up with their hands in the air trying to break the beams of coloured light. Jimmy and I jumped up and down in time to the music laughing and falling over each other. He broke a few beams and I got nowhere near. When a pink beam pulsed above my head Jimmy grabbed me by the hips and lifted me up. I broke the beam with both arms and a whoop. He lowered me down, but kept his arms around my waist and looked at me intensely. Then his lips were on mine.

My sensible side, who'd clearly not been in attendance when I was visiting the beer vans, and who was sitting soberly on a straight-backed chair in her Mary Janes, spoke up.

You can't do this. You have a boyfriend. You owe it to Pete to either work it out or extract yourselves from each other's lives like grown-ups before you go around kissing hot guys who have been so kind and have the nicest family and a fucking bitch of a dog.

I allowed the kiss to continue a bit longer, hoping my wicked side would turn up, but she didn't. She was probably at the front of the stage doing yard glasses with her cleavage out.

I pulled away from Jimmy.

'I've been wanting to do that since—'

'Oh please don't say "*since we first met*"!' I laughed kindly.

'No, you had a boyfriend. And I thought you were uptight and a bit crazy.' He grinned. His arms were still round my waist. The heat from his hands warmed my skin where my top didn't quite reach the waistband of my denim shorts.

'I still have a boyfriend.'

'And you're still crazy.'

We stood in each other's arms while people leapt about around us.

'I'm sorry,' I said, looking up at him. 'I can't do this. Not when Pete and I are ...' I didn't know how to finish the sentence. I didn't know what Pete and I were. We hadn't broken up (yet), but we weren't exactly a happy couple either. I needed to be sure we were officially over before I did anything with anybody else. 'I've got some stuff to sort out before I can ...' I shrugged. 'You know ...'

The laser lights illuminated Jimmy's face in pulses: pink then dark, green then dark, purple then dark. In the flashes of light I could see his disappointment. It was an intoxicating turn-on.

'I understand,' he said, his voice low. 'I ...' He looked down at me, his hands still on my waist. 'I really like you.' He smiled. 'But you know that.'

I put my head against his chest and his arms folded across my back. He let out a sigh.

'Can we hang out tomorrow?' I said. 'Before you go to work?'

Jimmy took a moment to answer. 'Sure,' he said eventually. 'I'll take you to my hangover place – it serves the best Bloody Marys and burgers.'

'That sounds perfect,' I said, genuinely gutted that in two more days I'd be on a plane flying away from Jimmy and Cape Town.

Jimmy's arms tightened across my back as though he'd read my thoughts.

The music stopped soon after and by midnight everyone had made their way back to the van in various states of sunburn and sobriety. We piled in with damp towels and swimsuits, dusty feet and missing flip-flops, empty beer cans and bags of rubbish (South Africans were very environmentally aware), and drove back along the dark highway to town. It was 3 a.m. when we pulled up outside Diego and Ian's and everyone was asleep except the driver and me. It took a while to wake Jimmy; he'd had much more to drink than I'd thought, and when I finally managed to get him inside we found Flora waiting at the front door. She trotted ahead of me as I guided Jimmy down the stairs to his bedroom and oversaw the removal of his shoes, shorts and T-shirt, which all came off with another gust of glitter, and the tucking of him into bed in just his boxers.

'Stay,' Jimmy said, patting the empty side of the bed. ''S too late to get an Uber home by yourself.'

'OK,' I said, looking around for something to wear.

'Wear one of my shirts.' He flapped his arm in the direction of his pile of clothes at the bottom of the wardrobe. 'He doesn't know what he's doing,' he mumbled.

'Who?' I asked, crossing past the bottom of the bed towards his wardrobe.

'Pete. He doesn't deserve you. You should be with someone who appreciates how kind you are. And who sees how much you love your sister and your niece and nephew.'

I stopped at the foot of the bed and looked at Jimmy. He lay on his back with his eyes shut, a half-smile on his lips.

'You should be with someone who likes eighties glam rock and mixes a mean margarita and can play the piano and knows how to make an origami Yoda and has really nice toes.'

'Should I really?' I said with a smile, thinking that I'd really like to see the origami Yoda.

'Just a suggestion.' Jimmy rolled onto his side and shut his eyes. 'Juuuuuust a suggestion.'

I rummaged through the bottom of Jimmy's wardrobe, found a clean-ish looking T-shirt and pair of boxers and went to the bathroom to wash the suntan lotion off my face and swish toothpaste round my mouth. When I came back Jimmy was asleep, snoring softly. I went to lift the sheets and climb in but Flora hopped up on the bed, curled into a ball of snowy fuzz on the empty side and fixed me with a defiant, black-eyed glare.

'Fine,' I whispered. 'You win.'

I grabbed a pillow and blanket from the hall cupboard, walked across the room and lay down on Oscar the Couch. Once comfy, I opened Instagram. I flicked through Giselle's photos, feeling a sense of loss at the images of Pete on rock faces, beaming at the camera. He'd developed a deep tan and it hurt to see how happy he looked. I moved to Goat's feed and scrolled through. Goat had more shots of himself, strategically framed to show a particular watch, or backpack-water-pouch, or climbing shoe, but there were still a handful with Pete and Giselle. As I scrolled through, one he'd posted that evening caught my eye. It was of Goat standing at the edge of a bonfire, obviously giving a speech to the gathered muscled, tanned, kitesurfing, shark-disregarding weirdos. I zoomed into the background and my heart sank. There, illuminated by the bonfire's glow, sat Giselle and Pete. Kissing.

I'd recognise those pineapple board shorts anywhere. I'd bought them for him but he'd always been too embarrassed to wear them, preferring his navy ones with the white piping down the side. I zoomed in with my fingertips. Pete's hand was at the back of Giselle's slender neck, her hair in braids again. She had a hand on his knee. It was such an intimate pose. They looked like a couple in love.

Even though I'd known it was pretty much over between Pete and me, I covered my face with my hands and wept, trying not to wake Jimmy with my sobs. After a moment I felt something wet and cold touch my hand. Flora stood, looking at me, her black eyes shining. She cocked her head to the side, making her puffball ears bounce, then hopped up and nestled into the curve of my body.

CHAPTER TWENTY-FOUR

'Good morning, sweet girl!' Diego said as I walked into the kitchen the next morning in a pair of Jimmy's boxers and his oversized T-shirt. He stood in the kitchen in a hot-pink vest, arranging fruit salad into two earthenware bowls. 'You're the girl who never leaves! Not that I want you to.' He pulled me into a bear hug then held me at arm's length. 'Big night, huh?'

Ian, who was not normally at home at 8.17 a.m. on a Friday, sat on a stool wearing impeccably pressed navy trousers and an ice-blue shirt, open at the collar. He stood and gave me a kiss on the cheek then returned to his seat.

'A *late* night,' I said, my voice hoarse from lack of sleep. It had been past 4 a.m. when I'd finally fallen into a fitful slumber, my mind spinning with images of Pete and Giselle. And Jimmy kissing me. I'd woken at 7 a.m. and couldn't get back to sleep. My eyeballs looked like I'd exfoliated them with hedgehogs. 'Jimmy's still sleeping.'

'Then you must join us for breakfast,' Diego said, getting out a third bowl and holding up his hand at my protest. 'We insist. Coffee?'

I nodded gratefully. 'This is strange,' I said, indicating the torrential rain outside and climbing onto the stool next to Ian with considerable effort.

'But needed,' Ian said, shifting a newspaper out of my way. 'Rain is good news in summer.'

'And it means your site inspections get cancelled and you can have fruit salad with your beloved,' Diego said, passing Ian his fruit salad, which had bits of decorative mint on top.

'That I can.' Ian's eyes twinkled.

Over breakfast Ian and Diego got on to the topic of why Jimmy had come to Cape Town and how they thought it would be better for his writing and music career to be back in London, but that Jimmy was reticent.

'Jimmy has always felt that he needed to protect me from any gay backlash,' Ian said, folding his napkin neatly and laying it next to his empty bowl. 'Even though, if you're going to be gay, Cape Town is *the* place to be.'

'*The* place,' Diego echoed.

'Jimmy knew I was gay before I knew.' Ian pushed his bowl to the side and picked up his espresso with hands that had been recently manicured. 'He used to get into all kinds of scrapes sticking up for me. But don't think he was the tough guy sticking up for the gay sissy. He might be big now but he was a scrawny kid, a foot shorter than all his mates. I was double his size.'

'Jimmy is a pussy cat,' Diego interjected. He stood and began clearing the breakfast bowls.

I smiled.

Ian nodded. 'But if he thought I was being picked on he was in there like a *feral* cat. Most of the time I wasn't even being bullied. Or if I was, it wasn't for being gay – just regular kid arseholery.'

'Kids can be *nasty*,' Diego fussed.

'I was twenty-four when I'd worked up the courage to tell Dad. But he didn't react well.' A brief sadness crossed Ian's face but dissipated in an instant when Diego laid a hand on his shoulder. Ian smiled and continued. 'He denied it and said I was trying to be fashionable or that I was copying things I'd seen in the movies. Admittedly, I did once dress up as Julia Roberts and pretend to accept a plastic necklace from the coat stand—'

'Who didn't?!' Diego exclaimed as he filled the coffee machine.

'But he was wrong. I'm gay to my bone marrow. I didn't just watch *Will and Grace* and think, "*My god he has impeccable suits, I want to be like him*".'

'You do have impeccable suits, though,' Diego said.

'Thank you,' Ian said with an affectionate glint in his eyes. 'Anyway, Dad was ashamed. And Jimmy wrote him off that day. It was either Dad or me and Jimmy chose me. And now it's been almost ten years.'

Diego shook his head and *tsk*-ed.

'Jimmy sees the situation with Dad as either/or, black or white. But life isn't like that. There are variables and grey areas and the only way through anything is to recognise that we're all different. A knee-jerk reaction is understandable – but it needs to be reassessed. And Jimmy just won't do that.'

I frowned. The Jimmy I'd spent the past ten days with was the most open-hearted, non-judgemental person I'd encountered. It seemed strange to hear he wasn't willing to forgive his father.

'Dad was shocked, that's all,' Ian continued. 'He didn't expel me from the family, but for Jimmy he may as well have.' Ian checked the time on his sleek watch and stood. 'Dad and I started talking a few years later. It took him time to understand. To accept me as Ian, his son who had always been his son.'

'He reassessed *his* knee-jerk reaction,' Diego said.

Ian smiled. 'We're OK now. And we've been OK for a number of years. We just need to get Jimmy on board.'

'Fucking stubborn, that boy,' Diego said, but he had a fond look in his eye.

'Yes, I am fucking stubborn,' Jimmy said, walking into the room wearing just a pair of shorts, his hair looking like a dog's breakfast that a fox had had a go at first. 'Did Ian tell you Dad is a Classics professor majoring in Greek History? You'd think he of all people would understand. The Greeks invented the gay stuff – it's all over their crockery.'

Diego and Ian exchanged looks.

Jimmy ignored them and pointed to the rain. 'My hangover place doesn't open in the rain. It's a beach place.'

'Oh,' I said. I didn't know what else to say. I didn't know if Jimmy would remember kissing me, or what he'd said about Pete before he fell asleep. I found it hard to look him in the eye and I felt the unsaid words between Ian and Diego watching us.

Jimmy scratched at his hair. 'Want to drink coffee and watch the rain instead?'

Downstairs Jimmy opened the sliding doors to the balcony off his bedroom. The room filled with the sounds of the rain hammering on the sand below and the angry surf beating at the shore. Despite the inhospitable weather the air was still warm. Jimmy pulled Oscar the Couch up to the open doors and sat at one end with a tiny guitar that may have been called a ukulele.

'Sorry about the rain ruining our plans,' Jimmy said, twanging at the strings.

I shrugged. 'I like weather,' I said, taking a seat at the other end of the shaggy sofa. 'Rain gives you permission to just be, not do. It reminds me that nature is in control. No matter what I try to organise, the world will do what it wants to do.'

'For a crazy person that's a pretty chilled-out view.'

For a while we sat on the sofa and watched the rain make date-sized dents in the golden sand. I sipped an awakening lemon-ginger tea while Jimmy sang Eric Clapton's 'Layla' but exchanged Layla for Flora, then moved indiscriminately through his favourite parts of 'Runaway Train', 'Black Hole Sun', 'Take Me to Church', 'Lola', 'House of the Rising Sun' and Talking Heads' 'Wild, Wild, Life'.

'Pete kissed the gazelle,' I said between songs.

Jimmy stopped strumming and looked at me with an expression that made my heart break. 'How do you know?'

I told him about the photo. And about Pete telling me he'd had doubts about us for a while, how I'd been totally blindsided but now that I'd had time to think, realised he was probably right. We had 'grown apart'.

'When I met you guys, I know it was only for a few minutes, but you seemed to be really different.'

'We didn't used to be. But I guess we are now. We were into all the same things when we were young – running and travel and stuff – but then I got distracted by Annabelle and didn't realise we'd . . .' A couple of tears ran down my cheek. I was embarrassed and tried to quell them with my fingertips but they kept leaking.

Flora, who'd been sitting on her silk cushion, trotted over, hopped up on the sofa and curled in my lap.

Jimmy smiled. 'She does that,' he said, reaching over and giving her an affectionate tickle behind the ears. 'It's the best thing about dogs. They have a reflective nature. If you're happy they'll join in, instantly ready to party. "*Where? What? Who cares! We're HAPPY!*" But if you want to mope they'll flop next to you, instantly more depressed than you . . .' Jimmy frowned. 'Actually, that part annoys me. I want to *own* my depression.'

I giggled through my tears.

'Is there anything I can do . . .?' Jimmy said, resting a hand on my knee. 'Or say . . .?'

I shook my head.

'Or sing?'

I opened my mouth to speak.

'Just not "The Sun Will Come Out Tomorrow", he said with a shudder of distaste.

'Then no,' I sniffed.

I smiled at Jimmy. His tactic had worked. My tears had dried. He smiled back and plucked at the ukulele/teeny guitar thing.

'Well, you turned me down last night and it looks like you needn't have.' He gave me a quick sideways glance but otherwise kept his gaze on the rain that was now easing to more of a patter.

'I didn't know if you'd remember that.'

Jimmy turned to me. 'Of course I remember.'

I waited to see if he was going to say anything else but he just kept looking at me.

'It wouldn't have been right. I didn't know if Pete and I were going to break up when he got back or . . . what was going to happen. As much as I wanted to . . .' I felt myself blushing. 'It would have felt like cheating. To me, anyway.' I shrugged. 'It's best to have a clean break before, you know, doing anything else with anyone else.'

Jimmy looked at me for a long moment. 'Do you always do the right thing?'

'No,' I said. 'I do what I want. And what I want is usually the right thing.'

Jimmy emitted a short laugh. 'What do you want now?'

I looked at Jimmy, waiting for an answer, and then shifted my gaze to the sky, now a pale grey-ish white. A rainbow appeared over the blue-grey ocean. It was a weak, pathetic one that was only a portion of a rainbow. Jimmy strummed his tiny guitar and started to sing 'The Rainbow Connection'. I looked at his profile. His eyes were always on the verge of crinkling into a smile. A smile he was generous with, a smile that had lifted my day so often recently.

I looked down at Flora. *What do you think?*

Do it, Bitch, Flora seemed to say. *I'd do it but I don't know how because, as you so kindly pointed out, it's hard to figure out which end is arse and which end is face in this fluff.*

OK. Do you mind fucking off then?

My pleasure. I can't think of anything I'd rather see less.

Flora jumped off my lap (OK, I helped her with a well-intentioned shove), crossed the room and headed out of the bedroom door. Probably to go upstairs and tell Lucy what a bitch I was. I looked at Jimmy at the far end of the sofa.

When did the sofa become so long?

He was miles away! If I wanted to kiss him I'd have to shuffle along for, like, an hour and a half. I might lose the inclination halfway there. Or get hungry and have to leave to make a sandwich.

Maybe it would be better to just look at him with 'meaning', then he'd know what I was thinking and we could rush at each other and meet, romantically, halfway across this expanse of shaggy green fabric.

I gave that a go. Jimmy kept strumming and singing, his eyes on the escalating rain.

Why isn't he noticing that I'm looking at him amorously?

I huffed out a sigh and looked at the rain. Why was it so hard to make the first move? I knew Jimmy wanted it. I was pretty sure he knew I wanted it. Why, then, could I not do the sofa shuffle? Why did Gus and Sam and André and Bryn make such a long sofa? I'd be having words next time I saw them.

'Jess,' Jimmy said.

I turned.

He leant forward and put the ukulele/baby guitar on the floor then held out his arm.

'Come here.'

I shuffled down the sofa, which, in the end, wasn't nearly as long as I'd thought, and tucked myself under his arm. He shifted so his back was against the armrest and I lay against his chest. He smelt of sleep and yesterday's suntan lotion and cologne and comfort. His heart was beating fast. It didn't take long for our fingers to intertwine and then we were kissing, uncertainly at first, and then deeper and more intensely. His hands were at the back of my neck, and on my cheek. I ran my hands down his chest, feeling a thrill as my fingers dipped and rose over each muscle. Within moments we were pulling each other's clothes off. The sound of the rain pelting at the sand and the waves thrashing against the rocks heightened the atmosphere. With my legs wrapped around his waist, Jimmy put an arm around my back and we moved towards the bed, slamming the bedroom door shut on the way.

'You know what you want now?' Jimmy said, his body pressing down on me, his lips on my neck and his voice deep and hoarse.

'Yes,' I said, pulling at the waistband of his boxers. 'You.'

CHAPTER TWENTY-FIVE

'You're beautiful,' Jimmy said, brushing my fringe off my face and kissing me delicately on the lips.

I lay next to him, smiling, naked and exhausted. It had been an energetic couple of hours. I was sweaty, hungry, thirsty and completely drunk on Jimmy. We kissed for a little longer, all the restraint we'd shown for the past few days cast off as we ran our hands over each other's bodies. We could have stayed in bed for the rest of the day but I was starving. And Jimmy was craving hangover food. I jumped in the shower, smiling to myself, and then got dressed into some spare clothes I'd taken to the festival.

'I've hidden some crisps at the very back of the cupboard with all the fancy china,' Jimmy said from his sitting position in bed, a sheet covering his nakedness, as I sat on top of the covers, nodding. He'd had to hide his emergency snack food from clean-eating Diego and I'd told him that at home I kept my unhealthy treats on Dave's shelf of the fridge so Pete wouldn't know I ate Jaffa cakes and cheap eclairs from the Tesco Metro. 'And there are marshmallows in an unmarked paper bag at the back of the liquor cabinet. And there might still be some ice cream hidden in the bottom of the freezer in a box labelled . . . you know what? It's probably easier if I come up. It's hidden *everywhere.*'

'OK,' I said, relieved. I'd already forgotten the location of the pretzels, the caramel waffles and something Afrikaans that sounded like 'coke sisters'; I didn't know if I was looking for a girl band CD, a food item or cocaine for ladies.

'I should probably have a shower,' Jimmy said, reaching for his shorts on the floor. 'But that can wait—'

We were interrupted by the door banging open and Diego holding up a clutch of paper bags stamped with the name of a café, his eyebrows raised in the universal eyebrow-language of 'look what I've got!'

'—because there's crescent shaped GLUTEN TO BE HAD!' Jimmy shot out of bed, dragging the sheet with him.

'Yoh! I don't need to see that!' Diego said, shielding his eyes from a flash of Jimmy's nakedness. 'And neither does our sweet girl here!'

From behind his hand shield, Diego's brow lowered and his eyes flicked from me, looking innocently back at him, to Jimmy, struggling with a pair of shorts, his bare butt white in comparison to the tanned rest of him. Diego gave one final side-eye look of suspicion before turning on his heel and leaving the room.

I leapt off the bed and followed him up the stairs, while

Jimmy hopped about on one foot trying to put on his shorts and panicking in case the gluten got eaten before he was dressed.

'I'm sorry you had to see that,' Diego said, climbing the stairs on his toes, his smooth calf muscles tensing with each step. 'But Jimmy gets very excited about gluten day.'

'Diego is very pedantic about when gluten can enter the home. Fridays only,' Jimmy said, catching up with us and trying to pass Diego, who was purposefully making his already large frame take up all the stairs.

After our heavenly gluten lunch of abundantly filled croissants followed by glazed handmade doughnuts, which Jimmy had devoured without uttering a single word, he and Diego sat at the kitchen island fighting over a crossword. Pamela pottered around the kitchen making bone broth, intermittently offering up possible answers, and I received a phone call from Pete.

I hopped off my stool, headed out onto the balcony and stood under the open brolly, sheltering from the rain. 'Hello,' I said coolly, catching Jimmy's brief glance of curiosity.

'I'm at the apartment, where are you?' Pete said.

'At a friend's.'

'What friend?'

'Just a friend.'

'Oh,' he said, sounding put out. 'When are you coming back? Soon?'

I looked inside through the open balcony door. Jimmy and Diego were stuck and Diego was googling. Jimmy was getting angry about the googling because googling is cheating. Diego was saying there was no disclaimer on the crossword that said it needed to be completed without Google. Jimmy was saying there should be and that it takes a while for society to catch up with all the corrections to laws the advance of technology necessitates. Diego was giving him a 'you're a dick' look and they were embarking on an adult squabble over the pen. Pamela was walking past with a bunch of carrots, laughing.

'No,' I said down the phone with a smile. 'No, I'm staying here.'

'Staying where?'

'I'll see you tomorrow morning.'

'But we fly out—'

'I'll be back after breakfast.'

I hung up, flicked the phone to silent and watched Diego and Pamela congratulate themselves for figuring out that seven down was 'Guadeloupe' and Jimmy sulk because googling was not 'figuring it out'.

I trotted back inside and stood next to Jimmy. 'Can I stay one more night?' I said in his ear, while Diego read out the next clue.

Jimmy grinned and slipped an arm around my waist. 'Of course you can,' he said, his lips close to my ear making all the tiny hairs on my neck stand up. 'I'll get my shift covered at work.'

'Seven down is fourteen letters for a 1974 comedy western and Google says it's something called *Blazing Saddles* but I think it's—' Diego looked up and saw Jimmy and me mid-kiss. 'Heeeeeeeeeeeeey?' he said, making the word last as long as *Django Unchained*.

After the crossword was completed (illegally according to a huffy Jimmy) and Diego had been updated on the fact that Jimmy and I were now 'people who kissed', and we'd watched Diego immediately get on the phone to Ian and excitedly (and somewhat like a fourteen-year-old girl) update him that Jimmy and I were now 'people who kissed', we looked out at the rain. It was still very much an indoor day.

'Movies and popcorn on the sofa?' Jimmy asked, and I couldn't have thought of a better way to spend a rainy afternoon.

Jimmy's idea of movie-watching was to bring out three DVD box sets of 1960s TV series: *Hogan's Heroes*, *The Munsters* and *Get Smart*. Their cardboard sleeves were tatty and well-used.

'They're hilarious!' Jimmy said off the back of my down-cast expression.

'They're ancient,' I replied, looking at the back of *The Munsters*. 'They're over fifty years old!'

'Timeless classics,' he said, taking it out of my hands and loading it into the DVD player, which was also a relic to my mind. 'You'll see.'

'They're all his father's favourite shows,' Diego said, walking into the room with a gym bag and his keys dangling from his index finger. 'They used to watch them at the weekend together when Ian and Jimmy were young. Jimmy watches them so he can feel close to his father even though the two of them are estranged.'

'Would you stop psychoanalysing me?!' Jimmy said, stalking back towards the sofa and taking his place next to me. 'I don't care how much *Dr. Phil* you watch, you're a personal trainer, not a psychologist.'

'You think I don't need psychology to get those *mafutas* back on the treadmill after squeezing out four babies and then having their husbands run off with a younger model who is actually a model?' Diego said, heading to the front door. 'I psychologise all day, my bru, and *you*,' he pointed an outstretched finger at Jimmy, 'are a poy-key of problems.'

I turned to Jimmy, who was scowling and making a fist-grinding motion in his palm at Diego, who, with a wink in my direction, swished his lycra-clad, muscled butt out of the front door. 'A poy-key?'

'Yep,' he said, turning his attention to the TV remote, his face still arranged in a glower. 'P–O–T–J–I–E. It's a cast iron pot you put over coals and cook curry in. It's delicious.' The anger seeped away from his features. 'Diego has the best recipe for Cape Malay chicken.' He paused to think. 'Shall we do one tonight? I'll ask Diego.' He affected a scowl but his petulance was being superseded by affection. 'When I decide to talk to him,' he said as he typed out a text to Diego about potjie for dinner that night, his eyes gleaming.

Towards the late afternoon, after surprising myself by laughing my head off at a whole season of *Get Smart*, the rain cleared and in the subsequent calm Diego made his Cape Malay curry in the potjie on the beach while Ian, Jimmy and I took turns to pop back into the house to refresh our drinks. We sat in cream-coloured canvas deck chairs and ate curry from bowls on our laps, our bare feet in the damp sand. Ian brought candles and luxurious blankets outside after dinner and we sat in the fading light watching the sea and sky become similar shades of blue-grey and the diehard surfers paddle across the gentle swells in black wetsuits. When Jimmy went back inside to get a last round of drinks, Ian turned to me.

'Jimmy really likes you,' he said.

Diego looked up from packing up the potjie.

I smiled. 'I really like him.'

'Maybe you can convince him he needs to be back in England. Maybe you're enough of a pull.'

I watched Diego put wet sand on the hot coals and thought about Pete and Annabelle and home. I wondered how SA-tanned, smiling Jimmy would fare back in brick-and-rain London. It would be like trying to plant a sunflower in rubble.

'Things with me are complicated,' I said.

Ian watched me for a moment then nodded, indicating he would speak no more on the subject.

At the end of the night, once we'd trekked our beach dinner kit back inside and were all heading to our beds, Ian turned to me once more.

'You're a very special girl,' he said, pulling me into a hug.

He smelt of Yves Saint Laurent and salt air. 'I hope things . . .' he glanced at Jimmy, who was watching us with a mixture of curiosity and fondness. 'I hope things work out.'

I smiled. I'd known him, Diego and Jimmy for only ten days but for some reason in that time I'd relaxed into their lives like that was where I was supposed to be. Like they'd been waiting for me to come along and I'd fitted in perfectly, like 'Guadeloupe' in seven down.

CHAPTER TWENTY-SIX

The next morning was Saturday. My flight home was at 7.30 p.m. that night. I woke to a text from Pete asking when I'd be back. I turned the phone off, shoved it in the drawer of the bedside table and curled my arm around Jimmy's naked, sleeping form.

He rolled over and smiled sleepily. 'You're actually going today.'

'Well, we've said goodbye a few times, so we should be used to it.'

We kissed, and then as the kissing became more urgent we moved on to more enthusiastic bed-orientated activities.

It was hard to leave the bed later that morning. We knew when we did that it was potentially the last time, so we lingered: kissing, chatting, laughing and kissing.

Jimmy had another writing class to get to so after showering we trudged upstairs to breakfast, Jimmy stopping me halfway up the stairs to press me up against the wall in a kiss so passionate it nearly had us heading back to bed again. But we did eventually make it to the kitchen, where Diego and Pamela were scanning recipe books and deciding on what to cook for a soirée Ian and Diego were having that night.

'Ah, sweet girl, you're leaving us today! For real this time,' Diego said, coming round the side of the island and pulling me into a hug. 'Say it isn't so!'

Jimmy hugged Pamela good morning and smiled at me.

'So, what does our sweet girl want for her last breakfast?' Diego said as he released me from his bear embrace.

I grinned. 'Your protein pancakes?'

Ian came back from a walk on the beach with Flora and Lucy and we all ate breakfast in the sun on the balcony. While Jimmy went to his bedroom to pack up his writing stuff, I sat on the sofa with Flora and we discussed how far she and I had come in our relationship. Diego and Ian reappeared in the kitchen in matching running gear and I walked with them to the front door.

'Our Jimmy, he's very keen on you,' Diego said, holding me by the shoulders, his arms outstretched.

'But what about the Tarantino Test?' I said, forcing a smile. 'Or the fact that I have *The NeverEnding Story* soundtrack in my playlist?'

'Unforgivable,' Ian said, giving my cheek a gentle kiss.

'Absolutely,' Diego pulled me to him in a strong hug, heavy with expensive cologne.

They left, making me promise, yet again, to keep in touch,

then Jimmy appeared with his bag and after a hug from Pamela, it was time to leave. As I walked out of the house, with its sea views, the smell of the sea wafting through the ever-open balcony doors and the loving family that cooked and bantered and laughed inside, I knew for sure it was for the last time.

On the drive back Jimmy was quiet. When we pulled up at the apartment for the final time I didn't move. I didn't want to get out of the car.

'I could give my class a miss?' Jimmy said. 'We can hang out together until I have to go to work?'

I gripped his hand. 'No, you need to finish your script. And I need to go and have a very awkward conversation and an even more awkward twelve-hour plane trip.'

Jimmy nodded.

'So,' I drew in a breath. 'Goodbye, then, I guess. For real this time.'

'I've stopped believing you,' Jimmy said with a smile that didn't quite reach his eyes.

'OK, I'll see you later today then.'

Our jokes were weak and self-conscious. We were trying to hold the emotion in as it was new and couldn't go anywhere. I made no movement to get out. The front seat of his crappy car had become my happy place.

'OK,' I began. 'I'd better—'

Jimmy leant across and kissed me. My senses were on high alert: the feel of his lips, the graze of his stubble, the smell of his soap. It all combined to bring me a premature nostalgia.

We pulled apart and I saw the same expression on Jimmy's face as I felt the sting of a missed opportunity.

I swiped under my eyes, stopping tears. 'Bye then.'

'I'll call,' he said, swallowing thickly.

I nodded, leant forward and gave him another lingering kiss on the lips then leapt out before I changed my mind. Walking away from that car was the hardest thing I'd had to do, bar comforting Annabelle when Daniel left her. It was as if an elastic bungee cord were pulling me back to the shitty Mitsubishi and Whitesnake. At the doors to the apartment I turned back. Jimmy was watching me. I waved, swiped my security pass and headed inside to the cool, empty foyer.

At the sixth floor I let myself into the apartment and Pete shot off the sofa. 'Where have you been? You said you'd be home in the morning and it's nearly lunchtime! I've been calling you.'

'Have you?' I said, looking in my bag for my phone, not finding it, then remembering that I'd put it in Jimmy's bed-side drawer.

My laptop was charging at the dining table so I flicked it open and sent Jimmy a Facebook message asking him to take my phone to the bar, saying I'd pick it up on the way to the airport later. I was going to see him again after all. The never-final goodbyes were getting ridiculous. Pete paced impatiently behind me.

'Where have you been?' he said, after I'd closed Facebook.

'You have no right to ask me that. I've been at a friend's.'

'A friend?'

'Yes. A friend, Pete.' I opened the British Airways website and began the process of checking in online. 'What did you expect me to do while you were away? Sit around in the apartment moping that you don't love me any more?'

'I do love you,' he said, but the sentiment lacked conviction. 'I'm just not *in* love—'

'Oh no, don't tell me you're going to say it. It's such a cliché.'

Pete rolled his eyes. 'Clichés are clichés for a reason. Because they make sense and are commonly—' he stopped and peered over my shoulder. 'Are you googling a cliché?'

'Yes,' I said, scrolling. 'The definition of a cliché is "*a phrase or opinion that is overused and betrays a lack of original thought*".' I looked up at Pete. 'That's you all over.'

Pete fumed. I went back to the British Airways page and completed the online check-in.

'Look Jess, we need to talk,' Pete said, once I'd shut the laptop.

'Oh yes?' I said, walking past him to the kitchen and getting a bottle of water from the fridge. 'What about?'

'Us,' he said, and then he launched into a quick, noticeably practised, monologue. 'I think we're going in different directions. It's nothing that either of us has done but sometimes people change.'

By the tone of his voice it sounded like he'd read an article on the gentlemanly way to break up with your girlfriend and was following the advice to the letter. He was playing Mr Reasonable as if I was the little woman who was going to lose control of her emotions. Well, I wouldn't let him have that satisfaction.

'We've grown apart. We were so young when we got together and I think we've become different people.'

He seemed like he was in a hurry to have the conversation. Like he'd worked out what he would say, how I would react and now he just wanted it to be over so he could get on with his life.

'It's not me, it's you?' I said, affecting a breezy casualness. 'We want different things? You will always love me, you're just not *in* love with me? You hope we can be friends and you'll always cherish the time we had together?'

Pete's face hardened. He hated being made fun of. But he had no right to be angry with me. He left me alone on our holiday, cheated on me with a girl who looked like she'd been computer-generated by a sexually frustrated, *Game-of-Thrones*-forum-frequenting gamer and now he was being clichéd in our official break-up conversation. My rational side didn't want either of us to be hurt. But she was still in the back putting on lip balm and moisturising with organic coconut oil, so the devilish side was in charge. I was done thinking that this was all my fault.

'Pete?'

'Yeah?'

'Fuck you.' I pushed past him and headed towards the bedroom to pack.

Pete followed. 'We *do* want different things,' he said through gritted teeth. He really was trying to maintain his 'I'm the good guy here' role.

'No,' I spat, while struggling to reach my suitcase on the top of the wardrobe. 'You want the direction of internet fame and girls with no cellulite or armpit hair and I want the direction I've always wanted. This is your doing. It's you. All fucking you!'

Pete sighed and got our suitcases down. I snatched mine out of his hands, threw it on the bed and fussed with the combination lock.

'I'm staying in Cape Town.'

'You're what?' I spun around.

He crossed his arms over his lavender polo shirt that he maintained was cornflower blue. 'For an extra week. My boss has already approved it.'

'Where will you stay? You can't stay here.'

Priya was due home the next day and there was no way he'd come out alive once I'd told her what had happened.

'Goat has a spare room.'

I narrowed my eyes. 'And where is his cousin staying?'

Pete went pale and averted his gaze. I could see it as plain as the day was hot and sunny. He'd fallen for her. Hard.

'Right,' I threw open the suitcase lid. 'Well, have fun.'

Pete stood behind me, twitching and fidgeting.

'There's something else.'

'Oh yes?' I said, pulling clothes out of the wardrobe and rolling them up like logs of sushi to save space the way Dad had taught me.

'OK ...' He commenced pacing. 'God, I can't believe I'm saying this but ... Fuck. OK. Shiiiit.' He dragged his hand through his neatly clipped hair but he wore so much gel the style barely moved. 'Oh fuck. OK. OK.' He stopped pacing and guided me to sit on the edge of the bed.

I looked back at him with a neutral expression. I wanted to let the 'confession' play out. I wanted him to squirm.

'OK. OK ...' He took in a deep breath then whooshed it out through tense nostrils. 'I cheated on you. With Giselle. Goat's cousin.'

He watched for my reaction but I gave none. I sat next to my open suitcase, waiting for more.

'Shit. Fuck. I can't believe this is happening. Fuck. God. Shit.' He paced again. 'I never meant for it to happen but it just did and, I mean, I thought we were pretty much over anyway. I never wanted to hurt you and, it's just, we connected on a whole other—' He stopped pacing and looked at me with wild eyes. 'Say something!'

I looked back at him.

'You have to say something! It's killing me that I did this to you! Shiiiit!'

I stood, picked up my bikini and towel, threw them in a beach bag and walked out of the bedroom.

'What are you doing?' Pete said, confused.

I continued walking through the apartment until I reached the front door.

Pete strode after me. '*WHAT* is going on?'

I turned around in the open doorway. 'I know you cheated on me,' I said, my voice calm.

Pete's face dropped.

'You really ought to learn a bit more about social media

291

if you're going to make it your new thing. People see everything.'

Half an hour later, probably after telling Giselle how it had gone, Pete came and found me next to the pool. He waved at the pool attendant then sat on a nearby lounger, his elbows resting on his knees.

'I'm really sorry,' he said. 'I'm sorry about ... about all of this.'

I shrugged. I was glad I had my oversized dark glasses on. After a lengthy silence, in which I pretended to read a magazine but was actually just flipping pages trying not to cry, Pete cleared his throat uncomfortably.

'I don't feel needed when I'm with you,' he said in a quiet, embarrassed voice.

'Needed?'

'Everybody wants to feel needed in a relationship. And you don't need me. It makes me feel ...' Pete searched for the word. 'Dispensable, I guess.'

'That's ridiculous,' I said. 'But you're right. I've never *needed* you – I'm independent. I've *wanted* you, though.' I made sure to use the past tense because, despite how sad and betrayed I felt right then, I knew that I didn't want him any more either.

Pete flicked his gaze to the approaching pool attendant, conveying that no, now was not the time to talk paragliding and abseiling and HIIT reps. The attendant understood and turned his attention to a slightly skew-whiff sun lounger.

'You're *too* independent,' Pete said.

'You can't be too independent,' I scoffed. 'I'm the right amount of independent. You should be happy I've not been one of those girlfriends who can't go to a party without attaching themselves to your sides.'

'We go to a party and you take off and I don't see you all night!'

'You mean like you on this holiday?'

Pete gave me a look.

I closed my magazine. 'Anyway, we see each other all the time. Parties are for talking to new people.'

'Well, I guess that's another area where we differ.'

'I guess so,' I grumbled.

We sat quietly for another few moments.

'So, you're here for another week?' I said.

'Yeah. There are a few youth group activities that Goat is going to and I really think it will help with what I have planned.'

'What exactly do you have planned?'

'I don't know. I just feel like I'm on to something and I know I want to do more for the kids, you know.'

'So then what? You come back to London and ... what?'

'There's a guy at work I can stay with for a few weeks till I get myself sorted.'

I nodded. Pete had this all planned out.

'This is all so fucked up.' I sniffed, trying to hold back tears. 'I thought we'd be leaving together.'

Pete nodded, looking saddened.

'I thought we'd be going home engaged.'

Pete nodded again.

'I thought we'd be together for the rest of our lives and we'd have a boy and a girl and I'd start a blog and get a dog, I'm not meaning to rhyme by the way, it just worked out that way, and—'

Pete looked less sad and more impatient.

'I thought we'd have a nice life together,' I finished off quietly. I looked beyond Pete's shoulder, across the tops of the apartments towards Table Mountain, monolithic and malevolent. 'It's all *that's* fault.'

Pete looked behind him at Table Mountain then turned back to me with an expression of practised regret. 'It would have happened anyway, eventually.'

I turned away from him and looked across the harbour at the dazzling ocean.

'Oh, fuck off, Pete.'

CHAPTER TWENTY-SEVEN

'I'm sorry I have to be quick! I'm late!' I said, rushing into Sylvie's restaurant and sidestepping waiters bustling about, setting tables. I navigated various dogs and headed to where Jimmy was standing behind the big gold bar with a serious expression. 'I realised I hadn't got Annabelle and the kids any presents so I quickly packed and Trust took me to the Waterfront, and oh my god the traffic getting out of there was mental, and—' I stopped, realising Jimmy's face wasn't its usual sunny and happy self, and that perhaps I should have come in a little less manic seeing as we were going to have yet another emotional goodbye. 'What?'

Jimmy came out from behind the bar, pressed my phone into my hands and pulled me to the side. 'I think you were right,' he said, his voice low and his face ashen. 'About the vagina artist.'

'What are you talking about?' I said, my mind on traffic/check-in time calculations.

'The vagina artist turned up and I think, yeah ...' He frowned in the direction of the gallery. 'I think you were right.'

'Right about what?'

'He's in there now, setting up.' Jimmy looked awkward. 'With his family.'

I slowed my racing mind and forced myself to think about what Jimmy was saying. Vagina Artist. In the Gallery. With his family. I was right ...?

'No,' I shook my head. 'He's a local.'

Jimmy looked nervous as I wove through tables and chairs to the open gallery door and looked in. Frankie, her pink hair tips up in a chignon, and a slim lady with her hair in a ballet dancer's bun, stood with their backs to us appraising the positioning of a vaginal sketch on the far wall, perhaps fifteen metres from us. There was no man. Two blond children sat on a leather bench nearby, their backs also to us, looking at an iPad. I turned to Jimmy, confused. He motioned for me to keep looking so I turned back.

Sylvie came out from behind a partition in the middle of the room, about five metres from where Jimmy and I stood peering around the edge of the doorframe. 'If you're allowed, you can ask the kitchen staff for some ice cream,' she said to the two kids.

The children, a boy who looked about nine and a girl of perhaps eleven or twelve, looked in the direction of someone behind the partition and said 'Can we?' in sweet little South African accents.

I turned to Jimmy and made to start the phrase, 'What the f—' when I heard my father's voice and my stomach dropped.

'Well, just this once. Aren't you lucky?' he said, just like he used to when Annabelle and I were young and someone had offered us something special and not of Mum's dietary specifications. Then my father stepped out from behind the partition. My father. The vagina artist, who'd been in Mozambique with his 'family'.

My breath caught in my throat and I felt dizzy. I put a hand on the doorframe to stop the room from spinning. Jimmy's hand rested on my arm.

It was him.

It was really him.

I wanted to run away. I wanted to keep watching. I wanted to faint. Time seemed to slow. My feet felt anchored to the floor. Dad accepted a hug from the boy, took the iPad from the girl and the children turned and skipped towards the doorway. Dad, without looking in our direction, walked to the far wall and joined Frankie, Sylvie and the lady with the ballet bun who was adjusting the information card underneath a painting. The kids bustled through the doorway, barely registering us in their pursuit of pudding. I felt like I might vomit as the bun lady placed her slender hand, which sported a large solitaire diamond, affectionately on Dad's shoulder and turned to Frankie.

'It took such a long time to convince him to exhibit,' she said in a melodic South African accent.

Dad slipped his arm around the slender-handed lady's

slender waist. She turned and smiled at him and I saw her profile. She was probably only about forty.

Just then Trust burst into the restaurant, rousing me from my nauseous trance. 'Miss Jess!' he called from the open front door at the other side of the room. I ducked out of the gallery doorway and fell against the wall. 'We must go!' He tapped his wrist urgently even though he didn't wear a watch.

I looked up at Jimmy and backed away. 'Did you know? Did you know this whole time?' I remembered him looking at the photo of Dad when Pete and I had first met him.

Jimmy shook his head, frowning with confusion.

'Miss Jess!' Trust said urgently.

I turned and ran out of the gallery, wanting to be far away from whatever the hell I had just seen.

Jimmy rushed after me. 'Wait!'

I dived into the open van door. Trust slid it shut and I turned in my seat. Through the restaurant window I could see Dad and the lady walk across the room and join the children at the bar. As Trust screeched away from the kerb I looked at Jimmy standing on the footpath watching me leave with a look of anguish, and the gravity of the situation hit me.

'I will drive fast, but traffic—'

'It's OK, Trust,' I said, turning on my phone. 'It's my fault. Just do the best you can.'

Trust nodded and made some decisive lane changes. My phone came alive with the apple chime and Jimmy rang through immediately.

'I didn't know, I *swear*,' he said as soon as I answered. 'When he came in with his English accent I just put two and two together. So that guy is your dad? Oh my god, you were right. I'm so sorry, are you OK? I can't believe it's your dad! Are you sure? Of course you know your own dad, but are you *really* sure?' He was babbling and I had to close my eyes to calm myself. I still thought I might throw up. Trust's hurried swerving wasn't helping.

'Yeah ...' I said, the words hitting home. 'That was my dad.'

'Christ,' Jimmy said. 'Do you want me to do anything?'

'Yes please,' I said, my chest burning with a sudden hot anger. 'I want you to punch him in the face.'

'Right,' Jimmy said. 'I'm not going to do that ...'

'Shit,' I breathed in and out. 'I don't think there's anything you can ... Actually, yes. Can you find out as much as you can about that lady he's with and ... actually no, I need to ... yes. No, I know ... no, that's not a very ...' I trailed off feeling both horribly in the moment and also like I was watching it all happen to someone else. Like how you feel after a night of missed sleep, which you've tried to counteract with far too much caffeine; distant and detached yet wired and keenly alert.

'Um ...' Jimmy sounded tentative. 'I'm not clear on the ... the, ah ... proceedings.'

I swallowed, trying to get my thoughts in order. 'Do nothing.'

'OK,' he said, sounding relieved.

'But maybe see if you can get the name of the lady he's with? And her age.'

'Right.'

'And also the names and ages of those kids. And also try and find out where he lives and if he has two mobiles, and also—'

'Hang on, I need a pen.'

'No, don't worry about it,' I said, pinching the bridge of my nose. 'Just do nothing like I asked.'

'Right,' Jimmy said, sounding confused.

'God, this is so fucked up.'

'I know,' Jimmy said. 'I really want to do something for you but I don't know what.'

'That's OK,' I said, and I began to feel nauseous again. 'I'd better go. I'll call you later.'

I got off the phone and saw that there were a bunch of missed calls and text messages from Priya asking me to call her back IMMEDIATELY. They were all from that morning.

'Babe!' Priya said down the phone. 'I've got something awful to tell you. I'm going to need you to sit down. And get Pete with you, OK, because, I'm really sorry babe, but this is bad.'

'Oh god, what?' I said. My mind couldn't dredge up a more horrifying scenario. I was all panicked out, it seemed. 'Are you OK? Is Laurel all right?'

'We're fine, babe. It's about your dad.'

'Oh.'

'OK, sorry about this, but Laurel and I were leaving our

resort today and we saw your dad. With a young family. Two kids. Hot lady. Babe, you know I always like to see the positive, but … It didn't look good. It looked … intimate, you know?'

I was quiet. Obviously I'd already seen what I had seen but this additional information made it hit home harder. That was really him: the local on holiday in Mozambique with his family. But he was *my* father. He lived at home with Mum. It didn't make any sense.

'Babe? Are you OK?' She said some panicked, muffled words to someone, I assumed Laurel. 'Oh god, babe, are you OK? Are you there?'

'Yeah, I'm here,' I said, my voice croaky.

'I would have gone over there and kicked his arse but we were getting on a ferry to go back to the mainland to get our flight tomorrow and he was boarding a sea plane. And it's Teddy Roberts! It's your *dad*! I know it doesn't make any sense but I saw what I saw, babe, and I'm so, so sorry.'

'That's OK.'

'Babe, put Pete on. I'll tell him you need lots of looking after. Are you at the airport?'

'We've broken up. He cheated on me and is staying here with that guy, Goat, from *The Bachelor* who he idolises and I'm stuck in traffic and might miss my flight.' I started to cry. 'Priya, everything has gone to shit. I just want to go home.'

'Whaaaaaat?!' Priya shrieked down the phone then turned and quickly told everything to Laurel. She came back on, incensed. 'Pete is a muthafucking cunty possum-faced wank bastard fuck-hole . . .' She kept ranting and I had to hold the phone away from my ear. 'What the fuck!?! Oh my god, I feel like this is all my fault! God, you were going to go back engaged and now Pete is fan-boying over Goat and your dad has a whole second family!'

I hadn't put that sentence together yet. Obviously those words were exactly the ones you'd use to describe the thin-handed lady and his two kids who were nearly the same age as his grandson, but I hadn't said them out loud. And neither had the psycho in my head. Where was she? Taking a lavender oil bath?

'What do you want me to do?'

I didn't know. I didn't know anything about anything.

'Nothing,' I said. 'Just get home safely.'

'OK,' she said, her voice calmer now. 'Love you, babe.'

'I know. I love you too.'

I hung up and looked ahead at the lanes of traffic. It was moving. Slowly. Trust threw quick glances my way while he navigated vehicles in various states of disrepair. I checked the time. It was going to be a fine line if I made the flight or not. Exactly how I started this trip two long weeks ago. Except in very different circumstances to those I found myself in now. No boyfriend, a cheating father and Annabelle not being constantly at the forefront of my mind. Plus a little tired from all the shagging I'd been doing with a bartending, scriptwriting muso who lived in the basement of his brother's place.

I dialled Annabelle's number.

'Hi. I'm just in the middle of the kids' dinner.'

'It's Dad,' I said miserably. 'He's got a whole second family. For real this time. Jimmy saw it, Priya saw it and I saw it. I don't know what we're going to do! What about Mum? What about us? He's got a *whole second family*, Annabelle!'

'OK,' Annabelle said, her voice soothing. 'OK. Just take a second to breathe.'

I took a deep breath in and eased it out.

'Good. Now tell me what happened. Slowly.'

Annabelle listened without judgement as I explained about Jimmy and the phone, Sylvie and the ice cream, the thin-handed lady and her diamond, Frankie and her pink hair tips, Dad and his arm around thin hand lady, about Trust bursting in and me being late for the flight, about how I ran out of there without confronting Dad and how I was currently regretting that decision because I was sitting in a van in traffic, probably going to miss my flight anyway, with a shit ton of accusations.

'And don't think you can convince me out of this disaster,' I said. 'It's exactly what I thought it was! I can't *believe* you made me doubt my intuition.'

'Well,' Annabelle said diplomatically, 'it's just that your intuition is generally, psychotically, paranoically, drastically incorrect.'

'I concur,' I said as Trust made a few brisk and frightening lane swerves. 'But this time I'm right. So what should we do about it? Should I call him? Should I forget my flight and go back there? What should we *do*?!'

I started crying, Trust got worried and kept looking away

from the road and making questionable driving choices, and Annabelle told me not to call Dad and just to get home and we would sort it out together. Then she had to go and get Hunter down from the top of the fridge, and suddenly the traffic opened up; Trust and I had a tearful yet brief goodbye, check-in was relatively empty and I made my flight.

CHAPTER TWENTY-EIGHT

I dragged myself off the plane and through the rigmarole of baggage collection, passport control and onto the tube without engaging with any of it. Is it possible to have your mind racing without actually thinking about anything? Fragments of thoughts came to me: Jimmy's face when we said goodbye the first, second, third and final time; Dad's young kids and how they looked at him; Dad's young *kids(?!)*; Pete and his eagerness to get back to Goat (Giselle); that super-large crepe from the market, shark flags, Ian in his white NSYNC outfit, Diego saying Jimmy liked me, Ian's cologne, Diego's pancakes, gluten day, Jimmy's face on gluten day, Pete's face on confession day. Dad and his kids. Dad and his kids. Dad and his god damned kids ...

I stood on the tube, my bag between my feet and my winter coat, which had been in in my suitcase, weighing heavily on my shoulders. It made me feel burdened and cumbersome after the last two weeks of shorts, flip-flops and summer vests. As the movement of the carriage jolted me back and forth I began to feel more awake and questions popped into my head. Are those kids my half-brother and sister? Did the little girl look a bit like a blonde Annabelle? Dad draws vaginas? Does he have a model? Was that woman with the thin hands his wife and vagina model? Was Mum ever his vagina model? Why in Christ's holy pyjamas do I have to contend with THAT mental picture?! The thin hand woman had a big diamond on her finger. Mum had never worn such extravagance, preferring to give money to those more needy (generally an obscure charity that nobody ever donated to, like 'slam poetry counselling' or 'save the British house spider' even though most people were busy flushing the things down the plughole) – so why did that woman get a big diamond? Did Dad *know* he had a second family? It sounded ridiculous but Dad was a little vague at the best of times. Perhaps he had some kind of weird affliction that caused a person to live a double life without ever fully knowing it? Maybe it was a new kind of brain tumour that, once diagnosed, would be named after him, and our family situation would end up in a celebrated oncology dissertation? Thoughts such at these flew in and out, but nothing stayed in my mind long enough to fully explore.

One hour and four train changes later I arrived at Annabelle's. I walked in and fell into her delicate arms, relishing the familiar smell of her Sunday-morning special:

cinnamon and coconut porridge. Katie, in pink flannel pyjamas, ran over followed by the thundering footsteps of Hunter.

'AUNTY JESS!!' He screeched.

Katie made excited squeals.

'Kiss sandwich?' I said, crouching down, and each of my flight-parched cheeks received a giggly kiss.

I was desperate for a Katie cuddle. I scooped her up. In the past I thought there was nothing a Katie cuddle couldn't solve but now, with her unyielding arms around my neck, I wasn't so sure. Tears trickled down my cheeks.

'So,' I said, leaning forward and setting my coffee on the polished coffee table fifteen minutes later. I sank into my favourite spot on the sofa, where the cushions were neatly lined up instead of in their usual haphazard manner. Hunter and Katie sat on the floor occupied with the gifts I'd given them. 'How are we going to tell Mum?'

'We just tell her.' Annabelle curled her legs under her in the armchair opposite and spoke over the top of her mug of herbal tea, the steam curling past her delicate nostrils. 'What else can we do?'

I nodded and wondered how Mum would react. She was nearly seventy and she'd been with Dad most of her life.

'Where's Pete?' Annabelle said.

I looked at her strangely then realised I hadn't even told her about him cheating and staying in Cape Town to find himself, become an internet sensation and fuck Giselle.

I huffed out an angry exhale. 'You know this trip, apart from Priya's wedding and shagging Jimmy, was a complete disaster.'

While Hunter helped Katie do a puzzle on Hunter's bedroom floor, Annabelle and I sat in the living room. I told my sister about seeing Pete kissing Giselle on Goat's Instagram, about Jimmy at the festival saying he really liked me and how I'd turned him down, about the rainy day on the sofa that ended up in an afternoon of unbelievable sex (which technically wasn't cheating because Pete cheated first and fuck him, anyway). Then I got distracted by describing Giselle and her airbrushed-like skin and said I was growing out my fringe and that Botox actually sounded kind of harmless, and somehow ended up on how pissed off I was that I got sat next to a man on the plane who had Alzheimer's and kept tapping his wife to ask the same questions over and over, keeping me awake. I'd felt bad about being annoyed by the Alzheimer's man and spent the rest of the plane ride worrying that I'd end up with Alzheimer's myself, which would be the universe's way of punishing me for being intolerant. Annabelle's expression told me I hadn't had enough sleep and needed to calm down. I turned down her offer of a 'smoothie' and went into the kitchen and ditched the coffee for camomile tea.

Around 2 p.m., as I napped on the sofa, the sound of a van door sliding shut alerted us to Mum's arrival. Annabelle and

I gave each other a fortifying look, then went outside to greet her.

'Oh my deary dears, hello!' she said, leaping out of the van and gripping me in a bony hug. She smelt faintly of ylang ylang and vegetable stock. 'You look so well! And tanned. Why are you tanned? Where've you been?' She frowned. 'Did you leave Annabelle *on her own*? Did you use sunscreen? You know that stuff is full of chemicals, don't you? It's best to just wear long sleeves and a big hat.'

'Hi Mum,' Annabelle said, taking the suitcase from the driver who looked only too keen to dump and run. I imagined Mum had gabbed the poor man's ears to bleeding point after being silent for so long.

Mum spun around. 'Oh my dear Belle-belle, have you coped? Did Jess leave you? I'm so sorry I stayed away longer, I had my eyes opened to the guilt we all carry and I had to do some serious inner work. Did Wayne call you? Where are my delicious grandchildren?'

We hustled Mum out of the cold, let Katie and Hunter leap all over her, chuckled at their faces when presented with dreamcatchers made of foraged plant matter, then Annabelle set them up in Hunter's bunk bed with a movie and the three of us made tea in the kitchen.

'Can we make you something to eat?' I asked Mum. 'A sandwich?'

'We have grain-free bread?' Annabelle offered.

Mum flapped her wrinkly hands. 'No, no, no,' she said. 'I don't eat like that any more.'

'Like what?' I said.

'Like that: this lettuce, with that tomato, with that bread, with this chicken. The body doesn't know what to do with all the different things at the same time! Oh, the poor body. It's called Mono Meal-ing. I'll tell you all about it. No, I shall just have the tomatoes, please, if you have them. And the lettuce a little later.'

'Right.'

While Annabelle got the tomatoes I made tea, then we moved to the living room, Mum chatting about the benefits of eating only one food item at each meal, giving the body the respect it deserves while it performs the 'wondrous, delicately balanced art of digestion'.

'You know, you can actually feel your body responding to the nutrients if you have them one by one,' Mum said, taking a seat at one end of the sofa. 'Now are you going to tell me where you had to go that was so important you left Annabelle *on her own*?' She frowned at me again.

I sat at the opposite end and turned to face her. 'Mum, we have something to tell you.'

'Is it about Katie?' Mum's face paled and she drew a worried palm to her pendant.

'No! Nothing like that. Katie's been doing really well, hasn't she, Annabelle?'

'*Really* well,' Annabelle said, settling into her armchair.

'So, then, what is it?'

'It's about Dad . . .'

Mum looked worriedly from me to Annabelle. 'Is he OK?'

'He's fine,' Annabelle said.

'Hardly,' I snorted at the same time.

Annabelle gave me a look. Mum glanced between the two of us, confused.

'This is going to be really hard to hear,' I said. Annabelle had thought it best I just come out and say it: succinctly and plainly. Annabelle said I was to stick to the facts and not get carried away with anger just yet. We needed to let Mum know that we would be here for her no matter what. With this plan in mind I began the succinct, clear speech I'd been practising in my head. 'I went to South Africa and I—'

'SOUTH AFRICA?!' Mum shrieked, looking horrified.

'Yes, and when I was there—'

'What on earth for?!'

'Priya's wedding. But Mum—'

'Priya got married? To that nice lesbian girl?'

'Yes, to Laurel. The nice lesbian girl. And Priya is a lesbian too, you know, Mum. That's how lesbianism works. Priya—'

Annabelle made a throat-clearing noise.

'Anyway,' I said, nodding to Annabelle. 'When I was in Cape Town I saw Dad.'

I waited for Mum's reaction but she just looked at me as if she was waiting for the real nugget of information.

'With a woman,' I continued. 'A *younger* woman. Who had a *really* big diamond and nice clothes and—'

Annabelle made a 'get back on track' little cough.

I glanced at her and nodded. 'And it's true, it's *all true*, because there was this dog hotel/restaurant/gallery-type place doing an exhibition. Of vaginas. And they were really—'

Annabelle coughed again.

'Anyway, they told me the paintings were by someone who was away in Mozambique "with his family". And then when I went in there to get my phone from this guy Jimmy, who I met and hung out with because Pete was up the Cederbergs with some bitch called—'

'*Jess*,' Annabelle said.

'Sorry.' I looked at Mum, her eyes flitting back and forth between her two daughters, a look of non-comprehension on her face and really, who could blame her.

'Mum,' I said, getting my thoughts in order. 'The thing is . . .' I paused. I just had to say it. 'Dad has a whole second family in South Africa. A young wife and two children. I saw them. I saw them with my own eyes.' Tears welled and I sniffed back a sob.

Mum sat very still. She blinked and breathed and burnt calories at her resting metabolic rate, but that was about it.

'Mum?' I said, searching her face for horror, hurt and/or anger.

She fiddled with her tiger's eye pendant, her eyes glassy and unfocused. Annabelle and I looked at each other. I ran my hand under my dripping nose.

'Mum?' Annabelle said. 'Did you hear Jess?'

Our tiny mother sat still, her knees pressed neatly together, encased in brown wool slacks. She seemed to take up no space at all on Annabelle's sofa.

'They drugged her on that course! I knew it!' I shuffled along the sofa and grabbed hold of Mum's hands. 'Did you leave your sherry unattended at any point?'

Annabelle shook her head. 'They weren't drinking.'

'Oh,' I said, nodding. I sniffed back my burgeoning tears and turned back to my spaced-out mother. 'Did you leave your lentils unattended?'

'What?' Mum said, clicking back to attention. 'Lentils? Yes, Plum, I think I could probably get you the recipe ...' Her eyes lost focus again and fell on a point somewhere between the floor and La La Land.

'They've brainwashed her!' I said. 'I *knew* it was some kind of cult.'

'She's in shock.' Annabelle said gently. 'Mum?'

Mum looked up. 'Yes?'

'Did you understand what Jess just said?'

Mum's eyes darted from me to Annabelle. 'Yes.'

'Then you ought to be reacting to this news a little differently than you currently are!' I cried.

Mum blinked at me. Then turned and blinked at Annabelle. 'I suppose I should ring your father,' she said.

'That's a good idea.' I shot into the kitchen, retrieved Mum's phone from where Annabelle had it charging and raced back to the living room.

It took her a few moments to get her passcode right, during which time I'd bitten nearly all my fingernails off and had starting chewing the edge of my sleeve. Once the phone was unlocked, Mum hesitated a moment before dialling. The room was silent while we waited for the call to connect. This was it. There would be tears. There would be anger. There would be accusations and denials and our family might never be the same again.

'Hello dear,' Mum said into the phone. 'We have a slight problem . . .'

I frowned. *Understatement!*

'No, she's fine, no need to panic.'

What?! Oh, I think there was a very real need to panic. In fact I'd been doing it for weeks, and was hoping the rest of the family would join me. I spun to see Annabelle's expression. She had her eyes narrowed on Mum.

'Yes . . . yes, I'm afraid so . . . I'm awfully sorry . . .' Mum twirled a finger round her necklace, her brows in the shape of concern, not utter fury like they ought to have been.

What the fuck was happening? I looked to Annabelle, whose face had hardened.

'OK, I will, love. I know . . . Yes we did, we did . . . Bye dear.' Mum got off the phone, placed it purposefully on the coffee table in front of her and after what felt like an age, lifted her gaze.

'What the fuck was that about?!' I squawked.

'Well, girls,' Mum straightened her already straight slacks, played with her pendant, pinched at her turtleneck collar. 'That was your father.'

I made a 'duh' face.

'And he . . . well, *I* . . . you see, your father and I . . .' Mum turned to me. 'Plum, the people you saw with your father . . .'

'Yes?' I said.

'Well . . . it's not what you think.' Mum shook her head, her neat grey hair bobbing back and forth. 'Those children are . . .'

'Are . . .?' I pressed.

'And that woman, Maryna is her name—'

'You know her?!'

'Not personally, but I . . . well, she's—'

'SPIT IT OUT, MUM!'

Mum jumped at the volume of my voice then blurted her explanation. '*Dein vater ist verheiratet! Die frau die du gesehen hast, ist seine tochter und die kinder sind seine enkel! Die wahrheit ist, ich bin die geliebte und wir sind familie nummer zwei! So, das war's!*'

'*In English,*' I said through gritted teeth.

'Of course.' Mum looked from me to Annabelle again. 'The thing is . . . The thing is . . .'

'What's the friggin' thing?!' I roared, making Mum jump again.

'Plum, it's very complicated but your father and I . . . well, more to the point *you two girls and I*, we're . . .'

'We're the second family,' Annabelle said, her voice quiet and loaded with realisation.

Mum's eyes widened behind her glasses. With her turtle-neck jumper it gave her the impression of a startled tortoise. Her stunned gaze flitted between Annabelle and me. Then her face dropped.

'Yes,' she said to her lap.

All the blood rushed from my head. I felt faint.

Mum's hands worried her pendant again. She looked from Annabelle, still and expressionless, to me, fighting back a panic attack. '*Schiessen*,' she muttered.

CHAPTER TWENTY-NINE

The whole room was silent save for the chink-chink-chink of Mum fidgeting with a new and unsightly beaded bracelet.

'That lady Jess saw with Dad is his *daughter*?' Annabelle said, stony-faced, leading Mum through the confession while I sat reeling and mentally scanning myself for signs of a stroke.

'. . . Yes,' Mum said.

'And those children . . .?'

Mum flicked her eyes around the room before settling them on her lap. 'Are his grandchildren.' Mum lowered her voice. 'Scarlett and Renzo.'

The fact that they had names shocked me. Scarlett and Renzo. Who were they to me? My half-niece and nephew?

After a long stretch of quiet Mum turned in my direction. 'It's not a young wife and young children, you see. It's not as bad as you thought, Plum.'

I glared back at her, feeling really quite unhinged. 'It's not great, Mum!'

'No . . .'

I fell back against the sofa.

Annabelle sat opposite in her armchair, her inner thoughts indecipherable on her blank face.

Mum looked up from her lap, affecting a problem-solving kind of tone. 'You know, I have a book at home I bought for such an occasion as this. Shall I pop back and get it?'

She tried to stand and Annabelle fixed her with a glare. Mum sat back down.

'I think you need to go back to that "work through your guilt" retreat for the next forty years, Mum,' I said. 'How . . . how did this even happen?'

'Well, that's a rather complicated story.'

'Then I'll need food,' I said, starting to feel a little peaky.

'That's a good idea. I've hardly eaten since the retreat. You know, I think they use starvation as some kind of mind control thing. I'm not sure I agree—'

'Mum!'

She flinched. 'Yes, sorry Plum. Not the right time. I'll tell you about it later. And you must tell me about your trip.'

I glared at her.

'At a more appropriate time,' she conceded.

'Yes.'

With a plate of lettuce for Mum and seeded loaf toast spread with almond butter for Annabelle and me, Mum began her confession.

'I met your father when my parents and I came to England for my last year of school. I guess you could say Teddy and I were high school sweethearts.' She turned to me, her eyes shining. 'Like you and Pete.'

I swallowed down a tacky mouthful of toast. I'd tell Mum about that calamity after we got to the bottom of the current one.

'I went back to Bavaria for university and your father stayed here. We spent all our money on train rides visiting each other,' Mum said, her expression wistful. 'Then, after university I moved back to London and we lived in a little studio flat in Angel. It was perfect. I had a research job at the local radio station and your father started with a small international real estate company that seemed to be going places. Then the company offered him a promotion but it came with a one-year placement in South Africa.' Mum's face dropped. She played with her pendant, seemingly lost in that particular moment of sorrow then continued her story, Annabelle and I listening attentively.

'I'd just gone back to university to get my master's so couldn't go with him. We planned to keep in touch as much as possible, but communications from South Africa were difficult back then. We didn't have all this chat on the face-booktime or the internets that your lot have, we had to rely on letters or costly phone calls.' She shook her head at us like our generation were somehow to blame for not coming up with Facebook Messenger earlier. Her jaw tightened and she continued. 'Teddy's one-year placement became two, and then three and before we knew it he was based in South Africa permanently and his once-a-year trips home were not enough.' Mum sniffed and dragged a sad-looking hanky out from her sleeve. 'I didn't hear from Teddy for over a year. I finished my master's, I got a job on the radio, I dated Patrick for a while—'

'*Patrick?!* Patrick from your radio show?' I spluttered. I looked over to Annabelle, checking she was as shocked by this additional bit of information as I was, but she remained, as she had been throughout this entire process, guarded and pensive. 'Patrick, your producer Patrick?'

Mum looked at me like I ought to have known that information. 'Yes, Plum.' She frowned. 'Oh, but Patrick was a nice enough man and very ethical and, of course, very dear to me, but it wasn't fair. I'd given my heart to one man and it wasn't ever coming back.'

My eyes flicked to Annabelle again. She sat very still, waiting for the rest of Mum's explanation.

'Then one year, I was at an old school friend's birthday party and Teddy walked in. I hadn't seen him for four years.' Mum blew her nose into her hanky. 'It was then I learnt that Teddy had married and was expecting his first child.' Her eyes watered and her face crumpled like she was experiencing the hurt all over again. 'I was broken-hearted,' she wept. 'I left the party immediately.' She paused to blow her nose again, then composed herself and continued.

'Your father phoned the next day but I hung up on him.

Then he turned up at my flat, calling to me from the street below. It was very romantic. He wanted to remain friends but I couldn't. I just couldn't!' She sniffed copiously. 'He told me he'd never stopped loving me. But I told him to go and leave me alone and never speak to me again! It was horrible! *Horrible*. I was a mess. I baked and ate two chocolate fudge cakes and then fell asleep for a day and half.' Mum sniffed and caught her breath. 'I didn't see him for perhaps another couple of years but then his father died and I went to the funeral.' She rested her gaze somewhere in the past. 'His wife and his two-year-old daughter stayed in Cape Town because they didn't have the money to all come out. It was very expensive in those days, you see.'

A lump formed in my throat. How awful it must have been for Mum.

She took in a shaky breath and continued. 'At the wake I went over to offer my condolences. He looked so sad and yet so happy to see me and we realised none of the feelings had gone. If anything . . .' Mum's eyes began watering again. 'If anything the time and the distance had made our halted love more intoxicating.

'Your father stayed in London for two weeks while he moved his mother into a home,' Mum said, casting her eyes downwards. 'He spent every night with me.' She twisted the ratty hanky in her wrinkled fingers. 'I am ashamed.' She looked up and wiped away a tear. 'But I have loved your father from the moment I saw him in his school uniform with his incompetently knotted tie and his text books falling out of his satchel.' She blew her nose. 'He was my first and only love.'

'But ... but what about us?' I said, feeling both terrible pity for my mother and also a growing sense of injustice. Annabelle and I were unknowingly made a part of an appalling, hurtful lie.

'Well, by that stage your father had been made a partner in the company and was spending many weeks travelling with clients. He'd move between the London and Cape Town offices so we saw each other regularly. When he was here he was with me. And we lived life like a normal couple. When he was there he was with ... with her.' She had the decency to look embarrassed. 'Then we had you, Annabelle.' Mum smiled mistily in Annabelle's direction. 'And you, Jess,' she said, turning to me with wet, adoring eyes. 'And it's been going on so long there never seemed the right time to ... to stop, I guess.' Mum sniffed, sat back on the sofa and gave a tiny shrug of her tiny shoulders. 'There, you have it,' she said, weeping openly. 'My most wonderful love affair is also a most terrible act of deception.' She dissolved into tiny hiccuping sobs.

I looked over at Annabelle in the armchair. She was pale and appeared to have gone inside herself, processing everything we'd just heard.

'I'm so sorry,' Mum squeaked from behind her hanky. 'I'm so very, very sorry.'

I edged along the sofa, sat next to my mother and put my arm around her shoulders. I had so many questions: did the other family know about us? Did Dad ever think about leaving us? Did he love both Mum and his wife equally? And if he did, how was that possible? But my main question was, WHAT THE FUCK WERE YOU THINKING?!

CHAPTER THIRTY

We paused the most shocking, life-flipping conversation I'd ever been involved in while we went through the process of getting Hunter and Katie fed, bathed and into bed. Annabelle seemed to have perfected the routine in the two weeks we'd been gone, and the kids had helped to set the dinner table and then eaten their meal agreeably. Hunter had organised himself in and out of the shower and even remembered to hang up the bath mat. Something my flatmate Dave didn't even bother to put down in the first place, and he was twenty-eight. Once the kids were in bed we got stuck into the wine (and by 'we', I mean I drank enough for the three of us) and I asked Mum question after question with her getting more and more defensive while Annabelle listened quietly. Mum attempted to raise various diverting topics, asking about the South African weather, if I was going to cure my own biltong, if I'd seen a shark, the South African's stance on plastic bag usage, if I'd ever consider mono-mealing, seeing as I couldn't cook to save myself; but I disregarded her off-theme enquiries and continued to demand more information. Mum, it turned out, had gone back to Patrick at some point during her forty-year 'affair' with Dad.

'So you had an affair on your affair?' I said, stunned. 'Who *are* you?'

'Mum, you're worse than me,' Annabelle said, and we all fell apart with inappropriate giggles. I blamed the bottle and a half of wine I'd mainlined, the 'tea' with a cannabis tinge to it that Annabelle had had in place of dinner and the fact that Mum was delirious from her mono-mealing.

'Well, I guess technically that is what it was,' Mum said. 'But again, my heart wasn't in it and again I had to push Patrick away.' She shook her head. 'I was not fair to him. I did help him companion-sow his allotment, though.'

I sat at the dining table picking the label off the second wine bottle. As the facts became solid truths in my head, my feelings, which before had been stunned into immobility, started to mould around them. I felt shame, fear, anger, loss, sadness, grief and betrayal. But also in there was a tiny, teeny, almost undetectable sense of relief. I'd always wondered why I was such an anxious child, and now adult. We'd all put it down to Annabelle being so unruly but perhaps my subconscious knew something was up. It made me feel like there was a reason for my anxiety and I wasn't just 'a bit mental' as Pete had called me a handful of times. Usually with fondness.

'Didn't you feel hurt that Dad kept going back to his wife?' I said, as Mum sat at the other end of the table polishing glasses that didn't need polishing because they were from Asda. 'Weren't you mad he never properly broke up with you in the first place?'

Mum frowned but kept her eyes on the stubby tumbler.

'I can't believe he married someone else . . .' I said, picking at the wine label with intensity. 'Dad's been so . . . so . . .' I searched for the right word. 'So *unfair!*'

'Plum, calm down,' Mum said, still polishing. 'I knew what I was getting into. This is no more your father's fault than mine.'

I looked over to Annabelle. She gave a small yet sad smile that said 'I know, this sucks' while she prepared carrot sticks and other kid-healthy snack stuff at the kitchen bench. I turned back to my wine bottle.

'My childhood is a lie,' I said, picking at the label. 'All my memories, my ideas about who I was, who I *am* . . .' I picked some more, realising, with shame, who Annabelle and I were in this new arrangement. 'My dad was never even really mine.'

'Oh would you just . . . *be quiet*, Plum,' Mum said, looking flustered. 'Do you have to make it all about you *all* of the time?'

I frowned. 'I just found out my dad has a whole second family, Mum. That I'm a product of an *affair*. That my life is a *complete* lie.' I shot Annabelle a look of incredulity.

'Listen to you,' Mum said, abandoning her polishing and moving across the room to the ironing pile but looking oddly redundant upon finding out the ironing pile was already ironed. '"*My* dad, *my* life".' She patted the top of the crisp sheets. 'Now, where's Pete?'

'We broke up and I slept with a piano-playing bartender,' I said, waving my hand nonchalantly at her and moving towards another bottle of wine.

'What do you mean—'

Annabelle shook her head at Mum and, despite her attempts at trying to talk about Pete, or Katie, or climate change, or to try and go home and get the self-help book that was evidently going to make everything all right, Annabelle and I continued to ask Mum uncomfortable but necessary questions until we all went to bed, emotionally spent.

'Aunty Jess . . .' Hunter's heavy whisper came to me through a fug of deep sleep. 'Aunty Jess. Aunty Jeeeeeeee-eeeeeessssss.'

I opened one eye, the merlot-flavoured 'medication' I'd administered last night making itself very much known. 'Shhhhh,' I whispered, trying to smile but probably looking like a one-eyed, slack-jawed pirate. 'It's still night time.'

'Aunty Jess . . .' He breathed a little louder. 'You fart in your sleep.' His upside-down face grinned at me from the top bunk. 'It smells like sausages.'

At 6.11 a.m. I pulled on a pair of Annabelle's woolly socks and an oversized jumper and dragged myself downstairs, where Annabelle and the kids were in full Monday-morning mode. Hunter had whispered non-stop from the top bunk from 5.37 a.m. until 6 a.m. on the dot. He wasn't allowed to be up before six but whispering loudly in my face with hot, spittled morning breath about how Thor and his adopted brother Loki didn't get on and that the Avengers were trying to send Loki back to his planet and Thor was trying to get Loki to stop being a baddie and go to Avenger's subsidised family counselling (or something ... I couldn't quite keep track of the whispered plot), wasn't considered 'being up'.

'Smoothie?' Annabelle said.

'Not one of your kind, thanks,' I said, choosing the seat closest to the radiator. The 25-degree drop in temperature was proving hard to adjust to.

I pulled Katie onto my lap and relished her uninhibited hug and kiss combo. The joy she could spread was boundless and I squeezed her and told her I loved her. She cupped her pudgy hand to my face and told me, in garbled speak and sign language, that she loved me 'too too too much', then sang and signed 'You Are My Sunshine'.

Mum pattered in, fresh from the shower and the pain and emotion from the night before washed over me again. This woman who had been the tiny yet tough, loving yet strict, fair yet unconventional backbone of our family was a big fat (actually small and bony, like a featherless baby bird, but you know what I mean) liar. And I couldn't seem to correlate my feelings. I felt sorry for her; she'd loved and lost and decided playing second fiddle to Dad's real wife was better than not having him at all – and yet I was angry. She'd lied to Annabelle and me for our entire lives and made us unwitting accomplices in an unforgivable act. I was also scared; what would happen to us all now that this was out in the open?

Were we still a family? What were our family friends going to think of us? Of her?

Strangely, and unexpectedly, I also felt in awe of my mother. I'd had a loving, happy childhood. Each time Dad left, Mum would comfort us, distracting us with fun games or outings. Not once did I witness her crying herself to sleep, as she'd admitted last night to doing every time he'd gone back to his wife.

'Morning, girls,' Mum said. She kissed her grandchildren and then, with a wary glance in my direction, headed towards the kitchen counter. 'Are you back to work today, Plum?'

My flurry of feelings dissipated and was replaced with hungover apprehension. In just under three hours I had to go back to work and be nice and sociable. *'My boyfriend left me, my father has a second family and my Mum has been his mistress for forty-odd years'* is not something a colleague needs to hear after enquiring politely about your holiday while in transit past your desk.

'Yes, unfortunately,' I said, helping Katie spoon in a mouthful of scrambled egg.

'Shall I make up Hunter's snacks?' Mum said, looking around for something to do.

'I did it last night,' Annabelle said, taking almond milk out of the fridge.

'Oh, good,' Mum said, heading towards the kettle. 'Shall I make you girls a coffee?'

Annabelle pointed to the full plunger, wafting steam on the bench. 'Done,' she said.

Mum looked at Annabelle, moving about the kitchen with

effortless efficiency and appeared to be feeling both impressed and superfluous.

Annabelle pottered through her morning routine while Mum and I tried to assist, but each time we went to start a job Annabelle had got there first. We were left standing in the middle of the kitchen with an unneeded plastic Moana bowl, or in the hall with one of Hunter's creased school shirts when he was on the sofa tying his shoes wearing a nicely ironed one. I thought Annabelle would be an exhausted wreck after two weeks without us but if anything, she seemed more in control.

The lack of having anything to do, plus Mum's defensiveness in the face of our questions, was making her irritable. I kept looking at her thinking, '*Mistress*' and not being able to marry the thought of my Oxfam-frequenting, composting, save-the-bees, apple-cider-vinegar-fermenting mother with the 'bit-on-the-side' image that came along with that word. Or that Annabelle and I were the product of a very well-concealed, long-term affair.

'Where's Hunter's drink bottle?' I asked while looking through a drawer that had previously been a mess of Tupperware, lids to long-since-disappeared thermoses and other assorted travelling food and drink containers, but was now a neatly organised tea towel drawer.

'We keep it here now,' Hunter said as he walked behind me with his hair combed. He opened an orderly cupboard, pulled out his drink bottle then filled it from the water jug.

As I watched Hunter diligently pack his school bag,

checking against a list of contents stuck to the fridge that hadn't been there two weeks ago, I contemplated whether Mum and I being there constantly for the past few years had stopped Annabelle having to do it all herself. Had we stifled her? And now, with the space to find her own feet, she'd stepped up and her little family unit was ticking along nicely, cannabis smoothies and all?

'So your father will be back on Saturday morning,' Mum said, once the door had shut on one of Annabelle's friends who was taking Hunter to school.

When did Annabelle have time to make friends at the school? Most of the mothers looked at her hyper son and her wrist tattoos and steered well clear. God, we'd only been gone two weeks, yet Annabelle's life seemed so different. *She* seemed so different.

'What?' I said, stopping mid-fridge-rummage. Saturday was five days away. 'Doesn't he want to come and explain himself?'

Annabelle stopped wiping Katie's face and looked at Mum. The night before we'd decided not to call or text Dad; that it was better to wait until he got here. It felt so unnatural not to call him but it made sense to be physically in the same room when he told us his side of the story. But I'd assumed he'd be on a plane immediately; wanting, if it was at all possible, to allay his daughters' hurt.

'He's with a client,' Mum said, measuring out exactly seven grams of her cleansing mushroom tea that smelt like mould covered in evil. 'It can't be helped.'

'A client or a second mistress?' I asked, pulling an apple from the fridge and shutting the door.

'Now stop that, Jess,' Mum said, getting back to her fungus with force. 'I've told him it's best to not call. Things can get so . . . miscommunicated without the benefit of facial expression.'

I left Mum in the kitchen, followed Annabelle to Katie's room and flumped on the pink princess duvet.

'Shall we call him?' I said while Katie picked out what she wanted to wear and Annabelle crouched on her knees on the floor approving or discouraging innumerable pink glittery items. 'Don't you think he should call us? Don't you think he ought to *want* to?'

'I think Mum might be right,' she said, nodding to a pair of pink, purple and cream stripy woollen tights that I wished came in adult size because the mere sight of them made me want to bounce around the room singing songs from the shows.

'How can not talking to Dad be right? I just don't get it! How can he not be on a plane right now? He's our *dad*!' He was the one I ran to when I was upset as a child, or called when I was upset as a teenager, or emailed when I was upset now, because Mum's advice might be to 'replicate the tide with your breathing' or 'try thinking about the sad thing and looking left'. I'd learnt my lesson when I was eleven; after saying I had a headache that wouldn't go away she had me hitting my head with a stick with a metal ball-bearing on the end of it, quoting some kind of ancient Chinese treatment.

I ended up with a headache *and* tiny ball-bearing shaped bruises all over my scalp.

'I know, but Mum's right,' Annabelle said. 'In this instance,' she added off the back of my look. 'Let's leave it till he's back. Then we'll have had time to process everything and can talk about it calmly. He may be having to deal with his other family at the moment.'

While Katie signed that she wanted pigtails and her strawberry hair ties and Annabelle set about locating them, I sat on the bed, stunned. His other family. I hadn't put much thought into how this would be affecting them. I hadn't put much thought into 'them' at all. I was only thinking about how it affected my family: Annabelle, Mum and me. How dreadful must it be for the other family? What would they think of us? Would they hate Annabelle and me just for existing? My stomach flipped. I hated being hated.

After showering and going through Annabelle's nearly all-black clothing trying to find something work-appropriate that would stretch across my bust, I headed into the kitchen, sliding my phone into my bag. Jimmy had texted the night before to see if I'd got home OK but I hadn't replied yet. Life had gone a bit ... mental. I grabbed my coat and scarf from the back of a dining chair and turned to Mum, who, for lack of anything else to do, was putting the magnetic letters on the fridge back in alphabetical order after I'd made a passive-aggressive drunken limerick about adultery the night before.

'So, before I go to work, do you have anything else you'd

like to confess to?' I asked, sliding my arms into my coat.
'You helped stage the moon landings, perhaps? You're a
hacker for Anonymous and need to leave the country because
you've pissed off Sony and now the American government
are coming for you? You're Banksy, and you keep your spray
cans at Patrick's allotment?'

Mum pursed her lips and frowned like I was being unjus-
tifiably dramatic. 'No,' she said firmly. 'That is it.'

'That's it, is it?' I said. 'Are you sure? Are you sure there's
absolutely nothing else?'

Mum looked uncomfortable as I pulled my sleeves down
from inside my jacket. 'Well, yes, actually, now that you
mention it. Just one.'

I stopped mid-toggle-fastening. 'You're kidding, right?'

With a confessionary expression, Mum stepped forward
and put a chilly hand on mine. 'Jess . . . Plum. Your birthday
isn't November the twenty-first.'

'Huh?'

'It's November the twenty-second.'

I blinked. 'What?'

'Your birthday. It's not—'

'I heard you, Mum! I just can't quite understand . . . how
can my *birthday* be wrong?!'

Annabelle stepped into the kitchen, Katie on her hip with
her hair in adorable pigtails that sprang out of the sides of her
head like little chocolate fountains, and watched us.

'Well, Plum,' Mum said, taking on a placatory tone. 'It
was a very busy time for me. Annabelle was such a difficult

child,' she glanced at Annabelle, whose only reaction was a 'fair point' kind of head tilt. 'And your father was away when I had to go to the registry building and fill in the birth certificate and . . . I guess I was just a bit forgetful.'

'ABOUT THE DAY YOU GAVE BIRTH?!'

Mum pursed her lips and glanced at Katie, who laughed and clapped her hands. 'Now Jess, no need to yell.'

'There is a need, Mum! I think there is a very *big* need. I can't believe it! I feel . . . I feel like nothing in my life is real!'

'Oh, pfft,' Mum said with a stern look. 'Pull yourself together.'

'Pull myself together.' I strode out of the kitchen and down the hall with Mum at my heels muttering in German. I took my phone out of my bag and did a Google search, a feeling of dread creeping over me. I stopped as I reached the front door. 'God dammit Mum!' I spun to face her. 'Now I'm a different star sign!'

CHAPTER THIRTY-ONE

My coat was barely off and I'd only said the word 'Have' (which was the beginning of the sentence: 'Have I got some *fucked up* shit to tell you') when Lana threw me into a meeting in her place.

'Sorry, sorry, sorry, I know you want to tell me all about your holiday,' she said as she chucked me a fresh notebook and quick-stepped me past the coffee machine and Steve-o the Australian office barista who '*G'day*'-ed me a welcome back, towards our glass-walled meeting room. 'And I do want to hear it,' she threw a quick glance in the direction of my ring finger, 'but I've woken Roger up in LA and he's on hold and he's not happy.' She ducked behind a pillar with an exposed metal pipe running down the side of it. 'And I canNOT handle that guy this morning.'

I looked in the meeting room at who she was referring to: a hectic young 'genius' (self-described) man/boy director we'd worked with a handful of times and who thought he was reinventing the three-minute music video, pontificating to some gathered peoples. He was tall, thin, achingly cool and had bought his entire outfit from 'Indie Directors R Us'.

Lana shuddered, grabbed a pen from a nearby desk and handed it to me. 'OK, take notes, shut down anything ostentatious and keep the meeting moving. We've got a big day today. And thank you!' She grinned, flashing naturally white teeth, then raced back to her office.

'I want no narrative. No imagery.' Directors R Us paced the room, the waxed floorboards creaking with each pointy-loafered stride, shouting out random shots. 'A horse standing in spaghetti. A girl with her feet in a tub. Toothpaste on a tree. A doll on fire. No. A ...' he continued his blah blah blah-ing and I began wondering why the hell I was sitting in a meeting when there were many other, much more logical options I could have chosen instead of coming into the office the day after finding out that my family was the opposite of the happy nuclear family I'd always believed us to be. I could have stayed at home and watched *Life is Beautiful*, eating jam on toast and cultivating a nice wee depression. I could have flown to Barbados and pretended none of it was happening. I could have booked in to have my spleen removed; *anything* would have been preferable to being at work listening to a dick director talk about dick shots.

'Sure,' I said to one of the dick shots without really hearing what it was.

'Absolutely NOT!' Steph, our three-dog-owning,

keeps-their-photos-on-her-desk, PETA-belonging production manager said, throwing me a look of disgust. 'You can't set a frog on fire!'

What?!

'No, no, of course not!' I shook my head vigorously and turned to the director. 'Sorry, no, we can't do that.'

'Well, get me one that's already slated for animal testing,' he said which made me immediately think of my mother and the time she'd purged our house of any product or company that tested on animals. Annabelle had had an epic, cyclone-like rampage upon finding her make-up in the bin, Mum had tried to wrestle the rubbish bag away from her and in the melee Dad had quietly popped out. He'd come home with a small pile of books, a bunch of strange ingredients and then spent the entire weekend helping Annabelle make natural blush, eye shadow and lip stains at the kitchen table.

'I think we should move on.' Steph's harried voice pierced through the memory that was playing like an old movie in my mind. She turned and gave me a hard glare, making me sit up a little straighter.

'Yes,' I said, trying to feign officiousness and 'with-it-ness'.

The director made 'why did you hire me, do you want creative distinction or not?!' kinds of noises then carried on listing his demands, his eager-to-please assistant scribbling furiously next to him. I looked around the table; to my left was Steph, her brow creased, tapping irately at her iPad; to my right was the annoyingly enthusiastic assistant, and across from me sat a couple of reps for the alt-rock band from

Newcastle we were making the video for, one making notes, the other nodding blithely and swiping right on his phone. Was he Tindering? Did Elsie, the other PA sitting at her desk outside the meeting room in her customary short skirt and heels, just get swipe approval? I looked through the glass; she too was on her phone. Was there Tinder flirting going on?

'Jess?'

I turned. Steph was looking at me expectantly. I looked around the table. Everyone was looking at me expectantly.

'Ummm, sure,' I said, venturing an answer and hoping it was the right one.

Steph glowered.

'No?'

The director glowered.

Shit.

'Let's come back to that one,' I said. I gave Steph a brief '*sorry, I'm here, I am SO here*' kind of nod then smoothed out a blank page in my notebook. 'What else?'

'I want someone licking a candle,' director dude said after looking at me like I was a very irritating bug.

I scribbled *candle*.

'I want a shot of clouds. Then one of water.' He stopped pacing. 'No. That's narrative opposites. Clouds then tiramisu.'

Tiramisu, I scribbled.

He recommenced his wide-stride march. 'Gimme someone putting on deodorant.'

Deodorant.

'Give me a road.'

'An ominous road?' the assistant offered.

'Don't say ominous – not *ominous*.' He rolled his eyes.

'So, a road to somewhere better? A happy road?' The assistant asked and I thought, hell yeah, I want a road to somewhere better. A road right out of Shit Town, thanks. And if that road could lead to Ian and Diego and Jimmy, that would be nice.

'A *nothing* road. No narrative.' The director scratched at his non-existent stubble.

My phone screen lit up with a text from Jimmy. I glanced at the others all either occupied with their note-taking or staring adoringly at the director, then slid my phone from the table, held it in my lap and opened the text.

> Hi Jess, I know you're probably going through hell right now but I just wanted to let you know I'm thinking of you. You don't have to reply but I'm here if you need to talk or whatever. I miss you. Xxx

'OK, scrap the road,' I heard the director say while I worried about Jimmy worrying about me and longed to be back in his bedroom getting those three kisses for real. 'Give me a French fry.'

Absent-mindedly I pushed a plate of untouched biscuits towards the director, who looked at them and then at me, as one might look upon crackers spread with water vole innards.

I glanced around the room. Everyone was staring at me again. 'Do you want me to order in?'

Half an hour later, with pages of half-formed notes and doo-dles of deodorant and tiramisu in Lana's previously very neat notebook, I entered Lana's office and sat in the velvet tub chair. She looked up from tinkering on her laptop.

'So, what are we shooting?' she said, glancing at her watch. I knew from her diary that she was about to race across town to bid for a three-video deal with an up-and-coming pop princess from the dodgy end of Ladbroke Grove.

'Um . . . anything,' I said, flipping through the (unusually for me) sparse pages of notes. 'Literally anything. As long as there's no narrative or symbolism, or theatre, or story, or imagery, or opposites, or similarities, or connections, or emotion, or—'

'So, what then?' Lana said, impatient.

'Well . . .' I said, flicking faster, trying to find anything useful. 'Ahh . . . he wants to set a frog on fire . . .?'

Lana sighed heavily. 'What's the song about?'

'Love.'

She rolled her ice-blue eyes then looked at her Rolex. 'So, tell me about your holiday. And be quick. I have nine minutes.'

I speedily regaled her with the whole scenario, only hitting on the main points: wedding, mountain, Pete and the cheating, Jimmy and the shagging, Dad and the vagi-nas, Mum and the lie, Pete still in Cape Town but moving out when he got back, Dad not coming home till Saturday morning to explain himself and the fact that I was now a Sagittarius and needed to re-evaluate my whole sense of self accordingly.

Lana shook her head, her Scandi blonde hair swishing. 'Holy shit. No wonder you never take your holidays if this is what happens. Are you OK?'

I nodded, emotionally checking myself. 'I'm not sure . . . So far, yes. I think so.'

'Why don't you go home,' she glanced at her watch again. 'I'm sure Elsie can continue to cover your workload.'

I shook my head. 'I'm here now. The distraction is probably just what I need.'

She gave a sympathetic nod and looked at her watch again. 'Can I do anything?'

'Just keep me really busy.'

'Not a problem.'

And she offloaded a bunch of production notes and I hid behind my computer giving an air of 'too-busy-catching-up-on-work-to-tell-you-about-my-holiday', booking crew, catering and studio time and ignoring emails from my friends asking how the holiday went.

As I left work that afternoon I called Annabelle to check she was OK if I went straight home and picked up my suitcase from her place another time. Annabelle said Mum was there teaching Katie to sign the words 'digestive juices' and trying to convince the internet that Mono-Meal Monday was the new Meat Free Monday, and that my suitcase was just fine as long as I didn't mind that the cat was sleeping in it.

My flat was cold and smelt like Burger King. I threw my bag on the sofa just as Dave was coming out of his bedroom dressed for work. Even with a supplied uniform he managed to look homeless. His hair was messy and his skin pale and waxy.

'Welcome home,' he said, picking up a couple of empty cartons of chips and burger wrappers. 'How was it?'

While Dave got ready for work (sniffed socks from the floor to see if they could last another wearing) I filled him in, starting with the Pete situation in Cape Town.

'So Pete is moving out?' Dave said after listening to my tale while collecting his belongings from various places around the flat.

'Yeah.'

He stopped in the door to the kitchen. 'So . . . I don't want to be a dick about it, but . . . what about rent?'

I hadn't thought about that. Despite Pete and I sharing a room and Dave having his own, we'd split the rent equally three ways, making it affordable for all of us. Paying half might make things a bit tight. 'You could always get a girl-friend?' I suggested.

Dave looked at me like I'd suggested he get Legion-naires' Disease.

'And what about my twelfth birthday, when Dad couldn't make it because of work?' I said five minutes later after I'd told him about my parents.

We stood at the open fridge taking turns to eat random ingredients. Dave and I considered this a perfectly viable way of eating dinner.

'Or the time he missed seeing me in the school nativity play? Or my interschool relay finals?' I said, waggling a pickle. 'Or any of the things he couldn't come to? I don't know if my dad missed me winning the English award because of a lie or because he really was working. Did he *choose* to miss certain things and then really was working on others? I feel like I want to get an inventory of my whole life events and tick them off with him – 'legitimate miss' or 'missed by choice'.

'What will that do?' Dave said, leaving the fridge with a wedge of cheese and heading into the living room with me at his heels.

'I don't know. It will help me make sense of everything, maybe? Mum and Dad were a lie, Pete and I broke up and Annabelle seems to have been fine without me. I feel a bit . . . I feel . . . like an unboxed jack-in-the-box, you know?'

'Yeah . . .' Dave nodded, then frowned. 'No, not really.'

'Pointless. And floppy.' I flopped onto the sofa to emphasise my point.

Dave, never one for talking much about feelings, collected his aged rucksack from the floor and left for work among mutters of, '*you'll be all right*', '*I don't suppose anyone meant any harm*', '*chin up*' kind of platitudes and I stayed on the sofa contemplating whose job it was to get the jacks in their boxes. I thought it would start off being the best job ever, but then the enjoyment would wear off and you'd end up hating those springy, cheerful bastards. You'd look at a jack-in-the-box and where everyone else sees joy and hilarity you'd see pain and frustration and a wasted life.

Tuesday passed much like Monday but with less sleep and more staring off into the distance. I kept thinking about the logistics of having two families, and trying to figure out how my vague father had managed it for so long. I wondered if he'd ever gone from one family to the next, woken up and not remembered which house he was in. Which bedroom he was in. Which *wife* he was in. Ew. And then my head had filled with *very* unwanted thoughts about the logistics of Dad's sex life. Did his SA wife ever want 'goodbye-I'm-not-going-to-see-you-for-a-while' sex before he jumped on a plane to Mum, who immediately wanted 'hello-I've-not-seen-you-in-a-while' sex? And what did that do to his emotions? Was there guilt during either of the sex times? And how unfair was it that I was thinking about my father's sex times?!

To get the thoughts out of my head I'd needed something shocking so I'd gone onto Giselle's Instagram and looked at Pete through her lens. Then ended up with some wrath that had Lana telling me to go outside and 'walk it off'. Dave wasn't home that night so I'd stayed up till 2 a.m. watching *Stranger Things* without absorbing any of it. Was it about aliens? Was it a comedy? Did it have hobbits? I didn't know.

*

On the Wednesday I was sitting at my desk with a pile of call sheets that I was supposed to be entering into the computer, but instead was doodling and mentally running through my past to see if there were any signs of the double life we had been living that I might have dismissed as Dad just being vague. Like, did he ever call Mum his wife's name? Did he ever ask me how a school project was going that was not mine but perhaps one his South African daughter was working on?

Lana passed my desk and I was partially aware of her saying something, then suddenly she was in front of me.

'Jess?'

'Yeah?' I said, clicking out of my reverie and focusing on her. She was looking at my doodle pad. I'd scratched an angry scar in the paper.

'Are you OK?'

'Yes, thanks.' I pushed the ruined doodle pad to the side and picked up a call sheet. 'You?' I asked through a yawn.

Lana watched me for a moment. 'Can I get you a coffee?'

'Ah ...' I said, looking between the call sheet and my computer screen. It seemed I'd already entered that one. 'Ahhh ... yes, a coffee ... Yes please.'

'Are you sure you're OK?'

I looked up at her. Wow, it was hard to focus. 'Yes, I'm all good,' I said with a smile as my mobile rang.

I smiled wider at Lana to show her that everything was just fine and she headed towards Steve-o with a nod.

'Hey,' I said into my phone.

'Turn on the radio,' Annabelle said.

She didn't need to say which station. If we said that, it meant Mum's radio show. I clicked on a tab that was always open on my desktop, put an earphone in my free ear and immediately heard my mother sobbing.

'Oh, the innocence!' Mum wailed. 'So easily betrayed. So easily hoodwinked! Their little faces . . .'

'Oh dear,' another voice came down the radio waves. 'Are . . . are you OK?'

'What's going on?' I hissed down the phone.

'A caller asked about natural stress relief and Mum said the usual.' By this Annabelle meant the list of stress-reducing things we'd heard many times over: take St John's wort and passionflower extract, stop caffeine, put your bare feet on grass, tell a house plant you love it, etc., etc. 'Then Mum said she'd been suffering from stress herself and had found that listening to children's choirs on YouTube was helping.'

'Right . . .'

'And then she started crying and saying adults must be careful not to "corrupt a child's innate innocence" and something about the "worlds we weave", and "we're all guilty" and then I called you.'

'Christ.'

'I'm going to call Patrick.'

'OK,' I said and hung up while listening to Mum blubber down the radio waves about a child being born an 'empty vessel of possibility' and how they are so easily and accidentally 'filled with the sticky tar of untruths', with the caller trying awkwardly to comfort her. I hung my head in my hands.

'And the singing!' Mum wailed. 'Oh, *dieser engelsgesang*!'

My desk phone rang and while keeping my head in one hand I lifted the receiver and banged it down again with the other.

'Jess?'

I looked up to see Lana with my coffee. She was frowning at the now silent phone. In the earphone Mum's wailing suddenly stopped and Patrick came on air. 'I do apologise, we seem to be having some technical difficulties but now we have someone on the line who managed to solve her gum disease with urine therapy.'

I pulled my earphone out while looking up at Lana. 'Sorry,' I said, and the look of concern on her face nearly had me in tears.

'How are you coping?' Lana said from behind her desk five minutes later.

'I'm OK,' I said from the tub chair.

'I disagree.'

I bit my lip.

Lana studied me for a while, her hands clasped under her chin. 'You used to run, right?'

I nodded, confused.

Lana then told me that to help her get through her messy divorce she'd started running. It had calmed her mind and ordered her thoughts. And it was while on a run down Abbey

Road that she'd come up with the idea for her all-female music video production company. She scheduled a run into every day now – it was as important as a business meeting. She suggested it might be a good way to help me deal with my 'situation' and the growing seed of wrath I was develop- . ing because of it.

So at lunchtime I entered a bra shop and a woman who could have been twenty-four or sixty-four approached me with a face so taut she looked as if someone had grabbed a fistful of the skin at the back of her head and was running in the other direction.

'I'm taking up jogging again but the last time I ran I didn't have these,' I said, opening my jacket to reveal my bust. 'I need these jiggly panna cottas to be rigid and immobile. Like toffee apples. Or bollards.'

The woman appraised my bust with heavily drawn-on eyebrows and walked towards some hanging bras that looked like they were made of bad-weather sailcloth.

'They feel like I'd get rather sweaty,' I said a few minutes later when I'd tried on the three options they had for my bust size.

They'd been so hard to get on that the lady had thrust aside the curtain, grabbed the back straps and hoisted and pulled so forcefully she may as well have pinned me to the floor, dug a knee in my back and forced the edges together. I'd suggested a bigger size and, with a mild sweat across her upper lip, she'd agreed. I looked wistfully at the small-bust sports bras in multi-coloured fabric designed to be shown off. Mine were in nude or black and intended to be hidden shamefully.

'Yes. Sveat is a problem for breaztez like yourz. You use panty linerz,' the lady said, walking behind the counter with my two reluctantly chosen bras.

'Excuse me?'

'In ze cups. Mozt effective for sveat. Other productz don't work so much.' She waved to a host of 'sweat wicking' powders lined along the counter. She reached to a shelf behind her and handed me a little pink bottle. 'Chafing problem too. You need ziz.'

I paid and left feeling a little grim. The last time I ran I did it in nice bright little crop tops. Now it was a shiny black material so thick a pair of hedge clippers would have a tough time getting through, panty liners in the cups and a product called 'lady slide' that promised 'silken-like sliding' in the cleavage area.

On Thursday morning, some scented liners up against the underside of my breasts, I programmed my run-mapping app and took off. I assumed I'd need some kind of Rocky Balboa montage-worthy struggle to get my pace back but actually, after a brief two minutes of empathy for asthmatics, I hit my stride and my familiar breathing rhythm took over.

I can do this, I thought, as I wove in and around tourists taking photos of swans on the Serpentine. *I can feel my wrath subsiding already. Wow, some people really need to pick a walking line and stick to it. Christ, lady, watch your kid! Who the hell walks five abreast on a London footpath? Single file, people – I've got places to go! Stop weaving from side to side, you indecisive fuck. WHY DOESN'T EVERYONE GET THE FUCK OUT OF MY WAY?!*

CHAPTER THIRTY-TWO

'So, how is everything, babe?'

'Oh you know, like genital warts,' I said, picking my way along the busy wet footpath. 'Absolutely ghastly, but I'll survive.'

Priya, in full triclops make-up, laughed her loud, honking laugh. She'd FaceTimed me from her set between lighting changes. Behind her some cast members in their animal hybrid costumes or grey motion-capture leotards covered in sensor points sat in canvas chairs talking on phones, reading from scripts or staring off into the distance. One bald, muscled guy was having a set of giant elaborately feathered eagle wings attached to a heavy-looking harness on his back by three burly men in SPFX uniforms. Crew walked to and fro lugging various props, lights and cables. In contrast to her vibrant surroundings I was heading home from work along drizzly Charing Cross road trying to avoid being buffeted by Harry Potter-loving, umbrella-wielding tourists outside the Palace

Theatre. It had taken a huge effort to get to the end of the week. Work had been horrible (zero ability to concentrate/ worried looks from Lana/terrible coffee from Steve-o); home had been horrible (Mum forcing me to do cross stitch to work through my anger/Pete's absence from the flat but his heavy presence on Giselle's glossy Instagram feed/Dave's dandruff on the back of the sofa), and the only time I felt even a seed of calm was when my mind wandered to Jimmy and Cape Town and Jimmy's abs and Jimmy's eyes and Jimmy's grin.

'Have you heard from Pete?' Priya said, scratching one of the three fat dreads that ran along the top of her head.

'No.' I pulled my coat collar tight against the cold. 'But he's due back tomorrow, so I guess I'll see him when he comes to pick up his stuff.'

'He's a fucktard,' Priya said. 'I mean, I still think he's ordinarily a great guy and he does make *the best* tamarind salmon salad, but his current behaviour can only be described as fucktardy.'

'I concur,' I said. 'Fucktardy.'

'There's no chance you guys will work it out?'

I shook my head. 'I think we drifted too far in different directions to go back. And anyway, I don't think either of us *wants* to go back. We got together so young, we're different people now, we grew apart, blah blah blah,' I said, bored of the whole cliché Pete and I had become.

'True,' Priya said. 'He didn't need to cheat, though.'

'No,' I said, skirting round a throng of busy businessmen. 'But he did.'

''Cause he's a fucktard.'

I laughed. 'He is.'

'So how's Annabelle coping?'

I stepped out of the stream of the busy pavement, stood under a shop awning next to the tube station and told Priya how, despite the fact that our world had imploded, my sister seemed to be doing better than she had in years. And seemed unusually, paradoxically content.

'And your mum?'

'I feel really sorry for her, actually. Dad is married to someone else. I just can't believe it . . .'

Priya's perfect eyebrows sloped with empathy. 'What's he going to do? Has he told his wife yet? Are your mum and him splitting up?'

'I don't know. I don't know anything about my dad's "real" life.' I shook my head, still not believing that these words were coming out of my mouth. About my own parents. My own, boring, read-the-papers-on-Sunday-morning, put-the-bins-out-on-Thursdays, always-wash-your-jars-before-putting-them-in-the-recycling parents. 'He arrives tomorrow morning. Mum and I are staying at Annabelle's tonight and Dad will head straight there when he lands, so I guess I'll find everything out then.'

'What do you think he's going to say?'

'I don't know.'

'What do you *want* him to say?'

I thought about that for a second then launched into my hopes with Priya's smile growing wider as I progressed.

'I want him to say, "Wake up Jess, you've been having a nightmare. Would you like me to bring you breakfast in bed? There's a box of orphaned baby raccoons downstairs and you need to nurse them to health. I'm pretty sure all of them are going to think of you as their mother so you may need to give up work to care for them. But don't worry, a BBC documentary team is interested, so you'll be fine for money and after that they'll probably offer you a job where you get to play with baby animals all day. Do you want your eggs scrambled or poached, and shall I tell the reflexologist to come in now? Oh, and the news was just on and it turns out doughnuts have zero calories and cure cancer so we will all need to eat at least two a day. The ones with extra sugar glazing are the healthiest. Also Trump's out, world peace is in, climate change has been reversed, snakes are severely endangered, scientists have eradicated all diseases and Jack Black is coming for dinner. By the way those new diamond earrings look fabulous on you".'

'Hmm,' Priya said with a thoughtful, three-eyed expression. 'I think you've set your expectations too high. Maybe just hope for "*I'm sorry, I love you, please forgive me?*" and any box of baby raccoons is a bonus?'

'Maybe . . .'

We smiled at each other, then Priya's expression became serious.

'I'm so sorry you're going through this, babe,' she said. 'I wish I could be there with you.'

I bobbed my head. 'Me too.' I looked at my gorgeous,

freakily made-up best friend. 'I wish your disgusting third eye really could see the future.'

'I don't see the future.' Priya sat up straight, shut her real eyes, slipped into her ethereal character voice and said, 'I navigate tiiiiime and spaaaaace', then spun her creepy forehead eye around and around which she could do via a little remote she kept in a pocket in her costume.

'Gross!' I giggled and Priya opened her real eyes and laughed her honky laugh.

Just then a girl with a headset approached Priya and said they needed her back in the chair to fix her loosened dread. We said our goodbyes and I joined the damp throng of commuters making slow progress into the bowels of Leicester Square tube station.

Twenty minutes later my phone rang as I turned the corner of Annabelle's road. It was Pete. My spirits, after six years of practice, immediately lifted. But then I remembered he wasn't my boyfriend any longer and therefore wasn't ringing to ask me if I'd like chicken or salmon for dinner. With a heavy heart I answered.

'Hi.'

'Hi, how are you?' he asked, his voice so familiar yet also strange, having not heard it for a whole week. The last time we'd spoken we'd been standing at the bottom of the apartment stairs saying an awkward goodbye with Trust standing next to the van looking uncomfortable and confused.

'What do you want?' I said, but not too harshly.

Mum had requested that should I talk to Pete, I not tell him anything about her and Dad as his parents were good family friends and we were all in a state of limbo as to how this whole thing would play out. So, Pete didn't know that his call was coming at a difficult time. I'd like to think if he had he wouldn't have said what he did.

'Well, I'm coming home tomorrow and I just wanted to let you know Giselle is coming too.'

'Right.'

'She's actually a Pilates instructor, so will get work easily.'

'Great.'

'We're not coming back together,' Pete said after a moment. 'We're just coming back together. At the same time together. Not as a couple together.'

'Pete, shut up.'

'Sorry,' he said and then launched into the logistics of me being out of the flat the next morning so he could pick up his stuff. Which worked out fine because I would be with Dad, learning all about his duplicity. I hung up from Pete, let myself into my sister's flat and flopped on the sofa in front of Annabelle, who was sitting on the floor rubbing some oily-looking cream from a recycled jar into Katie's elbows.

'Where's Mum?'

'In the kitchen making dinner,' Annabelle said. Katie was singing along to a song playing on the family iPad in front of her. 'She's been crying again.'

'What about this time?'

Mum had been crying all week and Annabelle and I had started exchanging WhatsApp messages entitled 'Reasons Why Greta Cries'. Yesterday's list had read:

- ate the perfect peach
- saw a dog without a bone
- realised David Attenborough was in his nineties
- was sad the perfect peach moment was over

'She's brought round the family photo album.' Annabelle placed the jar of cream on the coffee table and helped Katie into her pyjamas. 'She keeps pointing at pictures and sobbing.'

'Right,' I said, not quite ready to head into the kitchen to comfort my mother. I picked up the open jar, sniffed and recoiled. 'What *is* this?'

'Mad Mandy made it. Marcus's sister.'

'She made it especially for Katie?' I said, reading the hand-written label instructing the cream be rubbed '*into Katie's delicate skin after a neroli oil bath*'.

'Yes,' Annabelle said. 'And she sends home-made bath salts that help Katie's skin condition and weekly numerology readings based on my birthdate. Which is a complete bunch of crap because this week I was supposed to have a windfall and find inner peace.'

I snorted my amusement and replaced the stinky jar on the coffee table. 'How does she know your birthdate? And about Katie's skin?'

'I guess Marcus told her.'

'Marcus is telling his sister all about you?' I asked. 'Why?' Annabelle shrugged.

'Well, I think he likes you.'

Annabelle dismissed my speculation with an eye-roll. She signed and told Katie that she was all done and to go play with Hunter. Katie gave her mama a kiss then toddled off with the iPad blaring an inspirational anthem about loving yourself and not needing anyone else, with Annabelle smiling after her.

'That song,' I said, getting off the sofa and heading towards the kitchen, 'is about masturbation.'

It was nearly 7.30 p.m. and the kitchen was clean, quiet and held no evidence of dinner-making happenings.

'Mum, have you started dinner?' I asked, glancing over her shoulder at the photo album laid flat on the table. She was tracing a picture of Annabelle and me in summer dresses with a short-filed nail.

'I got the meat out.' She waved a thin hand in the direction of the kitchen, turned a page and uttered a little German moan.

I looked around the kitchen and saw a hunk of frozen beef sitting on a retro plate.

I knocked it with my knuckles. 'It's frozen solid.'

'Yes, Plum,' Mum said vaguely.

'How's dinner going?' Annabelle walked into the kitchen holding Katie's iPad. She sniffed the non-aromatic air. 'I can't smell anything.'

'Mum, what have you been doing in here all afternoon?' I

said, opening the oven hoping to find a secret, fragrance-free, fully prepared dinner.

Mum looked up from the photo album with tears in her pale blue eyes. 'What's that, Plum?'

'We'll have to order in,' I said, opening the cupboards and fridge and finding nothing but salad, grain-free crackers and smoothie ingredients.

Annabelle put the kids to bed while Mum sat at the table pointing at various family events in the photo album where Dad was absent, making comments like 'we lied then', 'and then', 'and then too'. I ordered enough Indian food to feed Calcutta then thought my stomach would collapse in on itself when they told me they were very busy and it would take an hour to deliver. I hung up and joined Mum at the table with the photo album, only to find out that Dad had missed my science presentation when I was nine because he was at his other daughter's graduation ceremony in Cape Town. Dad had had all these big events in his life, his other daughter getting married, his other grandchildren being born, birthday parties, buying houses, anniversaries, and I couldn't get my head around the fact that there was such a huge part of his life he hadn't shared with us. How would it have felt to be at his daughter's wedding one weekend and the next be back with us, not mentioning anything about that wonderful day? It made my mind swim and caused constant nausea. I tried to stand, felt faint, wobbled on my feet and fell back down on my seat.

'Stop!' I said, wrestling with Mum who was trying to push

my head between my knees. 'I just need something to eat, I missed lunch today. Get off!'

'I can make smoothies?' Annabelle said, coming back in the room.

'That's a good idea,' Mum said, still trying to push my head downwards. 'Why don't you put some ashwagandha in it? To calm us.'

I managed to fight off my tiny mother and sat up, my hair stuck to my sweating face. 'How are you so strong?' I puffed.

Half an hour later Mum, Annabelle and I lounged in the living room, the lights low and Annabelle's record player emitting something soft and jazzy.

'I'm feeling much calmer,' I said from my prone position. 'That ashwa-up-ya-gunga stuff really works.'

'Ash-wa-gunga.' Mum said, trying to enunciate but bursting into giggles.

'Ashwa*gandha*,' Annabelle corrected with a smile.

'I don't think I'm even that worried about Pete bringing Giselle home tomorrow.'

'He is?' Annabelle said from her armchair.

'Yep,' I said, tucking a pillow behind my head. 'Together six years and it's all over, pfft, just like that.'

'I guess the women in this family don't have much luck with men,' Mum said, sipping her smoothie.

'Oh, I got lucky in South Africa,' I said, thinking of Jimmy. 'And it wasn't cheating. No one can say it was cheating because Pete cheated first.'

'Are you ever going to tell me what happened with Pete, Plum?' Mum asked. 'Or do I have to call his mother and find out from her?'

I gave her a very condensed version of what happened while Annabelle sipped her smoothie and listened, having heard it all already.

'And no, I don't see us getting back together,' I said as Mum opened her mouth to add some off-the-wall insight. 'He's made it very clear that he doesn't see a future with me. And after that holiday I don't see myself with him either.'

'But you're nearly thirty, dear,' she said with concern. 'What about children? You know your prime fertility years are already behind you.'

'Oh I've never been worried about that,' I said, airily. 'If I don't meet the right man my plan was always to just get some sperm from a bank.'

'A bank?' Mum frowned.

Annabelle sniggered.

'Yes,' I said. 'I think HSBC has the best sperm.'

Mum scowled.

'Either that or I'll find some cool, good-looking guy, have an unprotected one-night stand and not tell him when I get pregnant. Although it might not work the first time. I'll probably have to have quite a few unprotected one-night stands.' I grinned at Annabelle, who smirked and shook her head. 'Actually, it sounds a fabulously fun way to have a baby. I don't know why everyone doesn't do it.' I looked over at

Mum for a satisfying reaction but she was fiddling with a Rubik's cube. After a moment she looked up.

'I stopped listening to you after HSBC, Plum,' she said, and went back to the cube.

We sipped our smoothies, listened to the jazz and talked in a meandering way about various topics.

'I've had successful relationships,' Annabelle mused. 'Before they became unsuccessful.'

'Your father wanted to be a pilot,' Mum said, clicking one side of the Rubik's cube fully to white. 'None of this would ever have happened if he'd been a pilot.'

'It would have been way worse if Pete and I had moved to freaking Egham and *then* broken up.'

'I think success in a relationship isn't longevity,' Annabelle said. 'It's the intensity.'

'Although pilots travel to South Africa ...'

'Imagine if we'd gotten married?!' I took a gulp of my smoothie. 'I'm better off like this, with you guys.'

'And the cabin pressure isn't good for digestion. No, that wouldn't have been good at all.'

'I don't even know why I haven't called Jimmy back. I should. But I don't want to talk to him while I've got the wrath.' I giggled at the thought of me being wrathful when I felt so, so calm.

'Anyway,' Mum said, putting the completed cube on the coffee table. 'Annabelle hasn't had a man for such a long time.'

'And she hasn't had an illegitimate child in such a long

time either. Well *done*,' I said, raising my smoothie glass in a toast fashion. 'We're so proud of you.'

Annabelle tittered and curled her delicate legs under her.

Mum turned to me in a confessional manner. 'She has low self-esteem, so pushes them away before they can reject her.'

'Mum, I'm *in the room*,' Annabelle said.

'Yes, of course you are, dear.' Mum gave me a look that said, 'What's she on?'

After an hour and a half I went into the kitchen to get away from Mum, who'd turned up the jazz and was showing me where I got my shocking moves from, and to ring the curry house.

'The curry's already been delivered,' I said, arriving back in the living room.

'I don't remember that,' Mum said, swaying in the middle of the room with all the fluidity of a rusted windscreen wiper.

'Because they had the address completely wrong! Some fuckers have our food!'

'They stole it,' Mum tutted and swayed. 'Terrible.'

'No, apparently they paid. They are paying stealers! Is that even illegal? Can you call the police?' I thought about how that 999 call would go and sniggered to myself at the idea of a serious police officer saying, '*Can you please describe the stolen gobi, ma'am?*' 'I've ordered it all again which they say could take another bloody hour. I'm *starving*, and you only have rabbit food here!'

'More smoothie?' Mum said.

'I guess so,' I said, falling back onto the sofa.

Annabelle collected the empties and left the room to make more while Mum and I sat listening to the jazz.

'Your grandmother knew how to treat a man,' Mum said after a while, seemingly continuing a conversation she'd been having in her head. 'Her boyfriend didn't write to her during the war so she sent him a saucy photograph. He came home and married her instantly.'

'If only a saucy picture carried the impact it once did. I'm afraid free internet porn and the Kardashians have ruined it.'

'Kardashians?' Mum said, taking a seat on the sofa. 'Are they the family who drove you to the beach for the day and forgot to bring you home?'

A gentle knock at the door stopped me from having to explain the pointless yet ever-present phenomenon that was the Kardashians to my mother.

'Yay! Food!' I leapt off the sofa, passed Annabelle carrying three smoothies into the living room and ran down the narrow hall. In two seconds I was back in the living room, grumpy and with a man in tow. He was wearing ironed jeans and had introduced himself as Marcus.

'It wasn't the food.' I fell onto the sofa and picked up my refilled smoothie glass. I was going to eat the coasters if I didn't get some naan bread into me soon.

'What are you doing here?' Annabelle said, straightening in her armchair.

'Well, I just . . . I wanted to . . .' Marcus looked nervously from Mum, to me, to Annabelle. 'Hello,' he said to Mum, who peered at him through her giant glasses as if he were some strange but fascinating creature.

Hunter suddenly hurled himself into the room and threw his arms around Marcus's waist. 'Marcus!'

'Hunter, what are you doing up?' Mum said, standing. She rocked on her feet. 'Goodness, I feel a little dizzy. Must be the up-your-gunga.' She looked over at me and tried to stifle a giggle, her eyes watering with the effort.

An excited WHEEEEEEE let us know Katie was also up and a moment later she ran heavy-footed and squealing into the room. She flew at Marcus, who bent down and picked her up.

'Katie ...?' I said, confused. Why were the kids so affectionate towards quiet, wearing-a-nicely-pressed-navy-sweater Marcus with the mad sister? How come I wasn't greeted with as much affection? I was more than a little miffed. 'I'm more than a little miffed,' I said, but as it was not in connection to anything I'd said out loud previously I looked crazy. I tried to stand up but also felt wobbly, so flumped back on the sofa. I looked at my smoothie.

'Is my smoothie plain?'

'What do you mean?' Mum said, sitting back down and smiling like a stoned madwoman.

Stoned!

'Am I ... am I *stoned*?' I said, incredulous. I'd never been stoned.

Mum fell sideways on the sofa with the force of her laughter.

'Annabelle?' I turned to my sister, whose eyes were still on Marcus.

'Yes,' she said frankly. 'You are stoned.'

'*What?!*'

'You were getting hyper so we decided you needed sedating,' Mum said from her sideways position.

'Roofied by my own family!' I was aghast. 'I'm aghast!' I said.

Mum laughed hysterically into a cushion.

Annabelle turned back to Marcus. 'Why are you here?'

'Did you come to give me another mission?' Hunter said, hopping from foot to foot. 'I figured the last one out easy!'

'Not this time,' he said, ruffling Hunter's permanently ruffled hair. 'I came because . . . I wanted to . . .' He looked at Annabelle, who seemed to be flushing around the neck.

'Yes?' she said.

'What's happening?' I said, looking from Marcus with Katie in his arms to Annabelle on the sofa with her eyes wide and an unsightly heat creeping across her collarbones. 'Mum, something's happening,' I said, tapping at her head but not taking my eyes off the confusing chemistry between Annabelle and Marcus.

Mum wiped her streaming eyes, muttered about being 'high' and convulsed into hiccuping giggles again. Marcus put Katie down then crouched at her level. He began signing and Katie's already beaming grin grew wider. Her eyes sparkled and flicked between watching his hands and looking up into his smiling face.

'How come Marcus knows sign language?' I asked Annabelle, who ignored me and watched her daughter and Marcus interacting.

'What's he saying?' Mum said, trying to right herself but getting caught in the cushions.

'I can't . . .' I leant forward and tried to read their hands. 'He says . . . he wants to play the harp . . . he says '*horsey do, horsey see*' . . . he says . . . no, that can't be . . . he says . . . Agh!' I fell back against the cushions, angry and frustrated. 'I can't figure it out, I'm too stoned!'

Mum howled with laughter and fell to the other side. I turned to Annabelle, who looked like she was either very happy or very sad. Or about to sneeze. Man, being high was confusing.

'He says . . .' I focused on his hands. 'He says . . .' then I gasped and looked over at Annabelle, who was tearing up. 'He says " . . . *tell Mummy I love her*" . . .'

'Ridiculous!' Mum wheezed, trying to straighten her skew-whiff glasses. 'You're too high. Try again.'

'He's a divorcee,' Annabelle said a few minutes later while Marcus was out of the room putting Hunter and Katie back to bed. Her cheeks were still flushed.

'Divorced?!' Mum said, appalled.

'He's not exactly getting a vestal virgin with me, Mum.'

'But still . . . *divorced*,' she tutted. 'Why?'

'His wife had an affair.'

Mum shook her head disapprovingly, still tut-tutting.

'From *where* do you get your moral standing?' I said to Mum, who pursed her lips in return.

'He's a property developer. He's thirty-six, has no kids and we've been seeing each other for eight months.'

'WHAT?!' I said.

'*WIE BITTE*?' Mum said.

Annabelle, tiring of Mum's incessant tut-tutting, looked her in the eye. 'Fucking for six.'

Mum's eyebrows shot up. 'No need to use such language!' she said primly.

Inexplicably, or perhaps explicably (on account of the weed), I began to get the giggles. Then Mum did too and we gripped each other's arms and tried to supress hysterics until tears streamed down our cheeks while Annabelle looked on unamused.

Marcus arrived back and stopped in the doorway looking uncertain.

Annabelle walked across the room, stood next to him and waited for Mum and me to regain our composure. Once we were under control, she spoke. 'We wanted to keep it quiet because we knew you'd both have your concerns.'

'And we do,' I said, getting righteous. 'He could have sleazy objectives. He could have dodgy money practices. He could have syphilis.' I turned to Marcus. 'No offence.'

Marcus, standing nervously beside Annabelle, reddened and waved my apology away.

Annabelle rolled her eyes and turned to Mum. 'The kids adore him. He and Hunter have this little challenge game,' she said with a fond twinkle. 'He gives Hunter sentences in comic-book speak and Hunter has to decipher them. The last one was "*Go to the centre of trade and retrieve the sunset orbs*", Annabelle said in an Ironman-type voice, her eyes shining with playfulness.

Mum and I frowned back.

'It means "go to the market and get oranges",' she said with an expectant grin.

'Hunter can't go to the market by himself,' Mum pooh-poohed. 'That's an irresponsible request. Marcus clearly isn't suited to childcare.' She turned to Marcus. 'No offence.'

Marcus again gave a feeble wave of dismissal. Annabelle's grin dropped. Just then the curry turned up and Annabelle and Marcus moved to the kitchen. Mum and I turned on the TV and with me on the floor eating my curry at the coffee table and her on the sofa munching her mono-meal of avocado, we tried to follow a documentary about stingrays while bitching about this newcomer.

'He doesn't look like the type to "shag and pack a bag", to "doggy-style then run a mile", to put "cock in hole then rock 'n' roll", but those are the ones you have to keep an especially close eye on.'

'What *are* you talking about, Plum?' Mum said. 'And don't use such language. Disgusting talk! You should be ashamed of yourself.'

I looked up at her. 'I'm not.'

Mum pursed her lips. 'I just worry,' she said, pushing her avocado aside and eyeing my plate. 'Annabelle doesn't have room in her life for a man.'

'Well,' I said, biting a folded chunk of naan bread and talking through the mouthful. 'Maybe she does if she doesn't need us so much any more?'

'Doesn't need us?' Mum looked unbearably hurt.

I felt the burn too. I turned back to the TV. Mum was already hurting; there was no need to say that I'd started to think that Annabelle might want some independence. From us.

'I used to be scared of stingrays until I watched *Finding Nemo*,' I said, and Mum nodded like I'd said something insightful.

'Are you going to eat that?' Mum asked, looking at my plate with its smudges of orange, two torn pieces of naan and a discarded onion bhaji.

'No, I'm done.'

Mum slid off the sofa, hustled me out of the way and began shovelling the food into her face.

'I feel like crisps,' she said, after swiping the last bit of naan across the last smear of curry and shoving it in her mouth.

'You've got the munchies!' I laughed.

Mum crept out of the front door and was back ten minutes later with her arms and coat pockets full of the kind of crinkly wrapped foods I'd never seen in her possession before.

'The nice man said I would like the Pringle so I got three.'

CHAPTER THIRTY-THREE

'Oh . . .' Mum groaned. 'Oh, it's awful. Oooh nooo. Oh dear.'

'Mum, shush, you're hurting my brain innards,' I whispered.

'Oh, oh, oooooooh . . .'

'Stop. *Please* stop,' I croaked. 'I have a hangover.'

'Cannabis doesn't give you a hangover,' she rasped. 'Oh, but I have one. Oh what *is* it? It's *terrible*.'

I tried to sit up. Mum and I had slept on Annabelle's pull-out sofa bed and as I moved I found Wotsits in my armpit.

'Well, what does it give you then?' I said, tossing the limp Wotsits onto the coffee table, which had been shoved to the side of the room.

'A low, dear. You've been high so now you have a low.'

I stopped moving, having made it only halfway to sitting. 'A low? Well, that's not great,' I said, feeling resigned to my fate. I located and flicked away another couple of Wotsits. 'I was already pretty low . . .'

'Oh, oh no, I can't sit up. Help me, please Plum?'

I tried to pull her up to the half-sitting pose I was in but only succeeded in shunting myself back down. We grappled with the blankets and pillows and each other and finally, amid groans, grunts and Wotsits, achieved sitting status.

'Oh, I really feel awful,' Mum said, touching a feeble hand to her forehead. 'It must be the E-numbers.'

'Now I know what it's like to be a drug addict.'

'Oh, the rubbish people eat! How do they hold down jobs feeling like this?'

'I need the next high to stop me feeling like this.'

'I wonder if there's a way to purge it all from my system . . .'

'But actually, because I know the low comes after the high, I don't understand why you wouldn't just ride out the current low and get back to normal, humdrum, everyday, middle-of-the-road averageness so you never have to feel this low again.'

Mum looked at me with bleary eyes.

'I've just talked myself out of normal averageness. I can totally see the benefits of being high now.'

'Are you quite finished?' Mum said.

I nodded.

'Good,' she said. 'Now, do you think if I made myself vomit I'd feel better?'

Hunter and Katie hurtled into the living room, dressed, fresh-faced and bouncy, with the health and vitality of those who have not been up all night getting stoned and rolling in Wotsits.

'I taught Katie a song!' Hunter said, helping his grinning little sister up on the sofa bed. 'Katie?' he said. 'Let's show Grandma and Aunty Jess, OK?!'

Katie clapped her hands and together they sang and signed 'The Rainbow Connection'. Katie's words were slightly garbled but the tune and her sign language were spot on. She watched her older brother with adoration. Annabelle walked in, also dressed and fresh, and stood at the end of the sofa bed mouthing the words. Mum, her huge-framed glasses on wonky, signed along with them, her eyes moist with pride. As they sang and signed the last words Mum gave Katie a huge squeezy hug, I got a kiss sandwich, Hunter started leaping across the sofa bed pretending to be Hulk and my thoughts went to Jimmy singing that same song on Oscar the Couch, the rain battering the sand below. Oh to be back in that simpler time when my only worry was Pete cheating on me with Giselle, and whether or not Jimmy had condoms.

'It's nearly time to go,' Annabelle said to the kids, signing for Katie's benefit. 'Get your bags, OK?'

Hunter and Katie leapt off the bed and ran out of the room squealing.

'Where are they going?' Mum asked.

Before Annabelle could answer, Marcus walked into the room looking formal in his woollen vest, slacks, his blondish hair combed and his face newly shaved.

'Did you stay the night?' I said, pulling the covers up to my unsupported chest and trying to hide my horrified judgement.

Marcus went to answer but Mum, also tugging at the jumbled covers, interrupted.

'Oh, I don't think that's appropriate. It's too soon for Annabelle.' She pursed her parched lips, the bunched-up covers pulled tight under her chin and her wrinkled feet sticking out the other end.

'Marcus has been staying over for the past six months,' Annabelle said airily, while handing Marcus Katie's portable respirator and a spare pair of bendy glasses. 'I'm thirty-three and allowed to have sex without getting your approval first.'

Mum's mouth dropped open and she looked awkwardly from Marcus, bristling with discomfort, to Annabelle, serene and resolute. 'Well, I . . .'

'But no, he didn't stay the night, seeing as you asked. He came over early because he's taking Hunter and Katie out for breakfast.'

'But he doesn't know about Katie's allergies!' Mum said.

'He does,' Annabelle said.

'I do,' Marcus said comfortingly.

'But what if Hunter runs away?'

'You won't, will you?' Marcus said, giving Hunter, who'd arrived back in the room with his backpack on, an 'all right champ' chuck under the chin.

'Nah-uh!' Hunter said, standing to attention, keen to have Marcus's approval.

Annabelle saw the kids and Marcus off with Mum chipping in instructions and ultimatums should anything happen to them, then Mum showered while Annabelle pottered about and I stayed on the sofa bed googling the effect of an influx of E-numbers on a mono-mealing, recently cleansed, my-body-is-a-temple system. Once dressed (Mum), with the flat tidied (Annabelle), and with 86 per cent of the Wotsits removed from the sofa bed and a fear that Mum might collapse at any moment from toxin-related epilepsy (me), we sat in the living room in silence. I was sick to my stomach about the imminent family meeting.

Just before ten a car pulled up outside and moments later Dad came into the living room walking with the weight of his past decisions.

He stood in the doorway, his bags in his hands, looking like he hadn't slept in days. Where usually we would have been rushing to exchanges hugs and kisses and stories, there was nothing except uncertainty. Nobody moved because we didn't know how to be with each other.

Eventually, after what felt like an age, Annabelle got up, crossed the room and gave Dad a peck on the cheek. He looked at her with astonished gratitude.

'Coffee?' she said.

'That would be lovely, Belle-belle,' he said, touching her arm affectionately.

'I'll help,' I said, trying to get out of the bed, but feeling woozy and flopping back down.

'It's OK.' Annabelle waved away my offer and padded into the hall.

I stared after her. I wanted to be with my sister. I didn't

want to be left in the room with Mum and Dad. But I also didn't trust that my 'coming down' legs could hold me.

After a quick glance in my direction, Mum got up and greeted Dad too. I watched from the sofa bed with a strange mix of emotions as they murmured to each other. I could only see Dad's face; Mum had her back to me, and his expression showed nothing but love for my mother. As usual. But sorrow was at the edges – and that was new. Mum led Dad to one of the armchairs and she sat in the one beside him. They were close enough to hold hands, and when in those chairs in happier, more innocent times, that was what they usually did. By the way they rested their hands in their laps, or stiffly on the arm of the chair, I could tell that to refrain felt unnatural for them.

Dad looked across at me. 'Plum ...?' He was the same man with the same voice and the same clothes and the same aftershave. But he was also completely different.

I looked back at him, fighting the urge to burst into confused, angry tears and rush to him for comfort.

'I'm ...' he began. 'I'm so, so sorry.'

'About the lying, or for being found out about the lying?' I said, shocking myself by how bitter I sounded.

'*Jess*,' Mum cautioned.

Dad patted her hand but kept his sad eyes with the crinkles round the edges that showed he smiled often on me. 'It's OK, Greta, love. She's hurting.' He focused on me. 'I'm sorry about both. The lies I've told and the way you found out. I—'

'Let's just wait for Annabelle to come back,' I said, not wanting to hear anything without her beside me.

Dad nodded. 'Of course,' he said and the room became still.

Mum played with her pendant, while Dad studied me with his kind hazel eyes. Annabelle came back in and handed out coffees for everyone except Mum, who wrapped her withered hands gratefully around a mug of pungent mushroom tea. Because the sofa bed was still out and my Wotsits and I were still in it, Annabelle had nowhere to sit but the floor or in bed with me. She chose the bed, and with Dad and Mum on the other side in armchairs, we looked a weird little meeting indeed.

'So, let's have it then,' I said once Annabelle had curled herself into a tiny spot beside me. 'You met Mum in high school, you cheated on Mum in South Africa, you cheated on your wife with Mum, and then it's been cheat, cheat, cheat ever since, with a handful of kids thrown in.'

Dad reddened.

'Jess, what's got into you?!' Mum said. 'He's still your father and you will show some respect, my goodness!'

'Cannabis, Mum,' I said. 'Cannabis has got into me.' I gave her a hard stare. '*Unsolicited* cannabis.'

She muttered a few things in German, which I think translated to me being unstable. Dad appeared to be both confused and alarmed and Annabelle observed the banter impassively from behind her coffee cup.

Mum gave me a terse frown then patted Dad on the arm. 'Dear, I think it's best just to start.'

Dad sighed, rested his gaze on Annabelle then on me before turning to Mum, who nodded encouragement. 'Let me paint you a picture—'

'Will it be of vaginas?' I said.

All three of them gave me a 'you're unhinged' look.

'Sorry. It's the drugs,' I said, shooting an accusatory look at Mum.

She let out a puff of frustrated air. 'Oh Plum, will you rein in the crazy for just a couple of hours, *please*!'

Three sets of eyes waited for my response.

'Go ahead,' I said to my father without looking directly at him.

Dad, the pain of his forthcoming explanation weighty in the furrows of his face, began his tale.

It wasn't too dissimilar from Mum's, just from his point of view. They met in school, they made frequent trips to see each other while she attended university in Germany, they lived together in a flat in Angel and then Dad moved to South Africa and got busy with work. And marrying other women.

'Your mother and I,' Dad said with a look of desperation for us to understand. 'We'd never fallen out of love. It was just distance. We didn't have the ways to communicate like you do now. It made the world a huge place, and when I was in Africa there were only letters. Or a very expensive, poor-quality phone call with crossed lines and terrible delays. I don't suppose it's something you can imagine but it really was the dark continent back then. South Africa was my home.

379

I got on with my life. I did what everybody does; I worked hard, I made friends. I fell in love.'

Mum flinched. As did I. As did Annabelle. It was good to know she was in there because up until then she'd been completely unresponsive and I was worried her past drug-taking had caused an emotional deficit.

'I got married,' Dad continued. 'And bought a house. I had a daughter.' He glanced at Mum, knowing his words were painful, then looked back at us for our reaction. But he hadn't said anything that we didn't already know from Mum and I found myself getting irritated.

'What about us?' I said, indicating Annabelle and myself with a flick of my index finger. 'Why did you decide to bring children into all this?'

Mum and Dad had told me that Annabelle was such a difficult baby that they'd waited four years before trying again. But now I wondered if this was in fact true. Mum and Dad looked at each other.

'I'd read about the pill being bad for you,' Mum said, playing with her tiger's eye pendant, her eyes on her lap. 'So we moved on to ... other methods. And they weren't as ... thorough.' She looked up. 'Annabelle, dear, you were an accident.'

Annabelle blinked. Dad's mouth flapped and his hand rose in Mum's direction as if to slow her progression but Mum barrelled right on.

'And Jess dear, we always told you the reason you and Annabelle have such a big age gap was because Annabelle was a difficult baby, but that's not true. You were an accident too.'

Dad patted Mum's hand. 'What Mum means to say is that none of this was intentional. And accident or not, you are two of the most loved children on this planet.'

'But we were both accidents?!' I exclaimed.

Mum began to snivel. 'Happy accidents.'

'*Wonderful* accidents,' Dad said, his eyes shining.

The room fell silent, save for Mum's snuffles.

'So, what now then?' I said, after glancing at Annabelle, who seemed to have been shocked into a blank silence. 'What do we do? We can't just all continue this ... this *bullshit* lie that we're a normal family!'

Mum began to weep. Dad passed her his handkerchief and rested his hand on hers. She gripped it fiercely.

'You're right,' Dad said, his voice breaking. 'We let it go too far.' He looked at Mum sobbing into her hanky. 'And I'm afraid all I've done is hurt the people I love the most.'

I glowered at my father.

'About six months ago, I realised I'd be retiring soon. And with my career coming to an end ... so would the travelling between offices.' Dad looked at us to see if we understood.

I didn't know about Annabelle, because her face was still a picture of neutrality, but I understood nothing.

'Which means,' Dad continued, 'basing myself in one place.'

'Oh,' I said.

I understood. He meant choosing where to live. Choosing a family.

'And where will that be?' I asked, my voice quiet.

I was keenly aware of Annabelle's unmoving presence next to me, waiting for an answer. Mum and Dad looked at each other.

'I don't know,' Dad said eventually.

That was unacceptable. Parents were *supposed* to know what to do. It was an unwritten part of the job description.

Annabelle, inert until then, had a sudden realisation. 'Is that what you guys meant when you said it was time to live honestly and let everybody know the truth?'

I turned to her in disbelief. Had I heard something like that I would have done some investigation. I would have assumed there was a secret that needed outing, but not Annabelle.

Mum looked up from her hanky, snivelling. 'When did you hear that?'

'About six months ago, when Katie had that reaction and we were all at the hospital.'

'Six months ago?!' I cried. 'When they were first discussing it?'

'It seems so, yes.' Annabelle was unfazed. 'That's when Mum started crying a lot and signing up for retreats and being weird.'

'I was not being weird!' Mum said, insulted to her two-faced core.

'Well, that's just great!' I said. 'You heard them talking

about revealing some big secret and you didn't click that it might be in any way significant?! If you'd told me what you'd heard, this could all have been over months ago!'

Mum, Dad and Annabelle looked at each other.

'What would that have achieved that is different to finding out now?' Mum said, her expression curious.

'Well.' I scrambled for a solid reason. 'We could have found out in a better way, you know, with a therapist present or something. I dunno ... We wouldn't have organised this big expensive party that we now have to cancel.'

Mum and Dad looked at each other.

'Oh no, the party will still go ahead, right Teddy?' Mum said.

'Yes, we should still have the party,' Dad nodded.

'But it's a lie!' I said, incredulous. 'Everything is a lie! You'll be standing in front of your friends and family lying. And you want Annabelle and me to do it with you?' I looked at Annabelle for backing but she had gone back to concentrated stillness.

'Why shouldn't we celebrate together?' Mum said. 'It's still our birthdays. It's still our anniversary.'

I scoffed at the word.

'We've had forty years together,' Dad said quietly. 'Nothing, *nothing* can make that untrue.' He looked at me, a note of determination in his voice. 'We should have the party.'

I looked at Annabelle. Her gaze rested on our parents, assessing the pair of them. I turned back to Mum and Dad sitting side by side, holding hands like they always did at dinner tables and breakfast tables, train rides and car journeys. Side by side like a couple of ducks. How could that be a lie? They were a couple. We were a family. It was a lie and it wasn't a lie. They loved each other. Without their explanation I'd already known it. Everyone who knew them knew it. My thoughts shot around my head like a room full of spooked budgies. And the fact that I couldn't pin even one of them down made me feel confused and powerless. And here were Mum and Dad talking about having a party?! I was suddenly furious. I leapt to my feet and threw my coffee cup at the wall. It smashed and the dregs of my coffee splattered on a retro lamp Annabelle had re-covered herself. Everybody jumped up, shocked.

'EVERYTHING IS ONE BIG LIE!' I shouted.

'Jess,' Annabelle said, suddenly at my side.

Mum's bony hands clung to Dad's arm. With Annabelle and I standing beside the sofa bed and Mum and Dad standing opposite us, their eyes wide and fearful, we were a family divided.

Dad looked at me for a moment then his chest sank like he'd been wounded. 'Jess, the love isn't a lie.' He squeezed Mum's shoulders. 'You can't help who you love.'

It angered me further. How could they be so selfish to think this little arrangement wouldn't affect anyone else? Couldn't they keep their pants on? Or at least a condom on?

'We're not even a family any more!'

'But Plum,' Mum said with an imploring look, tears trickling down her face. 'Did you ever feel unloved?'

I looked at them both, my eyes burning with fury. My answer was simple and easy. No, I hadn't. I'd always felt very loved. And somehow that made it seem even more of a betrayal. Tears pricked my eyes. Hot angry tears.

'How could you?' I shook my head. 'How *could* you?!'

I grabbed my bag, flung on my jacket and shoes, and, after throwing a look to Annabelle asking if she was OK and receiving a stoic nod in return, I flew out of the door.

CHAPTER THIRTY-FOUR

'I'm sorry, I just had to get out of there. Are you OK?' I said into the phone as my taxi turned down my street.

'Yes,' Annabelle said. 'I think so.'

I'd called Annabelle as soon as I was in the cab out of the rain. She said Mum and Dad were very upset and that Dad was almost inconsolable.

'What do we do?'

'I don't know,' Annabelle said.

'Me neither.' I passed the driver some money and slid out of the car. 'How do you feel?'

Annabelle waited a beat before answering. 'I don't know.'

'Me neither.' I stepped over some bin bags that a fox had clearly had a go at. 'What are they doing now?'

'About to head home. Mum's rubbing baking soda on the lamp.'

'God, sorry about that.'

'It's OK.'

I reached my flat and looked up at the cracked bricks above the front door that I'd repeatedly told our landlord could collapse at any moment and decapitate someone. 'We'll get through this, won't we?'

'Yes.'

'How?'

Annabelle let out a delicate breath. 'I don't know. But we will.'

I stood at my front door, my house keys in my hand. 'Yeah.'

'I'd better go,' Annabelle said. 'I've got to meet Marcus and bring the kids home. I'll call you later, OK?'

I hung up, entered my flat, hung my coat on the hallway hook and noticed the change immediately. It felt, apart from Dave sitting on the sofa watching a zombie movie and eating cornflakes from a salad bowl, empty.

'Hey,' I said, dropping my bag on the dining table and scanning the room.

'How's it going?' he said, not removing his eyes from the TV.

'My whole life is a lie and I've been roofied by my mother and sister.'

'Stink,' Dave said, twisting in his position to see the roofie damage. 'Wanna talk about it?'

'No.'

He bobbed his head as if to say 'I get that' and turned back to the TV while I walked around the flat. Pete had been and gone and removed almost all trace of him having lived there. And it was only 11.17 a.m. To be fair, he hadn't ever been much into home decor, all the little unnecessary touches that make a house a home had been bought by me (or upcycled and gifted by Annabelle), so he didn't have much stuff that was 'his'. Pete was more a functional item owner. If it didn't do anything practical then he wasn't interested in the ceramic vase that stood on chicken feet. Or the crocheted owl so ugly I had to buy it and give it a home and a name (Rastus, in case you're interested), and who now lives on the recovered 1930s sofa I'd found at Camden Market before it got expensive and touristy.

So even with Rastus untouched and the chicken-feet vase still on the dining table that Annabelle and I had bought on eBay then spray-painted glossy white, I knew he'd taken everything that was his. The weights that usually sat under the coffee table for his evening reps while watching a sports documentary were gone; only a dent in the carpet where they'd been kept for the past four years remained. The *Men's Fitness* magazines he kept in date order on a side table were gone too.

I moved to the bedroom. His drawers were empty, as was his side of the wardrobe. He'd taken the hangers because he was very fussy about what kind of hangers he hung his uniform shirt on. Too long and they created a sticky-out bit down his arm, too thin and they stretched it and did something else but I'd stopped listening, telling him I was getting closer to death with each passing second and I didn't want to devote any more of them to talking about hanger damage in what was effectively a school sports uniform worn by a grown man. His manscaping products were gone from the bathroom; his ankle weights, therabands, skipping rope and various other fitness apparatus were no longer under the bed. The top of his bedside table was bare. In the kitchen, all he'd taken was his super-powered blender, his industrial-sized cans of protein powder and a fridge magnet his sister had sent him from Bali of a lizard on a surfboard.

I walked back through the flat looking at all the holes left by Pete's departure. I thought about my childhood and all those times Dad wasn't there – supposedly working but actually living his 'real' life with his 'real' family. Holes in my childhood, holes in my home ... *Man, I'm grim*, I thought, shocked at my mood. The Verve were right: the drugs don't work, they just make you worse. I was not cut out for come-downs. After googling how to fast-track a cannabis purge from the body I arrived back in the living room and stood behind the sofa watching the credits, dripping like blood, roll up the TV screen.

'Were you here when he took everything?' I asked.

Dave twisted in his seat again. 'I was in my room,' he said, watching my reaction. 'He had someone helping him. A girl.'

'Yeah, I know who she is.'

Dave took a bite of his toast sandwich and watched me as he chewed. 'Wanna watch the new *Evil Dead* again?' he said after swallowing his mouthful.

'Definitely.' I climbed over the sofa, pulled a crocheted blanket onto my lap and curled up among the cushions.

*

We ordered pizza, watched hours and hours of zombie stuff, then Dave got ready for work (ate toothpaste) and left. In the subsequent silence my mind went immediately to Jimmy. With everything else falling apart, leaving me feeling completely powerless, that was one area where I could take action. I flicked open my laptop and called him on Skype.

After a mere two rings Jimmy's face appeared, the sun in the faultless blue sky shining bright behind him. From the angle, I could tell he was sitting at the kitchen island.

'Hi,' he said, his expression loaded with unspoken questions.

I hadn't seen or spoken to him since I'd raced out of Sylvie's restaurant a week ago. So much had gone on in that time that it felt simultaneously like it had been an age and also like it was just yesterday. His face was still beautiful.

My stomach erupted into frenzied butterflies.

'Can I talk to Flora, please?' I said, affecting a polite enquiry.

There was a moment where he looked confused, then his eyes sparkled and a small grin appeared.

'Sure,' he said, his voice warm. He disappeared for a moment then came back and positioned Flora on his lap. 'She's a bit tired from our walk this morning so if she doesn't say much don't be offended.'

I giggled. 'So, Flora, I wanted to ask your opinion on a guy.'

'*Oh yes?*' I imagined Flora to say. '*Fucked something up did you? It doesn't surprise me.*'

'I slept with him and said I'd call but didn't,' I said. 'So I want to apologise but I don't know how to go about it.'

Jimmy smiled behind Flora, who gave her customary black-eyed assessment with muppet-eared head tilt.

'I hardly think the male in question would have waited around for someone like you, but should he have low enough self-esteem to do so, I suggest you go up to him and sniff his butt.'

'Uh-huh,' I nodded. 'Then what?'

'Turn around and let him sniff yours. Then lie on your back and expose yourself.'

'That sounds kind of desperate.'

Jimmy made a quizzical face.

'It works a charm for me.'

'I might go for something less . . . forward,' I said, glancing at Jimmy, who was grinning.

'Lame,' Flora put a paw to Jimmy's chest. *'I'd like to get down now, this conversation has been a waste of good crotch-licking time.'*

'You two girls done talking?' Jimmy said.

'Yep,' I said as Jimmy ducked out of view to lower Madam Floof to the floor then reappeared. 'She wants me to sniff your butt.'

'I wouldn't advise that,' he said, seriously. 'Diego made beans for breakfast.'

I smiled. 'So, what do you say? Can you forgive me for not replying to your texts or calls?'

'Or Skypes, or Facebook messages?'

'Yes, all of those,' I said, feeling truly sorry. 'I've had a bit going on.'

'I know,' Jimmy said. 'I wanted to see if you were OK.'

I cringed. 'Sorry.'

Flora ruff-ruffed in the background. Jimmy looked down at her then turned back and faced the screen again. 'She really wants you to sniff my butt,' he said, then cracked into a winning smile.

'Jimmy, I cannot take this any more! I refuse to be caught in the middle of—' Diego's voice boomed from somewhere in the room and then stopped as he passed behind Jimmy and spotted me. 'Oh hello there, sweet girl! We miss you – when are you coming back?'

'One day, hopefully,' I said, grinning.

He grinned back then turned to Jimmy and his smile fell and his brow lowered. 'Well, thank *god* you've called – we need someone who this domkop will actually listen to!'

Jimmy reddened and I felt myself flush with the compliment.

'Jimmy got his script in on time, you know. And guess what? He got offered one of the placements! He has to be in London in May to do that summer course at the production company.'

My hopes fluttered at the thought of Jimmy coming to London. 'That's amazing! Congratulations!' I beamed at Jimmy, whose face was not the picture of glee you'd imagine. 'What's the problem?'

'Ex*act*ly,' Diego said, his muscled arms folded across his huge pecs. He looked at Jimmy expectantly.

'I can't take the placement,' Jimmy said, his expression one of firm resolve.

'Of course you can!' Diego said.

'I can't,' Jimmy said. 'I can't afford the course fees. And I can't afford to live in London for three months unpaid. I can barely afford to live here in your basement!'

'Argh! You're talking kak!' Diego leant his elbows on the counter next to Jimmy and spun the laptop his way. 'Jimmy's Dad has offered, via Ian, of course, because those two still can't get their shit together, to lend him the money and for Jimmy to stay at home but *he*,' he gave Jimmy some heavy side-eye, 'is refusing.'

Jimmy spun the laptop towards him. 'I am not *refusing*; I'm saying I won't go.'

'That's refusing!' Diego said, pushing back into the frame.

'Yeah, but when you say refusing like that it makes me sound like a child.'

'You're *behaving* like a child!' Diego shoved Jimmy to the side so his face filled the screen. 'Ian and Jimmy have been at each other like a couple of fishwives for days. I can't take it any more, sweet girl. I can't take it!' He glanced at his watch. 'I have to go to a class. Please convince this idiot he is behaving like an idiot.'

He fell into Afrikaans, stalked back and forth in the background collecting his phone and keys, picking up Lucy and Flora and giving them kisses while throwing exasperated looks in Jimmy's direction, then he blew me a kiss, gave Jimmy a quick final scowl and left.

'Why won't you stay at—' I began.

'What happened with—' Jimmy said at the same time.

'You go first,' I said.

'No you,' Jimmy said. 'You owe me. You slept with me. And then didn't call.' He folded his arms across his chest making his biceps bulge. 'And now you're refusing to sniff my butt.'

I smiled and in one big monologue told Jimmy everything that had happened from the moment I drove away from him in Cape Town right up until arriving home and finding the flat completely Pete-less.

'That's . . .' Jimmy sought for a suitable expression of consolation. 'Fucked.'

'Yes,' I said with a slow nod. 'And I feel like I'm developing a lot of wrath about it.'

Jimmy frowned. 'You look very unwrathful at present . . .?'

'It's probably the drugs,' I said. 'I forgot to tell you Mum and Annabelle roofied me.'

After I explained the familial drugging and exfoliation-by-Wotsit, we moved on to Jimmy's placement and why he was refusing his father's offer.

'I didn't think about how I'd fund it because I never really thought I'd get in,' he said.

'But you worked so hard on getting it finished.'

'I know,' he said with a shake of his head. 'But it's just so expensive. There are the course fees, flights and living costs. Apparently they work you really hard so there's no spare time to get a job on the side. Not even a bar job because sometimes you have to work on a script overnight. I'm earning South African rand – I'd be better off if they paid me in pistachio nuts.' He shrugged. 'I'll never be able to save enough by then.'

'But your dad is offering to help.'

'I can't accept,' he said. 'I've barely spoken to him in ten years.'

'Can't you borrow money from Ian and Diego? I'm sure they'd be happy to help.'

'They've offered. But I don't want to take anything more from them. They already do so much for me. And I don't know how I can ever earn enough to repay them. It's three months unpaid in probably the most expensive city in the world. Plus, don't say anything but I've heard them talk about getting married and I know Diego is going to want some big, colourful, ostentatious affair with acrobats and face painters and ice sculptures and a professional dress-up booth.'

'How exciting!'

We chatted for a little longer, Jimmy only gently scolding me for ignoring his attempts to make contact, and after we said goodbye a small feeling of lightness lingered and I decided it would be my new mission to get Jimmy to come to London.

As it headed towards late afternoon, Annabelle texted to see if I was OK and did I want to come back for dinner at her house with Mum and Dad. I couldn't understand how she could look those two Liar McLiarsons in their lying eyes. Then Mum texted. Dad had misplaced his phone again so Mum texted on his behalf. I replied that I was fine but no, I didn't want to join them for roast beef lest some MDMA be hiding in the gravy.

CHAPTER THIRTY-FIVE

I spent Sunday rearranging my things into the empty spaces so I didn't feel so depressed when I saw Pete's unoccupied side of the wardrobe or his bare bathroom shelf. I checked in on Annabelle but she was the epitome of that overused 'Keep Calm and Carry On' saying that was on every mug, tea towel and meme. She and Marcus were taking the kids on a walk along the Thames and then having a cosy pub lunch. I was kind of hurt that she'd kept her relationship with Marcus a secret from me, but my happiness at her happiness overrode that hurt. I told myself that I had enough to contend with without adding 'miffed' to my list of new emotions. After Dave left for his night shift I donned a onesie, curled up on the sofa with a snack and FaceTimed Jimmy.

'I'm just on my way out so I hope you don't mind if I keep getting dressed,' he said, setting up the phone on what I thought was probably the top of his drum kit and removing his T-shirt.

'Oh, I don't mind,' I said, my expression, I'm sure, the extreme opposite of minding.

Jimmy grinned and dropped his shorts.

'Where are you going?' I said, nibbling on my snack and watching Jimmy zip around his room in his boxers locating clean clothing items.

'Up Lion Head with Ian and Diego,' he said, referring to a peak next to Table Mountain that Pete had said was supposed to be stunning and that Google had said was dangerous.

'But it's going to be dark soon,' I fretted, noting the colour of the sky out of Jimmy's balcony doors behind him. It was the burnt orangey-yellow of a gloriously hot Cape Town sunset. I ached to be back there.

'It's the full moon hike. We take torches.' He pulled a T-shirt over his head. 'Hundreds of people do it. It's totally safe. Kids do it!'

'Hmmm,' I said, nibbling some more.

'What are you eating?' Jimmy said, picking up the phone and putting his face closer to the screen. His grey eyes sparkled.

I looked down at my bowl. 'A salad.'

Jimmy narrowed his eyes. 'That's a bowl of cookies.'

'Yes,' I squared my shoulders. 'It's a cookie salad.'

Jimmy gave me a look.

'A salad is merely a mixture containing a specified ingredient,' I held up a cookie, 'and served with a dressing.'

I received another look.

'For the purpose of this conversation I researched the definition.' I sniffed.

'Right.' Jimmy shook his head with a wry smile. 'Well, you have no dressing.'

I held up a pot of chocolate sauce I'd been dipping the cookies into, poured it over the bowl then grinned into the screen.

While Jimmy found shorts and socks and batteries for his head torch we discussed my mother and father and my life of lies, then when he had to go, his bustling activity had me feeling slothful so I pushed my cookie salad to the side and spread my running gear out for an early-morning run. Don't be stupid. Of *course* I went back and finished my salad. I'm no quitter.

After work on Monday, a day in which I stared at the computer achieving nothing, I went to Annabelle's, as I had done every evening for the past three and a half years, but this time I'd called first to make sure Mum and Dad weren't going to be there. Annabelle had said they were going to one of their friend's houses for dinner. They were having a normal couple's night out at another normal couple's house, doing normal couple-y things like a normal, non-lying couple would do. Oh, how the deceit continued!

After feeding and bathing the kids, Annabelle and I sat cross-legged on her living room floor playing Monopoly Deal with Hunter and Katie, who were both sitting inside a polyester pop-up *Frozen* tent in the shape of a castle. Hunter played all card games from inside the purple and turquoise tent so he could strategise in secret. It also meant he could run all his moves past Katie in sign language.

'Have there been any updates on . . .' I glanced at the tent. 'On the "situation"?'

'Derek . . .' Annabelle began, looking up at me for confirmation she'd said the right name, 'hasn't told the A Team yet.'

'What?' I said, placing down a card. 'They're just sitting over there in the sun not knowing anything of this is going on? They're probably planning Derek a seventieth party as well!'

'Probably,' Annabelle said, frowning.

'What if Derek tells the A Team everything and they decide they don't want him?' I said, placing my money cards on the floor. 'Then what? Derek and Magdalena stay together and everything just continues as it was before except over in Cartagena a whole A Team is falling apart?'

While Annabelle blinked and tried to decipher what I'd said Hunter's hand shot out of the tent, grabbed the cards and disappeared back through the polyester door flaps.

Eventually she just shrugged and I didn't know if it was because she didn't know the answer, or was struggling to follow the code I'd created so we could discuss Mum and Dad in front of the kids without them knowing what we were talking about. Magdalena was Mum, Derek was Dad, the A Team was his first family, and Annabelle, Mum and I were the B Team. And Cartagena was Cape Town for no other reason other than I liked how the 'g' was pronounced as an 'h', and saying it made me feel like I was in a movie about drug lords.

'How do you think the A Team will react once they find out about the B Team?' I said, and then had a sudden and horrid realisation. 'The B Team will be the A Team's dirty secret!'

I'd prided myself on never having dirty secrets and now I actually *was* one. Gross. I felt like showering.

Annabelle placed some cards down and Hunter's face peeked out of the flaps to assess the play then disappeared back inside. She rubbed her temple. 'This code is giving me a headache.'

After we put the kids to bed we did the dishes while continuing our assessment of the situation, but not in code so the conversation moved faster and nobody needed migraine medication.

'Her name is Annika and she's sixty-seven,' Annabelle said of Dad's wife. 'She's an interior designer and travels a lot. She does up rich people's holiday homes in places like the Seychelles and Zanzibar. She's apparently quite highly regarded in South African design circles.'

I shook my head and placed a clean pan on the dish rack. 'This is so weird.'

Annabelle picked up the pan and dried it while telling me about the rest of his family. His daughter, Maryna, was forty-one, and also tall and blonde. But I already knew that. She was a stay-at-home mother, a nutritionist and blogger, and was working on her first healthy-eating cookbook. Her husband, Dad's son-in-law, worked in finance and was apparently a really great guy. Annabelle then moved on to Dad's grandchildren, Scarlett and Renzo, but I stopped her when she started listing what sports they did.

'How are you able to have this information in your head and not go crazy with anger or jealousy or feel that you are living in a David Lynch TV series with a parallel universe?' I said, genuinely mystified.

All this knowledge made me more and more mad. Dad had a very real life in another country with another family, and Annabelle seemed to be OK with it all. Or in denial. I was worried that she was compartmentalising a little too hard and this was going to come out later as a drug abuse relapse. Or worse; strict religious-ness (is that a word?). It was flipping me out.

'Why aren't you more . . .' I did a four-limbed crazy seizure-type dance, which, if I'm totally honest with myself, was exactly the same as my normal dancing, and a cricket-ball-sized floof of suds fell from my soapy hands into my hair. 'Aren't you mad? Don't you feel, I don't know . . . ashamed? I know I do.'

Annabelle wiped some suds from my eyebrow. 'Who am I to judge?' she said. 'Look at my family.' She waved in the direction of her fridge, which was covered in photos of the kids, their artwork, play-centre newsletters and magnetic letters spelling words like 'cat' and 'truck'.

I placed the last dish in the dish rack then dried my hands and sat down heavily on a dining chair.

'Jess,' Annabelle said, after putting away the last dish and sitting down next to me. 'Do you love Hunter and Katie?'

I glared at her. 'How can you even ask me that?!'

'Well, they aren't in a mum and dad/son and daughter family from a Ladybird book, are they?'

'No,' I said, picking at a groove in the table.

'And I know you know that family doesn't only come in one format.'

'But we've been lied to,' I said. 'Don't you have questions? Shouldn't Dad be making a decision so we don't have to sit around in this horrible limbo situation? I feel sick, like, *all the time*. And I just don't understand why you aren't angry. I'm furious!'

Annabelle put her arm around my shoulders and I leant into her. 'Things are starting to go right for me,' she said. 'And it's taking all my energy to keep it that way. Also,' she released my shoulders and leant back to look me in the eyes. 'You haven't seen him, Jess . . . Dad is frightened. He's terrified he'll lose both families.'

I blinked away a tear. It hurt to think of my gentle-hearted, loving father afraid his families, whom I *knew* he loved fiercely, would reject him. Yet I couldn't see how I would be able to forgive him. How *any* of us would be able to forgive him.

'But you're still talking to them both. It's like you're condoning it!'

'I'm not condoning it. I'm just aware that people make mistakes.'

Another tear ran down my cheek.

'You don't understand because *you* don't make mistakes,' Annabelle said, passing me a tissue from a box with the *Frozen* characters on the side.

'I do too!' I said, blowing my nose. 'I drank weed smoothies, I slept with a musician, I skip to the end of crime novels.'

Annabelle gave me a look that said '*you don't know the meaning of mistake till you've woken up in the Gare Du Nord with a Latvian Dubstep band, a ferret in a box and three extra earring holes.*'

'I post photos of myself on Facebook that make it seem like I'm having a great time when actually I feel shit, so am feeding into the FOMO culture that is causing one of the biggest spikes in mental health problems society has seen since the war. See? I'm a total rebel.' As I blew my nose I was suddenly stuck by a thought. 'Do you think Maryna is on Facebook?'

Annabelle and I looked at each other, then at my phone sitting on the kitchen table.

'We shouldn't,' I said, but Annabelle was already typing in my passcode.

'She's really pretty.' Annabelle clicked through the photos while I looked over her shoulder.

'I know,' I said, remembering seeing her in the thin-handed flesh.

Maryna didn't seem to use Facebook often but she'd been tagged in plenty of group photos. One image showed her with her daughter, our half-niece, Scarlett. I recognised her from that horrible day at Sylvie's restaurant. Annabelle lingered on the photo, staring at Scarlett with her long blonde hair and her sweet pre-teen face.

'This feels a bit . . . icky,' I said. 'Don't you think?'

Annabelle nodded yet continued to click through the images.

'It's weird to be looking at pictures of our half-sister when she doesn't even know we exist. I think we should—' I stopped.

Annabelle and I saw it at the same time. It was a family Christmas photo. About twenty-five people of all ages were gathered around a vast outdoor table, wearing shorts and vests and looking tanned and merry. Maryna, holding a platter of what looked like lobster, stood behind Dad, who, with a paper hat from a Christmas cracker on his head, was sitting on a chair with a little boy not much older than Hunter on his lap. Renzo. Dad's other grandson. Annabelle and I stared at the photo for a long time. Dad's arms were around Renzo's waist and they were both looking down the lens laughing, like the person taking the photo had just said something hilarious. Renzo was wearing a Thor T-shirt just like the one Dad had brought home from Dubai for Hunter. I slipped the phone out of Annabelle's trembling hands. She looked up with tears in her eyes and let out a shaky breath.

CHAPTER THIRTY-SIX

'I really think Steve-o needs to take another barista class,' I said, walking into Lana's office on Wednesday morning. 'Your matcha espresso looks mucho depresso.' I placed the watery, green, over-spilling shot glass on a napkin on her desk.

'Can you close the door?' Lana said, moving some papers to the side and closing her laptop. She never closed her laptop. Something serious was going on.

'What's up?' I said, shutting the door. I pulled the tub chair close to her desk, sat down and leant forward. 'Are you pregnant? Are we getting the Rita Ora video? Did you go out drinking with Ed Sheeran again? Is there really a limerick about James Blunt hidden in his tattoos?'

'I want you to take some time off,' she said levelly.

I sat motionless for a second. Lana looked back at me with steady blue-grey eyes.

'What?' I said eventually.

'I think you could do with a few personal days. You've had a lot going on and—'

'I'm fine!'

'You're not.'

'I *am*.'

'When the Sony rep came in yesterday and asked you how you were you said you were still coming down from all the weed.'

'I am, though!'

'Yes, but you have to stop telling people that,' Lana explained calmly. 'I know this is the music industry and a certain level of drug-taking is almost mandatory but you've got to stop bumming out all the clients. They come here for buzzy, zeitgeisty ego-boosting and you're giving them the moody blues.'

'They're actually a great band,' I muttered.

Lana fixed me with her unwavering gaze. 'Instead of sending Universal the final cut of the "Taking You with Me" video you sent them a link to an online quiz you'd filled out to see what kind of serial killer you were.'

'*What?!*' My hands flew to my cheeks. 'Oh my god.'

Lana listed a few other gaffes, which included me wailing '*I don't want it to be over*' in front of a very important investor after my favourite pen had run out, bitching to her about a needy, demanding artist in a 'Reply All' email that included the needy, demanding artist, and keeping 'Roger from LA' on hold for fifteen minutes while I cried because the instructions on the back of a Pot Noodle were too bossy.

'Jess, I know this isn't the usual you,' she said, then gave an apologetic smile. 'But this is my company and I have to protect it.'

I couldn't believe how many mistakes I'd made without realising. I was devastated.

Lana got up from behind the desk, pulled the second tub seat close and sat down. 'You need time to come to terms with your family situation,' she said, her voice quiet and comforting. 'And you haven't properly dealt with your break-up yet either.' She stopped for a minute to let the words sink in.

They didn't sink, though. They plunged.

'This is not a request, Jess,' Lana continued in a firm voice. 'I'm telling you to take the rest of the week off. And maybe next week as well.'

My eyes shot up from staring at Lana's watery matcha disasta. 'Are you *firing* me?!'

'Of course not!' Lana said, incredulous. 'Jesus, Jess, you're a woman on the edge.'

'I know! I know!' I flumped back in the tub chair. 'I think it's the drugs . . .'

Lana gave me a look.

'Sorry, sorry! I'll stop talking about it. I promise I'll stop. Just please don't make me go home. My job is all I've got holding me together. I need to be here and I need to keep busy so the thoughts don't drive me crazy.'

Lana stood, smoothing down her cloud-grey pencil skirt. 'No,' she said, 'your thoughts are exactly what you need to spend time with.' She walked back behind her desk and flicked open her laptop. 'I've given your work to Elsie. Go home, Jess.'

I stood and watched Lana clicking at her silver keys.

She looked up and her face softened. 'I need you, OK? Go home, get your thoughts into order, watch some of that awful zombie shit you like and come back like my old Jess: feisty, faintly psychotic and better at the job than me.' She flashed her perfect Scandinavian smile. 'OK?'

I smiled back weakly. 'OK.'

As I left the office mid-afternoon I called Annabelle.

'I'm on forced compassionate leave,' I said, heading to Leicester Square tube station. 'I'm supposed to be thinking about my problems and working through them but I don't want to think about Mum and Dad's lies. Or Pete and I breaking up, and the last time we slept together or the last time we kissed.' I wove through a clutch of tourists. 'When you sleep together you never know if it's going to be your last time, and my last kiss with Pete was just a boring goodbye one and our last shag was just a quick functional one after we went out for dinner. How depressing is that?'

'It's like that with kids too,' Annabelle said and I could hear her tapping at her keyboard in the background. 'One day you're lugging your four-year-old around on your hip, complaining about backache and telling him he's a big boy and shouldn't need to be carried. And then all of a sudden you realise you don't carry your son around on your hip any more; that he's eight and you will never carry him on your hip again. And you've already had your last time and you didn't even know it. You put him down one day and you never picked him up again. It's sad.'

I stopped outside the tube station. 'That is sad. I think I'm more depressed now than I was before.'

'Sorry,' Annabelle said. 'Do you want to come over?'

'Yeah, OK.'

'Mum's here.'

'Then no thanks,' I said, realising that I felt angry with my mother for this 'compassionate-leave/crying-about-a-pen/ making-mistakes-at-work' situation I found myself in.

I told Annabelle I'd see her later then called Priya, but she was on set and could only say, 'Love you, babe. Got a big night shoot tonight. I'll call you tomorrow.'

So I FaceTimed Jimmy and asked if he was coming to London.

'No.'

'Did you turn down the placement?'

'Not yet.'

'That means there's still a chance.'

'I don't know. I'm not sure I even want to live in London.'

'But London has pubs and beer.'

'We have *beaches* and beer.'

'We've got history and architecture.'

'Beaches and beer.'

'We have seven Whole Foods Markets at very easy-to-get-to locations.'

'You can eat organic here for an eleventh of the price.'

'West End shows?'

'Cape Town has an acrobatic musical show run by drag queens in a giant velvet tent with an eight-course meal served in time to the music by waiters in fancy dress.'

'Seriously? How come we never went to that?'

Jimmy laughed. 'It gets sold out a year in advance. Next time, maybe?'

I felt a thrill at the thought of there being a next time. 'There has to be something that you like about London,' I said with a defeated sigh.

'There is,' Jimmy said with a twinkly grin. 'You're there.'

CHAPTER THIRTY-SEVEN

For the rest of the week I kept pretty much to myself. Dad had gone with a client to somewhere in the Canaries so it wasn't difficult to avoid him. He'd tried to call a few times but I hadn't answered. Mum was a little harder to avoid because there was always the chance we'd bump into each other if we were visiting Annabelle. I missed her, though, so found myself listening to her radio show in the mornings. She was fabulous and her callers loved her; that lying, recycling eco-witch. Both Mum and Dad still wanted the party to go ahead. But how could we stand in front of all the people who'd watched Annabelle and me grow up, whose children's weddings we'd gone to, who we'd been on family camping holidays with and who'd dropped round casseroles when Mum was sick and Dad was away, and lie to them all that everything was normal. That *we* were normal. And Annabelle felt the same. I think. It was hard to get her to take a firm stance on anything. She always saw the variables in any situation whereas I believed there were two sides to every story. Well sometimes there just wasn't. Goldilocks stole food, Harry Potter was nice/Voldemort was naughty, Ross and Rachel were definitely *not* on a break, and Dad had lied to us our whole lives. I hadn't cancelled anything yet, though.

At home I worked hard at keeping positive. Or at least not depressed, bitter and wrathful. I followed every recommendation I could to cope with stress. I watched comedies and read Martha Beck. I made lists of the positives:

1. *I have a sister in Cape Town and that was close to Jimmy*
2. *I have a sister in Cape Town and she might get me free diamonds*
3. *I have a sister in Cape Town, which means when I get old and infirm I have one extra person who can bring me prunes*

I bought brightly coloured flowers, I played happy music and planned a weekend in Cornwall with Priya and Laurel for when they got back. I read Oprah's *What I Know for Sure* three times and ended up grumpy at the story of the window of her private plane cracking. I wanted a private plane. I did all the things suggested by the half-page Life Coaching column from *Be Happy* magazine.

After three nights of barely sleeping I reluctantly made an appointment to see the doctor. He offered me a variety of scary-sounding hypnotic sedatives with a variety of scary-sounding side effects (black hairy tongue?!), and I said 'no thanks, I've got the internet' and went home and looked at baby raccoons, before-and-after pictures of dog adoptions and YouTube videos of elephants helping other elephants. And it did make me feel better. And my tongue remained pink and hairless. I have my own Diazepam, thank you very much.

But I was most at peace (well, the least wrathy and crazy) when I was running. And, I was starting to realise, when I was talking with Jimmy, Diego, Ian and Flora on Skype. Which I did every day. I felt like I belonged with them. I'd completely been myself at their place. But I couldn't just turn up in South Africa and say, '*My family . . .? Yeah, that didn't work out. Can I join yours?*' Well I could, but I'd be viewed as very strange indeed.

The weekend rocked around and I stayed at home watching movies with Dave (and ignoring his advice: *if life knocks you down – just stay there and take a nap*), only leaving the house for runs and to pick up croissants; which reminded me of Diego and Jimmy on 'Gluten Day'. I received an email from Dad asking to see me when he got back which I didn't reply to. And Annabelle texted me an updated 'Reasons Why Greta Cries':

- not enough people realise the benefit of mono-mealing
- she was sad about all those years she abused her organs by eating meat and three veg

- daffodils
- she just realised she could follow David Attenborough on Twitter

On the Monday I swung by Annabelle's after an afternoon run hoping I could play Monopoly with Hunter and have a Katie cuddle. I needed one and the need outweighed my desire not to see my mother. But when I arrived Mum had taken Katie for a walk, and Hunter was at a play-date after school with Annabelle's new mum friend (apparently they'd bonded over their back tattoos), and Annabelle was sat in the kitchen doing accounts at the dining table. I grabbed a glass of water and sat in a chair that didn't have a box file on it.

'I don't think I can forgive either of them,' I said, continuing the conversation that had been going on all week.

'Nobody's perfect,' she said, shuffling a pile of receipts, her eyes on her computer screen. 'Look at me,' she waved a hand around. 'And nobody means any harm.'

'Rubbish. Hitler did. Charles Manson did.'

'Yes, but Mum and Dad—'

'Those kids at Columbine did.'

'Our parents have travelled their journey and it's not *your* journey but—'

'The Boston Bomber did.'

Annabelle looked over the top of her laptop. 'Fuck it. Let's watch *Weekend at Bernie's*.'

*

Towards the end of the movie Mum came home with Katie, and Hunter got dropped off a couple of minutes later. I watched Annabelle's face light up as she chatted to her new friend and I was so happy for her. Mum eyed me warily as I sorted a pile of ironed clothes. We'd not spoken or seen each other since the meeting with Dad a week ago.

'I'm not at work because of your lies, you know,' I said, putting Hunter's clothes in a neat pile. 'Your affair is ruining my career. If I end up on benefits I'll fill in the form saying Reason for Benefits: *Big stinky affair.*'

'Oh, surely you can still go to work,' Mum said, as she joined me and began making a pile of Katie's mostly pink items. 'Why should that stop you?'

'Lana says I need to work through some things before I'm allowed back in the office. And I do. Because you've been lying to me my entire life.'

'Well ...' Mum said, folding tights and looking like she was scrambling for a good defence. 'Not your *entire* life. You were a very late talker so it really wasn't until you were about three and a half.'

I glared at her.

'I think you should try some meditation.'

'No thanks,' I said, putting the neatly sorted piles back in the laundry basket for delivery.

'It will be a good outlet for your ... prickly emotions. It's an excellent tool to learn, and once you've mastered it you won't believe you ever coped without it.'

'Rihanna singing her recent songs is probably my level of

enthusiasm for meditation,' I said, holding the laundry basket in front of me.

Mum looked perplexed. I explained that in her latest songs Rihanna was so unenthused she barely finished the words; instead just moaning an approximation of the lyrics with as much vivaciousness as a slow-draining sink. I'd imagined her lying on silk sheets (they'd be rose-coloured) with some minion music producer holding up a microphone from his crouched position on the floor, another assistant holding up sheet music and Rihanna droning out the mumbled. half-formed lyrics while appraising her talons and wondering what her personal chef was making down in the kitchen, and thinking she'd probably get down there around 2 p.m. Mum looked more perplexed.

'Meditation is not for me,' I summed up.

'Meditation is for everyone.'

And because I had nothing else to do and I really wasn't comfortable being angry with my cute, weird little mother, I allowed her to lead me into Annabelle's bedroom.

I sat on the floor and crossed my legs like Mum instructed. 'Annabelle and Marcus have had sex in here,' I said, still feeling somewhat antagonistic towards my composting, worm-farming fraudster of a mother.

Mum looked scandalised. 'Shhh!' she hissed through tight lips.

She gave me a hard little glare then arranged her features into a vision of calm, closed her eyes and told me to do the same.

'The intention is not to get involved with your thoughts,' she said. 'Or to judge them. Simply be aware of each mental note as it arises.'

'OK,' I said and immediately thought of the Blue Footed Booby from the Galapagos Islands and wondered who had been given that word first: the breast or the bird. If it was the breast, then I wanted to know what sicko pervert anthropologist had named the Booby after a boobie. And if it was the bird then that was *really* weird because a boob looks nothing like a Booby.

'Muuum,' I said, feeling overwhelmed by all the boobies in my head. 'I think I accidentally got involved with a thought.'

I told her about all the boobies. Mum listened with one eye open, passed no comment then shut it again and I followed suit.

'Think of your thoughts going past on a conveyor belt,' she said in an airy-fairy spa lady voice. 'Observe them and let them pass.'

'Is it a supermarket conveyor belt, or like the ones at the airport?'

'Doesn't matter.'

'Weeell, the supermarket ones go in one direction but the airport ones come back around. Do I want the thoughts to come back around?'

'No. Go for the supermarket one.'

'OK.'

I sat with my eyes shut watching my imaginary thoughts

slide past on a supermarket conveyor belt. I imagined someone boop-booping each thought's barcode and then I wondered where the thoughts get put. Do they end up in a big supermarket bag (reusable and probably made of hemp), which would mean I'd then have to collect my thoughts and carry them out? No, they were supposed to be going past, observed and discarded. So did the conveyor belt just finish and all the thoughts fall off the edge into a big thought pit? Did they rot or could they be recycled? I ran my concerns past Mum.

'OK,' she said, taking a deep breath in through tense nostrils. 'Think of thoughts as wisps of wind that dissipate after you've recognised them.'

'Outside or inside?'

'What?'

'Are the wisps of wind outside and is the wind making the trees move and are the leaves fluttering to the ground and has my brolly just turned inside out and—'

'They're inside. Inside a nice, calm, peach room.'

'Oh, that's much better,' I said, thinking of a wispy thought floating across a peach wall. Gross. Who painted that wall peach? Who, apart from hospital boards and old folks' homes, would ever think of painting a room peach?!

Five minutes later Mum and I entered the living room where Annabelle was sitting on the floor doing a puzzle with the kids. Mum walked past me, grim-faced, and collapsed on the sofa.

'Some people are not made to meditate,' she said, resting

a palm over her eyes. 'I'm exhausted. How do you live in that head of yours?'

'I'm constantly entertained.'

Later, after Annabelle had fed and bathed the kids and Mum and I had tried to assist but just ended up tripping over each other, Annabelle sat in the kitchen helping Hunter with his reading homework, and I sat on the sofa watching Mum rubbing Marcus's mad sister's home-made cream into Katie's elbows with all the tenderness I remembered from her as a child and thought, *'Why couldn't you have just decided not to love him?'* Why couldn't she have looked at Dad and thought, *'That door has closed. There will be others but that particular one has closed and locked and I need to walk the hallway of life looking for others.'* I was very proud of my analogy and sat down next to Mum and said it.

She looked shocked, but pleased that I was talking to her in a nice gentle manner, and also confused about the doors.

'Why didn't you just tell yourself not to love him any more?' I said. 'Then we wouldn't all be living this lie.'

Mum looked at me through her giant glasses. 'You wouldn't be living at all, Plum,' she said in her clipped Germanic tongue. 'Did you think about that? And neither would this little love bug.' She smiled and touched a finger to Katie's nose, making her giggle.

I winced at the thought of Hunter and Katie not existing.

'But didn't you ever think you could have had it better?' I said, treading carefully. 'A real relationship that wasn't based on lies? Someone who was all yours? Like, truly yours? Didn't you ever think you were … short-changing yourself?'

Mum turned to me. 'You can despair that roses have thorns or you can rejoice that thorns have roses.'

I frowned; did she just get the words to 'Every Rose Has Its Thorn' spectacularly wrong? 'What?'

'You can either see the bad in the situation – the thorns,' she explained. 'Or the good in the same situation – the rose.'

'Is Dad a rose or a thorn?'

'He's the rose.'

'And the fact it's all a lie is the thorn?'

'No. His wife is,' Mum said, then looked up in shock that she'd said it, gave a guilty titter and we both cracked up.

After telling Katie to go and get a memory card game, Mum turned to me, her little wrinkled hands resting on her little corduroy-covered knees. 'You need to talk to your father, Jess,' she said. 'He told me you haven't been answering his calls or emails.'

I sighed. 'I don't know what I want to say to him. I have too many questions and I'm not sure I'm ready to hear the answers.'

'Your father's actions, they were never malicious,' Mum said. 'He did what he did *because* he loved everybody.'

Mum watched me for a reaction but I didn't have any. 'Well, you'll have to talk to him soon,' she said, reaching for the lid of the smelly cream and putting it back on. 'The party is coming up.' She glanced sideways at me, a hopeful glint in her eyes, which I chose not to respond to. 'Then he goes back to Cape Town. And I'm not sure how it's going to work out after that . . .' Mum stopped screwing on the lid of the cream and the corners of her mouth dropped.

I took the jar, put it on the table and held her bony hand. 'I know.'

She gripped my hand and gave a watery smile. Then Katie came running back in and began setting up the Moana memory cards on the coffee table, her breath heavy and raspy. She signed to me to play and I signed 'yes' back and gave her a kiss. I shuffled closer to Mum, pulled Katie onto my knee and the three of us took turns flipping over cards.

'When are you going back to work?' Mum said after a short while when we'd played in harmonious peace.

'When my wrath has cleared up,' I said with a smile.

Mum smiled back.

I found a matching pair and received a congratulatory kiss and hug from Katie.

I was lying on my bed later that evening, surrounded by my old tween diaries and feeling microscopically happier now that I was talking to my mother again, when Jimmy rang through on Skype.

'Hey,' I said after his face appeared, tanned and grinning.

'Hello! What're you up to?'

'Going through my old diaries to see if any of my behaviour was more Sagittarian than Scorpion,' I replied.

I'd told Jimmy about the incorrect birthdate and

consequent star sign identity crisis. Jimmy had sympathised. He heavily identified with being an off-the-wall Aquarian.

'Right. What will that achieve?'

'Nothing!' I tossed my diaries to the side and pulled the laptop closer. 'But if I don't keep my mind busy I'll spiral into self-pity and self-pity is ugly. I refuse it.'

'OK,' Jimmy said, nodding. 'I get that.' He smiled. 'Do you want some external pity?'

I grinned. 'Yes please.'

'Oh there, there,' Jimmy soothed. 'You'll be a fabulous Sagittarian.'

CHAPTER THIRTY-EIGHT

On the Wednesday of my second forced week off work I got a knock at the door at 10 a.m. I opened it up to a crisp late-February morning to find my father holding two takeaway coffee cups, his breath a white fog against the blue sky behind him. I hadn't spoken to him in nearly two weeks. He looked older.

'Your mother says it's easier to have difficult conversations when you're side by side, something about the no eye contact making it easier to open up, so I thought we should go for a walk.' He held out a coffee with my name written on the side in black Sharpie. 'Shall we, Plum?' His words were firm but his eyes pleaded.

I stood in the doorway in my running gear contemplating the coffee steaming between us.

Dad's idea of a walk was to drive up to Battersea Park and sit on a bench next to the boating lake surrounded by inch-thick duck poo.

'Why aren't we having this conversation with Annabelle?' I asked, after a period of silent duck contemplation.

'You seem to have taken this the hardest,' Dad replied.

'That's because I'm the lucid one. Annabelle seems like everything's all fine and dandy,' I said, a tad more bitter than I'd intended. 'What does dandy mean, anyway . . .?'

Dad ignored my question. 'Annabelle and I have had a few chats. She's hurting too, Jess. She just shows it differently. Annabelle understands . . .' He searched for a word. 'She understands making mistakes and living with them. But look at Hunter and Katie. Would you have it any other way?'

Why did everyone keep bringing up the children? They were hitting me where it hurt and it worked. I would have to concede that I would change nothing about my existence (except I'd probably ask for less anxiety, more height and for less of a lady moustache. Correction: *NO* lady moustache) and I couldn't even allow the thought to settle in my head about Hunter and Katie not— No! I wouldn't even finish the sentence.

Dad looked at me. 'You've never done anything really wrong, Plum, so this is hitting you harder.'

'I have too done things wrong,' I said, indignant but not really sure why.

Dad gave me a 'let's hear it then' look.

'I've . . . I . . .' Again I found myself searching my un-chequered past for something, *anything* that proved I was an uncontrollable badass. 'Sometimes in supermarkets I change the herbs around so they read Parsley, Sage, Rosemary and

Thyme,' I said in tune (but dramatically out of tune) to the song. I admit it wasn't all that rebellious, and in some lesser-stocked supermarkets, ones that hadn't branched out to exotics such as Saffron, Sumac and Tarragon, it meant I only swapped around the Sage and the Rosemary.

Dad nodded, looking flummoxed, then angled himself towards me. 'Your mother thought you might have a lot of questions and that I should find a neutral place in which you could ask them.' He said this with a glance around at the mothers and babies, joggers, dog walkers and people talking loudly on their phones, wondering if this counted as neutral. He turned back to me. 'So, Plum, I know you've been struggling with this . . . situation we find ourselves in. And I want to do anything I can to help you come to terms with our unique . . . ah . . . position.'

I sat at the far end of the bench with one leg bent, the foot resting on the knee of my other leg, and picked at a thread escaping from my sock.

'Ask me anything,' Dad said, his voice hopeful. 'No subject is off limits.'

I hated my brain right then for wanting an explanation of the expression 'the world is your oyster'.

'Plum?' Dad said after a few minutes in which I neither said nor did anything more than sip my coffee and play with my sock. 'Maybe I should start.' Dad fumbled in his pocket and pulled out a piece of notepad with Mum's handwriting on it.

'You mother thinks you probably want to know if I ever felt guilty and if my wife—'

I shook my head. No, no, no, no! I wasn't ready to hear this! 'Stop,' I said.

Dad stopped and waited, his expression nervous.

I looked up. 'I only want to know one thing.'

Dad took a deep breath then nodded.

'Who is your real family?' I said. 'Who do you want to live with?'

I waited while a host of painful thoughts traversed my father's tanned face.

Then his face fell and he looked at his hands. 'I don't know,' he said quietly. 'I can't make that decision. It's too hard.'

I picked at my sock. I knew how he felt. *Everything* was too hard. But this was a situation created by him. My father. The man who'd wiped away my tears and put plasters on my knee. The man who'd taught me to ride a bike, who'd built Annabelle and me a tree house where I'd played Barbies with the girl next door and where Annabelle had smoked joints and drunk Carling. He was the man who'd helped me win the Year 3 geography project prize by bringing back stamps and maps from his exotic travels, and clapped the loudest when I got my certificate. He was the man who made me feel loved, and safe, and important. He was the man who'd shattered my world. Who had broken my heart.

'I look at you and . . .' I swallowed. 'I don't see the dad I used to know. I see a stranger.'

Dad's face crumpled. The agony at seeing him so distressed

was overshadowed by my need to self-preserve. I was about to majorly fall apart and I wanted to do that alone.

'I want to go home now,' I said quietly.

As soon as Dad pulled up at my flat I flew out of the car, through the front door, fell on the sofa and my body convulsed and shuddered with huge, breath-stealing sobs. I stayed there crying until my body had completely run out of liquid then dragged myself into the kitchen and gulped down glass after glass of cold water. After checking my blotchy skin in the mirror I took off to Tooting Bec Common and ran round and round the fields, pushing myself harder and harder, but still I couldn't escape the image of Dad's face, desperate, terrified and crestfallen. I hated hurting him. But I was hurting too. I ran as fast as I could, thumping my feet on the pavement all the way home, but when I got there, breathless and exhausted, the thoughts and emotions had come with me.

I jumped in the shower and was in there so long I had no idea how much time had passed. Once dressed I stood in my room, my father's anguished expression came into my mind again and I had to use all my emotional might to fight back another round of sobbing. I needed a bigger distraction. I called Lana.

'How do I get Jimmy to come to London?'

'Tell him how you feel.'

'I don't think it's enough. I know that sounds romantic and

all that but in reality, once you've said all the lovey-dovey stuff, you've still got to pay your bills, right?'

'OK, give me more background info.'

I told her about Jimmy being brought up by his Classics professor father, about Ian coming out, his father's reaction and the ten years Jimmy hadn't communicated with him, bar the odd unemotional Christmas card, because of it. I told her about the course that he couldn't afford, the potential of a job offer afterwards and the most important part.

'*I* want him here.'

'OK, here's what you do.'

A mere two hours later I called Jimmy.

'Your dad is awesome.'

'What?' Jimmy said.

'He joined a group for fathers who have gay sons. He joined it, like, *eight* years ago, going by the date of his posts.'

'Dad posts on a gay website?'

'Gay children *support* website.'

'How do you know?'

'I googled him.'

That had been Lana's advice. Google the dad and see what I could come up with.

Jimmy was quiet for a moment. 'So,' he cleared his throat. 'What does he say?'

I smiled. 'He says amazing stuff. He gives advice to other fathers now. He says he hopes by sharing his mistakes that other fathers won't lose the years he's lost with his sons.'

'He says that?' Jimmy's voice broke.

'Yup,' I said, gently. 'And he mentions you a lot.'

I listed some of the posts I'd read, then the phone line was silent for a while. I was just about to ask if he was still there when I heard quiet weeping. It broke my heart. I wanted to jump through the phone and hold him in my arms and kiss away his tears. And once that was sorted, jump on him and shag him stupid.

'One of his posts was to a father who had said horrible things to his son and hadn't seen him for years,' I said, wanting to tell Jimmy all about the great things his father had posted. 'The son had gotten married and adopted a baby. The dad wanted to take it all back and get to know his new son-in-law and grandchild. Your dad wrote that when a relationship has broken down, and horrible things have been said and done, the best thing to do is apologise and ask if they'd like to try and start again; to build an entirely new relationship from the ground up.'

Jimmy sniffed.

'I reckon that's pretty good advice . . .' I waited and allowed Jimmy the time to process. I heard nothing but his irregular breathing and the odd sniff. 'Maybe you could do that with him?' I said after a while. 'I can help you, if you like.'

Jimmy sniffed again. 'Maybe you could do that with your dad too?'

CHAPTER THIRTY-NINE

After speaking with Jimmy I'd sat on the sofa at home and thought about my father. Really thought about him, as a person. I tried to imagine a life that he wasn't part of and if that was what I wanted. I put myself into future situations, like having a baby. I forced myself to imagine that future day; me sitting in bed holding my new-born, looking around the room at my husband (he was totally hot), at Annabelle, Hunter and Katie, and perhaps Marcus (in my mind I'd re-dressed him), at Mum and then at the gap next to her where Dad should have been. And I realised, although I was still very angry, and I didn't know how it would all work out, that I didn't want that gap beside Mum. I didn't want that future . . . But I also didn't want that gap filled by a lie. Dad needed to tell the truth. Then we could all learn to live with whatever our new reality was. It took me another two days to pick up the phone and arrange to meet my father.

'You have to make a decision,' I said. 'It's not fair to any of us. To Mum, to me, to Annabelle, or to Hunter and Katie.'

Dad's face softened at the mention of the kids.

I swallowed. 'And it isn't fair to your other family either.'

My exhale was wobbly but I held it together. That sentence had been hard to say. I didn't know if I'd actually be able to form the words 'your other family' without crying or fainting or vomiting.

Dad looked at me across the old wooden table, then his anguished gaze fell to the hot chocolate sitting untouched in front of him. I'd chosen a quiet spot at the very back of a local café. A shaft of afternoon sun fell across Dad's right shoulder, highlighting the silver hair at his temple.

'You married Annika,' I said, making Dad look up, surprised, I presumed, that I knew her name. Or surprised that I'd used it. 'In good faith you promised to love her forever and never cheat, and obey her rules about where the kitchen utensils go and which towels are for guests only, or whatever you say in wedding vows.'

I'm always completely bored by that part of a wedding and will usually be glazed over, running *The Rocky Horror Picture Show* through my head to keep from napping.

'The point is, you have to make a decision because ... because you just have to. You can't avoid it because it's difficult. And also ...' I paused, looking at my father, hanging on my every word. 'You may have told us the truth but you're still lying to your wife and daughter.'

Dad winced, like it caused him physical pain to think

of his wife and daughter hurting. His face was a terrain of suffering.

'I think it's time for a new start. A truthful start.' I bit down on my lip, pressing hard with my teeth to stop it from trembling.

'I'm—' Dad began, but the words got stuck in his throat. 'I'm afraid if I tell the truth I'll . . .' He studied his hands for a while, then raised his gaze and looked directly at me. 'I'm frightened I'll lose everyone.'

'Well,' I drew the courage in as I took a deep breath, 'I'm still really, really angry but . . . I'm here, aren't I?'

Dad blinked for a few seconds then he grasped my hands across the table and nodded.

'What's your . . . other family like?' I asked, as we walked across Streatham Common towards the car on the other side of the park, Dad slow and considered and me fidgeting and double-stepping beside him. 'No, don't tell me! I'm not ready.'

Dad nodded.

'How . . . how did you meet your wife?' I asked. 'Don't tell me!'

Dad frowned, nodded and continued putting one deliberate foot in front of the other. He had an unhurried way of walking, an unhurried way of talking. Next to him I was a flibbertigibbet.

'Is your daughter . . . is she anything like me? Don't answer that!'

'OK,' Dad said, looking distressed.

'Do I look like her? Don't tell me,' I said, my head swimming.

Dad stopped and held me by the shoulders, a look of torment on his well-weathered face. 'It hurts me that I've done this to you. Sometimes . . .' He shook his head, more to himself than to me. 'Sometimes I can't believe what I've done. How I let it all happen. How *did* I let it all happen? I've never considered myself a dishonest person,' he paused. His gaze drifted over my shoulder and he seemed to go within himself. 'But . . . I guess I am . . .' His attention was caught by a group of primary school kids running past us, swinging each other round by their backpacks and using language I hadn't even heard of till I was in my teens, then he blinked and brought his eyeline back to me. 'Lying to people I love . . . And walking away . . .' His eyes watered. 'Walking away each time and saying goodbye, I knew it meant I was going to see my other family but the disgust I felt for myself, that I was happy . . . happy and at the same time so very sad . . . it tore pieces off my heart every time.' He swallowed. 'But I *promise* you, it will be OK one day. We just have to get through this tough part. As a family.'

I wiped away a tear. 'A family. Yeah, right.'

'We *are* a family, Jess,' he said, looking into my eyes with his brown dependable ones. 'An unusual one, which is going through something that I . . .' he faltered. 'Something that I've done to you all and I can't ever take it back.' A tear ran down his cheek, following the groove of a well-used smile line. 'But we're a family nevertheless and I love you with all, *ALL* of my heart, Plum.'

He looked so very tired as he eased himself down on an ornamental rock.

I stood watching him for a moment then sat down next to him and contemplated my shoelaces.

'Your mother was fine,' he continued. 'She was always off doing things, seeing people, doing courses. Busy, busy, busy, your mother.' He looked up at me with a fond sparkle in his watering eyes. 'She's always had so many interests. She's been fine. She's always been fine.'

'But she *isn't* fine, Dad. She's signing herself up for weird mind-altering retreats, she's mono-mealing and now she's talking about going on a road trip to Vegas. She's never even been to Brighton and she wants to go to *Vegas!*'

Dad looked shocked at this information.

'She knows she's losing you,' I continued. 'And I don't know what this is going to do to her. I just can't see how either of you thought this was ever going to be an acceptable situation for anyone.'

Dad studied me for a moment, then rubbed his chin and looked at a mother chasing a runaway toddler. 'And I regret that. I do.'

'It doesn't help, though, does it?' I said.

'No, Plum. It doesn't.'

'I feel like an accomplice to your big lie and it makes me feel terrible about myself. And so, *so* angry.'

Dad looked at his hands.

I sighed. Regrets wouldn't help but I realised, with a maturity I was really quite chuffed with, neither would my anger. We needed to find a way through this or the resentment would destroy what had been, up until now, a loving family unit. Family . . .

I turned to Dad, ready to ask my questions. 'How can someone love two families? Why couldn't you stop yourself? Why didn't you use a frigging condom? Why didn't you use a frigging condom after NOT using a condom and ending up with Annabelle?' I stopped and thought for a second. 'Did they have condoms in your day?'

'Well yes, actually,' Dad said, taking on his you–may–find–this–interesting–to–know fact–regurgitating voice. 'They've been around for quite a while. In France, after the syphilis outbreak in the fifteenth century, they used a linen sheath soaked in chemicals, which they tied on with a ribbon. It was called a "glans cover" as it only covered the . . . ah . . . the tip. They used a variety of other materials around that time; like leather, intestines and bladder. These were mostly used to protect against disease, though, not birth control. The first rubber condom was produced in the 1850s. The earliest ones had to be made to measure for each individual . . . ah . . . man, by a doctor. Latex condoms were made a little later and were given to soldiers in the war. Again, mainly to protect against disease. Durex made the first lubricated condom in 1957, I believe, and by 1960 Japan used more condoms per capita than any nation in the world. Although the French were the first to add texture to the condoms.' Dad stopped, seemingly only just aware he'd been talking about condoms, rather loudly and near mothers and toddlers, to his youngest daughter for going on two long minutes.

'This conversation has taken a very weird turn,' I said.

'Yes, Plum, I agree.'

'And I'm still the same amount of angry and also now a little grossed out from the penis and intestine talk.'

Dad nodded.

Again we sat in silence.

'I can't tell you how someone can love two families,' Dad said after a moment. 'I can only tell you that I do. I love you all very much – equally, if that is possible to understand. How could I stop myself loving your mother? I've loved her since I was sixteen years old.'

'But ...' I sniffed back a threatening sob. 'But I thought we were an open family. People who shared everything, and now I find out that half of your life you kept hidden from us.' I started to cry. 'And it hurts so much.' Heavy sobs shuddered themselves out of my body.

Dad's hand hovered near my shoulder. He was frightened to do what he'd done for so many years without thinking. Everything may have changed, but I didn't want *that* to. I leant towards him, giving him permission, and his warm hands pulled me closer and gripped me in a strong, honest embrace. He smelt like Dad. He smelt like home. I sobbed and sobbed and sobbed.

I don't know how long it took me to get my crying under control. It could have been a matter of minutes or I could have been there for half an hour, unleashing the hurt and confusion from the past couple of weeks. I pulled back from Dad, all cried out. He ran a thumb across my damp cheek, his face familiar and full of tenderness.

I blew my nose on his offered hanky. 'I just want everything to go back to normal,' I said once I'd got myself under control. 'And I'm afraid that will never happen. I *know* that will never happen because . . . because it wasn't normal to begin with.'

Dad drove me back to my flat in silence. But a less prickly silence than before. I sat in the passenger seat of his very tidy Mercedes contemplating the fatherly face that I'd thought was all mine, but had also been some other child's all along. He was still my Dad. Just not *all* mine.

We pulled up outside my flat and just as I was about to get out of the car Dad's hand fell on my arm.

'Will we be OK?' he said. 'Do you think you'll ever be able to forgive me?'

I looked at my father's troubled face. 'I want to,' I said. 'And I think if you want to then that's a good place to start.'

Dad's eyes softened. 'It is a good place to start,' he said in a quiet, almost relieved voice.

'I don't think I'll ever get over the art, though.'

'The art?'

'Why vaginas, Dad?' I said, shaking my head. 'You were great at landscapes.'

CHAPTER FORTY

'I've been walking all around Notting Hill and not once have I seen Hugh Grant,' Steve-o said, while he frothed my milk. He looked mystified about Hugh's reticence at hanging around Notting Hill for the benefit of Aussies on their two-year work visa, and I couldn't tell if he was absolutely dry and hilarious or serious and very weird. 'David Beckham nearly bumped into me on the street once,' he said, looking dejected.

'Most people would be excited to have David Beckham nearly bump into them.'

'Nah, not into soccer. We play Aussie Rules back in Bondi. You know it?'

I shook my head then got stuck listening to the rules of a game that sounded like open caveman warfare in lycra tank tops.

I carried two terrible coffees into Lana's office and two almond biscotti that Steve-o had made over the weekend. I had felt a weight off my shoulders having spoken to Dad on Friday, and so on Saturday, after chatting with Annabelle, we'd emailed Mum and Dad saying we were OK to go ahead with the party but that after that we would no longer be willing to lie; and whatever they decided, we'd be ready for it. Then that afternoon, after a mind-cleansing run followed by a quick skype with Jimmy and Flora, I'd called Lana to tell her I was ready to come back to work.

'And you won't talk about being roofied by your mother?' Lana had checked.

'I'll save it for my day on *Jeremy Kyle*.'

'Mmm, nasty,' Lana said after testing her long black that looked more like tar soup. She pushed it to the side and broke off a piece of biscotti. 'So you're doing better?'

'Yes,' I said. 'Much better. You were right. I definitely needed the time off. I'm still working through everything but I'm much less wrath-y.'

Lana smiled, producing two crescent-shaped wrinkles at either side of her mouth. 'That's really good.'

It *was* good. After talking with Dad I had felt that I might just get through everything with the majority of my sanity intact. I still had times where I got a full range of emotions. I'd be trucking along thinking I'd finally reached an emotional status quo when suddenly out of nowhere another scenario would pop into my head. The song Dad used to sing to me at bedtime, for example; did he sing the same song to Maryna, altering Elton John's 'Your Song' to feature Maryna instead of Jess? I'd become hot with rage, followed closely by grief for a lost reality. Then emotional numbness would arrive, then apathy, and finally I'd reach a state of fatalistic calm. '*What can I do? Nothing. Must forge on with life.*' And I would. Until the next memory and the next cycle of emotions. But they were becoming less frequent and I was developing tactics to deal with them. Like drinking. Or looking at baby foxes on the internet. Or drinking *and* looking at baby foxes on the internet.

I rattled all of this off to Lana while she sat listening, nodding, smiling and making faces of commiseration in appropriate places.

'And what about your parents? How are they doing?' she said.

I told her that Dad had flown out to meet a client in Dubai but would be back in time for the party the next weekend. He hadn't told his other family yet but would be doing that after the party; when hopefully he'd have made a decision about which family he would choose. The look Lana gave me when I'd said that had me swallowing thickly but I'd managed to fight off the tears. Mum was still going to her radio show every morning, except weekends, and spent her spare time feng shui-ing her garden shed or researching foods that healed frazzled emotions. She'd try them out and write her findings in a diet diary. So far we knew that tomatoes made her feel mad, cucumber made her feel pensive and onions caused her to pass wind with alarming frequency, which on an emotional level inspired both liberation and shame.

We knew this because Mum would call in on both Annabelle and me to update us with her food findings. If I ever asked her how she felt about the future she would suddenly remember something she had to do that was very important and nowhere near me. Or she'd tell me not to worry and bury her nose in a book on the herbal healings of Hippocrates. Sometimes we'd find her gazing off at nothing, tears dampening her soft cheeks. Often she didn't even realise it was happening and upon trying to comfort her we were told it was nothing to worry about, she probably just had weak-celled tear ducts or needed more curcumin in her diet. Or she'd developed an allergy to marzipan. Never mind that none of us ever had any marzipan on our person.

'And,' I continued, 'I've decided that although I love them both, I disagree with the decisions they've made, and just because they've had affairs and spent a lifetime lying to people they love, it does not mean I am headed for a relation-ship disaster future; even though I have just been in a spot of relationship bad luck with Pete the Cheat.' I squared my shoulders. 'My parents' past will not determine my future.'

'Very mature.'

'I read it all on a support forum for second families. Plus there are other people with majorly fucked-up situations and it makes me feel heaps better.'

'That is not.'

'I don't care.'

Lana and I grinned at each other.

'And Pete?' Lana said, nibbling on another piece of biscotti.

'He's called me a couple of times.'

'That's nice.'

'Yeah, he says it's to check up on me but it always ends up that he can't find his running socks, or favourite boxers, and wants me to search through Dave's stuff.'

'Oh.'

'I say I'll look but I never do. I'm not going into Dave's room. I'll catch jock itch or fleas or bump into a cousin that visited and couldn't find their way out and now has a four-foot beard, jock itch and fleas.'

Lana, her elbows resting on her desk and her delicate chin resting on her clasped fingers, grinned and shook her head.

'Of course I feel really sad that we broke up, and I think he's a real arse-munch for cheating on me, but I think the fact that it all happened at the same time as finding out about my parents did make me go a bit ...' I spun my fingers around my temples and rolled my eyes like that freaky little girl in *The Exorcist*, making Lana laugh her tinkly, white-toothed laugh. 'But I do see now that we were probably not right for each other.'

Lana gave a smiling nod of commendation.

'And I've stopped Instagram-stalking Giselle every day, which I think is healthy,' I said with pride.

'Good,' Lana said.

'It was getting boring anyway. She keeps posting pictures of all these touristy London places with millions of hashtags and exclamation marks, and Pete grinning like he's never stood under Marble Arch or sat at the foot of a Trafalgar

Square lion before. Although yesterday they did the zombie experience in Greenwich. I can't believe she got him to go! He would *never* have gone with me, and ...' I stopped at Lana's singular raised eyebrow.

'I'm getting a handle on it,' I said, picking up my coffee. 'I'm down to every second day and am intending to take that down incrementally week by week.'

Lana narrowed her eyes. 'Glad you've got yourself a plan.'

I nodded and grimaced at the intense sweetness of my 'no-sugar-thank-you' almond milk flat white.

'How's Annabelle coping with everything?'

I smiled. 'She's the happiest I've ever seen her. Which is weird considering everything that's been going on. She's been seeing Marcus for eight months. *Eight months*, and Mum and I were pretty much there every day. I don't know how she did it. He's very sweet with her and the kids seem to adore him.'

'Do you like him?'

'He wears woollen vests. And not in a hipster way. In an "I-don't-want-to-catch-a-chill" way,' I said, as if that were all the explanation needed. 'He's made Annabelle and the kids happy, so I like him for that.'

'And no more spiked smoothies?'

'Nope. I take my own food to Annabelle's now. Hermetically sealed.'

Lana laughed.

'I don't trust either of those drug pushers. They don't even see that what they did was wrong! But I'm not talking about that any more.' I pretended to lock my lips with an imaginary key.

'It sounds like you are doing very well, all things considered.'

'Well, between Pete's cheating, Mum and Annabelle's roofie-ing, and Mum and Dad's life of lies, I've definitely got some trust issues but I'm trying to be distant from it. You know, view it from afar; observe and analyse without getting emotional. I've started reading articles and watching documentaries on cheating.'

'And what have you learnt?'

'A European beaver mates for life and remains monogamous but the male American beaver, who also chooses a mate for life, will cheat and father more babies while remaining in a relationship with their original mate. And a blue whale can have a cock up to eleven and a half feet. That's two of Steve-o.'

'What's two of me?' Steve-o said as he walked past Lana's open door with a tray of empty cups.

'A blue whale's penis.'

'Oh, yeah,' he said with a slow nod like he'd been told he was half the size of a whale's phallus many times before and now it was just getting boring. He tipped a finger to his head in a salute, grinned and disappeared.

'What kind of documentary on cheating talks about whale penises?'

'None. That was purely for entertainment. Did you know they have a penis museum in Iceland that has dried-out erect animal penises mounted on the wall like trophy heads?'

Lana shook her head, indicating we weren't going deeper into that topic, even though I had sooo much more to say on the matter. 'And what about Jimmy?' she said, her over-forties crow's feet creasing as she smiled.

I sighed like a corseted heroine in a romance novel. 'He's lovely.'

And I launched into a soliloquy about the wonder that was Jimmy; his father, gay support websites, Diego and Ian's secret/maybe wedding plans, Flora and her butt-sniffing advice, Jimmy's musical, Jimmy's singing, Jimmy's stubble, Jimmy's abs, and when I'd reached the limit of my Jimmy knowledge many, many moments later, Lana handed me a pile of work, which included booking Steve-o in for another barista course, and we beamed at each other, happy to be getting back to normal.

'Oh, Jess?' Lana said just as I was about to leave her office.

I turned in the doorway. 'Yes?'

'Now that Annabelle seems to be doing OK, would you like to think about training for that producer role?'

I went back to my desk with the job description outline and a little seed of excitement.

CHAPTER FORTY-ONE

At 6 p.m. that Friday evening I arrived at Annabelle's to go over the final points for the party the next day.

'Now what?' I said as I entered the living room and found Mum on the sofa quietly sobbing.

'We're not sure,' Annabelle said from the armchair on the other side of the room. Marcus was perched on the edge of the armchair next to her, an uncomfortable expression on his pale face. 'We've been through all the usual stuff it could be.'

'Mum, is it Dad?' I dropped my bag on the floor and crouched beside her. 'Has something happened with Dad?'

Mum stopped to blow her nose then continued sobbing.

'She won't answer,' Annabelle said.

'Did David Attenborough like another one of your tweets?' Still nothing except sniffs and sobs.

'Is it the catering?' I said, putting my hand on her arm. 'Because if you really want to have some mono-mealing options, I'll put them back in, but I honestly think nobody's going to be interested in a bowl of spiralised carrot.'

Mum carried on snivelling, her face buried in her handkerchief.

'Is . . . is it . . .' Marcus looked tentatively from Mum to me to Annabelle. 'Could it be . . . *the menopause?*'

Mum's head shot up.

'Christ,' I said.

Marcus reddened. Annabelle patted his arm.

'Menopause?!' Mum gave Marcus a contemptuous glare. 'That was years ago!'

'Well then, perhaps it's . . .' He turned to Annabelle. 'What comes after the menopause?'

'Nothing!' Mum spat. 'I'm a hormonally depleted husk. I'm barely a woman!' She dissolved into shuddering sobs.

I rubbed Mum's shoulder and made soothing noises while giving Marcus a death stare.

Marcus's blush deepened.

'Where are the kids?' I mouthed to Annabelle.

'Movie in my room,' she mouthed back.

Eventually Mum stopped blubbing long enough to utter a few stilted words.

'I'm . . . losing . . . him,' she said between sobs.

Annabelle and I looked at each other. With the party happening the next day, Dad's decision was upon us. Mum would potentially lose her best friend and the love of her life. But until the decision was made it was still a big fat question mark, and it was turning Mum into a basket case. She'd recently checked out seventeen self-help books from the library yet spent the entire week engrossed in *Fifty Shades of Grey*.

'But Mum,' I said in a gentle voice. 'He wasn't ever yours to lose.'

Mum lifted her wretched face from her hanky and Annabelle gave me a look that said I was being harsh. I turned back to Mum and grabbed hold of her hand. With Dad not having yet made a decision and Mum rapidly spiralling into (further) lunacy I needed to appeal to her to do the right thing.

'Mum,' I said.

She continued to sob into her hanky.

'Mum, look at me.'

She looked up, sniffing and hiccuping.

'You need to do the right thing,' I said. Mum continued to sniff. Under the watchful gaze of Marcus and Annabelle I continued. 'You need to step back and let his wife decide if she wants to forgive him. Girl Code, Mum.'

She studied me through her giant glasses, looking like a lost little girl. Then she nodded and dissolved into sobs.

'He's the only man I've ever loved,' she said through sniffs and hiccups. 'I don't suppose either of you know what that's like. To be with only one man.' She looked at Annabelle. 'Especially you, dear.'

Annabelle rolled her eyes. Marcus shifted uncomfortably in his seat.

'What am I going to do?!' she whimpered into her handkerchief.

448

'Why don't you take up a new hobby?' Annabelle said.

'I already do all the hobbies I like.'

'You could become one of those people who help the elderly?' I offered.

'I *am* the elderly! Aren't I, Marcus?!' Mum said with an accusatory glare.

Poor Marcus shrank into the armchair.

'What about doing extra radio slots?' I said. 'Or you could do a course? Or there's always—'

'No, no, no!' Mum flapped her hands at us. 'What I need is some guidance and there's no self-help book to help the mistress of the second family!' Mum stopped flapping her hands mid-air and her eyes widened. '*I* could write one!'

While Mum got out her paisley notebook and furiously wrote notes on her new 'Mistress Self Help Book', I made dinner (rang the curry house and cut up Mum's avocado) in the kitchen. Marcus had taken Annabelle and the kids out for a quick supper before going to *Matilda* in Covent Garden. They'd piled into Marcus's Prius in their theatre-going best, smiles stretched wide on their faces and excitement dancing in their eyes. It was weird to have Annabelle acting so sorted while the rest of us seemed to be falling apart. Now that their relationship was out in the open Marcus had been taking Annabelle to all kinds of plays, galleries and restaurants. At the weekends they took the children for picnics and walks and to museums. They were like a miniature romance movie from the 1990s that probably should have starred a middle-aged Tom Hanks and Meg Ryan, and a couple of kid actors that would grow up to have drug dependencies and bankruptcies and 'took-home-a-hooker' scandals.

Dinner arrived and I assembled my curry, laid Mum's sliced avocado as appetisingly as I could across a plate and headed into the living room to eat in front of the television. After we'd eaten, Mum continued to scribble in her note-book, her passions ignited by the thought of writing the first self-help book of its kind, and I watched a documentary Mum had put on about the evils of dairy farming. I looked away from a cow's swollen teats to the laundry basket in the corner. In the past it had held a mountain of clean clothes that only ever got sorted when Mum or I tended to it, but now it contained a neat pile of ironed and folded clothes ready to be distributed. I knew the fridge was stocked with healthy food, that Hunter had done his homework and that Katie's therapies were all booked in for the coming month and had been recorded on the calendar on the fridge. Why were we here? Annabelle was out. The kids were out. And when they came back it would be to a tidy, well-run, warm, happy little home. Annabelle didn't need us any more. It was Mum and I who turned up every day, like we had done for the past three and a half years. It was Mum and I who were unwilling to let go of what used to be.

The idea that Annabelle might not need my help any more made me feel sad and a bit . . . redundant. *Dispensable.* And it dawned on me in that moment that Pete had been right. You do need to feel needed in a relationship. It's just that I'd obviously made my primary relationship with my sister.

'Mum,' I said, turning the TV down with a remote. 'We need to move on.'

'Yes,' she said, still scribbling. 'Good idea, Plum.'

'Mum?'

She continued her outpouring of 'mistress' advice.

'MUM!'

'Yes, Plum?' She looked up, confused.

'Why are you here?'

'I'm having dinner with you,' she said, mystified.

'Well then, why aren't we having dinner at your place? Or at my flat? Why are we *here*?'

'We always come here, because Annabelle needs ...' she trailed off, looking around the tidy living room that had been vacuumed that morning.

I watched her thoughts work their way across her features. Her eyes, behind her giant glasses, darted to and fro. The corners of her mouth fell and she turned to me, bewildered.

'Annabelle is fine,' I said. 'Isn't that great? Annabelle is finally fine.'

Mum blinked for a moment then dropped her gaze to her lap.

'Annabelle needs to be allowed to move on,' I said. 'Which means we do too.'

'Yes,' Mum said quietly.

We sat there with the TV on silent, pictures of cows and

milking machines and earnest-looking enviro-journalists on the screen.

'We're at a crossroads, aren't we, Mum?'

'We are, Plum,' she nodded, her gaze now somewhere in the middle distance. 'We are.'

I could sense the plates of my emotional universe shifting and producing a feeling of lightness. I could feel the pride at having come up with that analogy and vowed to start recording my incredible insights. My brief feeling of redundancy shifted and another feeling took its place.

I. Was. Free.

A buzz of delight played in my chest. But Mum looked bereft. Her hands sat unmoving in her lap, her note-scribbling abandoned. Life was changing too quickly for her. I shuffled along the sofa, moved Mum's notes and laid my head on her lap.

'Let's watch something funny,' I said, turning off the cow documentary with the remote and searching for a comedy that Mum would appreciate.

A little while later, my head still on Mum's bony little lap, I pulled a cushion close and hugged myself around it. I missed cuddling Lucy on Jimmy's sofa. And, towards the end, when Flora and I had come to our understanding, I'd been permitted to sit cuddling her too. I looked up at Mum.

'How come we never had a dog growing up?'

'Oh, we didn't think it would be fair on an animal with your father away a lot of the time. It might have got attached. It would have broken its little heart.'

I stared at Mum. It took her a few minutes to take her eyes off Jim Carrey in a tutu to look down at me. She raised her eyebrows in question.

'Not fair on an *animal*, Mum?' I said. 'What about us?'

'Well,' Mum said, trying to tread carefully but failing dismally. 'We could lie to you. An animal *feels*.'

CHAPTER FORTY-TWO

The next morning was Saturday, the day of the party. And I woke early to a text from Dad calling a family meeting at Annabelle's. I left my local bakery with a bag of croissants and stepped into the sunny but cold morning with my stomach cramping. What was Dad going to say? He must have come to a decision. Or maybe he had something else to confess to? He had a third family? He had cancer? He had a secret bunker and classified information from the government that chemical warfare was imminent and we needed to take what was in front of us and move immediately to an indefinite subterranean lifestyle?

As I hopped on a bus I scanned the party checklist on my phone. Everything was running smoothly. Nearly all of the 150 people had confirmed, the caterers had finally got their heads around the menu, the function room at the local pub had been decorated, Mum's dress had arrived from the online eco-shop, Dad's tux had been dry-cleaned and the

Van Morrison cover band had been given their playlist. All we had to do now was turn up.

Annabelle's flat was quiet when I let myself in. Marcus had taken Hunter and Katie to the park to give us some space. Dad and Mum were in Annabelle's armchairs, side by side, holding hands, and Annabelle was sat on the sofa across from them. I put the paper bag of croissants on the coffee table next to a tray of untouched tea and took my spot on the sofa next to my sister. It was pretty much the same configuration as three weeks ago except the sofa bed wasn't out, I wasn't covered in Wotsits and suffering a roofie comedown and Mum wasn't 'soiled by E-numbers' as she'd taken to saying.

'We've come to a decision,' Dad said. He had dark circles under his eyes and his skin was ashen. It had taken its toll on him.

'And?' I said, impatient to hear the outcome so I could book my therapy accordingly.

This was it. Make or break.

Which would we be? The 'made it' ones or the broken ones? Dad's eyes rested on me, then Annabelle and finally fell on Mum, who instantly erupted into agonising, inconsolable tears.

I gasped.

Annabelle, who had remained stoic through the entire period, crumpled like a discarded string puppet.

We were the broken ones.

I was stunned. Even though, in the back of my mind, I

knew this was the choice he would make, the choice he *should* make, I didn't think it would ever actually happen. My dad, who I knew loved me, who I knew loved Annabelle, who I knew *adored* my mother, was leaving us.

'I'm so sorry,' Dad said, his voice cracking. 'I'll ...' He gripped Mum's hand. 'We'll start to tell people after the party. I'll go back to Cape Town and tell Annika and Maryna.' He wiped tears from under his eyes. 'I'm so sorry ... about everything.' His mouth twisted and he covered his face with a wrinkled, tanned hand, his shoulders shuddering with his muffled sobs.

Annabelle, tears streaming down her perfect cheeks, rushed across the room and fell at his feet, her legs tucked underneath her. 'Dad, no,' she cried. She gripped him with her thin arms, her head resting on his lap and her chestnut hair falling across his knees.

Dad clutched her. Tears dripped from his chin as he said sorry over and over again.

CHAPTER FORTY-THREE

'If your dress is so tight we can see your pudendum then it is not a dress it's a compression bandage,' Pete's mum, Wendy, said through disgusted crimped lips, her eyes on Giselle.

I choked on my drink and pulled at the low neckline of my own dress.

Pete's dad looked like he didn't mind the pudendum at all. 'I think she looks nice,' he said, while chomping on a vol-au-vent, the flakes catching in his bushy moustache.

'I *know* you do.' Wendy's magenta lips crimped further. 'The whole *room* knows you do. Stop staring, Gary!' She glowered at the flakes of vol-au-vent falling down her husband's substantial stomach then turned to me. 'It's very bad taste bringing her here and I told him as much, but he wasn't listening to his old mum, was he? I'm so sorry, pet; it's not ruining your night, is it?'

I glanced across the room at Pete and Giselle. With her tanned limbs, tight red dress and elaborate French braid up-do, she looked like a *Baywatch* babe on a night out. Pete had turned up in an ensemble unfortunately similar to the waiters' uniform; black suit trousers, navy shirt and maroon waistcoat. Mum and Dad's friends (the ones who didn't know him) kept asking him for Campari and sodas, and even though he was attempting to be good-natured about it, his tight smile and glances towards Giselle made me realise he was dying of embarrassment. And that gave me a small comfort.

'It's OK,' I said to Wendy. 'Well, it's a bit shit, but he did call and ask and I said yes so I can't really complain, can I?'

'No, I guess not,' Wendy said, and she appeared to be embarrassed on behalf of her son. 'Oh Gary, would you stop staring!'

I nailed my Campari and soda (I'd wanted to see what all the fuss was about), made my polite excuses and left Gary to be chastised for being male and in possession of eyes and a heartbeat. Giselle had at least had the grace to come over and introduce herself and tell me how kind I was to invite her. I managed not to point out that I hadn't invited her, and that I was actually quite shocked Pete had still wanted to come. Had I not had a knot in my stomach knowing this was the final time Mum, Dad, Annabelle and I would be together in front of people who thought of us as a normal family and not a shameful 'B Team', then Pete and Giselle's presence would have had me shallow-breathing into a paper bag in the corner of the room, which, by the way, doesn't work and is just something they do in the movies. But, as it was, I almost didn't care. Almost. Luckily Mum had already informed everyone who knew Pete and me that we were no longer together so I had no awkward explaining to do. I did get lots more hugs from fragrant ladies 'in the prime of their lives', though. And the dapperly dressed men gave me 'chin up' nods after their watery gazes flicked disapprovingly from Pete and Giselle to me.

It was weird not having told Pete about what was going on with Mum and Dad. I'd always told him everything about everyone in minute detail for so many years. Now, the biggest thing in the world that could ever happen to me had happened and I wasn't sharing it with him. As I wove through the partygoers looking for a waiter, and trying to contain my boobs in a dress I'd bought six months ago but, because of all the running, was now too big for me, I thought not about Pete and Giselle, who were at the buffet table, their heads inclined towards one another, giggling at Mum's mono-mealing options I'd asked the long-suffering caterers to put back on the menu, but about Jimmy.

After Dad had dealt the blow that he was going to stay with his original family, if they'd have him, I'd felt like I had nothing left to lose. I'd called Jimmy as soon as I got home from Annabelle's with the intention of telling him exactly how I felt; that I liked him more than baby hedgehogs. And perhaps even elephants. And that he should call his dad, tell him he knew about the 'we've got gay kids' support group thing and that he was proud of him. And sorry. Then borrow money, get on a plane and come and be with me. But Jimmy didn't answer his phone. Or any of my texts. So instead I'd called Diego.

'He's not here, sweet girl,' Diego had said.

It had only been 11.30 a.m. in Cape Town; a time when Jimmy could usually be found wandering the house in his boxers, Flora trotting behind him, or out on the sun-soaked balcony sipping coffee and intermittently singing or playing an instrument.

'Do you know when he'll be back?'

'No,' Diego had said and he'd sounded oddly taciturn.

'Do you know where he is? His phone is off.'

'No, sorry.'

I braced myself. 'Did he come home last night?'

Diego made noises of discomfort.

'Oh,' I said. 'Right.'

I'd hung up from Diego, who'd made weak promises to tell him I'd called when he next saw him, and felt unbearably, despairingly heartbroken. Like I'd missed out on something that could have been truly special. But I had no claim over Jimmy; we'd only had that one time together. And I couldn't expect him to . . . what? Wait around for me in South Africa, a place I loved but had no intention of moving to?

I found a roaming waiter and asked for another Campari and soda.

'Make it two, actually,' I said and the guy winked his approval.

When he returned three minutes later I slurped down

the first one before he'd even left me, then handed him the empty glass and began on the next one while scanning the room for Annabelle. I spotted her across the bustling room, introducing some old family friends to Marcus. She looked beautiful in a 1990s-style navy shift dress and a new necklace Marcus had given her that evening. It was a tiny heart on a delicate gold chain and was something the old her would have thought cheesy. But her fingers were constantly reaching for it and she'd look at Marcus and radiate bliss.

I was just about to head over to her when a short lady in swathes of floaty turquoise approached me, her wrinkled coral lips in a sweet smile. 'Are you Greta's daughter?' she said, wafting Chanel No. 5.

'Yes,' I said, plastering on a smile that felt contradictory to my mood. 'I'm Jess.'

'What a lovely party,' she said, taking my hand in both of hers. 'Your mother told me you pulled this all together by yourself, you clever girl.'

I made 'oh, it was no big deal' and 'yes, they are a happy couple' kinds of noises while she enthused about the music, the catering, Mum and Dad and told me she was a friend of Mum's from pottery classes and had heard all about my thrilling job in the music industry and my clever schoolteacher boyfriend (obviously someone Mum hadn't remembered to inform), and '*Is marriage on the cards, my dear?*' and '*I know you young people like to leave it all to much later but best be getting on with things, I say*'.

'Now that looks interesting,' she said as I took a large, *very large*, swig of my Campari. 'Where can I get one of those?'

'From him,' I said, pointing across the room at Pete.

'Lovely,' the turquoise lady replied, then said a multitude of goodbyes and 'clever girl's and made a beeline for Pete. I watched with amusement as Pete went to the bar and irately ordered a Campari and soda because it was easier than explaining to a ceaselessly yakking old lady that *his* waistcoat was maroon and the waiters' were burgundy.

Still sniggering to myself, I turned and scanned the huge network of friends Mum and Dad had made in the four decades they'd been together, looking again for Annabelle. And with a start I realised Dad must have something like this in Cape Town. The thought hit me like a hurricane. With bricks in it. But I was getting used to these kinds of thoughts. They were a fact. A fact that shocked me in that split second when I first realised it, then became yet another piece of reality I filed in my brain as 'fucked-up shit that will come out later as cancer'.

'Do you think any of these people knew about Derek and Magdalena?' I said, finding my sister and sidling up to her.

'Nooo,' Annabelle said, turning around with Katie on her hip and an anguished look on her face. 'Not the code again.'

'Do you think people will take sides?'

'There aren't any sides to take,' Annabelle glanced down. 'Jesus, I can almost see your nipples!'

'Do you think they will think we're simpletons for not

suspecting anything was up?' I said, hoisting my neckline up with one hand and trying to bring my Campari to my mouth with the other. It was an awkward manoeuvre that had Campari spilling, Annabelle frowning and me looking like a simpleton.

Annabelle suddenly spotted Hunter serving himself a Hagrid-sized portion of chocolate cake. 'I have to go.' She turned back to me and watched me drain my glass. 'Go easy on the drinking, OK?' she said, a wrinkle of concern between her delicate eyebrows. Then she glanced down again and the wrinkle became a furrow. 'And cover yourself, you look like a page three.'

Annabelle drifted towards Hunter and I stood alone again, contemplating the roomful of people who may or may not have known about my parents' big lie. Ruth and Bert, our old neighbours, were dancing to 'Brown Eyed Girl'. Did they ever overhear an incriminating conversation between Mum and Dad as they sat in the garden in the summer sipping gin and tonics? Patrick, the producer at Mum's radio station, was at the buffet struggling with a pair of tongs. He'd had a relationship with Mum. Did he know about Dad's other family? And what about Dad's business partner, standing close by talking to Marcus? Surely he, if anyone, would have had an inkling at least. Every thread of enquiry brought forth a torrent of questions and I had to order another Campari and soda to quiet the noise in my head.

*

At 9 p.m., as I'd scheduled, the band stopped and everybody took their seats to listen to the speeches. I'd decided against giving mine. Prior to my trip I'd been writing it during quiet moments at work. But although every word in it was true: what a great mother Mum had been, a great father Dad had been, and how I wished I would one day have a relationship that made me as happy as they made each other; all those words were attached to a lie. Mum wasn't emotionally strong enough to give a speech and Annabelle had a deathly fear of public speaking. So that just left Dad. He took to the stage with Mum at his side in her shapeless eco-dress that was probably made out of something Annabelle would have once tried to smoke. Whoops and cheers erupted from the Campari-merry crowd.

'Here we go,' I said, standing next to Annabelle behind the kids' table.

She turned to smile at me but her smiled dropped. 'Put your bosoms away.'

'They aren't bosoms,' I said, pulling up my dress while Dad started talking about his friends, happy times and getting through tough times. 'Bosoms are older and get hefted around to Neil Diamond songs. These are tits,' I said, pointing directly at my cleavage and making Annabelle hiss at me to be quiet. 'And they want to twerk to Nicki Minaj.' Dad had moved on to talking about surviving teenagers and stock market crashes. I frowned. 'Only butts twerk. What do tits do?'

'How much have you had to drink?' Annabelle whispered, looking at my half-filled Campari glass.

'Enough to make me talk about tit-twerking. Not enough to quiet the dramatic stage production of our ridiculous life that's going on in my head right now.'

Annabelle looked at me blankly.

'Winona Ryder is playing you. *Reality Bites* Winona though, you know? With the spiky hair and the 1990s waif look? Not *Stranger Things* Winona with the screaming and the running and the really ugly coat.'

Annabelle gave me a stern 'shut-up' kind of look and I turned my attention to Dad.

'I've made some mistakes in my life,' he said, getting serious.

'You don't say,' I muttered.

'Shhh!' Annabelle whispered.

Dad's eyes scanned the crowd and stopped when he found us. I stiffened.

'My life, as I'm sure happens to everyone, has had its ups and downs,' Dad continued, his voice wavering. 'I've spent a lot of time away ... working. And as I've reached this age, I look back and ...' He faltered and reached for Mum's hand. 'We've got two beautiful girls ...'

'Three,' I whispered to Annabelle, who scowled.

'... whom I've had the privilege to watch grow into remarkable young women. And two grandchildren ...'

'Four,' I whispered in her ear again.

Annabelle took my drink off me and handed it to Marcus. 'Pull your dress up,' she hissed.

'... who mean the world to me. And if it all ends now,'

he looked at Mum, then out at Annabelle and me. I grabbed Annabelle's hand and gripped it hard, trying to overcome the desire to flee the room. She wrapped her arm around my waist. 'Well . . . I wouldn't have changed anything for the world.'

Mum stood next to Dad with tears trickling down her lightly rouged cheeks and catching in the overhead lights. She seemed so tiny. Dad looked at Mum and I could see the words were stuck in his throat. He appeared to lose his thread. 'I'm . . . I . . .' He turned back to the crowd. His hand tightened its grip around Mum's. 'I'm just so happy to be here with my family and friends. Who knows what tomorrow will bring? All I know is that I am where I want to be right now. Thank you for being with us on this special night to celebrate love, life . . .' His gaze fell on Annabelle and me. 'And family.'

Dad stepped down from the stage as the band took up their positions. Annabelle and I stayed side by side, her dabbing at her moist eyes and me fussing with my neckline.

As the dance floor filled up to the sound of 'Gloria', Mum and Dad arrived in front of Annabelle and me.

'That was a good speech, Dad,' Annabelle said as she handed Mum a napkin from the kids' table.

'Your maths needs some work though,' I mumbled, making Annabelle smile despite herself.

'Thank you, Belle-belle,' Dad said, with a look of relief. 'And Plum, I have a surprise for you.'

'Your last surprise sucked,' I said, smiling to show I meant it light-heartedly. Sort of.

He smiled back then pointed behind me. Holding the neckline of my dress up, I turned around. And in the doorway across the room stood Jimmy, tanned, tall, grinning and filling out a navy suit in an exceptionally attractive manner.

'H-wh-?' I managed to stutter.

Dad gave me a kiss on the cheek. 'Time for a new start for you too.'

Mum laid a bony hand on my arm and whispered in my ear, 'Go get him, Plum.'

I turned to Annabelle, who was smiling, Marcus's arm around her shoulders. The dance floor began to fill with lively, Spanish-countryside-cycling, Swiss-mountain-hiking, let's-book-a-walking-wine-tour-of-Umbria active couples in their seventies. I stayed still, rooted by shock. And Campari consumption. And the fear my dress was going to fall down. Jimmy began to move across the room. There was a moment when he was lost from view in the gambol of dancers and then he was there.

'You're – you're here!?' I stammered. 'How? Why?'

He grinned. 'Because this is where you are.'

CHAPTER FORTY-FOUR

'It was so hard to lie to you, sweet girl!'

After kissing Jimmy and getting the most urgent details out of the way: yes, he'd taken the placement; yes, he was here to be with me; and yes, he did like how my dress wasn't containing my breasts, he said we had to FaceTime Diego immediately because the guilt at lying to me was eating away at his paleo-perfected stomach lining.

'I felt terrible! I wasn't sure I could do it!' Diego said, his face filling half of the screen.

'I knew you could,' Ian said.

Diego and Ian, also at a Saturday night party, were cheek to tanned, moisturised cheek in the frame of my phone. Coloured lights reflected off the inky ocean moving gently behind them and samba-like music played in the background.

Annabelle came up and introduced Marcus to Jimmy and while it was just Diego, Ian and me, Ian spoke.

'I don't know what you said but after he talked to you Jimmy called Dad.'

'Two days later he borrowed money from us, took the placement and booked his flights!' Diego beamed.

'He and Dad still have a lot of ground to make up but they will get there,' Ian said. 'And it's all down to you.'

I looked over at my own father, dancing with my mum and high-fiving a friend as he jitterbugged past him. 'Well, I know how that feels.'

Diego smiled. 'We know you do, sweet girl.'

'And we're thinking of you always,' Ian added.

After I hung up from Diego and Ian, I joined Jimmy, tucking under his outstretched arm, and listened, with an increasing sense of happiness, as he told Marcus how Annabelle had called him to see if he'd consider coming to London a mere hour after he'd booked his flights.

'You did that?' I said to my sister.

She nodded and I threw my arms around her petite shoulders.

'Careful!' She laughed, and when I stepped back to Jimmy she checked her necklace was still there.

Marcus and Annabelle gave each other 'let's leave these two alone' glances then left, and I felt so happy that my sister had found someone to have those silent, knowing exchanges with.

'Come here,' I said, dragging Jimmy by the sleeve, intending on leading him to a darkened corner and planting my lips on his.

'Hi.' Pete suddenly appeared in front of us with a look on his face that meant something was just dawning on him.

'You remember Pete?' I said to Jimmy.

'Yes, of course,' Jimmy said, extending his hand and smiling. 'Hi, mate.'

'Yeah, hi,' Pete said, pumping his hand up and down, his face a plethora of unanswered questions. He flicked his eyes from Jimmy to me.

'And this is Giselle,' I said, indicating the vision of perfection arriving next to Pete.

'Nice to meet you,' Jimmy said, shaking Giselle's hand. He shot Pete a look, which made Pete wither with shame.

Jimmy noticed a passing waiter then looked pointedly at Pete's outfit.

'Can I get a margarita?' he chuckled.

Pete reddened. 'It's actually quite a different colour, this is maroon and that's, well, theirs is more burgundy but, you know.' He gave a stiff shrug. 'Ha, ha. I get it.'

A couple of older ladies walked past on their way to the bar. 'Hello, ladies, you look lovely tonight,' Jimmy said. The women tittered and called Jimmy wicked. 'This man,' Jimmy pointed to Pete, 'makes a mean Alabama Slammer.'

Pete stormed off followed by Giselle and a gaggle of Alabama Slammer grandmas.

I laughed and Jimmy pulled me towards him. 'I missed you,' he said, leaning down, his lips close to mine. 'So much.'

'I missed you too,' I said, and drew him into a kiss that made the rest of the room disappear.

A couple of hours later, as the band neared the end of their set, Jimmy took Hunter on stage to watch the musicians close up and I stood at the edge of the dance floor watching Mum and Dad swaying cheek to cheek to Van Morrison's 'Bring It on Home to Me'. They looked like a happy couple heading into their twilight years with boozy brunches, trips to southern France and brochures of retirement homes made to look like land-bound cruises. But all was not as it appeared. And only Annabelle and I knew it. Dad had to confess to his other family in Cape Town and Mum had an unknown future. I would never really know what it must have felt like for them. For her to have made this decision to love someone who would never fully be hers. For him to have to split his heart and his time. But they weren't my decisions to understand. I didn't know how the future was going to play out. Would my mother cope without Dad? How often would I see my father? Would I be allowed to visit him? To call him? Would I be allowed to invite him for Christmas? How could these questions be part of my life? How could I even be contemplating the access I'd have to my own father?

I felt a slim arm slip around my waist.

'It's going to be all right, you know,' Annabelle said in my ear.

We stood side by side watching our parents. A tear trickled

down my cheek and Annabelle wiped it away with a delicate thumb.

'It'll never be the same again,' I said.

'Who said life is supposed to always be the same?'

I smiled at my sister. 'Yeah.'

The song finished and the band started playing 'Moondance'.

'MAMA!'

Annabelle and I turned to see Katie in Marcus's arms signing and calling out, 'MAMA DANCE!'

She looked at me.

'Go, dance,' I said. 'I'm fine.'

She hugged me, adjusted my neckline then skipped over to Marcus and took Katie in her arms. Although Marcus was as stable as they come and Annabelle seemed very happy, I knew I would probably never stop worrying about her. You may cease with the destructive consumables but do you ever lose that wild aspect of your personality? Annabelle felt my gaze and looked up. She seemed to know my thoughts and her face softened and her smile said all I needed to know. It was going to be OK.

'Hey!' Jimmy said, arriving at my side with a margarita. 'Doing all right?'

I watched Dad looking adoringly at Mum while she attempted a very rigid kind of swing dance. I looked at Annabelle holding Katie and laughing at Marcus who was dancing with Hunter on his feet. I looked at Pete explaining the difference between burgundy and maroon to a confused elderly lady from Mum's weaving group. Then I turned back to Jimmy, with his white shirt open to reveal a triangle of tanned chest and his face in a perpetual smile.

'Yep,' I said, and took the margarita out of his hands, dragged him across the room and joined my sister and her kids and her boyfriend on the dance floor.

EPILOGUE

ONE YEAR LATER

'You big bloody rock; you didn't get the better of me! I'm showing you. I'm showing you right now! Take that you hunk of—'

'Are you talking to yourself?' Jimmy said between great gasps of air.

'Nope,' I said, heaving in another breath. 'I'm talking to Mr Thinks He's So Big and Fancy Table Mountain.'

'I always thought Table Mountain was a girl,' Jimmy panted. 'They call Cape Town the Mother City, so her mountain is probably a girl.'

'Shhh, I'm concentrating on climbing this bitch or bastard.'

After sixty-seven minutes of climbing upwards in roasting heat I scaled the final few rocks, reached the summit and spun around to watch Jimmy claw himself over the last rock, his

474

T-shirt removed and tucked into the waistband of his shorts (thank *you* Cape Town for being so hot).

'I made it! I made it! I made it!' I bounced from one rock to the other, ignoring the bemused looks from other climbers collapsing on rocks and gasping for breath like spent marathon runners. 'I made it and I didn't die of snake!'

'Where do you get the energy to leap about like a flea after a climb like that?' Jimmy flumped on a rock in the shade of a scrubby bush and necked a bottle of water.

'I fricking made it!' I said, springing over to him. 'I want to take a photo.' I held up my phone in selfie position. 'Get up.'

'Shall we wait for the others?' Jimmy said, hefting himself off his rock and standing next to me in the sun.

'I want one of you and me. The winners.'

'Your lack of humbleness is grossly unattractive.' Jimmy pressed his sweaty cheek to mine and we beamed at the camera.

I checked the photo with a grimace. 'I look disgusting,' I said, and I was being kind to myself.

We took a series of photos, all beetroot red with hair a-fluff, and all equally horrible. While Jimmy collapsed back on his shady rock I sent one off to Pete with the caption 'Told you I'd climb it!' He sent a text back immediately saying, 'I'm glad. You look happy.' And then followed it with a picture of Giselle and her teeny-tiny baby bump that they were annoyingly calling Poppy Seed because it was a girl and would most likely come out with French braids. I said 'Awwww' then pressed delete with a little scowl that made Jimmy laugh.

I slipped the phone into my pocket just as Mum's German complaining sounded from behind a rock.

'*Nie und nimmer . . . wer klettert den auf so einen berg? Das ist doch folter! Verdammte scheisse, sind wir endlich da?!*'

'Don't swear, Grandma!' Hunter's voice echoed through the opening in the rocks.

I skipped across the dusty ground and peered down the rocky path that was more like a rocky ladder and saw Mum's clammy, pained face followed by a tomato-red Annabelle, a determined Hunter and Marcus taking up the rear in a cricket hat and chino shorts, his pale legs thickly plastered with factor fifty.

'I won! I won! I won!' I proclaimed as I pulled Mum up the last few steps by her hand.

'Of course you did,' Mum puffed and wheezed. 'I'm seventy-one.'

'And you left while we were still getting out of the car,' Annabelle said as she put one dainty foot in front of the other and reached the top.

She turned and helped Hunter scramble over the final rock, followed by Marcus, his pasty skin sizzling like pork crackling, and I did the little winning routine with them too. Nobody gave a crap.

We drained our drink bottles, took a million commemorative selfies then commenced the walk across the top of the behemoth towards the cable car that would take us back down.

Jimmy sent Ian a text saying we were on our way back

and received a photo in return of Diego and Katie sitting among the mountain of toys they'd bought in preparation for our stay.

The cable car descended and blew a cool breeze through the open windows. Annabelle told Hunter not to lean so far out and Marcus, turning a sickly shade of green, looked like he might suffer from motion sickness. I watched Mum at the open window of the cable car, Jimmy next to her pointing out landmarks, and thought of how far we'd all come since that difficult time a year ago.

After the party Mum and Dad told a few close friends everything and asked them to discreetly tell others. I can only imagine how busy the phone lines must have been in the ensuing days. Like us, our friends had struggled to deal with the truth. They too had been lied to for a very long time. Most were supportive. A handful took moral umbrage and sent sternly worded letters before cutting contact, but on the whole people had been sympathetic. And we'd got through the worst of it. As a family. Like Dad had said we would. Albeit a broken one.

Annabelle and I still saw Dad when he came to London, but one of his wife's stipulations if they were to remain together was that he didn't see Mum. Ever. The loss I'd felt when realising the four of us might never be in the same room again was like a death. And Mum's grief was awful to witness. The worst part was removing Dad's belongings from the family home like he no longer existed. Or we no longer wanted him around. I was angry at first and hated Annika for breaking up our family. But like Ian had said about Jimmy and his dad: '*a knee-jerk reaction is understandable. It just needs to be readdressed*', I realised that her reaction was probably perfectly justified. But I hoped that in time she would see that we were a family also and 'readdress' the decision. So, for now, we saw our parents separately. We hadn't had any big events like births or weddings but I didn't think Annabelle and Marcus were far off wanting to and I knew she would never get married without both Mum and Dad there.

Mum was now on the fourth draft of her ridiculous self-help book on how to navigate being the second family, complete with diet tips and recipes that help 'heal the guilt in your gut'. Apparently ghee works wonders if you're harbouring a deception. She was spending some time with Patrick, and while she would probably never have the sparkle in her eye she had when she and Dad were together, she seemed relatively content to go on long walks or take trips to the organic garden centre with him.

Dad was still going through counselling with his original family. Maryna had initially cut contact with him and stopped him seeing his grandchildren, but with therapy they were now on more cordial terms. There was vague talk of Annabelle and me meeting our half-sister, but I don't think any of us were ready yet. Often, in quiet moments, I'd think of Maryna and wonder how she had felt when she found out. Maybe her self-worth had plummeted too. I felt terrible. I didn't want her hurting. I didn't want her to think she wasn't enough for Dad.

And as an only child she didn't have a sister to turn to like I had. But I didn't contact her. For some reason I thought that should be her decision.

Annika's interiors business kept her travelling and Dad was attending a lot of the counselling sessions alone. She was still very, *very* hostile, apparently. It made me sad to think that Dad was so busy loving everybody that he might end up with nobody. Although, despite Annika's ban on Mum and Dad seeing each other, I knew they still communicated. Sometimes Annabelle and I would walk into a room and hear them on the phone together. Mum would quickly get off and say, 'Oh, that was just your father ringing to ask after Katie', or 'to see how Hunter did in his relay race'. She'd tap the phone with a wistful look then take a bracing breath and carry on.

Jimmy had finished his three-month course and was offered a job in the writer's room. It was a junior role, yet highly sought after. But in the meantime his tutor had shown his script to a well-connected animator friend of his in LA, and the friend had shown it to a producer. The producer had asked if Jimmy was prepared to work on another couple of drafts because he thought he could get some investors interested. So Jimmy had turned down the writer's room job, gone back to Cape Town, back to Sylvie's restaurant and knocked out those other drafts. It was now with some execs in LA who were very excited about it.

And me? Well, I've been doing OK. I can still vacillate

between total acceptance and total dismay. But I mostly settle with acceptance because it's an easier place to live. My therapist says I'm doing really well and, surprisingly, my paranoia and anxiety have lessened, which makes me think on some subconscious level that I knew something was up. The three months Jimmy was in London were the happiest three months of my life. He'd pretty much lived at my flat. His SA tan had faded but none of his innate sparkle had, thank goodness. When he went back to Cape Town I'd stayed in London to continue with my producer training and we did the long-distance thing. I was keenly aware of the parallels with my parents' relationship. Except we had FaceTime. And honesty.

I love Jimmy. I really do. I love his attitude to life and I love who I am when I'm with him. And I love that our children will have at least a 50 per cent chance of being able to sing in tune. Yes, I am talking about children. No HSBC sperm bank or millions of one-night stands with hot guys trying to get a sperm donor for me! Which is a real shame, but we all make sacrifices for the ones we love.

I've finished my training and have produced a handful of music videos by myself. Lana was very pleased and so was I. I loved my new role. But I wanted to be with Jimmy.

'I always knew you weren't going to be mine forever,' Lana had said as we'd sat in her office and she pressed send on an introductory email to a contact of hers in LA.

'Thank you,' I'd said with proper fat tears rolling down my cheeks.

*

'We're going now,' I called down to the beach, an hour after we'd returned from climbing Table Bastard Mountain.

Jimmy, freshly showered and with his SA tan restored, joined me on the balcony. On the white sand below Hunter and Katie were building a sandcastle with Pamela, who was wearing a giant multi-coloured sun hat and had already learnt a handful of baby sign words. Flora sat on her own deck chair under a brolly and Lucy lay next to her in a patchy bit of shade, half-covered in sand. Annabelle, Mum and Marcus sat in deck chairs nearby, drinking iced tea, luxuriating in the late-morning sun and listening to Diego and Ian explain the next day's proceedings. They were getting married, and as Jimmy had predicted, Diego was having his loud, proud, ostentatious, colourful affair. Jimmy and I were heading to the airport to pick up his father. It had been hard at the beginning but in the end, Jimmy and his father had found a solid foundation to start from. And they'd built that new relationship from the ground up.

'BYE!' Hunter stood and waved, tripped on the sandcastle, knocked Marcus's drink out of his hands and lost his grip on his plastic spade, which went flying and hit Mum on the head, coating her in a tsunami of fine white sand.

'*Kruzifix, verdammt und zugenaeht!*' she shrieked.

'Grandma!' Hunter said, getting up from his tangle of limbs and buckets with a stern look on his sand-covered face. 'Wash your mouth out!'

Everybody cracked up. Mum scowled and pulled her sun hat lower. She had stopped mono-mealing and the night before had been quite happy to knock back one too many of Diego's vodkas, once he'd told her the garnish was a local medicinal herb.

I laughed and turned away from Annabelle dabbing at a soaked Marcus with her towel, Katie clapping, Hunter telling Mum off, and Diego and Ian watching on in fascination. 'Ready?' I said, putting a hand on Jimmy's chest, the sun catching the diamond on my left ring finger.

He'd given it to me in his bedroom five minutes earlier. Nobody on the beach knew yet; Jimmy wanted to tell his father first.

He looked at the diamond, then at me and he grinned. 'Yep,' he said, then put a tanned arm around my shoulders. 'Back soon!' he said to the rumpus on the beach.

As we walked away from the balcony I saw Diego and Ian exchange an extremely knowing look. My family on the other hand, and as per usual, had no freaking idea.

ACKNOWLEDGEMENTS

I'd like to start the acknowledgements by finishing off the dedication. It should have read:

> *For Mama (She will be SO mad if I don't put*
> *her actual name, so to keep Mama happy:*
> *For Tricia Helen Brown) – for always*
> *making our family feel unbroken.*

But of course I couldn't put that right at the beginning in case it gave away what was going on!

OK, so on to the acknowledgements: (My family have demanded lots of 'airtime', even if their only contribution was to send a sugar-free, grain-free coconut and chocolate slice that nobody liked.)

But first, I'd like to thank my agent, Alice Lutyens. She's mad and fun and bloody good at her job. Knowing you're there (on the other end of the email) gives me confidence, so thank you.

And big, big thanks to my editor, Emma Capron, for being brilliant and patient and always so positive. Sorry I make you have middle-of-the-night work panics!!

I'd also like to thank Sally Partington for her eagle-eyed copy-editing and chatty, informative little notes down the side.

And thank you to Pip Watkins for all her hard work on the super-cute cover!

THANKS SO MUCH to the following people:

Janene Wolfe, for her expertise in how to deal with a naughty passenger who keeps trying to get up to business class.

Dave Scott, for sharing hilarious stories about his 999 job. And for being awesome.

Justine Barker, for answering all my really naive music questions. You're awesome too.

Natalie Daglish-Cooper and Callum Campbell, for answering my South African and Afrikaans questions. Miss you guys!!

Gerhard Schiele, for helping with translations and providing me with German swear words. And for the borrowed last name.

Thanks to my sister, Stephanie Brown, for responding to my panic attack by booking a flight to help me, and to Mum (Tricia Helen Brown – it's in here THREE TIMES now, Mama!!) for paying for it.

And a 'gee thanks' to my other sister, Andrea Cammell (do *not* pronounce it camel – she doesn't like it) for the yucky slice.

Mum, I'd also like to thank you for the ongoing inspiration – you know which parts are you. And Lithuania is in the next one! Keep being weird.

I have truly lovely neighbours who I feel so privileged to have met. They gave encouragement, wine, BBQs and a really delicious casserole that turned out to contain meat from the pet food aisle. Thanks Mia Taumoepeau, Sam Chapman, Amanda Neale and Campbell Read.

A huge thanks to the city of Cape Town. It's such a wonderful, inspiring, spellbinding place that I couldn't *not* set a book there.

And finally to my husband, Edd Bennetto, and my two spirited, weird and awesome sons, Jonnie and Wolf. You guys made finishing this book way harder, but your support and encouragement cancels out your disruptions and man, I love you anyway.

Catherine Bennetto has worked as an Assistant Director in the film and television industry, working on shows such as *The Bill*, *Coronation Street* and *Death in Paradise*. She can generally be found travelling the world and spends her time reading healthy cookbooks (not necessarily cooking from them) or at the beach. *Make or Break* is her second novel.

To find out more about

catherine bennetto

Visit her website: www.catherinebennetto.com
Or follow her on twitter: @cathbennetto

booksandthecity.co.uk
the home of female fiction

| BOOKS | NEWS & EVENTS | FEATURES | AUTHOR PODCASTS | COMPETITIONS |

Follow us online to be the first to hear from
your favourite authors

booksandthecity.co.uk

books and the city

@TeamBATC

Join our mailing list for the latest news, events and
exclusive competitions

Sign up at
booksandthecity.co.uk